BOOKS BY KRISTIE COOK

SOUL SAVERS

Recommended Reading Order:

A Demon's Promise

An Angel's Purpose

Genesis: A Soul Savers Novella

Dangerous Devotion

Dark Power

Sacred Wrath

Unholy Torment

Fractured Faith

Age of Angels Part I: Awakened

Age of Angels Part II: Lost

Age of Angels Part III: Marked

Prophecy of the Wolves: (A Soul Savers Tie-In Novella)

Wonder: A Soul Savers Collection of Holiday Short Stories &
Recipes

KNIGHTS OF SOULS AND SHADOWS

Knights of Souls and Shadows

HAVENWOOD FALLS

Recommended Reading Order:

Forget You Not

Lose You Not

Break Me Not

The Collector: Awakening

Savage Salvation (Sin & Silk)

Sun & Moon Academy Book One: Fall Semester

Sun & Moon Academy Book Two: Fall Semester

The Winged & the Wicked (with T.V. Hahn)

Havenwood Falls Short Story Anthology 2018

Havenwood Falls Short Story Anthology 2019

Havenwood Falls Short Story Anthology 2020

BOOK OF PHOENIX

The Space Between

The Space Beyond

The Space Within

KNIGHTS
OF SOULS and
SHADOWS

BESTSELLING AUTHOR OF THE SOUL SAVERS SERIES

KRISTIE COOK

To Belinda,
My Soul Sister,
I can never thank you enough

LOVE.
Always.
WINS.

CHAPTER 1

*T*he moment I stepped through the gates of Misery's Edge, my inner beast lifted her head, twitching her ears and sniffing the air. She undoubtedly felt what I did: a trace of something dark and dangerous slithering in the shadows, almost like it followed us. Perhaps it did. We tended to attract such things of darkness and shadows. After all, we were one, too.

Dark, dangerous, and sometimes feral—

"*Elliana,*" Brielle hissed in my mind, "*you're doing it again.*"

Glancing sideways at my identical twin as our combat boots thudded on the cracked asphalt, I scowled at the accusation in her mental voice. Unlike our mother, we weren't telepathic, but we could mind-link with each other. It was a twin thing.

"*Doing what?*" I asked, annoyed. "*Walking?*"

"*Scaring the natives.*"

She often teased me about how easily I could terrify people with a simple look. Mom called it my RBF—resting bitch face —that I couldn't help. Brielle called it my IFOF—intentional fuck-off face. She was a lot closer to being right than Mom, although it wasn't always intentional.

As we followed our parents down the avenue toward the center of town, all of my senses had been sweeping the area non-stop, always remaining vigilant, as we'd been taught. I slowed my gaze now to better see the people eyeing us as we passed by, watching each one I made eye-contact with as their pupils flared before they immediately turned and hurried away. One young mother with a red scarf over her dirty blond hair squeezed a scruffy-looking toddler against her chest and ducked into a doorway. What the hell? Did she think I'd eat her child if she didn't get away fast enough?

My scowl morphed into a frown, but I shrugged. "*Whatever.*"

"*You feel it, too, don't you? That something's not right here?*" Brielle's brown eyes shifted in my direction as her head tilted, causing her long black braid to fall over her plaid-covered shoulder. My sister had no fashion sense. Not that we had many choices, enchanted black leather comprising most of our wardrobe, but I swore she wore the ugly flannel shirt over her leather tank and that plain, fat braid just to irk me. At least it set us apart, our clothes and hairstyles being about the only things that made us distinguishable to most people. My own hair fell loosely in waves down my back as I nodded. "*Do you know what it is? Where it's coming from? I can't nail it down.*"

I shook my head before glancing over my shoulder. The armed guards remained at the gate, and several others were spaced apart along the protective wall that encircled the town. They had watched us with curiosity as we entered, but now they'd returned to observing beyond the border, to the outside world where zombies and violent gangs remained threats. The sensation definitely came from within the walls, where we passed rows of what appeared to be housing—lines of arranged rusty train cars, semi-trailers, and silos—where more curious eyes watched us, although most people simply went about their day. They were all human, as far as I could tell. Normans, as we called them, or norms for short.

Until recently, Misery's Edge only allowed humans through its gates. The founders of the town despised all supernaturals, because the supes—the demon-led Daemoni, more specifically—changed everything when they came out of secrecy two decades ago. Shortly after came nuclear and black magic bombs, sending any survivors underground for years. The norms heard rumors of the big battle between angels and demons that followed, but since most had remained in their bunkers, they hadn't witnessed it themselves. The humans couldn't see the demons in their true forms, and they wouldn't know if one possessed their own loved one. All they knew was that the vampires, mages, and shifters caused the end of the world as they'd known it. That all happened before I was even born, but to many, such as those here at the Edge, we were still the enemy.

Then along came Camila, the new mayor who walked with our parents now. She was human, but one of those who'd gained abilities from the lingering black magic, so not quite norm, but not quite supernatural either. This gave her a different perspective of the supes, and she opened the Edge's gates to us for the first time ever. Thus, everyone's curiosity.

Well, that and the fact that my family was practically royalty, a whole entourage of guards surrounding us. The angels themselves appointed Mom, commander of their army, also known as the Amadis, to lead the rebuilding of humanity. She had done her best, but things had been deteriorating and the threat of another war loomed—with Brielle and me at the center of it all.

"*It's nowhere and everywhere,*" I replied to Brie, also unable to pinpoint the sensation. "*But we were promised safe refuge here. You know Mom and Dad wouldn't have brought us otherwise. Dani wouldn't have, either.*"

Brielle let out a soft snort at that. She liked Dani, but not in the same way I did, which meant she didn't quite trust her like I did. I understood that we hadn't exactly known her for long, but I didn't need to. We had an instant connection. I knew Brie would come around eventually.

I glanced at the young woman on my other side—Daniela, my girlfriend. The idea of me having a girlfriend still felt unreal, but here she was, looking back at me with eyes so dark they were almost black, but in a soft, sparkling *human* way, not like the flat black void that filled demons' eyes.

"We're almost there," she said, her Portuguese accent thicker than usual with her excitement. Her hand swung out and brushed against mine, sending a web of tingles up my arm. I was tempted to grab hers, but Dad had already warned us that we were on a diplomatic mission and we needed to be careful of showing any kind of special treatment or alliance prematurely.

I understood Dani's enthusiasm when the avenue finally opened up to Market Square—the wonders of which I'd only heard stories about until now.

"Oh, my angels," Brielle gasped.

"Holy shit," I said more bluntly at the sight before us.

We had "merchants" at the Loft, the enormous underground bunker where we'd grown up and called home. They had "shops" to trade their goods, things they made out of scavenged scraps, offering little extras that went beyond the basics Mom and the council provided for all of us—shelter, food, water, and clothing. The rumors about Misery's Edge said Market Square was like our merchants' section of the Loft, only times fifty. They'd totally undersold it.

"I knew you'd love it." Dani's full lips stretched into a wide smile, revealing gleaming white teeth against her dark golden skin, as my own mouth parted in awe.

Rows and rows of tents and tables filled what appeared to have been a park in the Before time, colorful though faded fabrics whipping in the breeze, and items of just about everything imaginable were stacked, piled, or hung in crowded displays. Tools, textiles, old tires, hunting and fishing gear, pieces and parts of broken furniture, dried meats and fruits . . . That's only what I could see in the first row. And I'd never seen so many people in one place, not even when the entire population of the Loft gathered at once. They talked animatedly with each other while they investigated offerings, some louder than others as they negotiated for the best bargain. The beat of a drum came from a place I couldn't see, and the melody of a string instrument floated from somewhere else. The fragrances of baked bread and cooked meat wafted on the air, almost but not quite disguising the sour odor of human sweat—and something else unpleasant that eluded me in the same way that I couldn't pinpoint the strange energy winding its way throughout the town.

"I can't believe Charleigh's missing out on this," Brielle said as we closed in on the first row of merchants.

A small pang of guilt stabbed at me, but I quickly dismissed it. Charleigh was our best friend, our cousin—by choice, not by blood—whom we'd grown up with, and a powerful witch. She'd been longing to come here as much as we had.

"She'll see it soon enough," I said. "You know Mom will make Uncle Owen go get her as soon as everything is settled here. She's now our sworn protector, after all."

"Tell me again why you need a sworn protector," Dani said at the same time Sasha, our *lykora*, jumped from her hiding spot in Brielle's backpack, landing on all fours. "Isn't that Sasha's job?"

I couldn't blame Dani's teasing tone, because in her current state, Sasha looked like a toy-sized white dog sniffing the ground ahead of us, wandering off as she followed the myriad scents of the marketplace. When we were threatened, though, she took her true form, an otherworldly creature that looked like a wolf, but with feathered wings and the black stripes of a tiger, able to grow to whatever size necessary to protect us. *Lykoras* were known for their unending loyalty to their masters, and Sasha belonged to Brielle and me. It was her current form that kept me relatively calm despite that strange energy. If something were wrong, she would surely know.

"Besides, aren't you supposed to be the biggest, baddest thing on this planet?" Dani's teasing continued as her gaze traveled over my shoulder, where she knew my wings and weapons were hidden under a cloaking spell.

"Us and our brother," I murmured as we sauntered past a shop offering containers of all kinds—buckets, crates, baskets, and jars to name a few. "He's part of the problem."

"You have serious family drama," Dani quipped. She wasn't wrong, but she didn't even know half the story. I hoped she never did.

I'd shared with her the news Mom and Dad had dumped on Brielle and me two days ago—right before we were attacked, punctuating their point of how much danger we were in. I hadn't told Dani everything, though. Not those things I knew would drive her far away, to never have anything to do with me. When we'd met in Ravenbury, a small town near the Loft, a few weeks ago, she hadn't immediately rebuffed me like most people did. She was the first girl I'd met who also liked girls, and we'd connected right away. I couldn't risk losing her. Not when I finally found someone who could possibly love me. No, some secrets needed to stay that way.

Like the one Brielle and I kept—how sometimes it felt like the very fabric of our beings was woven of the darkest threads. And it wasn't just because the DNA of demons, vampires, shifters, and sorcerers tainted our angel blood. We inherited that from our parents, plus fae blood from our dad, but they didn't harbor this kind of darkness. They had their own, but not like ours. We were an anomaly. Some believed we should have never been born, and perhaps they were right. We attracted the worst kind of energy, pulling it to us as energy does—like to like—even across dimensions and worlds. I wasn't kidding, either. At six years old, we unintentionally opened an inter-dimensional gate to a world of evil. That same energy seemed to live inside us. Or, at least, inside me—my beast, whom I could never unleash. As our parents had revealed to us the other day, if not suppressed, our powers could literally destroy worlds.

Not that the news had surprised Brielle and me. We'd always suspected our powers were beyond anyone's understanding—or control—and it was probably a good thing we were cursed by a spell that bound them.

No, I didn't tell Dani any of this, nor other secrets about the darkness, some I even kept from Brielle.

I did tell her how the Daemoni, the demons, and the fae all wanted to capture my sister and me—how they wanted to use us for our powers or kill us because of them. How close they'd come the other day, when they attacked. It wasn't like the potential of our powers was a secret. After all, everyone knew who our parents were, both their leadership roles and the forces they could wield, which were unlike anything in the world. At least, until they had Dorian and then Brielle and me. Our brother Dorian was like us, but he embraced the evil energy fully, abandoning our family to lead the Daemoni, our sworn enemy.

"Enough drama to fill a book or two," I agreed. "You and Papa Miguel are lucky in that regard."

She snorted. "I suppose that is the silver lining of losing everyone you love."

Shit. I hadn't meant that.

"But I have you now," she continued, assuaging my guilt with that brilliant smile of hers. "And I'm not scared. Your powers are bound. Everyone just needs to realize that and relax. You can stay here with me until then."

If only it'd be so easy. Our powers weren't completely bound, though. When the Daemoni warlock blasted the curse that put Brielle and me in a coma two years ago, the spell had only suppressed some of the magic within us, diminishing its strength. We still had enough sorcery, fae, and angelic magic, and it was growing stronger every day. Mom and Dad had been training us relentlessly the past couple of years, teaching us how to use that magic and control it. To the point that I knew they were scared. Of us, their children. I had a feeling they were about to tell us why the other day, but then the Daemoni attacked, their first outright attempt at trying to capture Brie and me.

If only everyone would understand that Brielle and I didn't want anything to do with our real powers. We really did not want to destroy the world.

Demons, though? That was a different story. I'd gladly destroy every last one of them.

We walked in silence past the next booth, where artificial limbs hung from hooks on the plywood walls. The shopkeeper watched us with one pale blue eye, the other covered with a patch, as he scratched his temple with a prosthetic hand. I thought about Gertie, the elderly woman at the Loft who used to make us dolls from scraps when we were little and who had lost a foot a year ago to a *colata* tree. I wondered if we'd ever see her again. After all, we didn't know when—or even if—we could ever return to the Loft. We couldn't take the chance of bringing our enemies to our home, to our people.

"You'll be out there fighting on your mom's demon assassin team when they do," Dani continued with her unending optimism. "I think it's funny you despise them so much, though, since you wouldn't exist without them."

I frowned at this. Nobody had ever put it that way. "They're demons. They destroyed the world. Do I need more reason?"

She shrugged. "I suppose not. And I see why they would

want to kill you—you're a threat to them. A regular demon-killing machine—"

"You technically can't kill demons," Brielle interrupted. "You can only send them back to Hell."

"Nobody can?" Dani asked.

"Nobody," I confirmed.

"Well, still. I understand why the demons fear you. But why the fae? I thought they don't even like this world."

I shrugged. "That's a good question . . ."

I lost all train of thought when a three-sided tent stopped me in my tracks, making my breath catch, and I couldn't stop myself from ducking inside. I'd never seen clothes so pretty. I didn't know fabrics in such vibrant colors and rich textures even existed.

"Someone's restored these beautifully," Mom breathed from my side, startling me. She stared admiringly at a soft lavender dress hanging on a hook. Mom appeared to be my and Brielle's age, so we could be mistaken as sisters, but her hair was a reddish-brown, the dark copper of a penny, as Dad had said one time when he showed us what a penny was. Ours used to be the same color, until the curse forever changed it to a black so deep it was almost blue. I'd only ever seen our mother in leather corsets with black leather pants or in sweatshirts and jeans. A bit of a shock rippled through me at the thought of her donning these colorful, feminine clothes, but I realized now she probably wore these in the Before time.

My own gaze caught on a blouse made of a red shimmery material that I couldn't help but stroke. I nearly groaned out loud at its softness.

"That's real silk," Mom said. "It's beautiful."

My fingers traced over the yellow and orange embroidery along the bottom of the blouse that looked like flames. I sighed, knowing I'd look amazing in it.

"What do you have to trade?" asked the curly-haired

woman who apparently owned the shop. She looked about Dani's age, a couple of years older than me.

I glanced over at Mom, who shook her head. In an unusual move—I normally blocked her telepathy so she wouldn't snoop on my thoughts—I opened my mind to her, and we silently debated.

"*We have nothing to trade,*" she finally said. "*Everything on us is highly valuable.*"

"Thread? Fabric?" the woman asked, as she scrutinized my clothes. "That corset would do."

My hand flew to my chest, pressing against the leather corset, and I laughed. "This is no ordinary leather. I don't think your entire inventory is worth this."

She scowled, and Mom quickly grabbed my shoulders and practically shoved me out of the tent.

"What?" I asked. "You just said so yourself. I'm pretty sure none of her beautiful clothes are enchanted like our leathers."

"You're right, honey. Just maybe next time say it a little nicer, okay? It's called tact. We don't want to tick off the locals our first day here."

I shrugged. "I was just being honest."

Aunt Vanessa, who'd been standing guard outside, snickered as she fell into step with us, her white-blond hair almost silver in the bright sun. "Some people can't handle honesty. But don't let it stop you from speaking your truth."

Dani and I hung back a little as they caught up with the others at the next tent with its table of old electronic gadgets that no longer functioned. All electrical components had been fried by the dirty bombs, but that didn't stop Dad and Brielle from gawking all over them.

"Look, there's Papa," Dani said, lifting her chin as she looked across the street to a three-story brick building left over from the Before time. "That's his new home, on the first floor. It was once the front half of a boutique." I didn't know what a boutique was but didn't ask when she took my hand and tugged me that way. "Come on. I know he'll be happy to see you."

Brielle told our parents where we were going before following us over, joined a minute later by Aunt Sheree and her mate, Uncle Aidan, neither of whom were technically family. Only Aunt Vanessa was actually blood related.

"Owen and Carlie are taking medical supplies back to the Loft," Aunt Sheree said. "Vanessa and Jax are guarding your parents while they meet with the mayor. So you're stuck with us." She grinned, knowing we wouldn't have a problem with that. Sheree, a tiger shifter, was the cool aunt we could go to with anything, and Aidan always kept us laughing, usually unintentionally. He'd been stuck in his gargoyle form on the side of a Scottish cathedral for a few hundred years, so this world often befuddled him.

Papa Miguel greeted us all in his broken English, then spoke to Dani in Brazilian Portuguese.

"He asked if you can stay for dinner," Dani said, translating. "We can help him make *feijoada*, a stew from our home."

The rest of the afternoon passed mostly in a blur, with certain moments seeming to freeze as they implanted themselves in my memory: Dani's infectious laugh as she teased her papa; Brielle and Aunt Sheree dancing in the courtyard as they set out tables and chairs; Uncle Aidan kicking a ball with a couple of local kids; Mom and Dad returning with Uncle Jax and Aunt Vanessa to enjoy the feast. I didn't know life could be so . . . vibrant. If Charleigh and her mom, Aunt Blossom, were here, it would have been perfect. I could tell Uncle Jax, Charleigh's dad, shared those thoughts as he sat quietly by himself, rubbing a hand over his bald head as he watched everyone.

"I have something to show you," Dani said after we'd finished eating. Night had fallen, and she tugged me into the small apartment. We dropped side-by-side onto an oversized chair, where her bag sat on the floor. She opened it, tilting it toward me to reveal red silk.

"Dani," I whispered, my throat tightening. "How? When?"

She gave me a small smile. "I didn't. I was going to, but your dad beat me to it. He and your mom wanted me to give it to you."

I swallowed the lump in my throat. I couldn't believe they'd done that for me.

"I don't deserve this," I whispered.

"Of course, you do. You should have something so beautiful, Elliana Knight. You never know when you'll get another chance."

My chest ached with a feeling I'd never experienced before, almost like my heart swelled too large to be contained. Our gazes locked for a moment before hers traveled down, snagging on my lips. The urge to kiss her became overwhelming, and I began to lean in, but then the door flew open, and we were no longer alone. Mom, Dad, Brielle, and Miguel took seats on the sofa and the only other chair. Sasha jumped between us and curled up on my lap. So instead, Dani and I shared a knowing smile, my stomach fluttering with anticipation for a moment I hoped we'd be able to steal later.

That moment never came.

Everything was fine one minute. Brielle had just come over from sitting with Mom while Dad and Miguel exchanged stories in Portuguese. Then the next minute, Mom and Dad were grabbing us and ordering us to flash away. Except we couldn't. The magic that should have taken us out of there in a blink of an eye was blocked.

By the deepest, darkest energy I'd ever felt.

My inner beast sprang to her feet, pushing against the restraints on her. Brielle looked at me with fear filling her brown eyes. She felt it, too—from within just as much as without.

"Girls, stay here!" Mom shouted as she and Dad flew out the door, Sasha right on their heels.

I jumped to my feet to follow.

"Elli!" Brielle snapped. "Mom said to stay here."

"Like hell I am."

By the time I reached the doorway, Sasha was gone, and Mom, Dad, and Aunt Vanessa were already across the road, running toward Market Square, where Mayor Camila stood in the middle of the street. Except she was no longer Mayor Camila. Rather, she was transforming and growing into a monstrous, towering beast of purple and black mottled skin with two horns curling outward from her black hair.

The mayor was a gods-damned major demon.

"You should not have rejected my offer, Alexis," she said to my mother, her voice deep and raspy as she continued to grow.

Mom's black and purple wings exploded from her back, her swords appearing in her hands. "Did you really think I didn't know, Shamara? You cannot have my daughters!"

Dad's gray and black wings appeared, too, and I knew all hell was about to break loose. Before I could move to join them, a dark fog poured down the streets and pathways, filling the space between the buildings until it obliterated my parents and Aunt Vanessa, trapping them with the demon.

Screams pierced the air from the opposite direction, down the street. Then more from other locations. The air froze in my lungs when the realization set in: Demons. They were everywhere. Dozens of them, maybe hundreds in human flesh, possessing the norms and wearing their bodies like suits, the only tell their pitch-black eyes. No whites. No irises. Just all deep blackness. So fucking many. How had we not known? The major demon—only she would have been powerful enough to hide them from us.

Chaos erupted.

Just down the street, the man with the prosthetic hand

had lost his eyepatch, both eyes filled with that flat black as he lunged for the curly-haired woman who'd wanted my corset as she tried to run away. The blond woman stumbled past me, still clutching her toddler against her chest, as another woman launched at her, tackling her to the asphalt, the screaming child smashed beneath them. Possessed norms attacked their loved ones and neighbors everywhere I could see.

Clashing energy careened and collided within me as my beast tried to push herself free while at the same time my angel powers felt like they were about to explode out of me. I could feel Mom pulling on my Amadis power—the power of all that is good given to us by the angels—and I fed it to her to boost her own as she fought the major demon.

I was about to snap my own wings out and reveal my weapons when something on the roof of the building next to us caught my attention, drawing my gaze upward. Nothing more than a swirling and twisting shadow, but somehow, I just knew it was something . . . more.

All of the noise, the chaos faded away as a whispery voice filled my mind. "*Remember me, little shade? We had a deal.*"

I blinked in confusion, and then spun when a scream came from behind me, from inside the apartment. Horror filled me at the sight.

Papa Miguel's hands reaching for Dani, and his eyes . . .

"No!" I screamed, tugging on the chains holding my beast, trying to break her free.

Everything suddenly went black, deadly silent, as I fell into a sea of nothingness.

Then a white light flashed beyond my eyelids, a blinding brightness.

My hearing returned first, screams coming from every direction. My vision began to clear, only to see bodies dropping to the ground. Dozens of them. Hundreds. What the hell?

All the sobs, the screams, the wails filled with immense pain . . . confusion and chaos continued everywhere.

The loudest of all came from Dani, as she sank to the ground with her papa in her arms, lifeless.

I reached out for her, but someone grabbed me from me behind.

"Get them out of here!" Dad bellowed from somewhere in the distance.

"No!" I cried, trying to lunge for Dani again, but Aunt Vanessa's hold tightened on me. I threw my head back and heard the crunch as I smashed the vampire's nose. I didn't care about my aunt's renowned temper. I'd like her to see mine right now.

But then Uncle Owen appeared, his straw-colored hair standing on end as though he'd been running, and he locked me down with his warlock magic. "There's more coming!"

Everything else happened in a blur. As they swept us out of there, I seethed in anger, cussing at everyone around us and screaming for Dani. But I couldn't fight. Not just because of Uncle Owen's hold—I had a feeling my powers could break through it—but because somewhere within, I knew the precarious position we were in. Norms shot at us. Passages were blocked. We took lots of twists and turns as fat raindrops fell, and we somehow managed to escape Misery's Edge.

As soon as we passed through its gates, I fully felt the dark presence surrounding us. Demons. Daemoni. Dark fae. All of them closing in.

"*Brie, what happened?*" I asked, halfway coming out of my daze, as Mom and her council debated what to do next. "*I . . . I blacked out or . . . something.*"

Brielle sidled up next to me, grasping my hand and giving it a squeeze, for my comfort or her own, I couldn't be sure. Likely, knowing her, both. "*Probably from Mom's pull on our power. She destroyed the demons. As in killed them for good.*"

"*Impossible.*" Not even Mom could do that.

"She did it, nonetheless. All of them except Shamara, anyway. She flew away. But the people of the Edge only saw hundreds of human bodies dropping dead."

"Fuck."

"Yes."

I tried to make sense of it, including what happened to me, but my mind filled with only one vision: Dani's eyes as they pulled me away from her. Scared. Grieving. Accusing.

We began to move again, going through one of Uncle Owen's portals and appearing on a beach of black sand, an icy wind cutting at my bare arms. I realized for the first time that my brother was with us, talking to my mom and the others. Another portal swirled about twenty yards away.

"It's a gate like yours," Dad said. "Dorian opened it, but it goes somewhere else. The world beyond is another Earth. A version like ours in an alternate universe, but it's also very different. It's a good place. You'll see."

Brielle said something. Dad and Mom both replied. My mind still struggled to focus on the here and now.

"Wait," I finally said, looking up at them in horror as their words sunk in. "You can't be serious! We're not going there, are we? To another *world?*" My head shook. This could not be happening. I had to get back to Dani.

Dad leveled his hazel gaze on me, his jaw muscle popping and his nostrils flaring as he inhaled deeply. "In case you didn't notice, Elliana," he said with a measured calmness, "war is imminent, and your and Brielle's lives are at the center of it all. Hundreds of souls were just obliterated to protect you. Do not make their deaths in vain. Do not make *Miguel's* death pointless."

His words, his tone silenced me, my chest tightening and the backs of my eyes burning.

Brielle took my hand again and tugged me forward, only to release it when Sasha dropped in out of nowhere. Dorian said something to the *lykora*, who shrunk to her toy-dog size.

Brielle scooped her up into her arms. But all I could focus on was the black demon blood staining her snout.

As we passed through the gate, from the beach of black sand at night to a snow-covered mountain in the blinding light of day, my stomach knotted with guilt. The first girl I'd ever cared about was in her biggest moment of need, and I had abandoned her, leaving her utterly alone in the world.

CHAPTER 2

"*E*lli." The soft voice came like a sweet song from a distance. Then it came as a near shout: "Elliana Knight!"

"Gah!" I yelped. "What?"

"Where'd you go?"

I scrubbed a hand over my face, finding electric blue eyes staring at me with concern. Not the dark, accusing eyes of memories I could never shake, nor the red eyes that had replaced them more recently in visions that felt entirely too real. Not memories, those ones. More like a premonition.

"You were there again, weren't you?" The electric blues belonged to Sadie Angrec, who stood directly in front of me, deep in the woods on the side of a mountain in a world that was foreign to both of us, yet we'd called home for over a year.

"Sorry. I can't help it. The prospect of going back, of seeing for myself . . ." My voice trailed off, my breath stuttering on the exhale. It'd been over a year since we'd left our own world, since the curse on our powers broke, since we'd seen our parents . . . one year, four months, and thirteen days since that awful night in Misery's Edge. The night I'd left a girl whom I thought I could love right when she needed me most.

And here I was again, leaving a girl when her own life was falling apart. A different girl, one I most definitely loved but had never been able to bring myself to tell her. Because we'd known from the beginning that this day would come. She was an elven princess from Faery. I was from an Earth in a completely different dimension. We both had roles to play in our very different home worlds, and we both needed to return to them now. Sadie because her father, the elf king, had summoned her home. Me because of the visions with the red eyes.

"You'll be home soon enough." Sadie sighed as she brushed a finger between my brows to loosen their tight pinch. "We both will be, I guess."

My heart cracked for the hundredth time in the last week, since the day she told me her people needed her and she had to go home. The same day Charleigh and Brielle finally agreed with me that it was time for us to go, too.

I leaned my forehead against hers, our hair cascading together in a curtain around us, black and white, dark and light, just like us. "I hate this."

She clasped her hands around mine, holding them at our sides. "Me, too. I give one star to being royalty. Do not recommend."

She managed to elicit the smile she'd been trying for.

"Excellent service, but the price is entirely too high," I agreed.

"Entirely too high," she echoed softly, leaning back enough to look me in the eye. "This is not goodbye, though, Elliana Knight. The Faery realms are connected, including the one that's linked to your world. If it's meant to be, we will find each other again."

She closed the space between us, our mouths meeting for one last breathtaking kiss that nearly had me abandoning all plans so we could run off to some unknown place where nobody from any world could ever find us.

"Sadie, we have to go!" one of her elven friends called from the lip of the ridge. "I really don't want to piss off your father if we miss the portal!"

Breaking the kiss, I stepped back and forced a smile. "Good—"

She pressed her finger to my lips, stopping me. "See you again, Elliana Knight."

"See you, Sadie Angrec."

Our hands remained linked as she pulled away, lifting and stretching my arm out until our fingers brushed over each other's palms, and eventually hers fell away as mine drifted to my side. She left without looking back, my gaze following the waves of light blond hair until she disappeared from sight.

"We have to go, too, Elli," Brielle said quietly from behind me.

My chest hurt so much, I struggled to breathe, but I forced myself to inhale as I retrieved my backpack from the ground at my feet and turned around to face my twin and Charleigh. The exhale came out heavily as they stared at me with pity in their eyes. Even Sasha, who sat in Brielle's arms.

"Oh, for shit's sake, I'll be fine," I said, marching forward.

"Of course, you will be," Charleigh said. The sunlight coming through the treetops enflamed her long orange locks, making it look like sparks flew as she turned to fall into pace beside me. "You're Elliana fucking Knight."

I laughed. Leave it to Charleigh to achieve that when my heart thought it was dying. I didn't know what I would have done in this world without her, especially in the beginning. Our parents had ensured she could stay hidden here with Brie and me as our sworn protector, arranging a deal for all three of us to attend a college for the supernatural. It had been quite the experience, and we'd made the most of our time here. But those red eyes . . . the vision I'd had about home during a class assignment early last semester . . . I needed to know . . .

"Let's go," Brielle said, as Sasha leapt from her arms and

led the way through the woods toward another ridge where our gate to home was hidden. The *lykora* was as anxious to go home as I was.

"I can't believe I'm having a harder time with this than you are," I griped as I followed my sister. "Did you even like Aithan?"

"Of course, I did," Brielle replied. "I mean . . . those curls and those lips and that—"

"Ass," Charleigh and I said along with her. Even I could admit Brielle's boyfriend had a wondrous ass—an ass of the gods, as many of the girls claimed.

"But he's the descendant of Aion, the god of unbound time and space," Brie continued. "After he graduates and meets his dad's expectations, he can travel to any dimension, any time, at will. He'll find me if he really wants to." She said it so confidently, reminding me of Sadie's assurance that we'd find each other again.

If it's meant to be. That had been the caveat. And I didn't know if it was meant to be with Sadie and me. In fact, I was pretty sure it wasn't. Because what kind of god or creator or fate that decided such a thing would bind a beautiful soul like Sadie's to mine?

"Are you sure about the part of meeting his dad's expectations?" Charleigh asked. "Aithan's not exactly known as the ambitious type."

Brielle laughed. "True. But like I said, if he really wants to, he will."

"And if he doesn't?"

My twin shrugged, but I noticed the slight falter in her step. "I don't know that he's really the one anyway."

She said it so quietly, I knew there was truth in her words. She didn't rattle them off to cover any pain, present or potential in the future.

They'd practically been joined at the hip since the end of fall semester, but then again, Sadie and I had been, too, for a good portion of the spring semester and the last few weeks of summer. We hadn't taken it very far physically, though. I'd never been so intimate with anyone emotionally, not even my twin or Dani, but we'd restrained ourselves physically, knowing this day would come. Thinking about it in hindsight, I realized how backward that was and regretted not knowing Sadie in every way I could. Then again, maybe it was better that I didn't. Brielle had probably been smarter than me, enjoying the physical but keeping Aithan emotionally at arm's length. She knew this day would come, too.

The side of the mountain teemed with color and life as we climbed for the summit under the July sun. Squirrels and other creatures, some possibly supernatural, scurried across the forest floor, and birds sang from the canopy of leaves and branches overhead that allowed yellow sunlight to dapple the ground around us. Our final hike in this world took us through a meadow of purple, pink, and blue wildflowers, then we weaved around green pines and the white trunks of aspen trees whose leaves were currently green but would turn golden yellow soon enough—a sight we would not see this year.

"I am so going to miss this place," Charleigh said as we reached the edge of the tree line about two-thirds up the side of the mountain. "It's just so . . ."

"Shiny?" I asked as I paused to turn and look down into the box canyon and the small town nestled within it. It wasn't exactly shiny. Quaint, charming, rustic, sweet—those were perfect words, but not shiny. Still, even when the snowplow piles were covered in a brownish-gray crust or when it all melted and turned everything to mud, it was like a shimmering dream compared to home.

"I was going to say *alive*," Charleigh said.

"Yeah, that, too."

"Shiny also works. Clean, bright, beautiful . . ." She trailed off again, and I glanced sideways at her. I sucked my lips between my teeth when I noticed her eyes—a strange brown that sometimes looked as orange as her hair—watering.

"Hey, we're going to see our family!" Brielle reminded her, giving her a shoulder bump.

Charleigh's mouth curled into a smile that stopped short of reaching her eyes. "The only reason you could get me out of here. I mean, come on, aren't you two going to miss the clothes here? And the food?"

"Gods yes," Brielle and I moaned at the same time.

It was a toss-up between the two for which I'd miss more. I *loved* the clothes here. And the makeup and hairstyles and the feeling of knowing I looked good just because I wanted to. The food, though—they had *everything* here.

"Chili cheese fries, chicken wings, cheeseburgers, and shakes," Charleigh listed off, making my mouth water.

"Tacos," I moaned, already missing them.

"And ice cream and lattes," Brie added.

All three of us groaned together, and I gave Charleigh a grateful smile. She'd purposely avoided naming what or *who* I would miss the most. The light blond hair that felt like silk between my fingers . . . the full, firm lips that tasted like heaven . . . the heart and soul that just got mine like no other ever had, not even my twin . . . the electric blue eyes that captured me every time I caught sight of them. Probably because through them I could feel that heart, that soul . . .

Shit. I'm a mess already.

"Are we sure we want to do this?" Charleigh asked, breaking me out of the thoughts she'd been trying to distract me from. We all tilted our heads back to look up the sheer rock cliff that towered a hundred feet or so over us. The top was our destination.

"We have to. We can't fly out here in the open," I said. At the thought of flying, my wings pushed against the magic that cloaked them, itching to break free. But supes remained a secret in this world, and keeping that secret was one of the conditions of our being able to hide here. This was a no-fly zone.

"I mean, do we really want to pick family over clothes and food, soft beds and fireplaces, pizza and parties? I'm sure they could survive just fine without us."

Even though I knew she said it in jest, I blew out a heavy sigh. "I wish I could know that for sure. Then we'd definitely be delaying our return. I just can't dismiss what I saw in the hall of mirrors. What I see every time I close my eyes since then. What I feel in my gut."

"I'm just hoping Mom doesn't kill us herself if we go back and everything is fine," Brielle said.

I frowned. "I'd be seriously happy if she did, because that means my visions are just that, no truth to them."

But we all knew nothing was fine. We'd been hiding in this world for nearly a year and a half while our parents and all of our loved ones had likely been fighting a war. What Mom did that night in the Edge . . . the norms would never forgive her. The other factions would seize the opportunity to undermine everything she'd accomplished in the last two decades so they could take control—and get to Brielle and me. I didn't need disturbing visions to know things were nowhere near fine at home.

If they were right, though . . . If my intuition was correct and what I saw during that class assignment when I'd been trapped in a hall of mirrors was some kind of premonition . . . We might not even have a home world to go back to. Because those red eyes had belonged to smoky figures riding enormous horses, charging out of the gate Brielle and I had opened to that evil world, invading ours and devouring everything in their wake. No matter how hard I tried, I couldn't shake the gut feeling that it was real.

We'd tried for months to reach someone at home. It wasn't exactly easy to communicate across dimensions, though. Faerie stone chips embedded in Brielle's and my chests were supposed to provide a magical connection to our mother, which could be boosted by a spell Charleigh had been given. She was only supposed to use it in case of emergency, and somebody would be sent to us. We waited for months with no response. Then when our parents were supposed to come for a visit over the summer break and never showed, I finally convinced Brielle and Charleigh that we needed to return home. Something was seriously wrong. I'd learned to trust my intuition, and it was screaming at me so loud that I was willing to give up everything I loved about this place. Everyone . . .

So here we were, approaching the same spot where we'd first entered this world. We hadn't been back since then—one of Mom's directives to ensure we didn't give the location away —and the memory of that day came flooding back. I'd been so angry and frustrated for being whisked away to this world, scared and worried about what we'd left, but as soon as we crossed through, both Brielle and I fell to the ground, rolling around in the snow and laughing. The curse on us had broken, and it had felt like a huge weight had lifted.

Our full powers did come surging forth, but we trained with an incredible mentor whom I'd miss almost as much as Sadie. She taught us how to use and control the ramped-up energy flowing through our veins—but not the beast that still lived inside me, no longer chained by the curse. Rather, I kept her subdued, sleeping in a cage of my own making deep within, because I didn't think she *could* be controlled. She was still dark, dangerous, and more formidable than ever. A part of me I would keep locked up forever, but a part of me, nonetheless.

"Are we ready?" Charleigh asked, already starting on the spell to reveal the hidden gate that would take us home, Sasha dancing in front of her.

As the air itself seemed to part, the three of us moved toward it, but as one, we paused to look across the valley to the mountain on the far side. I could barely see a few glimpses of sunlight hitting the waterfalls. Behind those falls, under the mountain was where the campus was hidden. Where we'd spent the last year having the time of our lives. Where we'd begun to come into our true selves and our powers. Where a piece of our hearts remained.

Then hitching our bags higher on our backs, we left the mountains of the sunny, shiny world and came out on a cold beach of black sand in our very desolate, very dark Earth.

The black beach of Dorian's gate in Iceland was thousands of miles away from the Loft, our childhood home and where we hoped to find our family, safe and sound. Charleigh was powerful, but she hadn't been taught yet how to create portals, so we followed the path for flashing that Uncle Owen had given her. Transporting about a hundred miles at a time in the blink of an eye was so much faster than flying, even if Sasha would have let Charleigh ride her, which she'd never done before.

Sasha immediately took off, flying out of sight before we could stop her. She had her own way of watching over us, and she'd probably been more anxious to fly than even I was. After all, nobody in that other world could know she was anything other than a dog, nothing more than Charleigh's familiar.

As the sun began to rise, we finally appeared near the Loft, back to what had once been the Midwest of the United States of America. Back to home.

And my stomach sank at the sight.

"Where is everyone?" Charleigh asked as we crossed the empty clearing to the roll-up door built into the side of a hill. Wide enough for a truck to pass through, it was the only entrance into the Loft, an underground bunker that had been the Amadis HQ since it was our home. Because our mom was matriarch of the Amadis and leader of the Earth's

Angels, many considered us royalty, but the Loft was no palace.

And now it appeared to be abandoned and forgotten.

"We can't even get in," Brielle said, inspecting the enchanted symbols engraved in the doorframe. Touching them in the proper sequence signaled the protective wards to unlock the door, but the sigils had been mutilated, as though someone had dug at them with a blade.

An ominous feeling tugging at my gut, I turned away, toward the forest that bordered the land around the Loft. My brows pulled down as I studied it. The sensation was both alien and vaguely familiar at the same time.

"You're right, Elli," Brielle said from behind me. "Something's definitely not right here." She felt what I did.

As though on their own accord, my feet had already started moving toward the forest, my hand lifting over my shoulder to retrieve the hidden sword strapped to my back under my backpack, as I tried to figure out what had changed about it. At first glance, it looked the same as I remembered, and I dropped my hand, leaving the weapon, but unable to shake the sensation that something was off.

"Why don't we take a quick aerial view?" I suggested. "See if anyone is somewhere close by." Such as someone watching us . . . "You go south and east. I'll go north and west."

Before she could reply, I dropped my backpack and snapped out my wings—my beautiful, glorious wings. When pulled vertical behind me, they arced higher than my head and the tips dusted the ground. Like our mom's, our wings were black at the quills, gradating to a deep purple at the edges. I hadn't been able to fly since we left campus for summer break, over a month ago.

No longer able to resist the anticipation, I launched into the sky, Charleigh yelling after me. "Be careful! And five minutes, no longer. Or I'll come after you!"

Not that she could fly, but she had a few killer tricks up

her magical sleeve that could take me down if she really wanted to.

Brielle and I crossed paths in the air as we each circled the area of the Loft, just to be sure our people hadn't created another entrance while we'd been gone or that nothing else had changed. Then we soared away in opposite directions.

I flew only a dozen or so feet over the treetops of the forest. They didn't appear much different than before, still a grayish brown, although the canopy was thicker with leaves. It'd taken many years after the war before flora and fauna above ground showed any signs of life and many more years before they actually grew. And while they'd been normal to my generation born after black magic permeated our world, our parents' generation had been surprised by new plants and animals that had grown or evolved as a result of it. Ones that were much more sinister than their predecessors, like the fuchsia *colata* tree.

A flash of memory crossed my mind—the three of us running through these very woods, chasing a demon, then getting caught up by a *colata* that ensnared and tried to eat us. The memory blinked out as fast as it came, leaving a metallic taste in my mouth and a sinking feeling in my gut, though I couldn't say why. I'd wanted to be a demon assassin since I was a kid, planning to one day qualify for Mom's elite team, so chasing a demon wasn't too surprising. Except I couldn't remember when those events actually occurred. If they ever had. Was it truly a memory or another vision, like the one in the hall of mirrors? Whatever it was, it seemed linked to something more. Something awful.

I shook my head, trying to erase both the vision and the feeling as I focused on the forest below. And I finally realized what was different about it. Some kind of black vine crawled along the floor and twined around the tree trunks and branches. I dropped down and alit on a broad branch to inspect the new growth that had taken over the entire forest.

Reaching out a finger to touch a leaf, I gasped when a tentacle snaked up to touch me back. Almost like it was sentient, which it very well could have been. As my finger slid over the black vine that felt almost metallic in its hardness, I yelped and nearly popped my finger in my mouth to suck the blood that beaded along the cut. I stopped myself short, just in time. What a grave mistake that could have been. Who knew what kind of poison had been left? Good thing my body could heal itself almost instantly, all evidence of the slice already gone.

"Another flesh-eating plant, just what this place needs," I muttered as I sprang back into the air.

Nothing else seemed to be different as I flew farther north. Nothing besides a strange whispering sound coming from below. The farther I flew, the louder it grew—and the clearer.

Elliana.

The damn vine was whispering my name.

Then clarity came.

"Oh, fuck." My heart stuttered, and I pulled my wings forward to stop myself in midair. "No, no, no."

Below me, the vine was thicker than ever, and energy black as night oozed up from it. A Darkness I was way too familiar with, so evil that it needed a capital D. A Darkness that found me wherever I went. That lived inside me like a monster constantly trying to claw its way to the surface. That sang a comforting, welcoming ballad to me, that made me feel like I belonged with it more than anything or anyone ever had. A Darkness I had to practice very hard to control before it overcame me and left me as Dark and empty as it was.

My beast.

"Shit." I knew where I was. I knew what was below.

The gate Brielle and I had opened. Unlike Dorian's gate, ours didn't go to a happy, shiny world that wasn't war-torn and post-apocalyptic like ours. No, our gate opened to a world much darker than our own. One overrun by evil, perhaps even Satan himself. We hadn't meant to open it. We'd only been six years old at the time. We didn't even know how we'd done it. When our parents discovered it, Mom ordered Uncle Owen to seal it shut and cloak it to ensure nobody ever found it again.

Except we had. Brielle and I, ten years later.

"No," I said aloud, shaking my head as I glared at the ground below, my wings swishing to keep me airborne. "That never happened."

I didn't even know where that thought had come from. From the vines, a new whisper in my head? From the gate itself, telling lies to lure me in? Was it opening on its own now? Were the horses coming?

"Fuck," I said again.

It hadn't happened, had it? We hadn't opened it again, had we? Why did I have this weird feeling that we had? And that the results had been disastrous?

With a quick survey of the surrounding area, I spun in the air and soared back toward the Loft, my heart pounding as fear curled into a tight ball in my gut. I decided as I flew that I'd keep this to myself for now. Brielle was terrified of that darkness that lived inside us, but the more she dwelled on it, the stronger it became. A lesson learned the hard way. No, she didn't need to know about this, and neither did Charleigh. It couldn't really mean anything anyway. Right? The razor-sharp vines were just another effect of the black magic still dusting this world. That's why they felt so dark and sinister. And I hadn't actually seen the gate. I couldn't say for sure that it was open or even still there.

Besides, there were no horses. No red-eyed riders. As far as I knew . . .

"Five minutes!" Charleigh yelled at me, throwing my backpack at me before I even landed. "I said five minutes, and it's been at least fifteen. Where the hell have you been?"

My heart had already settled, my resolve solid as I dropped to my feet beside her. "Sorry, I just wanted to see beyond the forest."

She dropped her hands to her hips and arced a brow. "To dragon territory?"

Shit. I'd forgotten about the dragon shifter lair that lived beyond the forest, by the lake. Our mom had managed to make peace with them, but unlike in the shiny world, the dragons here weren't nice.

"Don't worry. I didn't even get close," I said.

"Did you see anything?" Brielle asked.

I shook my head. "Nope. Nothing out of the ordinary. None of our people hiding anywhere. You?"

"Nope."

"So what now?" Charleigh asked, looking between us. "Ravenbury?"

"No," Brielle said, her dark hair shifting over her shoulders as she shook her head. "If the Loft was in trouble with all the factions, Mom wouldn't have brought that down on Ravenbury."

She stared at the ground, which she often did while sifting through the facts and the options, but we didn't have to be Brielle or my dad to know the best answer. They had a sixth sense for that kind of thing, but this solution was an easy one.

"Misery's Edge," I said when they didn't. "Maybe somebody there knows what happened here. Maybe that's even where everyone is."

Doubtful, but not completely impossible. Shamara had vanished that night, and the lesser demons had been eradicated by our mother. There was the slightest chance enough of the norms understood what truly happened—or that the Amadis took over the town to protect it from happening again.

"I don't think so," Brielle said. "My guess is Amadis Island, but that's halfway around the world. We may as well start at the Edge."

"Are you sure, though?" Charleigh asked me, her motherly

worried look filling her light brown eyes. "You're ready for that?"

"I have to be eventually. Pull it off like a Band-Aid, right?" I shrugged, though I knew they saw through the façade. "Besides, we need to know what happened there, too, after we left. It could be tied to what I saw in the mirrors."

"Or maybe everything is fine, and our family is hanging out in Market Square, laughing and having a good time." Though she said the words herself, Brielle knew just as well as I did that that was a fairytale dream. But she also knew why it was important for us to go back. We had to know.

She'd been there that night. She'd seen what our mother had done. And she wasn't stupid. Nothing was fine. In fact, I was pretty sure that while we'd been having a fabulous time in the other version of Earth, everyone here had paid the consequences of Mom's actions, including Mom herself. And now we needed to step up and help.

"Of course," I added as one last thought before we flashed, "they could have burnt it to the ground, and it's nothing but ashes."

CHAPTER 3

"Huh." My hands dropped to my hips as we stood on a ridge that overlooked the town of Misery's Edge and the wide river beyond it to the east that carved the continent in half. From here we could also see the old broken and overgrown highway to the west that drew a concrete line to what had once been St. Louis about fifty or so miles to the north.

"This is . . . unexpected," Brie said.

"Could be promising," Charleigh added as we surveyed the wall surrounding the town and the dozens of people entering and exiting through the gates.

"The wall's much farther out than it used to be, right?" I asked.

"Definitely," Brielle said. "Look on the far side—it's right up to the river. There used to be an area for camping over there."

"I can't see as far as you," Charleigh reminded her. "And unlike you two, I've never been here, remember?"

"Well, it's definitely grown since we've been gone," Brie said.

The protective walls surrounding Misery's Edge were

pushed out every few years as more people settled in, requiring more housing and a bigger market. We'd been impressed that one fateful day, our first and last time ever here, but the growth in the short time we'd been gone was astonishing. Especially after what happened here that night.

"That's good news then," Charleigh said. "I mean, it hasn't been decimated by war, so there's that."

"Do you notice what I do, though?" I asked.

Brielle nodded. "That there are a hell of a lot of supernaturals?"

"Yep. Quite a mix, too." From here, I could easily identify a handful of mages, some in hooded cloaks, and a dozen or so shifters—and that was just near the gate. Unfortunately, though, I couldn't tell if they were Amadis or Daemoni, which meant they were probably neither—which in turn meant they weren't our people.

"That could also be good news," Charleigh said, and I gave her a sideways glance. Charleigh wasn't normally so . . . upbeat and optimistic. She was a little more cynical, like me. Then again, she did enjoy a good party, something that became quite apparent while we were away at college, and the Edge's energy today definitely gave off a sort of party vibe.

"So . . . let's go check it out," I said, shifting my weight from one foot to the other as nervous energy churned in my gut.

"Shouldn't we glamour ourselves?" Brielle asked. "There's a good chance we're still wanted. You and I might stand out, Elli, and Charleigh's hair gives her away."

Our fae blood gave us fae magic, which meant we could change our appearances, from a few tweaks to our clothes to a completely different look.

I shrugged. "You're the one who can see the best solution. What do you think?"

She stared at the ground for a long moment before finally shaking her head. "We're looking for our people. We need them to recognize us. If we run into trouble, Charleigh can cloak us."

The witch wiggled her fingers in the air as magic sparked over them. Her cloaking powers were much stronger than ours. "I'll be ready."

"But maybe we should at least glamour our clothes," Brielle added. "The fighting leathers might be too much."

So we adjusted our black leather pants to look like ripped-up black jeans tucked into knee-high boots and our leather vests to appear as tattered tank tops. Then she decided to give us hooded cloaks, after all, not unlike what those mages wore, to at least semi-disguise us. They also provided cover if we needed to draw our weapons.

"There," Brielle said. "Now we blend in."

"Raggedy and all," I muttered, already sorely missing the beautiful fashion of the shiny world. More than tacos, though? I still wasn't sure. At least, until my stomach growled with hunger. Yeah, tacos sounded amazing.

Charleigh snorted. "Maybe there's a food stall and we can grab something to eat. Not Mom's cooking, but we'll find her and get that soon enough."

Her confidence in that last bit sounded a little thin.

A few minutes later, I kept my senses on high alert as we passed through the gate, prepared to fight if we were recognized. Last time, every pair of eyes at the gate and on the wall had watched us enter. This time, we weren't even noticed. I released a long exhale as we followed the crowd down the road toward the center of town, toward the market . . . toward ground zero.

More rows of train cars and semi-trailers had definitely been added, even stacked on top of each other to create additional housing for what appeared to be an exploding population, much of the supernatural kind. In between those were lean-tos and other makeshift buildings made of repurposed materials for additional living space. Rows of dirt paths separated each layer, intersecting with the road that led to Market Square.

"Four more rows added," Brielle said, keeping her voice low. She would know. She counted everything and forgot nothing. "If each one goes all the way around the perimeter, that's easily another five thousand people, doubling its population in a year and a half. I wonder what made so many people flock here in such a short time. Especially so many supernaturals."

Neither Charleigh nor I had an answer, but I couldn't help but think it had something to do with that night and our parents.

"Maybe a lot of those people are from the Loft," Charleigh said, though we hadn't recognized anyone yet.

When we reached Market Square, I noticed it had also expanded. Some of the close-in train cars and trailers had been moved, which might have changed Brie's calculations, but some were also overtaken by merchants rather than used as residences. Most of the shops, though, were still three-sided tents and huts created by scrap wood and various faded fabrics. Fabrics that were often taken home each night to double as bedding. The difference between this world and where we'd been hiding slammed into me. While this was home and the way we'd lived all of our lives, it was almost like a third-world country compared to that of the other world.

Actually, it really was third-world type living, but it was like this globally. The war had destroyed civilizations across the planet, wiping out all electrical systems and the technology that required them—computers, digital networks, motorized transportation . . . everything. And the black magic that still remained, no matter how hard Mom's people tried to remove it, kept frying any attempts at rebuilding the grid and technology. While angel blood had counteracted some of the nuclear fallout, preventing the earth and humanity from completely dying out, that which spilled during the war hadn't been enough to overcome the black magic. Then terrible storms and other natural disasters frequently stirred up the dark energy and flattened entire towns. Brielle had intended to learn how to successfully transmute the black magic and meld it with technology while at college, but we hadn't been there long enough.

My gaze swept over Market Square, taking it all in. It was almost unrecognizable compared to last time, which I found comforting. My tense muscles relaxed some, and I could fully exhale when the emotions of that fateful night didn't slam back into me at the sight—because nothing was the same. The market's growth brought a bigger variety of products for sale and larger crowds, and other changes—mages, shifters, and the occasional vampire weren't the only supes that had moved in.

Charleigh leaned in close to me and whispered, "Do you see what I see? Pointy ears and tilted eyes?"

"Since when did fae hang out in our realm?" I murmured.

They supposedly hated our realm, especially after the war because the dark energy was too much for their natures. Then again, as we passed a few while scoping out the area, I realized these fae felt a little dark themselves. That didn't stop a trail of humans practically throwing themselves at the otherworldly creatures. Even Charleigh started to go doe-eyed, her feet shuffling forward toward a male whose back was turned to us, his silky black hair flowing over his shoulders.

"Hey!" I grabbed her arm and yanked her back to us.

"Shit," she murmured, then she mumbled what sounded like a spell. "Protection."

"I can't believe they're just out here in the open," Brielle whispered.

Neither could I, especially with all their features on full view. Not just the pointy ears and tilted eyes, but the faerie stones embedded like jewels in their skin and colorful markings in elaborate designs that looked like tattoos but moved, some giving off a faint glow. These fae weren't even trying to hide or blend in like they did at school.

Most everything we knew about the fae was from the shiny world, where we had some as classmates and friends. There were multiple fae realms across the dimensions, though, so I didn't know if those fae were the same as ours here. Sadie was an elf from Faery, which technically made her a type of fae. As far as I knew, the Faery realm of our dimension didn't have elves. Of course, the fae connected to our world had always been super secretive, so that didn't really mean anything.

All we knew about ours was that they were mischievous but could be malevolent, and as a rule of thumb, they stayed out of human affairs as well as Amadis/Daemoni and angel/demon business. Some leaned one way or the other, though, and could be helpful—for a price, of course. Giving a fae your word and then breaking it not only put your own neck on the execution block, but those you loved, as well. Even Dad's mom, who was full-blooded fae herself, cautioned us to never make a deal with any of her kind.

We'd also been warned about the fae's *special* effect on others, even other supernaturals. We hadn't noticed it in the other world, but I definitely sensed it here, even when those around us now must have dialed down the intensity of that effect. Otherwise, pretty much everyone in the market would be naked and throwing themselves at the glorious forms of the sex gods. Er, the fae. I meant the fae. *Shit.* The effect's intensity may have been muted, but I still caught a taste of it.

"Hey, look," Brie said, thankfully distracting me as she tilted her head toward a shop a few stalls down, where an older woman hunched behind the table. "Isn't that Gertie?"

"Yes!" Charleigh nearly squealed, and we rushed toward the booth selling knitted goods, including replicas of the dolls we used to play with when we were little, made from scrap yarn and material. The elderly norm was definitely from the

Loft, her gray head with the thinning hair and milky blue eyes familiar, even if her face seemed more creased than before.

"Gertie?" Brielle called out when we were nearly there.

Her head lifted, her eyes narrowing on us for a moment before recognition filled them. I expected a grin to greet us. She'd always liked us. Instead, her eyes widened, filled with fear, and she shook her head.

"What's wrong?" Charleigh asked as we entered the stall.

"Get out," she hissed.

"Don't you—" I began, but she cut me off.

"I said to get out!" She waved her hands at us, shooing us away, but we didn't move at first. "Go away! I have *nothing* for you."

The three of us exchanged a glance before hurrying out of the stall.

"That was weird, right?" Brielle whispered.

"Do you think she has dementia?" Charleigh asked as we moved along. "She does look like she's aged a few years since we last saw her."

I snorted. "More like a decade."

"And that was less than two years ago."

"Maybe something happened to her," Brie suggested. "Maybe she had a stroke. Or something caused by the *colata* tree that ate her foot. That could be why she doesn't remember us."

"Whatever happened, she's obviously no help. Let's keep going," I said, nervous energy ramping up again. I felt like we were buying our time here, and we'd soon run out of currency.

As we searched for more familiar faces, I couldn't help but inspect some of the goods for sale, even if the clothes were nothing like what I'd become used to. Charleigh was especially drawn to the tents selling witchy wares—which there were several of, compared to last time, when there'd been only one.

"I'm officially ruined," Charleigh lamented as we left one such stall, tugging on the straps of her backpack. "I should have raided the apothecary at school and brought more supplies with us. I only grabbed a few of the rarest and most versatile."

"The magic is in us," I reminded her, echoing one of our mage teacher's favorite things to say. "Who needs tools?"

She snorted. "Maybe not you and Brielle, but I'm just a lowly witch and still need supplies for potions."

We entered another tent selling mostly healing salves, herbs, and oils, where a pretty girl about our age haggled with the vendor. Her blond braids and dreadlocks trailed down her back, over a large bag, a quiver of arrows, and a bow. I couldn't get a read on her—if she was human or something else, which made me think something else but hiding her true energy.

"Okay, okay, Sky, you wore me down. I'll take the burn salves," the vendor, a middle-aged woman with graying red hair, said. "But do you have any of those dreamcatchers?"

The blonde leaned back on her heels and gave the woman a pointed look with a single brow arched upward. "I thought you didn't believe in them."

The vendor pulled her lips to the side and shrugged. "My son's been having terrible nightmares. I heard yours work."

"Of course, they do." The girl named Sky dug into her bag and pulled out a gorgeous dreamcatcher with stones that looked like green jade and prehnite woven into the indigo string, blue and green ribbons and feathers trailing from the ring. "I need to set the intention, though, so you'll have to give me more details."

Mage—she must have been some kind of mage. They were all about setting intentions.

The vendor looked over at us, her brows raised high. "Can I help you?"

"No, we're good, thanks," Charleigh replied, ushering my sister and me out. The woman obviously wanted privacy.

We'd just stepped back into the road when a commotion broke out a dozen yards or so to our right.

"What the hell, Breandán!" a man called as another came running in our direction, his long black hair flowing behind him, exposing the pointy tips of his ears.

"Oh, no," gasped a voice behind us. I glanced over my shoulder to see Sky stare at the fae running toward us, people shouting and cursing at him as he pushed his way through the throng of shoppers. Panic filled Sky's face before she spun and took off in a sprint in the other direction, darting through the crowd until she disappeared.

When I turned back toward the fae, he'd stopped running a few stalls down, his hands on his hips as blue-violet eyes glared this way. Not after Sky, but directly on Brielle. And then on me.

"You," he mouthed, a terrifying grin filling his inhumanly beautiful face. And murder filling his eyes.

"Fuck," Charleigh gasped. "Run!"

She shoved us forward, and we sprinted after Sky, following her path. We never caught up to her before Charleigh grabbed Brielle's wrist and tugged her to the right. I followed them into an alley between real, brick-and-mortar buildings. She pushed us into an alcove and immediately whispered a spell between gasps.

"Okay, we're cloaked," she said, her voice low.

Though we knew we couldn't be seen by anyone else, we remained statue still and silent until we watched the black-haired fae run past the alley. And then we waited another few minutes, just to be sure. Finally, my patience snapped.

"Who the hell was that?" I demanded.

"I don't know, but I'd say we're still wanted," Brielle said. "The fae were one of the factions who wanted to kill us before we left."

"Are you sure? Some just wanted to enslave us for our powers," I reminded her. "I don't think we were ever told who wants what from us, though. It's all so confusing."

She leveled me with a glare. "It's not a joke, Elli. Either way, we have a problem. So what now? And don't say fight."

We didn't have a chance to answer. We pressed up against the brick wall as a tall, broad man with greasy red hair and pocked skin sauntered down the alley, passing within inches of us.

"I know you're here, little girls," he called out, his gaze sweeping around.

Pure hatred filled me when he looked our way with eyes that were completely black. A demon in a human suit. I still hated demons with a passion, that fateful night fueling it even more. Not even the nice ones in the shiny world had been able to change that.

"No, Elli," Charleigh warned quietly, even if it couldn't hear us through her spell. She knew me too well. And she could probably feel the need to kill it pouring off of me. My beast inside me lifted her head with intrigue. A part of me wanted to call on her. Waking her might be worth the chance to rid the world of another demon.

"I can easily take it out," I said through clenched teeth, already drawing on my magic, my fingers inching inside my cloak and under the tank to the secret pocket. A spelled throwing star should do the deed. "Send it back to Hell where it belongs."

"With what just happened, we don't need to cause a scene," she said. "Besides, it's in a human suit. That could be a major demon in there."

The demon spun, its gaze aimed right at us as we pressed ourselves against the rough brick. If it could see us through Charleigh's cloak, it was no lesser demon. I didn't care, though. I'd been wrong—the market had been a distraction, but the emotions of that night still swirled, now moving closer to the surface. My hands clenched into fists, aching to unleash my magic. I couldn't defeat Shamara then, but I was much more powerful now.

Just as it lifted a hand toward my face, a boulder dropped from the sky right behind it. All three of us gasped.

No, not a boulder. A gargoyle.

"Uncle Aidan?" Brielle whispered, though he couldn't hear her.

The stone figure rose to its full height, towering over the demon in the human suit. Its wings spread outward, tripling its size, as its carved lips bared jagged teeth.

"Mine," the gargoyle grumbled, the sound of rocks falling over each other.

The demon shot down the alley, the gargoyle lifting into the air to follow. They disappeared around a corner, and we exhaled a collective breath when a loud roar echoed off the brick walls. A few moments later, a tiger rounded the same corner and stared in our direction with large yellow eyes, its orange and white fur striped in black raised along its back.

Relief swept over us. I could tangibly feel my sister and cousin's energy change just as much as my own. The tiger's ears twitched, and the tail flicked, then it turned and waited. Without a word, we followed the feline down the alley and turned onto a path where we had to be careful to avoid the people giving the beast a wide berth—a testament to how much had changed in the Edge that a tiger walking down the road was barely noticed. We made another turn and then entered one of the train car residences. As soon as we did, the tiger huffed then shifted, a tall, thin brunette replacing it.

She quickly lit a candle before drawing the car's door closed, then turned and dropped her hands to her naked hips. "What the hell are you girls doing here?"

CHAPTER 4

*a*unt Sheree stared us at expectantly, her long fingers tapping on her bony hips.

"We're looking for you," Brielle answered her. "Well, for our parents, but you're the next best thing."

"What are you even doing in this world, though?" Sheree demanded as she slipped behind a room divider. The narrow train car provided barely enough space for a sink and a couple of cabinets in one corner to the left and cushions piled on some kind of hobbled together frame to form a wide chair in the other corner. I could see the edges of a bed beyond the divider at the far end to our right, where Sheree had gone. "Did something happen? Were you in danger where you were?"

"We weren't sure," I answered, not quite a lie. Like Aunt Blossom, Sheree was one of Mom's best friends and on her inner council. Unlike Aunt Vanessa—who could be terrifying sometimes—or Aunt Blossom—whom we couldn't spill too much to, being Charleigh's mom and all—Aunt Sheree was the one we could go to and know we wouldn't get in trouble or feel judged. She'd listen, and she'd help. I'd normally have no problem telling her why we'd come back, even if it did sound a little overreactive, but as soon as I started talking, I stumbled over my thoughts and words, wondering if I was making a big mistake. "I saw something. During one of my classes. I was supposed to be developing my intuition. Seeing beyond what's right in front of me. And what I saw . . . I didn't know then if it was a vision of what was already happening or a premonition of something to come or . . . I don't know what, but it scared me. Truly scared me."

"What did you see?" she asked as she pulled back the room divider to join the sleeping area with the main room. Now wearing faded jeans and a black T-shirt, she dropped to her knees and plunged her arms under the bed, fishing for something. Her dark brown hair was cut much shorter than the last time we'd seen her, barely touching her shoulders.

I hesitated. Though I knew I could trust her, I also knew how ridiculous it sounded when I said it out loud. "Horses— black, smoky horses, enormous, at least two stories tall, and riding them were giant, black smoky figures with red glowing eyes," I began. She pulled out a backpack and a duffel bag, turning on her knees to stare at me. Her mouth was already opening, but I hurried on. "It's not really *what* I saw, though. It's how it *felt*." I shuddered at the memory of the terror they'd evoked while I was in the mirrors. "Complete and utter darkness. Like they were pure, unadulterated evil personified, spreading over this world and pouring into that one, too."

I purposely left out what else I'd felt—the little thrill in my belly at the magnificent sight of them. The desire to give myself over, thoroughly and completely, just for the chance to bathe in their energy. The longing to become a part of them . . . one of them.

"And you're sure it wasn't just a dream?" Sheree asked.

Crossing my arms over my chest, I eyed her dead-on. "Absolutely. I was wide awake, fighting for my life and everyone else's at my school."

Her dark hazel gaze flicked to my sister and cousin before

landing back on me. If she could see and feel what I had, she'd understand, but there was no way to do the whole experience justice. Brielle and Charleigh understood only because they'd been there when I'd stumbled out of the hall of mirrors. They knew, as Sheree did, how hard it was to rattle me.

Still sitting on her knees on the floor, she braced her hands on her thighs. "So you thought leaving the one place where you couldn't possibly be any safer was the right action to take?"

"We didn't know what to do," Charleigh intervened. "If you saw Elliana like we had . . . We had to know what was going on here. I tried to contact Mom with the charm she gave me, but I don't think it worked. The twins' faerie stones didn't work either—Aunt Alexis never responded. Nobody did."

I pressed my fingers to my chest, over my heart, where a chip of faerie stone was embedded. According to the story, the stone came from Faery, imbued with certain qualities from my grandmother, Bree, and enhanced by the angels themselves to emotionally connect the holder of the stone to the original keeper—our dad. He'd been instructed to give it our mom, which strengthened their soul-mate bond. When we'd gone to that other world, Dad had ordered Owen to come back for Charleigh, so she could serve her role as our sworn protector. Before our parents left, she divided Mom's stone into three pieces and embedded one into each of our chests, hopefully connecting us, even across dimensions. We'd felt Mom's energy at first . . . and then one day, not all that long after they'd left us in that world, it was gone.

When I glanced at Brielle, I noticed she also pressed her hand to the same place on her own chest. Looking back at me, she shook her head, her eyes filled with fear.

"We still don't feel her," I whispered.

Sheree frowned.

"Then when our parents didn't show up to visit like they'd promised, we knew something was wrong," Brielle added.

I cleared my throat and shifted on my feet, not wanting to admit the next part, but Sheree had to understand that we needed to come back. I looked at Brielle while silently warning her through our mind-link what I was about to disclose, and she gave a small nod. We couldn't deny this any longer.

"Besides, if nothing else," I said, "I knew for sure one thing: the darkness not only found Brie and me in that world, but it's growing stronger. The leaders of that safe haven only allowed us to stay as long as we didn't bring trouble to their town. I was afraid we could no longer ensure that. They would have made us come back soon anyway."

Sheree's frown deepened into a scowl. "Well, shit."

We stood in silence as she pushed her hand through her hair and stared at the floor, seeming to be contemplating what to do with us. I wasn't surprised that last bit would find its mark. Brielle and I hadn't been the perfect princesses everyone had hoped for to save the Amadis and the world.

"We really just need to find our parents," Brielle said, breaking the drawn-out silence. "Are they here?"

Sheree's head snapped up, her eyes focusing as though she just remembered we were even there. Then she leaned forward over her knees, pulling clothes, weapons, and other items out from under the bed.

"What happened to everyone at the Loft anyway?" Charleigh asked. "We went there first."

Sitting back up, our aunt blew out a breath. "A lot has happened since you've been gone. Well, of course it has, as long as it's been. I really wish we could have been there to see you graduate. Ah, I've heard so much about that world and how amazing it is. Makes me miss the Before time so much, but I'm happy that you three got to experience something like it."

"Aunt Sheree," Charleigh interrupted, "you're rambling like my mom."

"Oh, yeah, sorry."

"What all has happened?" I persisted. Unlike Blossom, Sheree wasn't exactly a talker. And she wasn't making a lot of sense, like about how long we'd been gone and missing our graduation. It hadn't even been two years since we last saw her. "And why are you packing?"

Glancing at the stuffed bags, she pursed her lips and rose to her full, quite tall height. In three strides, her long legs carried her over to the cabinets, where she pulled out a jug and cups. She poured us each a glass and handed it to us—a light brown liquid sloshed around inside. The smell just about got me, but I took a sip anyway—and nearly spit it everywhere when I tasted what might have been the worst moonshine ever. Or maybe it was just because my taste buds had been spoiled rotten the last year. Sheree motioned for us to sit. Charleigh and Brielle shared the chair, but I just leaned against the wall.

Our aunt pressed her butt against the countertop across from me. "As you can imagine, things got pretty bad after the massacre here at the Edge. Both your mom and Shamara, that demon bitch, violated the peace treaty. Unfortunately, a lot more people in most factions are taking Shamara's side, including a lot of norms."

"What?" Brielle and Charleigh gasped. I, however, wasn't surprised by this.

She frowned. "A lot of humans died that night. Other beings, too. While the supernaturals know the truth, not all of the humans believe that demons had set up camp in their loved ones' bodies. Your mom looked like the bad guy, only out to protect herself and you two, no matter the consequences. They don't get that she'd been protecting the humans, too. The demons and Daemoni have exploited that perception, driving a wedge between factions, including humans. The dark fae are taking advantage of it all, more and more of them coming to this realm and joining their side. Your mom managed to prevent war, but tensions were growing worse and worse. She had to seek out allies."

"So where are Mom and Dad?" Brielle demanded.

"And where are my parents?" Charleigh asked.

"Last I heard, Alexis and Tristan went to talk to the Light fae, to try to get an audience with the Seelie king in the Summer Court."

"Wait, what?" I said. "Seelie fae and Summer Court?" I knew these terms from Sadie and her Faery realm, but I didn't know the fae of our world used them.

Sheree sighed. "Right, I forgot. The fae have become so common now, and we've learned so much. I forgot you didn't know about them when you were here."

"We do now," Brielle said. "From school." She looked at me with a glint in her eyes. I knew what she was thinking— this meant Sadie could be right. Our Faery realms could be connected. I didn't want to lift my hopes too high, though.

"So your grandmother Bree is Seelie fae," Sheree continued. "I didn't catch it all, but Bree is part of the Summer Court. Your parents, along with Owen and Vanessa, were going to see if Bree could help facilitate an alliance between the Amadis and the Seelie fae, while the rest of us headed to Amadis Island to regroup with your uncle Noah. But then Blossom left to catch up to your parents because . . ." She drifted off, and the corners of her mouth turned down a bit as she crossed over to Charleigh and squatted in front of her. I straightened as I watched them. "Charleigh, honey, there was a skirmish on our way to Amadis Island, and Jax was hit with some kind of black magic."

"Oh, no!" Charleigh clapped her hands over her mouth, her words coming out muffled. "Is he . . . ?"

Sheree shook her head. "No, he's alive. Last I heard, anyway. But your dad's hurt badly, and nobody can figure out how to cure him. It's either demon magic or fae. Your mom hasn't been able to counter it with any of her own magic, so she went in search of the Seelie Court."

I gnawed on my bottom lip, wondering if Charleigh realized what this meant—if her mom could even find her way to Seelie Court, she would have to make a deal with a fae.

"So you don't have to be fae to go to Faery?" Brielle asked. We already knew that was true for the fae we'd met in the shiny world.

"Anyone a fae wants in Faery can go to Faery," Sheree said. "So your dad—and probably you two, as well—can take anyone you want there. And as you've seen, fae seem to be everywhere these days. Blossom only needed to ask for Bree, and she might have found a way in."

"So when will they be back?" I asked.

Turning, Sheree opened the cabinets, retrieving a few items, then strode back over to the bags on the bed. "That's the question of the decade, apparently."

"What do you mean?" Brielle asked.

Sheree hesitated, her back to us as she fiddled with the items in the backpack. "We haven't heard from them in . . . a while. When the Loft was raided, we all figured it best to disperse and go underground again until your mom returned. Alexis left Noah in charge, but all of the Amadis have been keeping a low profile. It's been the best way to keep the peace until we know we have allies."

I could feel her coming closer to the truth, but still sidestepping. "Aunt Sheree," I said, my voice low, "are our parents okay?"

She finally turned around, blinking rapidly, the corners of her mouth pulling down. "We don't know. They could be perfectly fine. They probably are. They're powerful and can definitely take care of themselves. And I mean, time passes differently in Faery, right? It's probably been only like a week there, but . . . it's been over three years here."

"*What?*" we all said again.

"How can that be?" Charleigh asked. "We left only a year-and-a-half ago."

Sheree shook her head, her brows coming together. "No, it's been four."

The three of us exchanged a look, then Brielle's eyes lit up.

"It's the whole timeline shift phenomena when passing through dimensions." She turned, her gaze bouncing between Charleigh and me as her nerdy self showed through. "Remember, we learned about it in class?"

Charleigh smirked. "Can't say I learned a whole lot in that class. I was a little distracted by the sexy teacher in the kilt—and what was under it."

I rolled my eyes. "I remember. Passing between dimensions can take you forward or backward on the timeline, even between two worlds that are near exact replicas."

"And in other realms, like Faery," Brielle continued, "time can actually pass faster or slower."

"So this at least explains why so much has changed here in what we thought was a short time," I said.

Sheree stared at us, her brows raised so high, her forehead crinkled. "Wow. Guess you did learn something. When your parents took you there, they said they'd only been there a few days, but when they came back, a month had passed here. That was part of the problem—it had appeared as though they fled, making them look guiltier. Your mom and dad did their best to keep the factions calm, but then the Loft was raided along with other Amadis strongholds around the world, and they knew they had to find help. So here we are."

"Not for long," came a deep voice with a Scottish accent, as the rusty metal door slid open with an ear-piercing screech. Uncle Aidan strode in. As if the space wasn't already small, he filled it completely. His bright blue gaze first went to Sheree. "Are we packed?"

"Just about," she said.

Aidan looked at us, crossing his thick arms over his barrel chest and shaking his head. "Don't know if I'm glad to see you lasses or if I want to strangle ya."

Then he opened his arms, and we each took a turn giving him a quick hug.

"You'll notify Noah?" Sheree asked as she shouldered the backpack and handed Aidan the duffle bag.

"Aye. I will. Tell the girls where to meet." He turned to us. "You lasses have weapons?" We all nodded. "Be vigilant." With a quick kiss to her cheek and a wave to us, Aidan left out the door again.

"What's going on?" I asked, sensing the tension as Sheree slid the door closed.

When she spoke, she dropped her voice to a near whisper. "We have to leave, but we can't go together. You three need to get out of town A.S.A.P. *Nobody* can know you're here or all hell will break loose. If Gertie hadn't delivered that message to Aidan in time, who knows where you three would be right now. Shamara may have fled the town and hasn't been seen here since, but for all intents and purposes, this town belongs to her. She'll find out you're here, and tonight is not the night we'll be starting a war. Too many powerful beings want to use you or kill you, and too many others have already died to protect you."

The mention of Shamara made the beast inside me stir, but the guilt Sheree had just laid down tempered the anger.

"Won't they already know, though, since you helped us in the alley?" Brielle asked, her voice quiet and laced with concern.

"How do they even let you live here?" I asked. "Surely there's still someone here from that night who knows you're part of Mom's guard."

"With a few memory adjustments by a warlock. We've been here right under everyone's noses for about a year, spying. Until today, we hadn't ever shifted in town, so nobody knew what kind of shifters we are. But a gargoyle and a tiger—there's a warrant out for those two. And helping three young women with your descriptions? Dead giveaway. So yeah, they know, which is why we can't go together." Sheree shrugged. "It's fine. I hate it here anyway. We'll meet up with Noah, your parents will return, Jax will heal, and everything will be okay."

She gave us a weak smile that didn't reach her eyes. She believed everything would be okay about as much as I did—not at all.

"But first you need to glamour yourselves," she continued. "Make yourselves look like fae. The Light and Dark are harder to distinguish from each other and apparently there's so much intermixing of their blood, as much as they try to deny it, that you won't seem off. They won't sense your true identities. And glamour Charleigh."

"I can just cloak us," Charleigh said. "You, too. Nobody has to see anything."

Sheree shook her head. "Aidan's already started a rumor about our departure. I need people to see me leaving. We'll meet up in two days across the river."

She told us where and the best way to slip out of town. Following her instructions, Brielle and I made us all look fae with pointy ears, upturned eyes, and colored hair—Brielle's lilac, Charleigh's silver, and mine a pretty teal green—and then we waited twenty minutes after Sheree departed before leaving ourselves.

We followed a different route out of town than how we'd come in, and my gut tightened as I realized where exactly it would take us. We hadn't made it to the far side of Market Square earlier—to the place where we'd been when all hell broke loose last time. As we approached it, the memory came clear as day, and now the emotions nearly swallowed me whole.

For a moment, I felt a false sense of joy as I was lost in the memory, but it immediately dissipated. Anger replaced it as Dani's screams from that night echoed in my ears and the vision of her papa lying unnaturally still as blood poured from his eyes and ears flashed across my mind. Then the anger was pushed aside by the overwhelming need to kill that fucking demon-bitch Shamara. She'd destroyed everything. Sure, my mother played a part in it all, but it came down to Shamara. Because of her, I'd lost Dani forever.

I kept my head lowered, watching the ground as we walked down the road where Dani used to live. I couldn't block the echoes of her screams in my head, though, and I knew the moment I passed Papa Miguel's door. I didn't look that way, but something had me looking to my left instead and upward. To the roof of the four-story brick building left over from the Before time, as though I expected to see something there, though I knew not what. And of course, there was nothing.

At first, as we neared the gate to leave this gods-forsaken town that I hoped to never have to return to again, I thought the flood of memories was responsible for the stench of brimstone and sulfur. But when I glanced to my right, I realized the odor was very real. Just inside the town's walls gathered a group of demons, not even in human suits, but in their natural form—seven or so feet tall with mottled, oily skin, leathery bat-like wings, horned heads, and hooved feet. As though they were one, they all turned to glare at us. Could they see through our glamour? Could anyone else see them? Surely not. Sheree said norms took Shamara's side. They couldn't possibly believe she was on the right side if they could see her demons like this. If they knew the truth.

My fists clenched at my sides as I talked my beast down

from the overwhelming urge to slaughter them all. Like Sheree said, this was not the night to start a war.

Just before we passed through the gate, a smaller figure in the middle of their group shifted and turned our way. And I let out a string of profanity while Brielle grabbed my arm and yanked me out of town.

"That was Dani," I hissed. "We have to help her!"

e passed through the gates, and Brielle dragged me into the nearby forest, refusing to release my arm the entire way, no matter how hard I tried to break free, and unfortunately, our strengths were matched. Charleigh threatened to use her magic to bind me if I didn't settle down. It was just like that night, when Uncle Owen had bound me after I'd head-butted Aunt Vanessa. Once again, I felt like we were betraying Dani, leaving her with those who would eventually devour her soul.

"We have to go back and get her," I insisted.

"No. We have to get as far away from there as possible," Brielle said, her grip on me tightening as her pace quickened, pulling me along.

"She's in this mess because of us," I reminded my sister. "I left her last time when she needed me most. I owe it to her!"

"Elliana, you heard Aunt Sheree," she said.

"I'm not sure I believe everything Aunt Sheree told us," I muttered. "Or, at least, she didn't tell us everything. Like how Dani is being held captive by Shamara!"

"We don't know that's the case," Charleigh said. "Or that

Sheree or Aidan knew about it. Maybe they just brought her in." She paused, then added, "Sheree did seem off, though."

"Exactly," I said.

Brielle sighed. "I noticed it, too."

We'd already traveled a quarter-mile or more out of town, weaving our way through the woods that bordered the wide river. After another fifteen minutes or so, I eventually slowed my pace, forcing Brielle to slow, too.

"Elli," she warned.

I jerked my arm free. "Just listen to me for a minute."

Before I could go on, a stick snapped nearby, and we all fell silent and still, listening and sensing. Something was out there. Had it been following us? The three of us exchanged a look, then I spun in the direction of the sound. A looming, dark figure strode toward us on four legs. Some kind of beast. I called on the fire within me, and a flame arose in my outstretched palm, illuminating the area better. A large, black wolf bared its long, sharp teeth as it growled, crouching lower to the ground with red eyes glaring at us. Daemoni. *Shit*. Did it know we were us? Or did it see three fae? Fae were powerful and drew on the elements, so I hadn't given us away with the fire. But were fae strong enough to defeat a Daemoni shifter? Maybe three would be, and we weren't fae anyway. They used to call us the Triple Threat for a reason. We could easily take this beast on. The wolf stalked closer, and I threw a ball of flames at it. The werewolf yelped and fell back, but then sprang at us.

Charleigh blasted a spell, but the wolf dove down, avoiding it and hitting the ground in a low crouch. A purplish-silver bolt of electricity jagged through the air as Brielle shocked the beast, and the stench of burning fur made my nostrils flare and my throat burn. She held both palms out, one paralyzing the creature while the other continued to shock it. The sound of running footsteps came from all directions, and I swore under my breath. We should have known the wolf wasn't alone. They tended to travel in packs. I felt confident we could have taken them all on, probably easily and efficiently, too, depending on how many there were, but we couldn't risk revealing our true identities.

I didn't wait for Brielle to flip through the options of drawing weapons and fighting or making a run for it. Taking the matter into my own hands—literally—I grew a larger fireball between my palms and shoved it at the wolf, surrounding it in a wall of flames, then yelled, "Run!"

We took off in a sprint as the other footsteps closed in on us, steering clear of an encampment to the west, dodging around the trees, and hurdling fallen logs until we found a large boulder. As we darted behind it and fell to our knees, Charleigh threw a cloak over us. Though the spell would muffle us, too, we remained silent as we squatted behind the rock, listening and waiting.

A moment later, a blur fell from the sky, landing on four legs and startling us all.

"Sasha," Charleigh breathed.

"It's okay, girl." Brielle reached out to try to soothe her, knowing she'd give us away, but the *lykora* seemed to disagree. The little white dog grew to the size of a wolf, her black tiger stripes and wings on full display. She flew off before we could stop her.

"That was a fucking Daemoni wolf pack," Charleigh hissed. "If they see Sasha, they'll know who we are."

"We should keep moving," Brielle whispered.

Several wolfish yelps sounded in succession, and a moment later, Sasha strode toward us, her muzzle stained red. Seeing through Charleigh's cloak, she rejoined us, shrinking back into her toy-dog form, the blood disappearing.

"Good girl," I praised, stroking her soft fur. As Amadis and Earth's Angels, we weren't supposed to kill unless there was no hope for the other's soul or it was a matter of life or death for us. I didn't know about those werewolves' souls, and I didn't know if it was really a situation of our lives or theirs, because the Daemoni had special plans for us. But I didn't care. They were dead. My sister and cousin were safe.

"Let's get out of here," Brielle said.

"No, wait." I grabbed her arm with a tight grip as she'd done with me earlier. "We need to go back to the Edge."

"Are you crazy?" she snapped. "We could have been caught just now. It's even more dangerous there."

"That wolf didn't recognize us. If it had, it wouldn't have attacked. It would have waited for its pack to surround us and take us in. You know the Daemoni wouldn't kill us. Not right away."

"So?"

"So they won't recognize us in Misery's Edge, either. Especially if we go in cloaked. We can listen and see if we can find out anything about our parents."

"Aunt Sheree said they're in Faery," Brielle argued.

"As far as she knows," I hissed. "But nobody's heard from them in three years, Brie. Three years! Do you really think Mom would let that much time go by without checking in on her people and this world? On us? That Aunt Blossom would make Uncle Jax wait that long?"

"No way," Charleigh whispered. "She'd go crazy wondering if he was still alive."

"Exactly." I nodded. "And they would know a lot of time has passed in this realm. They're not stupid. So either they're being held against their will, or they did come back and the demons have them. Or . . . worse." My voice dropped on the last word. "Until the end, Brielle. That's our promise to each other and Mom and Dad. It is not yet the end. We can't turn our backs on them!"

Brielle gnawed on her lip, blinking rapidly. I thought my words might have hit their mark. Our parents used to always tell us they'd love us until the end of always and forever—and they'd fight for us for just as long. It had become our family motto, so to speak.

My words definitely hit home with Charleigh. She looked away, her shoulders curling inward. Maybe I should have felt guilty for making them worry or for manipulating them, but I didn't. We could have potentially worse issues to deal with.

"Let's go back and do our own spying," I continued. "We can be cloaked, unlike Aunt Sheree and Uncle Aidan, and get closer to the enemy."

"You just want to save Dani," Brielle said.

"I do, but that's not the only reason. What if they have our parents, too? Or they at least know where they are?"

My twin seemed to be considering the idea more. I glanced at Charleigh, and she gave me a slight nod. She was in. We just had to convince Brielle.

"It's too dangerous," she finally said. "We'll meet up with everyone in two days and find out more. Noah might have other information, and he can send a whole team in to extract Dani."

I suppressed a growl. "She could be dead by then. Or become some demon's meat suit."

"How do you know she's not already?" Brielle leveled me with her weirdly violet gaze, glamoured from her normal brown.

A lump formed in my throat. If she expected that to dissuade me, she was dead wrong. If anything, it only made the need to go back stronger. I had to at least know if that was still my Dani or if she was already long gone.

"Why don't we find a place to camp for the night?" Charleigh suggested. "We can discuss it more and decide. It's probably not safe to do anything at night anyway, when those who want us most will be out in bigger numbers."

We stared at my sister for a long moment before she finally let out a harsh breath and nodded in agreement.

"There was a camp about a quarter mile back, right on the river," I said.

"We should probably stay away from anyone," Brielle said.

"We're glamoured. And who knows what we might learn?"

"I agree," Charleigh said. "Even if it's nothing about our parents, this world has changed a lot while we were gone. We need to know as much as possible, so we don't come across as complete morons and give ourselves away."

So we headed back toward the camp. It was more like a tent city, a permanent settlement, it appeared, where travelers came and went as needed. With no factories to produce materials for proper rebuilding of the infrastructure and housing, many people still lived a vagabond type life, scrounging for goods to repurpose and use or to trade so they could live another day or week or month. The contrast of this world to the shiny one once again was pronounced. The people in that other world had no idea just how good they had it.

Expecting to return to the Loft, we hadn't packed anything like a tent or bedroll. Just the clothes on our backs and in our backpacks, and weapons, of course. We stopped on the edge of the camp, claiming a spot and discussing what we could possibly trade for food and something to sleep in—or at least on. Sasha sniffed around the area, drifting away.

"Well, aren't you the cutest thing?" The female voice sounded vaguely familiar, and I glanced over my shoulder to see a young woman about our age squatting in front of Sasha and petting the white dog. Her hair was in braids and dreadlocks, and I recognized her from the market earlier. "I think I saw you in the forest before. Did you find your humans?"

I shot to my feet and spun to face her. I still couldn't get a read on what she was. She *appeared* to be human, but something told me she wasn't. I would have smelled wolf on her if she was one of the shifters, but I didn't. She was either a mage, who could easily pass for human, or a glamoured fae. At the stall this afternoon, she'd spoken like a mage, but that didn't necessarily mean anything.

"Oh, hey," she said, offering me a smile. She gripped her bow in one hand, and a quiver of arrows hung on her back. Two dead rabbits swung on a rope from her belt on one hip and a knife on the other. "Cute dog."

She didn't seem to recognize us from earlier, which meant she couldn't see through our glamour.

"Are you camping here?" she asked when I didn't reply. She peered over my shoulder where Charleigh and Brie sat on the ground.

"I don't think that's any of your concern," I said, still trying to get a feel on her.

She shrugged. "I was here last night and made this my spot." My hackles rose, my own weapons feeling quite noticeable all of a sudden, but she hurried on. "I was going to say there's plenty of room for all of us, and strength in numbers and all that."

"If you can trust the people who make up those numbers," I muttered.

"Let's start with names. I'm Skylar." She lifted the two rabbits hanging on her hip. "And I have dinner."

Ugh. It was a far cry from cheeseburgers and fries, but we were all starving. We'd brought a few treats from the shiny world, but it wasn't like we could pull them out in front of other people. We wouldn't be able to answer the questions that would surely bombard us. Claiming to have found a hidden stash somewhere while scavenging wouldn't have made sense. The food would have been inedible, hard as rocks.

"We're Bella, Penny, and Iris," Brielle chirped.

Skylar eyed each of us in turn with an olive-green gaze. She didn't buy it. Brie wasn't exactly the greatest liar.

"It's nice to meet you," Skylar finally said.

We settled in and cautiously questioned her about where

she was from and where she'd been. She was a traveler, creating items from nature and selling them when she came upon the markets, such as the dreamcatchers and salves she'd been selling to the vendor earlier in the day. She frequented Misery's Edge because it was one of the biggest trading towns in the region. Only Crescent City, where New Orleans had once been, was bigger.

"I don't know which is more dangerous, though," Skylar said. "I try to stay away from any town as much as possible, until I'm out of necessities."

Brielle gave me a pointed look.

"*Which means even more dangerous for us,*" she silently quipped. I chose to ignore her.

Skylar offered a couple of blankets to us, which Brielle and Charleigh took.

"I'll take first watch," I said.

Brielle narrowed her eyes at me, but she didn't argue. Perhaps she understood that as soon as I closed my eyes, I'd see one of three things—the massacre of that night, the red eyes and black smoky horses, or Sadie's face—none of which would allow sleep to come.

"Wake me up in two hours," my twin said. "I'll take next watch."

She probably thought me more likely to take off later in the night. She was wrong. As soon as they were all asleep—I tugged on our twin connection to ensure she was truly unconscious—I crept away, leaving my backpack behind so if Brielle woke, she'd think I'd gone to the bathroom or something. Hopefully, I'd be back before then, though. I'd make this as quick as possible, and when she woke to Dani and me here safe and sound, she wouldn't be able to say a thing.

Sasha started to follow me, but I ordered her to stay before flashing to the outskirts of Misery's Edge, to a place in the woods where I could see the gate we'd exited hours before.

Charleigh appeared right next to me, apparently following my flash. I wasn't surprised. Charleigh always had my back.

"You should have stayed with Brielle," I whispered, patting my glamoured fighting gear, taking stock of my weapons—throwing stars in my vest, the dagger on my thigh, and the sword on my back. Of course, I always had other weapons at my disposal, too. "I'm not sure that I trust that Skylar."

"Brie has Sasha to protect her. You need me."

I wouldn't argue with her. Two sets of ears were better than one, especially since she could cloak us.

"Thank you," I said with a grateful smile. "So I thought we'd find where the demon-fuckers are congregating and listen first, see what we can learn. We need to find out where Shamara is so I can kill that bitch. Send her back to Hell, anyway."

"Not even your mom could kill her, Elli, and wasn't she charged up with Earth's Angel power?"

I frowned. As our leader, Mom was the only one who could pull on the power of all Earth's Angels—all of our kin spread around the world. When she did that night, she unleashed a powerful blast, but Charleigh was right. It hadn't killed Shamara.

But Mom didn't have a beast like I did. When the time came, annihilating the demon would be totally worth freeing her.

"I'll figure that out later," I hissed. "For now, we listen. If they have our parents, you know the demons will brag about it. They can't help themselves. Then we kill them and get Dani."

"Got it."

"We're not leaving without Dani."

She squeezed my hand. "I know what she means to you."

I shook my head, denying her implication. The thought of Dani in that way only made my heart ache more for Sadie. "I owe her is all. I couldn't be there for her then. I can now."

"Then let's do it."

That's what I loved about Charleigh. Brielle over-analyzed and worried too much. Charleigh was more like me—no fear. Well, at least, we disregarded our fear and did what was necessary to take care of business. She knew we could handle this.

Our reconnaissance revealed nothing, though. It didn't take long to find the demons and listen in on their conversations, but all we learned was that they held a lot of people captive. Like a whole stockpile of meat suits, as one had said, for when their current ones "expired." *Ew.* I fucking hated demons.

Even more, I hated how I was drawn to them just as much as I was appalled by them. Their dark energy called to mine. The beast within was definitely awake, pushing against the holds I had on her. It made me want to destroy them all the more.

"If you attack them, you expose us," Charleigh warned, knowing me too well.

"Then let's move on," I snarled between clenched teeth. "Let's find Dani."

Too much time had passed, and Brielle would be waking soon and discovering we'd left. If she hadn't already. We needed to hurry and return to the camp before she did something I'd regret forever.

Finally, we found Dani by peeking in the back window of a lean-to propped up against a semi-trailer. She was curled up on a cot. Around the front of the one-room building stood two demons in human bodies, guarding the door. The norms' souls were completely gone, thank the angels. That meant I could kill these two. I retrieved two throwing stars from their hiding place in my vest, and with a swish of each wrist, the stars' flew, the edges sliding across their throats, finishing them both. Well, I ended the existences of the bodies. The demons inside plumed out in a cloud of black smoke and disappeared, sent back to Hell.

"Stand guard," I told Charleigh before I slipped inside the lean-to.

Dani shot upright on her cot. Good, I didn't have to wake her. "Who's there?"

Shit. She wouldn't recognize me. I had to drop the glamour.

"It's okay, Dani," I whispered. "It's me, Elliana."

Her dark brows furrowed together as she tilted her head, her dark brown ponytail falling over her shoulder. "Elli? Is it really you?"

I tried to smile, though tears stung my eyes. "It is. I'm going to get you out of here."

Her nearly black eyes blazed with anger. "What the hell happened to you? You left me when . . . when . . ."

Guilt crushed me inside as she choked on the words. "I'm sorry! I know leaving you was horrible, but I'll explain everything once you're out of here and we're safe. Then you can decide if you want to hate me. I'll understand."

As she sat there glaring at me, I began to think it was too late. She already hated me with the heat of a million suns, and as much as it broke my heart, I couldn't blame her. But I really needed to get her out of here.

"At least let me help you now. Then you can be free to do whatever you want. You don't have to listen to my lame excuses or anything. Just please, Dani. I can help you this time. Let me."

Her gaze swept around the small room, then she finally stood. I cracked the door open to find the area outside empty.

"Charleigh?" I whispered, unable to see through her cloak.

She dropped it for a second before cloaking all of us. "Let's get the hell out of here."

With Dani between us, we hurried for the town's gate, demons nearly running into us on more than one occasion.

Dani grabbed my hand, her entire body trembling. I could only imagine how terrified she'd been, a human held captive by these evil abominations. I hoped it hadn't been for long. If she'd been here since I left . . . I already struggled with the guilt of leaving her. Finding out they'd had her all this time just might kill me. I started to wrap my arm around her shoulder to calm her, but she shrugged me off. I couldn't say that didn't hurt.

We picked up our pace when the gate came into view, and Charleigh went ahead a few strides to scope out the other side. She'd just passed through and we were only a few yards behind her when suddenly I couldn't move forward. I couldn't move at all, as though an invisible cage surrounded me.

"What the fuck?" I gasped.

Charleigh turned toward us, her light brown eyes filled with fear. Her cloak on Dani and me had dropped, and we were surrounded by demons in human form, their empty black eyes giving them away.

"No!" Charleigh screamed. They paid no attention to her, thank the angels.

"Go!" I yelled back at her, and she did, flashing away. I stepped in front of Dani, my arms held back behind me to try to protect her as I moved in a circle, assessing the enemy. "Let her go and deal with me. She's only human. You want me, not her."

Dani laughed from behind me. "Who do you think summoned them?"

CHAPTER 6

I deserved this. I knew I did, but it still pissed me off that Dani had betrayed me like this. Why? What could she have possibly gained? Of course, she was mad at me, but getting us both locked up accomplished nothing for her but more misery. She could have at least waited until we took her out of town and she was safe. I didn't think she was stupid, but now I began to wonder because it just didn't make sense.

The demons bound my arms to my side with their grotesque black demonic magic that made me feel all gross inside. Calling on all of my elemental power, I tried to fight it, blasting them with fire, ice, and air the best I could with my hands pinned to my sides, but there were a dozen of them, too many to fight by myself. Even my Amadis power wasn't enough. They tensed and a couple even groaned in pain, so I knew they felt it, just not strongly enough to take them all down. These assholes were powerful, way up on the demon hierarchy. The intense dark energy oozing off them made me heady. I just didn't have enough goodness in me to fight them all at once. Maybe Brielle did, but not me. In fact, the desire to just give in to them grew with every step we took toward wherever they were hauling me.

We came to a brick-and-mortar building, and I realized it was the city hall. Mom and Dad had come here that awful day with the mayor, Camila, who'd actually been Shamara. A mix of dread and anticipation swirled within me at the thought that she might be here. Maybe my chance to kill her had come sooner rather than later. The demons dragged me down the steps into the basement, to what must have been the town's jail. They shoved me into a cell, then cast some nasty demon magic, ugly markings that glowed crimson on every wall and the single exit—spells that locked down my powers and warded the door, preventing any chance of escape.

Then they left me in the small, dark space.

I had no idea how much time passed. It felt like hours, days maybe. But possibly only minutes. I sat in the corner, my back against the wall, and curled my legs into my chest as my eyes drooped, then fell closed. Sadie's face faded in and out and then . . . sweet unconsciousness.

Bolting upright, I gasped for air. I sat in a bed, or a cot was more like it, the mattress thin and lumpy. The space was dark, a dull light shining in from another room. It was unfamiliar, tiny, with three stone walls and the fourth comprised of vertical bars. I jumped to my feet, sharp pain ripping across my shoulders and down my spine. My wings. They were gone. They'd been hidden since I was a baby, but the last thing I remembered until waking just now was my wings exploding from my back for the first time. Had I already lost them again? How? Could I bring them back? With that thought, they burst free. Big, as tall as me, and black and purple, just like my mother's. Whew. They weren't gone for good. I had the power to bring them back. Maybe this meant I was coming into my other powers, too.

Was this the Ang'dora? Mom didn't know if Brielle and I would experience the enigmatic change that the previous Amadis daughters went through to receive their powers, or if they would just come on their own during adolescence, like they did for the males. We were anomalies, nothing like any of our ancestors, so there was no telling. But maybe, just maybe, this was it.

I crossed from the cot to the bars in one stride and reached for them.

"Son of a bitch!" I yelped, jerking my hands back as soon as they touched the metal, my skin sizzling and smoking. What the hell were these things made of? They looked silver in the dim light, but only demons and the Daemoni were allergic to silver. I'd never had issues with it before. Could they be iron? We were part fae, but iron had never bothered us before, either. Of course, if I was coming into all of my powers, maybe they were strong on the fae side and iron had suddenly become a weakness. I could sense a magical energy permeating the area, though, and especially circulating around the bars. Maybe they were simply enchanted, a magical assurance that I couldn't break free.

Where the hell was I anyway? And where were my sister and cousin?

I leaned as close as I could to the bars without touching them, trying to make out what was beyond them. Some kind of corridor. The dim light shone from an orb hovering near the stone ceiling a few yards to the right and another one several yards to the left, creating deep, dark shadows beyond their reach.

I had the sense I was underground, but there was nothing like this in the Loft, and the smell was all wrong. Too dank and sour for our home. Other barred openings lined each side of the corridor. Was this some kind of prison? How did I get here? Why? And again, where the hell were my sister and Charleigh?

"Brielle?" I called out, unable to sense her through our twin bond. Noises came from the other . . . cells. That had to be what they were. Scuffing, shuffling noises. A hiss from one. A groan from another. "Charleigh?"

Neither answered me. I yelled louder for them. An unfamiliar voice told me to shut up, but I paid them no attention. I needed to know they were okay.

"Brielle!" I shouted again. "Charleigh!" Were they even here? Maybe they'd been lucky and had eluded whatever mess I'd found myself in.

"You're asking for it," a female voice hissed. Some kind of threat. Like anyone in those cells could do anything to me. Because we were in cells. Mother-effin cells!

Was this some kind of supernatural prison? At least, one controlled by magic? Did our parents know where this place was? If they did and had any idea I was here, I would have been out already. They would have come for me. For us—if my sister and cousin were here, too. Or maybe that's why I couldn't feel Brielle through our bond, because they'd already freed her and were still searching for me.

That made sense. It had to be the case. Right? Unless . . . unless this was my punishment. Dad had warned us before we left. Was this his way of scaring me into being a little less wild and a little more obedient, like my sister?

I grabbed the bars again, ignoring the pain this time as my skin sizzled and melted. I needed to know, damn it. "BRIELLE! Where are you?"

An electric shock blasted from the bars, and I went sailing across the cell. My back slammed into the stone wall, and I sunk to the floor next to a built-in toilet I only now noticed. Springing to my feet, I charged for the bars again. I didn't even notice the pain this time as I tried to shake them, screaming for my sister. Another zap sent me across the room, but I wasn't giving up.

The beast within me clawed at the walls of my soul, threatening to break free. One I normally kept suppressed, shoved into the deepest, darkest corner of my being. I couldn't stomach the thought of calling it my demon side, but deep down I knew that's what it was. I ignored it most of the time, but sometimes it could be helpful. Like maybe right now, especially as I felt it stirring stronger than ever. As if it had also come into its real power.

"WHERE. IS. MY. SISTER?" I roared as I sprang for the bars, the only opening, the only way out.

"That's enough out of you," came another voice, male—deeper but flat, void of any emotion.

Then a silver haze filtered into my vision, disintegrating everything.

Blinking, I looked around, disoriented, dazed. I wasn't in the stone cell but in a boring one with walls made of cement blocks, those gnarly runes still glowing blood-red. What had I just seen? Was that where I was going next? Or had I nodded off, dreaming about the school under the mountain and mashing it up with my current predicament? My brain didn't seem to be working properly to figure out what was real and what wasn't. The dark magic surrounding me was too much.

My beast mewled from deep within, wanting out. She could handle this. I always thought of her as my hybrid version of an animal's soul, a gift from the shifter DNA in my blood that wasn't like any animal in this world. I fed her my darkness, but she often wanted to give it back. Like now. Perhaps she couldn't take anymore while imprisoned inside of me. Perhaps I should just let her free. At least one of us could be.

I'd almost given in when I opened my eyes to find Dani standing outside the cell.

"You have no idea how many times I dreamed about this," she said, practically spitting the words out. Still feeling confused, I only stared at her. She glared back with expectation.

"Why?" I finally obliged, not moving from my corner.

She laughed. "It's the least of what you deserve. You and your cunt mother killed my papa. *Killed* him, Elliana. And then you just ran off, protecting your own asses instead of owning up to what you did. I thought you loved me!"

"I thought I did, too," I whispered. As much as we probably did deserve it, I wanted to throat-punch her for calling my mother that. "She'd only been trying to protect us all," I said, louder now.

Dani's laugh sounded like a shrill siren. "*Protect?* You expect me to believe that? She only wanted to protect you and Brielle. Your mother doesn't give a flying fuck about anyone else!"

Without thought, I sprang to my feet and flew at the bars between us. When I touched them, dark magic blasted through me. At the same time, my vision swam, and I was in that stone cell again. I felt my spine crack against the back wall after I'd touched those bars and went flying from the shock. I shook my head, trying to erase the vision, not knowing where it came from.

"She protected you!" I shouted at Dani. "Not just Brielle and me, but all of the humans, too. Including you!"

"Then why is my papa dead?" she snarled.

My mouth opened to explain, but the words lodged in my throat, and my chest tightened. I had to spit them out, as much as it hurt me and would hurt her.

"Your papa was no longer your papa," I said quietly, the truth carving through me. I'd adored Papa Miguel. He hadn't deserved what had happened to him. "He was possessed, Dani. A demon had taken over his body, probably devoured his soul, long before that night. What my mother did—she destroyed the demons. Not just sent them back to Hell but actually destroyed them. Unfortunately, that means their human hosts died, too. But it wasn't him anymore. It wasn't him. Camila . . . Shamara did that to him."

Her eyes narrowed as she glared at me, shaking her head. "I can't believe you think I'm stupid enough to believe that.

Camila was Papa's childhood friend. We came all the way from Brazil *on foot* to find her. She wouldn't have hurt him."

"But she did. Camila wasn't Camila. Don't you remember? Didn't you see her transform into that three-story tall, purple-skinned demon named Shamara?"

"No," she seethed. "I apparently missed that when my papa dropped dead in my arms. Because of your mother. Because of *you*."

My body trembled as I tried to maintain control, to stay calm and explain, when part of me wanted to shake her silly until her common sense returned because apparently they'd brainwashed it out of her. My words came out as measured as I could make them. "Yes, our mom was trying to protect us when she realized Shamara had us surrounded. I told you Brielle and I were wanted by a lot of powerful beings. Even the dark fae had come to this realm for us. Shamara had hundreds of demons possess the humans of Misery's Edge. Including your father. They would have killed everyone here. *All* of the humans, including you!"

"But your mom did it for her."

Tears of frustration burned the backs of my eyes and thickened my throat. "You're not listening to me. My mom killed the *demons*. We don't harm humans. Our purpose is to protect them, and that's exactly what she did that night."

"For fuck's sake!" Dani shouted. "Maybe you really are the stupid one here. I know exactly what happened that night."

"Then you know that wasn't your father!"

"No, I don't know that! I don't care about all the others who went crazy that night. Maybe they were possessed. But you spent the afternoon with us that day, Elliana—with him. Do you really think a demon could have faked that?"

My breath caught as I stared at her, my heart thundering in my chest. No. What she was saying couldn't be true. Right? Papa Miguel had been so sweet. So warm and kind, sharing his home and food with us, even though he had so little. And wouldn't Mom and Dad have sensed the demon inside him? We ate at their freaking house!

No, this can't be right. The only thing that had kept me from completely hating my mom was knowing that Shamara was the reason Dani's papa had died. That her demon-minion had killed him long before his body ever dropped. Mom wouldn't have done what she did if Shamara's demons hadn't basically seized the town, but had she been a little careless? Why would an innocent human have died?

"Your mom killed a lot of humans that night," Dani said, as though reading my mind.

"No. Her power doesn't work like that."

"Well, it did. And my papa was one of them. She's going to pay, though."

Before my eyes, Dani began to transform, her skin taking on a bluish hue I could see even in the dark space. Two small horns sprouted from her head, curling inward as they grew, and her cheekbones sharpened as her brows curved in a severe arch. As though she'd flipped a switch from off to on, dark power flowed from her, turning me on and making me sick at the same time.

"Lucky for me," she said, "I'm not human. Only half. I told you my mother died when I was little, but I'd been wrong. Shamara is my mother. That's why papa had brought us here. He didn't know what to do with me as I started coming into my powers. And no, not stupid evolving human powers. *True* power." Her lips curled in a proud smile. "Your mother killed the wrong man, Elliana Knight, and that's too bad for her. I *will* have my revenge on her, but for now, I can have it on you. And she can know what it's like to lose someone *she* loves more than anything in this world."

With that, Dani strode off, a barbed tail flicking out from the waistband of her jeans, as my jaw gaped open. I'd fallen for a fucking demon. A half-demon, anyway. Still—*ew.* My whole body racked with a disgusted shudder, and it took everything I had to not puke up my measly dinner.

I had no idea what this meant. I hadn't sensed the demon in *her*. Was she just that good at suppressing her power? Maybe, if she was really Shamara's offspring. Shamara was possibly the most powerful demon on this earth. At least equal to the Ancients, the major demons who had originated the Daemoni millennia ago. Maybe Papa Miguel had also been demon. Dani could have easily been lying. That's what demons were best at, after all. Lies and deceit.

Lies and deceit that possibly could have gone back to the beginning, from the moment I met her. Had she ever cared for me? Or had she been setting us up all along? After all, it was because of her we'd even come to Misery's Edge in the first place that day.

Dropping back into my corner, I tried to untangle the web of everything that had happened between us, searching for the tiniest clue that indicated any of it had been real between us. But I should have known better, even back then. I'd always known I was difficult to love. Why had I thought she'd be any different?

Or Sadie for that matter.

Not going there, I admonished myself. It would do no good.

One thing I knew for sure: Dani was wasting her time with me. If she really wanted to make my mother feel her pain, she needed Brielle, not me.

Of course, I'd never tell her this. I'd die here or go wherever they took me before I'd give up my sister. I just hoped Charleigh didn't lead the demons back to Brielle. She was smart enough not to. But she'd return to Brie eventually. She was sworn to protect us. She'd take care of my sister.

Again, I didn't know how much time passed. More visions or dreams or whatever they were of the stone prison danced in my head. Eventually, five demons in human flesh came to my cell.

"You're being transferred," one of them growled.

It was still night when we left the building, and they threw me up on a wooden wagon, binding me to the floor. Some kind of demonic beast pulled the rickety contraption through the town's gates. I watched the moon overhead as we traveled for an hour or so, then stopped. A pale face surrounded by white hair peered over me. The male version of my aunt Vanessa—her twin brother Victor. Unlike my aunt, Victor was still with the Daemoni.

"Hello, love," he said, his vampire fangs slipping down. "The Ancients will be pleased."

I couldn't tell what was going on, but a few minutes later the wagon started moving again. My eyes rolled up as far as I could see. Victor's white hair bobbed ahead, leading the wagon.

Shit. Shit, shit, shit. I really didn't know which was worse— Shamara or the Ancients. I did know, though, that the Ancients never operated alone. Not like Shamara did. That might have been her arrogance at play, but it made the Ancients ten times scarier. Or however many of them there were. I didn't even know that. I could hope my brother would step in, but I doubted it. He'd made his place in this world clear to our parents years ago, solidifying his position as leader of the Daemoni with a string of atrocities. His soul was even darker than mine and belonged to the Ancients. Then again, he'd helped us escape to that other world through the gate he'd opened, so there was that.

On the other hand, I knew I could take Victor, if he were alone. I just needed to break through these magical bindings.

My chance came when we stopped again, and a moment later I felt the bindings released. I sprang to my feet, prepared to shoot a fireball, but I froze.

My father stood in front of Victor.

CHAPTER 7

I blinked.

No, not my father. My brother.

Before I could move, Dorian flew at me, wrapped his muscular arm around my middle to hold me to him, and flashed. As far as we knew, only my mom and dad could take someone with them in a flash. It appeared as though Dorian had inherited that special trait as the path in the woods disappeared, and our surroundings were replaced by the inside of what looked like an old movie theater. Most of the seats had been removed, only a few rows remaining. The tattered curtains had also been pulled down, probably for repurposing, a few torn scraps dangling up near the ceiling. I saw that much before we flashed again, now appearing in the middle of a swamp. Possibly the bayou. Was he taking me to Crescent City? I'd half-hoped he was taking me back to Brielle and Charleigh.

"Where are we going?" I demanded when we didn't flash again right away.

Dorian was a spitting image of our dad—light brown hair, emerald green eyes with specks of brown and gold that technically made them hazel, a square jaw, tall, broad, and muscular. He wore his hair closely cropped, though, and sported a short beard. He also wore a silk suit, which our dad would never don, not even for his and Mom's wedding. Where Dorian could get silk suits these days was beyond me, though I supposed silkworms had likely replenished by now and there were definitely plenty of seamstresses and tailors. Ugh. My thoughts were rambling, my brain and heart confused and unable to focus on what it should have been—freeing myself.

Rather than answering me, Dorian glared at me with hard hazel eyes, his arm still like a metal band across my back.

"You're not going to tell me?" I asked.

He still didn't answer, but another vision flashed in my mind: Dorian soaring at me, his hands gripping my head, his wrists twisting, snapping my neck. Blackness filled my vision for a moment before his face was in front of mine again. What the actual fuck. Was I seeing the future with all these visions? I cursed our witch professor, the one who'd prodded me to open up to my intuition, which had apparently unlocked a new power, and one I was sure I didn't want. Seeing into the future could be quite handy, but like Mom's telepathy, it certainly had major drawbacks.

Wait. Was my brother actually going to *kill* me?

"What's wrong with you?" Dorian growled.

"What's wrong with you?" I shot back lamely. "Are you just hell-bent on making Mom and Dad hate you?"

His brows lifted, then he smirked. "I don't give a fuck what they think, but if that was my goal, don't you think I'd take Brielle?"

Ouch. Dickhead.

Grabbing my bicep with a large, strong hand, he twisted me away as he glanced around, as though looking for someone. Or something, actually, which became apparent when his gaze zeroed in on a point on the ground a few yards ahead of us.

"There," he murmured.

"Where? What?" I squinted, trying to see what he did, but all I noticed was a small scattering of leaves and twigs—although, I supposed *scattering* wasn't quite the right word. It almost appeared to be a purposeful arrangement, with four twigs creating a diamond shaped frame, blades of grass and stones assembled into the form of a snowflake, or perhaps a mandala. The whole thing was no bigger than my palm. Who the heck out here in the middle of the bayou had done this? More importantly, why did Dorian care?

He ignored me, dragging me toward it, and I tried calling on my fire magic, hoping to burn him into releasing me, but as we stepped over the tiny arrangement, the swamps of the bayou disappeared. We suddenly stood in a frozen tundra.

Snow carpeted the ground and covered the trees surrounding us. Low, dark clouds blanketed the sky, obliterating any sun and making it impossible to tell if it was morning or dusk.

"Whoa. Was that a portal?" My breath plumed out in front of me as Dorian finally released my arm. I would have made a run for it, except I had absolutely no idea where we were or where to go. Never mind the fact that Dorian could easily overtake me. Of the three of us, he was surely the most powerful.

"Welcome to Faery," he said after glancing at my confused expression. "More specifically, to the Winter Lands, home of the Unseelie king."

My eyes widened, and I shook my head vehemently. "No. No, Dorian! You can't do this!"

"Would you rather go to the Ancients? Or to Shamara?"

"At least they wouldn't kill me. The Dark fae want to *end* me." I still didn't know why. I could understand why the demons and Ancients would want Brielle and me. They assumed we'd be like Dorian and just needed to go dark like he had. Then they'd have all three of us to help them take over the world and whatever other nefarious wet dreams they enjoyed. But the fae? Nobody had ever explained their interest, but we'd seen them in Misery's Edge on that fateful night, coming for us.

"Not yet," Dorian said as we stood on the edge of a forest, staring across a snow-covered field at a mountain whose height put the Rockies and Alps to shame. Near the top of it, overlooking a deep chasm, was the most beautiful piece of architecture I'd ever seen. A glass castle. Probably not glass, but ice. It wasn't transparent, but white and gleaming, made up of several elaborately designed round buildings interconnected to each other. A bridge crossed the chasm to a smaller structure on the opposite mountain. Between them, through the ravine ran a river and a series of water falls down the mountain and toward the forest we stood in.

"Not yet," I echoed. "So you're going to let them torture me first and then kill me? You really hate us that much?"

"You're safer here. Now shut up." Not giving me a chance to retort, he grabbed me again, and we soared toward the palace. I could have flown myself, but he obviously didn't trust me. I hated flying with him. It was disturbing—Dorian didn't need wings. Mom had told us how Dorian had been able to fly since he was a kid, long before even Mom or Dad were given their wings.

The landscape below distracted me. Gray rock, green pines, and every once in a while, red berries or even a flower colored the otherwise snow and ice-covered terrain. Frosty mist hung over the tops of the trees, and we passed through layers of it stacked along the mountainside. The beautiful wintery scene reminded me of the mountains surrounding our college, but this was even more magical. And felt all the more dangerous.

Dorian didn't fly to the front of the palace grounds, which were surrounded by a high wall. He swooped to the side, near the chasm, and dropped, making my belly drop too. We landed on a ledge toward the bottom of the castle but still high above the river flowing below. A door opened in what had been a blank wall a moment ago, and Dorian ushered me inside.

We strode through dark corridors that twisted and turned. I expected to be thrown into another cell, but then we climbed stairs, passed through more darkened hallways, and ascended more steps, silence surrounding us. Maybe the Winter Court had been abandoned. Maybe our parents assassinated the king, and they had to deal with the aftermath to ensure everything was good here before returning to the earthly realm. And maybe—no, definitely—I was too old to be believing such fairy tales. The hauntingly beautiful palace was getting to me.

Finally, we stopped in front of a closed door, and Dorian turned around to me.

"I hate this for you, but it's necessary." With those cryptic words, he pressed his palm against my forehead for a brief moment, then threw open the door and shoved me inside. He didn't follow, and when I turned for him, the door slammed in my face. Of course, it was locked.

"Hate what?" I wondered aloud as I turned back around. My breath caught. Well, I supposed this was better than a typical cell, if I were going to be imprisoned somewhere. "You hate *this* for me? Just when I thought you couldn't be a bigger ass."

I'd never been in a bedroom so spacious or seen a bed so large. Who the hell needed such a big bed anyway? The room was decorated in blue and white, with white wooden furniture, including the bed, a dresser, a table with two chairs by the massive window, and a blue-upholstered settee in front of the fireplace, which was surrounded by a white wood mantel. Thick royal blue velvet drapes framed the floor-to-ceiling windows that spanned the entire opposite wall, and a thick comforter and pillows topped the bed in various shades of blue and white.

The windows beckoned me, and I strode across the thick,

white carpet to consider my options. The window overlooked the chasm, but if I craned my neck, to the left I could see toward the far side of the mountain, where white crests of ocean waves undulated in the distance. To the right I could see a bit of the palace grounds and beyond them the expanse of snow-covered field that led to the forest where I was sure Dorian and I had first appeared.

The windowpanes were solid and not freezing cold as I expected them to be. None opened, not so much as a latch. Turning, I surveyed the room again and went over to a door on the side wall. It led to a closet the size of our extra-large dorm room that the three of us had shared. Another door opened to an opulent white marble bathroom with silver and blue accents.

"One door out, and it's locked," I murmured to myself. I considered the windows again. Could I break them? Possibly, especially if I used magic. Then again, we were in Faery, *Dark* Faery specifically, and I had no idea what magic was in use here nor how my own magic would behave. And even if I did manage to escape, where would I go? Dorian had said we were in the Winter Lands. I assumed that meant there were Summer Lands, possibly where my parents were. But I had no idea where that was in relation to here. I knew nothing about the Faery lands. I didn't even know how to return to the earthly realm.

Shit. We'd been home for what—a day?—and I'd already been caught by the demons, handed over to the Daemoni, and taken to the Dark fae. Always the fuck-up, I was. At least this time I'd managed to keep Brielle and Charleigh out of it. I hoped like hell they were safe.

I'd figure this out. I wouldn't let them hold me forever. I was nobody's prisoner.

And in the meantime, I couldn't deny the flutter of excitement at being in Faery. I was always a sucker for adventure, but more than that, if my parents were really at

Summer Court, I was at least in the right realm now. I just needed to learn the lay of the land and anything else that would be helpful. How I'd learn, I didn't know yet, but I'd figure that out, too.

If I were really lucky, I'd find Sadie, as well. But I refused to get my hopes up, and if I were being honest with myself, I knew it was for the best that I didn't find her. I'd inevitably hurt her again, just like I had Dani. Perhaps we were all better off this way.

When night fell outside, bringing fat snowflakes with it, the door to my room finally opened.

"Dorian?" I said, turning from the window.

"No," squeaked a waif-like figure. Barely more than the size of a ten-year-old, she carried a wooden tray laden with dishes, delicious scents wafting my way. My stomach growled audibly, and I nearly drooled as she crossed the room and set the tray on the table by the window. "I'm sorry to bother you. My lady thought you would be hungry."

She dropped her head, and I couldn't tell if it was a bow or to keep herself from being seen.

"Who is your lady?" I dared to ask, wondering if she would divulge anything.

"Princess Maeve she be," she replied, to my mild surprise. She still didn't lift her head, and I realized it was in deference to me. I could hear respect in her tone when she stated her mistress's name. "Sister to the Winter king."

"I see. And your name?" I asked.

The tips of her pointed ears, poking through her stringy black hair, reddened. Her voice came out so tiny, if I didn't have supernatural hearing, I might not have heard it. "Ena."

"Well, thank you for the food, Ena."

She tilted her head even more, in a definite sort of bow. "Shall I draw you a bath?"

I about choked on my own spittle since I'd yet to go near

the food or carafe of what appeared to be juice or perhaps wine. "No, that's not necessary. I can draw my own."

I couldn't believe I just said that—*draw a bath!* I hadn't had a bath since I was a kid, if you didn't count the hot tubs at college. And I'd never *drawn* one. I snickered to myself.

"As you wish," Ena said. She remained perfectly still, standing by the table.

"Um, anything else?" I asked.

"I do not know. Is there?"

Oh. She was waiting on me to request anything, and since I had the opportunity, I might as well try. "Uh . . . I'm new to Faery. If you didn't know. I'm not familiar with things here. Are there books and maps you could bring me?"

Her thin lips turned down briefly, her eyes still glued to the floor. "I will ask my lady."

"Ena, you can look at me."

She instantly shook her head. "It is not my place."

"I'm the prisoner here, not you."

"Mmm . . ." was all she replied. She fell silent and still again. Maybe I was wrong about the respect I'd heard in her voice moments ago. Maybe she was just as much a prisoner here as I was. Maybe I was staring at my future.

If I had a future.

"That is all," I said, hating how the words sounded even without any arrogant intent.

Ena's head dipped again before she scurried out of the room. I repeated the words out loud to myself in different tones, but no matter how they came out, they sounded quite bitchy.

Despite how loud and painfully my stomach growled, I didn't dare touch the food. I'd heard the myths about fae food and wouldn't take any chances. I didn't take a bath, either. I wasn't about to make myself vulnerable in the tub naked. I did crawl into the bed that felt like I was laying on a cloud. Besides dozing off in the jail cell, I hadn't really slept since leaving the shiny world, and I had no idea how long ago that was anymore. I was exhausted. Still, guilt wormed its way in, settling heavily on my chest and making it impossible to fall asleep.

I wondered where Brielle and Charleigh were. My soul actually hurt, being this far away from my twin. I could usually feel her presence in some way that had always been comforting, but not now, not even when I pressed my fingers to the faerie stone in my chest. I hoped that didn't mean the worst for her. I hoped she was pitching a fit, livid at me and freaking out. She was probably feeling a heavy dose of guilt herself, although it wasn't her fault. She wouldn't have been able to stop me, and she knew that. It was just a good thing I'd gone without her and that Charleigh had ran ahead. Otherwise, they would have been here with me. Or worse.

Like Dani and Sadie, Brielle and Charleigh were better off without me. I only brought trouble to them. Now, they could meet up with Noah, and Charleigh could help her dad. She didn't have to worry about protecting Brielle as much as she did me. Brie would stick close to Noah and do whatever was expected of her, making Charleigh's job easy.

Yes, this was better all around. As soon as I could get the hell out of this castle.

CHAPTER 8

"*Unless you plan to starve, get your ass up.*"

A male voice broke through my sleep-hazed mind as something prodded said ass.

A bright light shone down on me, and I blinked up at him, coming to the realization that I was back in the stone cell. Glancing over his shoulder and noticing the bars were gone, I jumped to my feet and launched myself for the opening but slammed into an invisible wall.

"Easy there," the guy said. Some kind of shifter, probably wolf, based on the yellow glow in his eyes. He was tall and muscular, filling out his guard uniform so that the fabric stretched over his muscles. His gaze traveled down to my feet and up again, lingering on my chest as a smirk lifted one side of his mouth. Ew. I fought a shudder. I had to play this right.

"Do you know where my sister is?" I asked quietly with a little tilt of my head and bat of my eyelashes.

He jerked his head toward the corridor. "Fall in line," was his only reply.

The other cells were open, too, and people were lined up in the corridor. Various ages, from teens to middle aged, both males and females. All giving off some kind of supernatural energy or another. *All dressed in skintight, gray clothing—so tight there was no way possible to hide a weapon except maybe up your hooha, but, uh,* ouch. *I noticed for the first time I was wearing the same, and no shoes. None of us wore shoes.*

I didn't get the point about weapons. Supernaturals possessed built-in weapons. The issued clothing must have been enchanted, preventing the use of powers and abilities. I mean, if that was the goal. I really wasn't sure. I really didn't know anything.

"Move it." *The guard's hand landed on my back and gave me a shove.*

"Hey!" *I growled as I spun on him.* "Do you realize who I am?"

He rolled his eyes. "Let me guess. Some kind of princess or chosen one or something? Betrothed to the king or an alpha? Think we give a shit here? We have all kinds of those." *He waved his hand, gesturing at the line of what I could only call inmates.* "You're a dime a dozen here. Get over it."

He shoved me again, into my place in the line, as several of the other inmates snickered. Another guard stood at the far end of the corridor, and when he turned and started walking, the line began to follow. Lost in my own thoughts, I traipsed along with them as we were marched down seemingly endless corridors, turning right here and left there, the stone floor rough against my feet.

Nobody spoke. I wanted to ask questions. So many questions. Like where the hell was here? And what did he mean about all these others being my equals? At the risk of sounding bitchy, which I really didn't care about because I was *a bitch, my sister and I didn't have equals. As our mother had told us many times, as well as anyone who dared to challenge her, we lived in the Age of Angels, and as the only angels on Earth, we* ruled *the Age of Angels.*

There would certainly be hell to pay once I was found. I didn't belong here. I wasn't exactly the most well-behaved child—that was Brielle's job—but I didn't deserve to be in a prison. *I mean,*

I'd always known there was something wrong with me, but I'd committed no crime. I wondered how many of these other people had and how many were innocent like me.

More and more questions.

The only sounds as we continued were the clunks of the guards' boots on the never-ending stone floor and an occasional dripping rhythm coming from places I couldn't see—we were definitely underground. Great. After growing up in a bunker, I was so tired of being trapped underground. Finally, the lead guard opened a door into a large, brightly lit, noisy room. The scent of food cooking wafted under my nose, though I couldn't really say it smelled appetizing.

I followed the line toward the service counter where more supes slopped something I assumed was supposed to be food onto trays. I barely glanced at them, though, my eyes scanning the room for my sister's auburn head or Charleigh's orange one.

Rows of long tables filled the space, hundreds of supes in their gray uniforms, eating with a few growls and snarls in between. There was a din of conversation, small groups keeping their voices low for the most part as they huddled over their trays. Tense energy crackled in the air. Dozens of angry, danger-filled eyes, some more animalistic and feral than human, darted to and fro, remaining on alert as though expecting something to happen at any moment.

And then it did. A fight broke out on the far side of the cafeteria, throwing everyone into a frenzy. A crowd gathered around the fighters, yelling and cheering and egging them on. That's when I saw her—my twin—close to the scuffle but trying to scurry out of the way.

I swallowed down a flood of emotions, including relief that I wasn't here alone, anger because she deserved to be here even less than I, and a bit of fear for how we even got here. I didn't see Charleigh, and I had no idea what that meant.

"Brielle!" I shouted over the ruckus as I ran for her, hurdling tables and people as I went.

I didn't make it very far before I was slammed to the ground by a heavy body. The guard tried to pin me down, but my combat training kicked in, and instincts took over. I threw my full weight into squirming just enough until I could shove an elbow back into the guard's face, his nose crunching from the blow. That gave me another second and space to heave him off of me and flip in the air, out of his reach. I landed on top of a table, one bare foot sloshing into someone's meal. While a small crowd was still hollering at the fight across the room, some broke off, their attention now on us.

A trickle of blood leaked from the guard's nose as he glared at me. The beast within me lifted her head at the coppery scent, and I swear she licked her tongue up the inside of my spine, leaving a trail of powerful but dark energy.

And I liked it. I liked the silky feel of it as it spread over my shoulders and into my blood.

The guard lunged at me. I threw a hand up in self-defense, only planning to block him. Instead, a ball of fire shot out of my palm. Oh, shit. *Either the uniform didn't dampen my abilities, or they hadn't expected me to have any. I hadn't expected to have any! I must have come into my powers along with my wings, and maybe they underestimated just how dangerous I could be. If I'd gone through the Ang'dora, I'd apparently slept right through it. This would explain the previous guard's dismissal of who I was. Was it possible they really didn't know?*

The guard ducked the flames before lurching at me again. I threw both hands up this time, and instead of fire, several sharp icicles shot out of my palms. One skimmed across the guard's temple, drawing more blood, but he deflected the rest, and they shattered with the tinkling of glass hitting the floor. I did a bit of a dance on the table, excited for more. *Bring it on,* I taunted. With the dark energy pulsing through my veins, I felt all powerful.

Anger shining in his red eyes—I didn't know what kind of supe this guard was, but my guess would be vampire—he growled, and then he was gone. Too fast for me to see, let alone stop, he took me down again, effectively pinning me.

"Elli, don't fight them. We'll figure this out." *Brielle's voice came in my head. At least our twin bond was back, and we could speak to each other.*

"Are you okay?"

"A little beat up, but I'll live."

"WHAT?"

"I'll be fine, El. Just do what they say, okay? And don't give away our bond. We'll talk later."

She shut me out with that, at the same time I caught sight of her again. One side of her face was covered with a purplish-green bruise. Anger coursed through me, and I heaved my body up, trying to shove the heavy guard off of me. When he didn't budge, I attempted the fireball again. It was weak, but the heat was enough to make him yelp. Just not enough to throw him off of me. Instead, he slammed my head against the stone floor, hard, and then another booted guard stomped up to us, bent down, and blew some kind of green powder into my face.

As though a switch had been flipped, all energy drained right out of me, into the floor. They had to drag my floppy, wet-noodle ass out.

So much for being all powerful.

I felt like one of those ragdolls Gertie made for the little kids at the Loft, unable to even twitch a muscle as they took me back to my cell and tossed me on the cot. I groaned as pain shot through the right side of my face, where the guard had pounded it against the stone floor. My cheek swelled, effectively forcing my eye shut. Closing the other one and trying to ignore the pain, I sank into a deep sleep and dreamt about home and my parents. I woke up with the heavy weight of guilt and shame.

If I had only listened, I wouldn't have ended up in this place, whatever it was. But what really carved a hole in my gut was that I'd dragged Brielle along with me. I hoped that since I hadn't seen Charleigh in the cafeteria, she wasn't here, too.

I had no idea how we got here or even how long we'd been here. I had no recollection of entering the bunker or cave or whatever it was, of coming to this cell, and nothing about changing into this ugly gray uniform. Where were my leathers and weapons anyway? And how much time had passed from our arrival to when I finally woke up the first time? The second time? Hours? Days?

"Where the hell are we anyway?" I mumbled out loud, frustration making it sound like a growl.

"The Vault." The whisper came from near the bars, to the right side of my cell, surprising me. I hadn't expected anyone to hear or care, let alone answer.

I scrambled to my feet and over to the bars, careful not to touch them. "What's the Vault?"

"A supernatural prison." It sounded like she sat on the floor on the other side of the wall that separated our cells. "They say it's controlled by the fae, but it's not in any Faery realm."

My brows pinched together. "What realm is it then?"

"From the stories I was told as a child, it's a pocket realm. It's connected to many other realms, providing a place to send the worst, most deadliest criminals away. Criminals who can't be killed."

"I'm not a criminal, though." And I was pretty certain I could be killed, but I wasn't about to divulge that piece of juicy information. It might be hard to do, but no one ever said we were immortal. Not even as Earth's Angels. "I didn't do anything to be here."

"Of course, you didn't," she scoffed, sarcasm dripping in her tone.

"You did?"

"I killed five guards and the fae prince they worked for." Her voice was monotone, cold, and she provided no further details. No justification, like he'd murdered her whole family or anything. I decided I was better off not knowing.

"So how do we get out of here?" I asked.

"There's only one way," she said. I heard her intake of breath before blowing it out dramatically. "Die."

"But you just said nobody here can be killed."
"Exactly."

Drenched in a cold sweat, my breath came out in short bursts. As I took in my surroundings, re-orienting myself, I watched the slight figure of a girl as she placed another tray of food on the table. I wasn't in the stone prison but still at the Winter Court. The dream had felt so real, though. Thank the angels for Ena—her entry must have woken me.

As I threw the heavy covers off and swung my legs over the edge of the bed, I felt her looking at me through the curtains of hair surrounding her downturned face, giving me the side-eye. I still wore my fighting leathers—not that abysmal gray uniform—and had no intentions of removing the protective clothing. I also had no intentions of eating, though my body moved toward the table of its own volition. Ena uncovered the dishes this time before she scurried out of the room again.

The food looked so normal. Well, normal for worlds that weren't post-apocalyptic. A spread like I thought I'd never see again since leaving the shiny world was laid out in front of me —eggs, bacon, sausage, biscuits, croissants, waffles with berries and whipped cream. My arms crossed over my stomach, which physically hurt from the need for food.

"It's not poisoned," a twinkling female voice said from behind me. "My brother doesn't want you dead. Yet."

I turned to find a woman who looked only a few years older than me, but it was hard to know for sure since she was fae. She could have been two thousand millennia old, for all I knew. Her hair—a bluish silver in a fae way, not an old lady way—was done in an elaborate arrangement of braids around the crown, the rest of it falling in a smooth sheet behind her shoulders. Her light blue eyes, ringed with silver, tilted up at the outsides at a sharper angle than I'd ever seen on any other fae. Or maybe it was the tiny blue faerie stone embedded in each temple that made her eyes look all the more dramatic, or how those light eyes contrasted against her dark skin.

Though the ground outside was covered in a fresh blanket of snow and more continued to fall beyond the plate glass windows, she wore a sleeveless dress held up only by a ribbon around her neck, exposing miles and miles of satiny, deep ebony skin. The light blue silk fabric widened enough to cover most of her breasts and fell to mid-thigh, displaying delicate lines and whorls of glowing fae markings on her arms and legs. When she turned to close the door, her bare back showed off more swirls enhanced with faerie stones embedded down her spine. Her full lips painted the color of mulberries stretched into a smile when she turned back toward me.

"I promise it's safe to eat," she said.

"If I want to be trapped in Faery forever," I replied. *As if I currently have a choice.*

Her eyes assessed me, then she shrugged. "Why would you want to leave? Especially with the condition of your world." She all but wrinkled her nose with the statement, the disgust clear in her tone. Then she waved her fingers in the air, dismissively. "But no, the food won't trap you here. On that part, I'm not sure about my brother."

"And your brother is the king?"

"Oh, my manners. Pardon me. Yes, I am Princess Maeve. You can call me Maeve, though. And you are Elliana Knight, with an impressive brother yourself."

I suppressed a snort. *Impressive* was one way to describe the ass, I supposed. "Yes, I'm Elliana."

"Well, please eat, Elliana. I beg it of you, or my brother may have my head if you die from starvation."

My gaze fell on the food, and before I could think any more about it, my hand darted out and grabbed a piece of bacon. One bite was all it took and the next thing I knew, my ass was planted in the chair, and I was scarfing down every dish in sight. When I couldn't possibly hold another morsel, I sat back in the chair, realizing for the first time that Maeve occupied the other. After a flick of her hand, Ena rushed in, and Maeve spoke to her in a language that sounded like it could have been Gaelic, if I were to guess, but with otherworldly sounds and trills weaved in. As the waif quickly cleared the table, I noticed the gnarly scars along her bony arms for the first time, a nick in the side of her ear when her hair fell away to reveal it. What had happened to her?

"Ena tells me you want to read about Faery," Maeve said once the waif had left with a pile of dirty dishes bigger than her.

I studied her for a moment as she gazed back with equal, though cool curiosity. "If you have anything, yes. I don't really know much about it."

"But you are part fae. Nobody taught you your heritage?"

"Nobody knew much about the fae to teach me when I was growing up."

She nodded once. "Yes, that is true. Now we are all about spilling our secrets, it seems. Making ourselves known and present in your world."

She didn't sound as though she approved, so I hesitated before asking, "So do you have books I can read? Maps of the lands?"

Her finger tapped against her lip. "I would need to speak to my brother first. I am unclear on the protocol for . . . *guests* of your . . . caliber."

"My caliber?"

"You are not fae royalty, of course, who are our usual guests, but you are not the same as the prisoners in the dungeons, either. *Those* I know how to deal with. But I am not quite sure what to do with you until Fintan returns. He sent word that Dorian was bringing you, and he was not happy about it, but those two have a strange tit for tat thing going on, and my brother owed yours."

"I see," I said, not seeing at all. "Is Ena a prisoner as well?" I asked, wondering if that was indeed her plan for me, to become another servant.

Maeve's head pulled back as she laughed. "Oh, no, not at all. Ena is one of our many slaves."

My brows shot up. Was there a difference? She laughed again.

"That's right. I forgot how your world views slavery anymore. Well, believe me, Ena and the other Shadow fae are grateful to be here. Their lives as our slaves are worlds better than anything else they could possibly experience in the Shadow Lands, without doubt."

"Shadow fae?" I'd only heard of them once, mentioned by Sadie. Was this another clue that our realms were connected? I shoved that thought deep down. Raising my hopes even a notch would only bring pain, especially considering my current predicament.

Maeve leaned forward, her eyes lighting up. "They are awful things, the Shadows. The demons of the Faery realm, they are, and the Shadow Lands is a place of nightmares. At least, according to Fintan and others. I have never been there personally, thank the gods and goddesses." Her body shivered before she continued. "They are born with the worst kind of powers. Powers nobody could possibly want."

"Like what?" I asked, leaning forward as well, curiosity snagging me. It was like this kind of darkness—of gossip and talk of dreadful things—was a safe way for me to feel a hit of what I loved so much and could not have. There was also something about Maeve that I couldn't quite pinpoint yet. Something magnetic, drawing me to her when I should have been staying far, far away.

The princess shook her head slowly, that sheet of hair tumbling over her shoulders. "They are too hideous to discuss. They feed off what most of us consider improper, things to be avoided or at least kept hidden in the darkest parts of our hearts and souls. Fortunately, the slaves come to us drained of all their power." Her voice dropped even lower in a conspiratorial whisper as she went on. "But I will tell you about the Shadow Court—King Caellach and his princes are the worst, especially the prince they call the Tormentor. He and the king, too, feed off of others' pain and anguish, so he torments his victims in order to grow their powers. The Shadow Court is all about torture and agony."

"That is . . . some dark shit," I blurted, both fascinated and disturbed. And I thought *I* had dark thoughts and leanings. I felt like a saint compared to that.

Maeve laughed, her voice lightening and louder again when she spoke. "Crass, but true. So stay far away from the Shadow Lands and beware of the king, but more than anything, of the Tormentor."

"Warning taken, but I suppose it's not necessary if I'm being held prisoner here."

"Oh, doll, you are not *really* a prisoner."

CHAPTER 9

his was news to me. My head tilted as I studied the princess. "So I can leave when I want?"

As though bored, Maeve held out her hand and studied her perfect manicure. "Well, not until my brother returns, at least. He wants to meet you."

I bet he did. "When will that be?"

"Wish I knew. He's been traveling throughout Faery, trying to stop this ugliness that's causing our world to be almost as dismal as yours." She flicked a finger toward the window, the view displaying dark storm clouds churning over the mountain peaks.

"The Winter Lands aren't always like this?" I'd assumed since the region was called *Winter*, it was always winter here.

"Not so . . . *dark*," Maeve said. "It's been so long since we've seen the sun or the blue of the sky. A darkness hangs over our lands, and while we're called the Dark fae in your world, we're not totally dark. Like you said—that's the Shadow fae."

I didn't exactly say that, but I caught her drift. Our grandmother Bree had explained how being distinguished as Light fae or Dark fae really meant little. She'd mentioned the

Dark fae used to get their kicks from causing real problems in the Earthly realm, while the Light fae were merely mischievous, but neither was good nor evil as a whole. And neither held much interest in our world, at least until recently. Now I understood that Light was a synonym for Seelie and Dark for Unseelie, and, it seemed, more about geographic territories than anything. Or, at least, royal courts and politics. I had to wonder if the princess conveyed the truth about the Shadow fae—that they really were so dark—or if it was more politics at play.

"We all know the cause of it," Maeve continued, giving me a pointed look. "That gate you and your sister opened."

The last we'd heard, when our parents had told us how every faction had an interest in my twin and me just before the attacks began that sent us to the shiny world, the fae hadn't known exactly what we'd done. Had they figured it out and that's why they attacked then? Or had they discovered this since we'd been gone? I considered lying, denying it, but the look in her silvery-blue eyes dared me to be so stupid.

"We were only six years old," I blurted. "We didn't know what we were doing. It was sealed shut and cloaked, and we would never open it again."

"Are you certain about that?" she asked, one slanted brow raising even higher, and a small voice in the back of my mind answered silently: *No.* I didn't dare say it out loud, though. Silence was probably the best answer to any of her questions from now on.

She turned her attention back to the window, staring at the dusky sky. "Fintan believes you're not the sole purpose of the gloom. He thinks the Shadows have a hand in it, too, so that's where his focus is currently. I told him, though, if it was anyone else, it's obviously the elves."

My ears immediately perked up. "The elves? There are elves in Faery?"

Was Sadie really here?

Maeve's head snapped toward me, her whole demeanor and energy changing as though a switch had flipped. Even her facial features had transformed—her cheekbones sharper than before, her eyes dark and sparking with anger, her lips pulled back to reveal a mouth full of pointy teeth. This was more like the Dark fae I'd imagined while growing up, and for the first time since arriving, I felt a finger of fear trail down my spine.

"We don't discuss the elves!" she growled, smacking her hands on the table as she leaned in so close, I could feel her breath on my skin.

I jerked back, her power smarting as though she'd slapped me across the face. She'd been the one to bring them up! "But you—"

"They are wretched, horrible things, even worse than the Shadow fae. Every single one deserves to die a slow, horrible death by the Tormentor himself." She spat each word with a deep hatred that rivaled my own for the demons.

I blinked, biting my tongue, not about to piss her off even more by arguing with her. But my Sadie . . . her friends . . . I could never believe them to be as awful as Maeve made them sound. They had to be of a different Faery realm. Or Maeve was insane. Either was quite possible.

As though catching herself, the fae straightened, her features softening and returning to her beautiful, regal, mesmerizing self. "Enough of the ugly bits. That is for my brother to worry about, not me and not you. You and I, Elliana, we are going to be good friends."

I blinked again, the swing of her demeanor giving me whiplash.

"Trust me," she added with a smile that could melt the snow throughout the kingdom as she reached out and took my hand between hers. Her fae energy had morphed just as much as her face, a pleasant warmth tingling into my skin where she touched it. "It is in both of our best interests, but especially yours. It could mean your life or your death."

And while her smile and energy were warm and inviting, those last few words were laced with ice thicker than that coating the walls outside.

With the king's absence and no set date of his return, I had no idea how long I had to escape from Winter Court, but I knew I needed to do it before the king came home. It would surely be easier to slip past Maeve and whatever second-tier army was left behind while the top tier accompanied the king. And the best way to do that was to give in and befriend her, even if I didn't trust one cell of her gorgeous body.

"Friends," I said, smiling with a warmth I hoped matched hers. Then to ensure she believed me, I added, "I love your dress, by the way. It's lovely on you." While it may have been manipulative, it wasn't in the slightest bit a lie.

Her eyes drifted downward, giving me a slow once-over. "If you would acquiesce to removing . . . whatever that is you are wearing . . . and take a bath, there are plenty of lovely clothes in the closet for you."

I'd been so preoccupied with being pissed at Dorian, frustrated with my situation, and then trying to plan my way out of here, I hadn't even noticed any clothes. My leathers were safe, enchanted for protection. And yeah, they were kind of sexy because looking like a badass was hot. But still. They were drab, and since I'd spent most of my life wearing leather, I was terribly bored of it.

"Clothes for me?" I imagined them at least as beautiful as those in the shiny world, if Maeve's dress was any indication.

"Of course, doll. Like I said, I want to be friends. And I don't allow my friends to gallivant around the palace looking like . . . that." She flicked a hand my way as she stood, then she turned and sauntered for the door, her perfectly formed ass making the silk of her dress swish as she walked, the faerie stones down her spine glinting in the light. My mouth went dry as my stomach dropped, my tongue unable to form words when she bade farewell and left me to bathe and dress.

Since it was clear I wouldn't be busting my way out of here anytime soon, I gave in and did both. I found a beautiful silk top that was pretty much a backless camisole, the way the soft, flimsy material draped down my sides and across my lower back. It was perfect if I needed my wings, though I doubted that would be the case today. I paired the gold top with a pair of black, tight-fitting pants. I thought I'd died and gone to heaven when I saw my shoe choices. I'd expected all boots, which there were some, but several pairs of stiletto heels lined the shelves, their designs like nothing I'd seen in either version of Earth I'd been to. What was this place, anyway?

When I was clean and dressed, Ena led me out of my room and through a maze of corridors and stairwells until we finally came to a broad hall of white marble, silver-framed paintings lining the wall, and an enormous, two-story tall arched wooden door at the end—the front of the castle, I presumed. We didn't go that far, though, almost immediately turning right into a circular room that Ena called the parlor.

Several separate sitting areas filled the space, all of them made of dark wood that might have been cherry and upholstered in a deep blue velvet-like fabric with delicate winter-motif patterns—snowflakes, stars, crescent moons, and diamonds. Three tall, arched windows let in the dull light of the outdoors, and Maeve and three other female fae lounged on settees in front of the center one. Maeve introduced them as her ladies in waiting, and I had to suppress a snort. We might have been considered royalty at home, but we'd never lived like royalty. Especially not like this, in a huge palace with servants and courtiers and ladies in waiting.

As foreign as it all was to me, I did my best to acclimate and make them accept me. I knew how to put on the charm and get them talking, learning as much as I could. At least, when Maeve convinced them to speak in English, though they often drifted back to their faerie language I dubbed as Faelic. Unfortunately, when they did acquiesce to my linguistic needs,

I learned more about the Shadow fae and their ongoing disputes than I did about the Seelie and Summer Court or anything about elves. I didn't dare touch that topic again, though I hoped it would come up on its own. There had to be a reason for Maeve's hatred of the elves.

Days became a week, maybe longer—it was hard to keep track of time, with the dark light that was supposed to be daylight hovering over the lands. If Summer Court was like this, too, then maybe Mom and Dad really had simply lost track.

As more timed passed with no word from King Fintan or Dorian, I began to think my torture was becoming Princess Maeve's bestie. While I didn't like the fact that slaves served us and she seemed to have no qualms about that, at least she was pleasant to them and to me. But the incessant chattering with her ladies in waiting over decadent brunches of more food than we could ever possibly eat and sitting in that same round room with the same spoiled faeries day in and day out quickly began to feel like Hell, even getting dressed. My love for fashion dwindled with each day that passed, as did my enthrallment with the fae. Maybe I'd grown too accustomed to their alluring effects—or maybe I was becoming more like them, my fae side dominating.

I needed to be making a plan, learning my way around Faery, and preparing an escape, but any time I tried to elicit new information from Maeve or anyone else, they changed the subject to parties and who wore what at the last one. Parties I wasn't invited to, of course, but heard from my room where I was locked in every evening. As droll as the days were, the nights were terrifying.

Awaking from another nightmare, my eyes peeled open to find light flooding the room and Maeve sitting next to me on the bed. Her thumb slid across my cheek, wiping away tears. I hadn't realized I'd been crying and tried to recall the dream. I'd been in the stone prison again, fighting for food, for an extra minute in the shower, for my freedom. I'd been curled up in my cell, my heart aching to see my parents again, my sister. The feeling was all too fresh and real now.

"Bad dream?" Maeve asked quietly as her hand lifted from my cheek and to my hair, pushing the wet strands away from my face.

I looked up at her, finding true concern in her silvery blue gaze. She was a strange creature—perhaps all fae were. Most of the time she seemed like a shallow socialite, the epitome of a faerie princess. But sometimes I caught something else in her eyes, in her expression. Something darker, fiercer, more like me. Every once in a while, it was more than a glimpse, when it was just the two of us, and while she'd never divulged anything personal and stayed far away from anything political, she was more than a party girl without a care in the world. I believed she could care very deeply, but like me, tried to avoid doing so. Of course, trying didn't always lead to success.

"I miss my parents and my sister," I said, rolling onto my back and staring at the ceiling. I'd never been separated from my twin like this, and it'd been far too long since I'd seen my parents. I didn't even know how long anymore. The ache of missing them filled my soul—or, rather, emptied it. Leaving a hollow feeling where my heart should have been.

Maeve slid down and lay next to me. "I know that feeling very well."

I turned my head on the pillow to look at her. "Are your parents . . ."

"Dead?" she asked when my voice trailed off. "Yes."

I'd assumed as much, since her brother was king and not her father and Maeve herself seemed to be the lady of the house.

"How long?" I dared to ask.

"How long?" she echoed, almost sounding confused, but then she chuckled, the sound humorless. "I have heard of the Earthly realm's infatuation with time. It is a human construct, you know. I suppose those with such short lives feel the need to measure it. The fae do not. When you live as long as we do, it is futile to try to track it. But I can tell you that the grief feels as fresh as though it happened yesterday."

The truth of her statement came just as clearly in the sorrowful tone of her voice as it did in her words.

"How?" I whispered.

"War," she said simply, then changed the direction of the conversation, obviously not wanting to discuss the details of the *how*. "I miss them deeply, so I understand how you feel."

I rolled back to my side. "Maeve . . ." I hesitated, but I'd been delaying the question for too long. "Do you know where my parents are? Do you at least know if they're alive?"

She turned onto her side, too, and lifted a lock of my hair from my shoulder, rubbing her thumb over the dark ends. "You know my rule, Elliana. I don't discuss politics. But I have an idea. You should come to tonight's party. I have the perfect dress for you."

My brows pinched together as annoyance prickled my chest and throat. Once again, she turned a serious conversation back to parties and fashion.

"And while you're there," she continued before I could reply, "listen carefully. You may just learn something. In the meantime, I thought I could take you to the library today."

My mood swung as sharply as hers, excitement overcoming me. Perhaps becoming her bestie was paying off. She'd never replace Brielle or Charleigh, of course, but the more I came to know her, the more I realized I wasn't simply playing a role anymore. She had her faults, but she had her graces, too. Or maybe I was simply falling under the spell that was Princess Maeve of the Winter Court.

"The princess is intoxicating, is she not?" the male fae beside me asked later that night as we both watched Maeve spin around the dance floor in the arms of a prince. Her dress was nearly the color of her dark flesh, the glimmering sheen of the sheer fabric and the faerie markings on her skin the only distinguishing factors. With the right shift of light, her breasts and the curves of her ass were on full display.

"I suppose that is one way to say it," I murmured, unable to avert my gaze from her.

Beautiful creatures filled the large ballroom, which was decorated in what I'd come to learn as the traditional colors of Winter Court—blue and silver. Ribbons curled down from the ceiling, faerie light orbs twinkling among them. An orchestra played from one end of the room, their sound melodic yet foreign to my ears. One wall consisted of all windows, illuminated by a full moon and deep blue sky, and on the opposite wall stretched a long bar backlit with pink and lavender light. Shadow fae threaded their ways among the partiers with trays of food and drinks.

"I am to marry her," the man declared, and I nearly spit out my faerie wine—which was the most divine liquid to ever grace my mouth, by the way, even better than the coffee of the shiny world. I looked at him for the first time, and a broad smile filled his doughy face. Fae didn't show their age, but something about this one made him feel ancient and not in a cool, mysterious way. In a gross, you-could-be-her-grandpa way. "King Fintan and I arranged it before he left."

Maeve had failed to tell me this. At least, I thought she had. Admittedly, when she and her ladies rambled on about social matters, I tended to tune them out, even when they bothered to speak in mundane English. Surely, I would have caught such a major piece of information, though.

"I'm sorry," I said, "but I didn't catch your name."

"Prince Cymbel of the Court of Goldwood," he answered proudly. "And you are Lady Lia?"

I gave him a small nod. Maeve ensured I was introduced as a local lady of the Winter Court, considering I was a wanted being. She also helped me perfect my glamour as a fae, and we chose a much more subdued dress compared to hers to make me less noticeable and quite a bit less memorable. The dark gray silk had a cut that was almost motherly next to Maeve's, which I appreciated because blending in allowed me to eavesdrop more easily. For my benefit, she'd insisted that everyone speak in English tonight as an amusing twist on the night. "Won't it be fun to be so crass?" she'd asked the crowd at the opening of the festivities. They'd laughed and teased each other all night, though many often slipped into speaking Faelic.

We hadn't much time in the library today before we had to ready ourselves for tonight's ball, which may have been Maeve's plan all along, but I did have a chance to study a map enough to determine a general idea of the geography—Winter in the north and Autumn in the west, Summer in the south and Spring in the east. The Shadow and elven lands were noticeably absent from the map she'd shared with me. Since there were a few small islands off the coast, toward the edge of the map, I figured this was only one continent of Faery. I wondered how much of the rest of the realm was missing.

I'd also learned that while the Winter Court ruled the Unseelie lands and Autumn Court was secondary, there was also a scattering of other, smaller royal families that served the major ones. Seelie was much the same way, with Summer ruling and Spring secondary. In other words, there were courts sprinkled all over the lands. I hadn't caught all of their names or locations, but I'd noticed a pattern. A name such as Goldwood indicated a minor court under either Summer or Autumn governance, and since he was here, at this party at the Unseelie court, it must have been Autumn. I wondered why King Fintan would marry his only sister to the prince of a smaller court that was already an ally.

"My mother is of the Autumn Court," he continued. Perhaps that explained it, though it still sounded fishy to me. But what did I know of courts and royals, especially in Faery?

"I still fail to understand the pairing," said another male fae on the far side of Prince Cymbel, echoing my thoughts. I'd met him earlier, a nobleman (noble-fae?) of the Autumn Court. "She is more than you could ever handle. Maeve is more of a warrior than you will ever be."

Prince Cymbel chuckled. "Yes, she is. Or was. I do not expect her to fight anymore."

"You would not allow it?" I blurted. I hadn't known Maeve had been any kind of warrior—she never gave even a hint that she'd fought more than a fly—but I doubted this fae could stop her. As old fashioned as everything else was about this world, though, I wasn't surprised that he'd try.

"He would not need to allow it or disallow it," the other man replied. "Not after what happened at the Battle of Wormwood."

"A shame that was," Prince Cymbel said, nodding. "To see her parents slaughtered in front of her like that."

I bit back a gasp. No wonder she hadn't wanted to talk about it before.

A woman joined in the conversation—apparently fae loved the gossip mill as much as the old ladies at the Loft.

"I heard she was so drenched in their blood, all you could see were her eyes glowing with hatred before she shoved a sword into the elven prince's heart. The one who killed her parents, of course," she added as though that wasn't obvious.

With my heart pounding, I excused myself from the group to search for a fresh glass of wine. A server passed by, carrying a tray of flutes. I grabbed two and downed the first in one gulp, placing the glass back on the tray before he even took a step.

Maeve was starting to make a lot more sense to me now. Why

she never discussed being a warrior and tried so hard to focus on lighthearted topics such as parties and fashion. Why she withheld pretty much everything about her parents. Why she hated the elves so much. I understood now, including why she'd driven a sword through a prince's heart. I would have done the same thing.

She found me much later, as the party wound down, sitting at a table in the corner of the ballroom. I'd been quietly drinking my wine, listening to a conversation at the next table, as I'd been doing all night. I heard nothing about my parents except a proclamation that they deserved to be executed after what they'd done (though I didn't hear what, exactly, they'd done). Nobody mentioned their whereabouts, in Faery or otherwise. The only other tidbit I gained was that they knew the Knight twins had been seen, but both had disappeared again. I hoped that meant Brielle had found Noah and was safe and sound with the Amadis. I didn't want to think about what else might have happened to her.

"Shall we be on our way?" Maeve asked me, taking my hand and pulling me to my feet. I stumbled right into her arms, and she giggled. Maeve the warrior faerie princess who'd been so covered in blood you could only see the whites of her eyes actually giggled. And I'd made her do so. That gave me greater joy than it should have. "I see you imbibed in your fair share of the faerie wine."

"How could I not? It was fabulous," I said, hearing the slur in my words. How much had I drunk anyway? "And on our way where? Are we going somewhere?"

"Yes, to your bed." She slid an arm around my waist, her fingers resting on my hip, and steered me out of the nearly empty ballroom, leaving the poor Shadow fae to clean up.

She guided me all the way back to my room, which was good because I would have surely become lost. I didn't know my way around the entire palace sober, let alone drunk on faerie shit.

"You didn't tell me about Prince Cyr? No, Cym? No, Simba," I decided on as we entered my room.

"Cymbel?" She groaned. "I will kill my brother for that. He can't possibly expect me to honor it."

"Do you have a choice?" I wondered aloud as I tried to escape from my dress that suddenly felt entirely too confining.

"If I find someone else, he will be the one who won't have a choice. Here, let me help you." She turned me around to undo the clasps along my spine that held my dress in place. As soon as the fabric loosened, I felt her step closer to me and her breath came hot on my ear. "The question is, who could make an alliance my brother could not refuse and neither could I?"

Her fingertips trailed down my arm, and I understood what the prince had meant earlier. She was intoxicating. Perhaps more so than the wine. And when I opened my eyes the next morning, I didn't know which regret hit me harder: how much faerie wine I'd consumed or the fact that Princess Maeve lay in my bed next to me, both of us naked.

CHAPTER 10

*S*adie.

Her name, her face were the first thoughts that popped in my head at the sight of Maeve lying next to me. The dagger of guilt pierced through my heart and into my soul. Logically, I knew there was nothing to feel guilty about. We'd made no promises when we left each other. Well, she'd promised to find me, but we both knew the likelihood of that actually happening was slim to none. We'd made no other commitments, no vows, parted with no expectations of the other. Still, I couldn't help but think of her, wishing she was the one lying next to me. Wishing she was the one I awoke to this morning and every morning hereafter into eternity. Wishing we'd never had to go our separate ways, to serve our very different obligations.

"Who is Sadie?" Maeve asked, her voice husky with sleep. *Shit.* I hadn't wanted Maeve to know anything about Sadie. "You keep saying her name."

"Oh, my angels." I slapped my hand over my face. "I'm so sorry."

"What? Why? Oh!" Maeve laughed. "Not during sex. We didn't . . . that didn't happen."

I dropped my hand and turned my head toward her. "It didn't?" I tried to hide the relief, not wanting to offend her. "Then why are we naked?"

She sighed. "Not that I hadn't would have minded. But the dresses came off, we got in bed and . . . you passed out. And I must have too, because next thing I knew, I woke up here with you."

Thank the angels.

"Maybe next time," she said with a seductive grin, but as she watched me, the smile faltered, and her brows pulled together. "Or maybe not. Have I misunderstood your preferences?"

"No, you understood."

"Is it Sadie then? Who is she to you?"

I gnawed on my lip. I had no answer. I knew who Sadie used to be to me, but that was in the past. I'd likely never see her again, and she would eventually become a distant memory. I was no good for her anyway. She deserved more, and the sooner I let her go, the better. "Just . . . someone I used to know."

My heart cracked as the words came out, my soul refusing to accept them even as my mind knew their truth.

"I see." Maeve lifted her hand to cup my chin, her eyes following her thumb as it brushed over my lower lip. Her voice came out low and husky as she said, "I sense you need a distraction. I happen to be very good at that."

My breath hitched as I waited, thinking she was about to kiss me, my heart shying away but my body practically begging for it. She rolled away instead, though, and slid out of bed. I couldn't tear my eyes from her luscious body and the faerie markings that only added to the appeal, but I was glad when she covered herself with a robe. I was too confused to know what I wanted anymore.

Thankfully she was right—she most definitely was good at distractions.

Gone were the afternoons spent gossiping with her ladies in waiting and other courtiers in the parlor. She'd been holding out on me before, but now showed off everything the palace had to offer. We swam in the indoor pool fed by underground hot springs. We raced each other on the indoor ice rink. Maeve magically changed the text in the books to English, so we could read out loud to each other in the library, and we ate and drank and kissed. A lot. She slept in my bed with me, but we never even discussed sex let alone had it. I liked her there because for some reason, I didn't dream when she was.

The remorse about Sadie faded. At least, that's what I told myself. But it was replaced by guilt about my sister and my parents. I'd become enraptured with Faery and this beautiful princess, pretending as though I lived in a fairy tale full of fun balls and parties, delicious food and drink, and a fluffy, warm bed while they were out there, somewhere, in who knew what kind of condition. The twinge of guilt became full-on shame gnawing a hole in my gut.

I had to focus. I had to figure out how to escape this place before the king returned, which would likely be soon.

I had to distance myself from Maeve.

Feigning ill, I locked myself in my room and focused on formulating an escape plan. Well, I tried to. It became all too clear that as much as I had learned, as much as Maeve had shared with me in little bits here and there, I really knew nothing about the surrounding land. I knew I needed to fly south, and since there was no sun, I'd have to use the coastline as my guide. But I didn't know how far south I needed to go to find Summer Court.

I didn't know what obstacles to prepare for along the way. The books told of terrifying fae creatures that roamed the forests and lands and even how to defeat them, but much of it made little sense. I didn't know what was real and what was nothing more than stories to scare faelings from wandering into the forests. Even if the suggested defenses worked, I didn't know where to find the necessary supplies or ingredients to create them.

The truth was blatantly clear: I knew no more now than I had when I'd first come here . . . however long ago that had been. Days? Weeks? Months? I certainly hoped not months! That could be years back home.

"I'm beginning to think you are avoiding me," Maeve said, popping her head around my door. She'd been knocking on it all day, and it said something about how things had changed between us that she hadn't just barged right in on her prisoner. "I am absolutely certain you do not fall ill. You are part fae, part angel, and we do not get sick."

I lay on my bed, feeling defeated. "Maybe not, but I just don't feel well. Maybe it's because I'm not supposed to be in Faery this long. I'm not of this realm."

She seemed to consider this, but then simply replied, "Would you like dinner in your room?"

I sighed. "I just want to be alone for a while." She opened her mouth, but I cut her off. "Please, Maeve. Just a night alone is all I ask."

"As you wish." Though the words were agreeable, I could hear the hurt in her voice, making me feel worse.

Ena brought dinner to my room, but I didn't touch it. I lay in bed and finally let the tears flow until I fell asleep. With Maeve gone, the dreams returned.

I crouched in the corner of my cell that was barely big enough to stretch out in, especially when the opposite corner contained my dung hole. A literal hole in the floor where I was supposed to relieve myself. It stunk like . . . well, like shit and piss, as did I. This wasn't my regular cell but one by the Pits. I didn't know how long I'd been here this time. A few days maybe? Weeks? It wasn't

my first time either. The Vault guards were short on patience, and my temper tended to get me thrown down here in the Pits quite often. Well, that among other reasons.

I didn't mind the Pits itself. The thrill of facing and escaping death provided a welcome break to the monotony of my normal cell block. The first time fighting other inmates to the death had been scary as fuck, but the euphoria of winning had become an instant addiction. It also gave me a chance to learn and hone my new abilities and powers. There was no better teacher than real-life experience when your life was literally on the line. The crowds loved me, too, probably because I always looked like the underdog going in. And because of their love for me, I'd been able to make a deal with the master of the Pits—if Brielle was ever sent here, I would take her place.

The cells where they kept us before our turn to fight were the worst part, in my opinion. They were surely illegal in any world or realm besides this one. Any humane world, anyway. If I held my arms up and straight out, my palms touched the walls on either side. I could barely lie down on the stone floor, and I wasn't exactly tall. At least I had that going for me. I couldn't imagine a full-grown were-bear in one of these.

As if the anticipation of the Pits and the fight itself wasn't punishment enough, we weren't allowed the luxury of showers or clean clothes or more than two meals of old bread and water a day. And I'd been down here for weeks at a time, waiting for my turn. It was gross and cruel. Some of the weaker inmates never even made it to the fights, dying in their own feces-covered cell.

But if you won? The winner not only gained another chance to live but also a long, hot shower, clean clothes, and a heaping plate of real food. Not gruel and stale bread from the mess hall, but real meat, vegetables, and warm, fresh bread with butter.

My mouth watered at the thought, and I wondered when I'd finally be given my next chance in the fights.

As if in answer, Morfin clanged his baton on the cell bars. "You're up, kitten."

I suppressed a snarl at the demeaning "endearment" as I leapt to my feet, grateful to finally be getting out of here.

"Who is it this time?" I asked after the lion shifter opened my grate, and I stepped out next to him, his huge, hairy frame dwarfing me. We turned down the short corridor toward the holding area off the actual arena. I could hear the crowd hollering and heckling, and my chest tightened. "Has it already started?"

Morfin didn't answer me. This wasn't good. He was usually much more talkative, giving me a bit of a heads-up of what I was about to walk into. They kept us isolated in the tiny cells so we couldn't talk to the other fighters before we faced off in the Pits. Morfin usually at least told me what kind of creature I'd be up against, but now he remained silent. And the fact that the show had already begun meant I'd be facing more than one opponent. I tried to listen as we stood in the holding room, but all I could hear was the crowd booing.

After my first win in the Pits, Morfin had explained that the crowd consisted of beings from various realms who came to see the fights at the Vault because they got off on watching other creatures kill each other. It was a sport for them, one they betted on. That's why they liked me—the regulars won much off of those who underestimated me. And so many tended to do that.

The boos became louder and angrier, and that's when Morfin shoved me through the doorway and out into the Pits.

I blinked in the bright spotlights glaring on me but lifted my fist in the air when the crowd burst into loud cheers. They loved me, and I loved being loved. But as my eyes adjusted, my heart sank at the sight before me.

Oh, no. No, no, no! This wasn't supposed to happen. I'd made a deal! Of course, I should have known not to trust them, the master or the warden.

I shouldn't have been so surprised to see Brielle, surrounded by four others.

She wore the prison uniform, the gray dark and stained with who knew what. Shit and piss, I knew that much. Half of her reddish-brown hair was matted to her head, the rest hanging in thick, clumpy ropes. Her brown eyes looked sunken in her skeletal face. She'd lost so much weight. I stifled the urge to vomit at the thought of how long she'd been isolated down here in a tiny cell, waiting for her first time in the arena.

The Pits was just that—a series of wide pits in the floor of a large cavern in the lowest levels of Shadow Vault Citadel. The holding room entered into the largest and deepest pit that was somewhat off-center of the cavern. My wings gave me an advantage against most of the creatures I fought, allowing me to see the other, smaller dips in the floor that I'd sometimes use to trap my opponent in a more confined space. But the stands climbed up the walls of the cavern, and the crowds loved to throw things at me when I flew. Especially when my opponents couldn't make it out of the main pit to reach me, the sides too steep for them to climb. The crowd wanted action. They wanted blood.

That was probably why there had been all the booing before I made my entry. Brielle would not give them the fight they wanted to see. And if they didn't know she was my twin and not me, they would have been boiling mad with disappointment. Now seeing that there were two of us surely had their interest piqued.

I snapped my wings out and kept low to the floor as I soared toward the group with my sister in the middle, taking measure of the others as I did. I quickly realized she wasn't exactly surrounded. More like she and another girl were cornered. No, not quite that either. The girl was cornered, her back pressed against the sloping wall of the pit, a stalagmite on each side of her. Brielle stood between her and the others. Of course, my sister would be defending someone she was supposed to kill. As soon as I landed next to her, I realized why—the girl was human.

What the hell was a human doing at the Vault?

The other three were demons, the bright spot in this otherwise disturbing situation. I couldn't wait to annihilate them all. And I did just that, the crowd growing louder with each one, cheering me on.

I'd grown used to killing. The Pits had done that to me. Each kill not only became easier but brought a sense of relief. The darkness in me, my beast, loved it. I gave her a little freedom as we fought, unleashing our worst on the enemies until we were the last ones standing and bodies littered the ground. It was kill or be killed here, and I gladly killed. I tried to assuage the guilt after each fight by reminding myself that if I didn't do it—if I didn't survive every turn in the Pits—they'd throw Brielle in next time.

Yet, here she was anyway.

As the last demon poofed into black smoke and disappeared, I pumped my fist in the air to celebrate another win, and the reaction was deafening. It only took a moment for me to realize their cheers weren't for me. At least, not because I had won.

I turned to find my twin with the human's lifeless body at her feet, tears flowing down my sister's face.

"I had to," she cried. "I didn't want to, but I had to!"

The norm held a spear in her hands, its tip made of iron and silver. Where she got it from, I didn't know, but yes, Brielle had to. And I couldn't be prouder. I stepped forward to embrace her, but—

Realization hit me as the crowd's cheers grew louder and more repetitive.

"Fight! Fight! Fight!" they chanted.

Brie and I stared at each other with wide eyes, both of us shaking our heads.

"You will fight each other or both be killed," the master's voice boomed over the Pits.

"I will not!" I yelled.

"You will," he bellowed.

"No! We had a deal!"

The crowd booed and threw their trash at us, metal goblets and animal bones bouncing off my head and Brielle's shoulder, more piling on the ground around us.

"So be it," the master said.

And the next thing I knew, my sister's mouth gaped open in a gasp as the spear exploded from the front of her chest, spraying blood on my face before it continued its trajectory into my own body. Iron and silver. It burned a hole in my heart and through my veins as we both went down as one, falling to the blood-stained stone floor. My hand reached out for my twin as I watched the light leave her eyes and an emptiness like no other consumed me.

We departed this lifetime as we'd come into it—together.

I awoke with a scream in my throat.

"They're not dreams or even premonitions," I whispered in the darkness, my voice hoarse as though I had actually been screaming. "They're *memories.*"

No, that didn't make sense. If they were memories, Brie and I wouldn't be alive. And if they were memories—why hadn't I recalled them before now? That was some pretty traumatic shit. No, it had to have been just a dream. An ongoing, recurring nightmare, no more.

"Are you okay?" a voice asked from nearby. Not Maeve's, though.

I could barely make out the face in the dark. "Ena? What are you doing in here?"

"You scream a lot. I know what it's like." She perched lightly on the mattress's edge, near the foot of my bed. It was the first time she'd said anything so personal.

"The scars?" I dared to ask. She didn't reply, but that was answer enough. "What happened?" She remained quiet. "Did your king do this to you? I mean, the Shadow king —Caellach?"

I didn't expect her to answer, but maybe the darkness gave her courage. "The prince," she whispered. "The Tormentor."

"What a fucking asshole. I'm sorry he did that to you."

"I . . . I don't think he wanted to—" she began, and I cut her off.

"Don't ever make excuses for a beast like that. He was awful to you. But you survived, Ena. You are strong. You're free from him. Maybe someday you can be free from here," I hinted.

That was the wrong thing to say. She bolted from the room, a wave of her fear slamming through me.

I fell onto the pile of pillows, doubting I'd be able to fall back asleep after the vivid dream. I was tempted to find Maeve, but at some point I must have dozed off, because I found myself back in a room of stone walls. Not either of the cells, but bigger with two tables in the center, my sister and I laying on each one.

Tendrils of dark power entered the room, slithering over Brielle and me, followed by two shadowy figures whose energy was so black, I felt like I was drowning in the deepest of oceans. Even my beast inside cowered from them.

"I knew you couldn't be killed so easily," one of them rasped. The more powerful one. A dark tendril of his force licked along my cheek, making me gasp from the cold pain. "Yes, you are still alive, aren't you, little shade? What do we do with you? Have you earned your release?"

Wait. What? He was going to free us?

"Please?" I whispered.

"No," said the other.

"Quiet," snapped the first as it drifted between our tables. The black fog swirled around it, flowing and parting, revealing glimpses of a male face and glowing gray eyes. "What would you do for freedom, little shade? Anything?"

"What do you want me to do?" I asked weakly. Had I really died? I thought I had, in the Pits with that spear. So had my

twin. I looked over at her, blinking away tears. Was she still alive, too?

"I want you to be mine," the dark form replied.

"Father," the other said, the tone one of warning.

"Or any of my princes. We need you for our kingdom."

So trade one prison for another. A jailor I knew for one I didn't? One this dark?

"I just want to go home," I murmured.

"I could make that happen. You can go home for now, but I will come calling when it is time."

I shook my head. That was not a deal I'd make.

The form grew and loomed over Brielle's body. "For your sister's freedom?"

"Please," I begged, unable to move, to stop him.

A black finger trailed over her throat. "For her life?"

"No!" I meant to say don't, but fear strangled me, consumed me.

"No?" The shadow seemed to find joy in this refusal. No, not in my refusal, I realized, but in the agony my sister was apparently experiencing as her body jolted and writhed on the table.

"Stop!" I tried to shout, but I still lacked any energy, any force. "Yes, okay, yes. For my sister's life. For her freedom, too."

"Father," the other said again, more sharply this time. He was still ignored.

"We will make this deal," the father said.

"Both of us get to go home?" I asked.

"For now. But when I call for you, you cannot refuse, or you both die. For good this time. Do we have a deal?"

I watched my sister's trembling body and nodded. "Yes. We have a deal."

CHAPTER 11

We have a deal.
We have a deal.

The words echoed in my mind throughout the next morning, drowning out anything Maeve prattled on about. I'd needed the distraction and had joined her for brunch, much to her delight. But not even she could distract me from the vivid visions.

Were those really memories? I was beginning to think they were as they grew more solid in my mind, along with others from our time at the Vault. I didn't know why they'd only now surfaced. Since they had, though, it would sure be nice to remember the full story. Like, how did we end up in the supernatural prison in the first place? *Why?* Did I really fight to the death in some kind of arena? Did I really kill all those beings? I mean, it kind of sounded like something I would do, especially to protect my sister. Not that she couldn't protect herself—she just wouldn't. Or, at least, she'd take so long analyzing the situation to identify the best solution that she'd be killed in the meantime. Especially in the Pits, where there was no other solution and no mercy. It was either kill or be killed, full stop. *Shit.* The fact that I could recall that only confirmed that this had all truly happened.

Perhaps it should have been more disturbing, the things I had done there. But I knew that kind of darkness lived inside me, so it wasn't all that surprising. I was more concerned about the suppression of the memories and how they were flooding back. Why now? How could I not remember being imprisoned and all those kills before?

And what was most disturbing to me of all—who the hell did I make a deal with?

I also couldn't remember what came after. We must have been freed, as promised. But when? The visions made it seem like we'd been in the Vault for months, perhaps years, but surely that topic of conversation would have come up at some point in our lives. Had our parents wiped our memories and kept it from us all this time? Why? And *when* had all of this happened anyway? Brielle and I were older, at least mid-teens, but we'd both still had copper-colored hair in the visions.

"Oh, my angels," I gasped out loud.

"What?" Maeve asked. She'd been rambling on about something but stopped and looked at me as though seeing me for the first time that morning. "Oh, love, you look awful. You know what you need? You need to get out of this castle."

I momentarily forgot my epiphany. She was letting me go?

"Fresh air should do you well," she continued. "Why don't we take a walk in the gardens?"

Oh. Well, it was better than another day in my room or that dreadful parlor.

After we finished eating, we bundled up in thick, fur-lined cloaks with deep hoods that felt as old-world as everything else about Winter Court. I'd wondered more than once if all of Faery was like this or if Winter Court had its own flair for eras gone by.

We left the main part of the palace through the massive arched front door that led out to a spacious courtyard. Planter boxes lined the inside of the high stone walls surrounding the fortress, where trees, bushes, and flowers I'd never seen before grew. Green needles and leaves, red berries that might have been holly or something native only to Faery, and blue flowers contrasted against the white of the snow and ice coating everything. My generation—those who came after the war—hadn't known white snow until we were older. For years after the bombs, snow fell in a variety of colors, more evidence of nature tainted by the black magic. I was a little surprised the snow here in Faery was so white. Kind of plain, yet still breathtakingly gorgeous.

"It's so much prettier in the sun," Maeve complained when I commented on the beauty. We followed a path to the side lawns, the opposite direction from the chasm and the door Dorian had used when he brought me here. "This darkness hovering over us makes it look so . . . *dirty*. But when the sun shines on the snow, each tiny crystal sparkles in blues and pinks and all colors of the rainbow. I can't wait for you to see it. It's a spectacular sight and just one reason I love it here so much."

She went on about other aspects she loved about her home as we meandered around the grounds, but I tuned her out again, my mind drifting back to the dream. No, the memory. Then I remembered what I'd realized earlier.

"Maeve, do you know how to reach my brother?" I blurted.

"Dorian?" she asked, bewildered, and I realized I'd interrupted her ramblings.

"I'm sorry," I quickly apologized, stifling an urge to snap at her. I was trying my best not to let her on about my off mood this morning, but I was failing. "It's just, something urgent has occurred to me, and I desperately need to talk to him."

"Is this why you were avoiding me?"

"I wasn't avoiding you. Not you, specifically. I—"

She held her hand up. "No need to explain. I might be able to send a message to him. What does he need to know?"

Shit. I wasn't about to discuss this with her. Even though we'd become friends, she was still, for all intents and purposes, my jailor. Different prison and circumstances, but another warden, nonetheless. I couldn't let myself forget that again.

"Please, Maeve," I said as sweetly as I could manage. "We fought right before he left me here, and if your brother returns and decides to kill me after all, I'd hate for that to be my last words with Dorian. It's very important I talk to him personally."

She studied me with that piercing silvery blue gaze of hers for a long moment, one slanted brow arched, then rolled her eyes. "I am familiar enough with your brother to know that you have absolutely no relationship with him. And I know you now, too. You have talked about your parents and your sister, but never Dorian. I am quite certain you could not care less if you had hurt your brother's feelings." I opened my mouth to argue, but she hurried on. "But I will see what I can do."

"I do appreciate it. And I promise it's not about him helping me escape."

She laughed. "I'm not worried about that. There is a reason you are here, Elliana. And if anybody has a tight brotherly bond, it is Fintan and Dorian."

"Really?" I asked with sincere surprise. I knew so little about my brother, which would be extremely sad if he weren't the leader of our enemy with a soul as black as ink. I was better off not knowing. I supposed it made sense that the leader of the Daemoni be allies with the king of the Dark fae. I just hadn't considered Dorian being tight knit with anyone. A slight pang of betrayal touched my heart. Not betrayal of me, but of our parents.

"I do have an idea, though, to keep you safe," Maeve said, stopping our stroll to turn toward me. She took my hands in hers. "It might seem a little . . . outlandish, I admit." She hesitated, her eyes averting, almost shyly. Though there'd never been anything shy about Princess Maeve in the time I had known her. When her gaze came back to lock with mine, she lifted a hand to my face, skimming the backs of her fingers along my jawline. "You're different, Elliana. You make me feel things I have never felt before. Things I think only—" She paused, seeming as though she was gathering courage for her next words. "—things only true mates feel. Fated mates."

My breath caught in my throat, and I somehow managed to keep it there before it burst out in a gasp, or worse, a laugh. I blew it out slowly as I tried to decide the best way to respond.

"You cannot tell me you do not feel it, too," she said, her slanted brows coming together for a moment before they eased as her face relaxed. "You probably just do not know the feeling. Did you even know fae have fated mates?"

I shook my head, still too shocked to form words. I knew about shifters, and I knew my parents' souls were actually created for each other by the angels. I hadn't heard that the fae experienced such a phenomenon.

She smiled, her eyes filling with joy as she explained with a dreamlike quality to her voice. "It's a connection deeper than any other, one that cannot be broken even by death. In fact, when one half goes, the other follows shortly after because it just cannot fathom continuing on."

That sounded awful! Who would want that?

She continued. "It is the feeling that the two of you can conquer the world because together you are stronger than anything you could ever face. It is love and passion and a deeply ingrained knowledge that there is absolutely nobody else out there who could make you feel the way you do with your fated mate. You are simply meant to be together and denying the fact only brings pain and agony to the point you both could die, not from a broken heart but from a broken soul."

Again, *ew*. "And you feel that way about me?"

She squeezed my hands. "The closest I have ever felt. We would have to bond to know for sure, which is why you might not feel it yet. Especially since you are only part fae. But I do believe it, Elliana. I have never felt this way with anyone before, and if it is true, Fintan could never kill you. By faerie law, he would have to protect you as one of his own, as well as your family. We could find your parents. You and your sister would be safe from all those who want to kill you both." She paused, then added almost as an afterthought, "Also, he could not force me to be with Cymbel if I am meant to be with you."

Ah-ha. That was the full truth. This made more sense— that she had found a solution to benefit us both—than actual, real-deal fated mates did. I just couldn't imagine any god or fate or whatever torturing another creature by forcing them to be with me. Nobody deserved that fate.

Maeve shook my arms. "Look. Fintan is on his way home. I received a message this morning. If we ignore what we have together, if we do not do this before his return, your future is in his hands. If he still believes a power such as yours should not exist at all, he will find a way to kill you, as well as your sister. Or, he could come to his senses and see that an alliance with your people could benefit us all—and *he* would take you as *his* wife. From what I understand, I do not believe you would enjoy that much. Especially when you and I can have all of that and so much more."

Unable to think as she pierced me with those strange eyes, I slid my hands from hers and turned away, staring at an ice sculpture in the corner of the garden without actually seeing it. Was the answer to all of our troubles really that simple? If the Seelie fae held my parents against their will, wouldn't the Unseelie king be willing to rescue them if we had an alliance? From what I had managed to learn, the Seelie and Unseelie were constantly looking for reasons to go to war with each other. Living such long lives made boredom come easily, and war gave the fae something exciting to do and to talk about for a while. And Brielle and I would be so much safer if we were protected by the Earth's Angels, the Amadis, *and* the Unseelie fae.

On the other hand, Maeve said Fintan and Dorian were close. Did that mean the Unseelie were already aligned with the Daemoni? If so, what would happen if the Unseelie then aligned with us? War? Or could an alliance between the Amadis and Daemoni ever be possible?

Ugh! I was too much like Maeve—not enough interest in politics to know what was best. And Brielle and I had been removed from it all while in the shiny world, so even she wouldn't know the best solution with her gift. We didn't have enough of the facts. If only I could speak to Mom and Dad and know what they would want me to do. But I was on my own. My decision could prevent another all-out war—or it could start one.

"You think about it," Maeve said, slipping her arm around mine and steering me back out of the gardens. "Just do not take too long. Fintan will return soon, and then it may be too late. In the meantime, I will see if I can reach Dorian."

What she'd thrown at me had me reeling nearly as hard as the memories that were returning, and I'd almost forgotten about my epiphany and the need to speak with Dorian. Supposedly, the curse that had put Brielle and me into a coma when we were sixteen—the one that suppressed our powers just when we'd come into them and turned our hair black— was cast by a Daemoni warlock. Dorian would know if this were true or if that was a cover story for the time we'd spent imprisoned at the Vault. And if the latter were the case, why? Why would our parents want our memories erased and our powers suppressed? I mean, our time at the Vault was truly awful, but we'd survived, and we were stronger for it. Or maybe they weren't a part of that. Maybe they didn't know either.

Damn it! My thoughts were all over the place. Frustration was quickly growing into anger, and all I wanted was to get out of this damn palace and be free. To talk to my parents and find out what really happened in the past—and know what to do for our futures. Although, if they'd done such a horrible thing to Brielle and me, maybe it was just as well I didn't know where they were because I might have the urge to strangle them. The thought made the beast inside lift her head.

The fastest route to learning the truth just might be accepting Maeve's proposal. If aligning with the Unseelie was a dumb move, nobody would be surprised anyway. I was the fuck-up of the family, after all. I didn't see any better option before me, especially if it meant my freedom. I'd marry the king if it protected Brielle—I'd hate it, but I'd do it—but I'd rather be with Maeve, even when I was absolutely certain that we were not fated mates.

I decided to sleep on it, taking my dinner in my room again, but barely touching it. Just as I was about to change for bed, though, Ena charged into the room, throwing my fighting leathers, my weapons, and a cloak at me. Before the door swung closed behind her, I could hear what sounded like a scuffle or fighting coming from somewhere else in the castle.

"They cannot know you are here," Ena said. "Hurry! Dress, and I will lead you out."

"What?" I asked, staring at my clothes as though I'd never seen them before.

"He has come for you! You must escape!" Desperation filled her voice while she began undressing me herself.

"The king?"

"Just hurry!"

I shook my head. "No, it's okay. Maeve and I have a plan."

"My lady sent me! She said to make sure you got away.

Please, miss, please just hurry! The Shadows will . . ." She trailed off, fear overcoming her.

"The Shadows? That's who's fighting out there?"

"Yes, and they cannot know you are here."

Shit. Now understanding, I hurried into my leathers as Ena packed food and other necessities into a messenger-type bag. As I slid my sword, knives, and throwing stars into their proper places, a sense of comfort, of home settled into me, grounding me, making me feel more like me again. I hadn't known they'd been holding my weapons this whole time. I assumed the demons had confiscated them. Dorian must have grabbed them, which was all the more perplexing. I didn't have time to think about it, though.

Donning me in the midnight blue cloak with its large, deep hood, Ena snuck me down a set of stairs I hadn't even known existed, tucked behind a suite of rooms I'd never been in before. The sound of clanging metal and magic spells finding their marks rang throughout the castle, and a deep, dark force pulled at me. My beast wanted to fight, and maybe I should have. But I didn't. I followed Ena instead. I chose freedom.

After descending many flights, we finally came to a door, and I thought for a minute it might have been the same one Dorian had brought me in, but it didn't open to a ledge above the chasm. Rather, a short expanse of a snow-covered field led directly to the woods, and a gray horse waited.

For a brief moment, the vision of smoky horses with red eyes sent my heart galloping. *No, it's not here. It doesn't fit.* I forced myself to calm. I still didn't know where that vision originated—it hadn't come up in a memory yet, and I didn't think it ever would. Because I was sure it was yet to happen.

"Hurry!" Ena barked in a whisper, gesturing at the creature.

"I've never ridden a horse," I hissed.

"You cannot fly. They will easily see you in the sky. Stay to the woods and go southeast." She quickly gave me more instructions about where to go and shared a few tips and commands for the horse. "He knows what to do. Now go!"

I sprang up on the horse's back and held the reins as she showed me. "Ena, come with me. You can be free, too. From both of them."

Her eyes rounded with fear, and she shook her head vehemently. "I belong here."

Preventing further argument, she smacked the horse on the rump, then slammed the door between us. Holding on to the deep hood to keep it from flying off my head, I leaned over the horse's neck as he galloped across the field. Just before we darted into the woods, I whispered a spell to the snow to cover our tracks and looked over my shoulder for one last look at Winter Palace.

CHAPTER 12

*T*he night sky was at its darkest by the time I found the cottage Ena had directed me to. With my crazy mix of DNA, I didn't need a lot of sleep—a few hours allowed my body to regenerate all of its cells—but Moonbutt, the name I'd given the horse since I didn't know his real one, needed a rest. I contemplated releasing him since I could run as fast on my own and I was much less conspicuous, but I didn't know what I'd face ahead. What I might have to fight. I figured it best to conserve my energy.

I'd also considered returning to Winter Palace. Part of me felt like a coward for not fighting for Maeve and her court when she'd turned out to be a friend, possibly something more. I also still thought her plan had been a valid one. But fuck it. That was before, and I was free now. Friend, lover, or whatever she would have become, she had still held me prisoner in her palace. I could not forget that.

Especially when I noticed that the farther I traveled away from her, the less appealing she became to me. Her intoxicating effect faded with each mile I put between us, and I wondered if anything I had felt had been real at all. None of the other fae had affected me in that way, which might have been her doing as well. No, I couldn't be soft with her. I could never go back.

Of course, she could still show up at the cottage and take me prisoner again. I'd cross that bridge if and when I came to it. For now, I had to stay on course: find out where my parents were and return to Earth and my sister.

For Ena had told me one other thing right before I left, which Maeve had conveniently failed to ever mention: "Find the Circle of Knowing and you will find your answers."

I'd learned about stone circles at school, in a fae magic class. They contained concentrated magic that could be used for various purposes, including portals between realms. They were supposedly scattered around Faery, and a small number were on Earth, such as Stone Henge, connecting the realms. The energy on the Earth side was quite faint in comparison and rarely used. They had completely escaped my mind until Ena mentioned them. If this Circle of Knowing had the answers I needed, as Ena said, then I could at least make a plan. Hopefully one that included reuniting with Brielle and Charleigh as well as our parents and the rest of our family. If it was a portal home, even better. But if it said returning to Winter Court was the answer . . . well, at least then I would know.

For now, Moonbutt and I needed to rest. Near the cottage was a small stable—just one stall with a mound of hay and a bucket. I scooped the bucket through the knee-deep snow, then warmed it with fire from my palms to make water for Moonbutt.

"Okay, boy, there you go. Get some rest while you can." I patted his neck, and he gave a soft whinny in thanks.

Inside the one-room cottage was a fireplace, a chair, and a bed. A pile of wood was already stacked in the hearth, and I only needed to call forth a flame from my fire magic to light it. I probably should have been concerned everything we needed was provided so conveniently, but I chalked it up to faerie magic. Maeve had sent me here, so surely, she'd made it hospitable. Which probably meant she would be coming for me when it was safe—or that she expected me to return on my own. Maybe this was a test to see where my loyalties lay. If so, I'd fail it. Once again, Elliana Ames Knight would be a big fat disappointment. This time, I didn't really care.

I dreamt about the Vault again. Dorian was there, visiting us, and I couldn't figure out if he was trying to get us released or if he'd been the one to send us there in the first place.

"Whatever you do, keep your asses out of the Pits," he'd warned. Yeah, that didn't happen. If he knew me at all, even at sixteen, he'd have known what an impossible feat that would have been. Perhaps he did and the warning was a way to cover his motives. I had no clue when it came to Dorian. Part of me wished Mom was right about him—that he was redeemable—but everything I knew before and experienced now made me believe she was dead wrong. If he'd really cared, he would have done whatever necessary not only to keep us out of the Pits but to keep us out of the Vault in the first place.

That place changed me, especially the Pits. The fighting . . . the kills . . . the blood . . . how much I secretly enjoyed it all . . . Maybe that was why they'd erased our memories and suppressed our powers. I'd been scary as hell, if I did say so myself.

I awoke pissed off at Dorian, and the feeling stayed with me all afternoon as Moonbutt and I hit the road again. Well, not a road. Just a path through the never-ending woods. I was beginning to wonder if Faery had anything else to see besides trees and snow, but even though the Circle of Knowing was nearly a full day's ride south of the palace, Ena said it was still deep in the Winter Lands. I wondered what the rest of Faery looked like but didn't plan to find out. Not on this trip, anyway.

Night had fallen and the moon had risen when the forest finally began to thin, and I saw them ahead—a ridge above us where several large, irregular shapes hung in the air. Hovering six feet or so over the ground, their edges glowed faintly in various colors. I squeezed Moonbutt with my legs, and he took off in a gallop. But before we reached the top of the hill, he suddenly whinnied and reared up, as though he'd slammed into a wall, tossing me off his back and onto my ass.

"Hey!" I shouted after him as he galloped off the way we'd come. Seemingly out of nowhere, an impenetrable wall of darkness pushed in from every direction, surrounding me. The feeling was familiar—like I was at the bottom of the deep blue sea where no light could ever reach.

I had barely enough time to conjure a flame to see by when I sensed the attack without seeing it. My beast within stirred as something airborne charged at me from above, and growing the flame into a ball, I blindly threw it. There was a screech of agony as a burst of flames flashed in front of my face, a clawed hand shooting from it and narrowly missing my cheek before there came a thud on the ground nearby. Probably within kicking distance, but I couldn't even see that far.

Before I could try to find it to know if it was still alive and remained a threat, I sensed another creature flying at me. I threw a fireball, but it soared out of sight, missing its mark. I conjured a long icicle, but I needed to see my target for it to be effective. While I couldn't see it, I still sensed it. Dropping the icicle, I called on my air magic, swirling my arms above my head until they created a powerful wind, drawing it around me into a cyclone. Snow and dirt rose into the air as the wind force strengthened. There were two more thuds, then nothing.

After waiting another moment, I slowed the air, unable to listen or feel beyond it. The next two came at me on the ground. I heard their footsteps but still saw nothing. Releasing my knives, I dual-wielded, taking them out easily. But they were followed by more and more—at least another half dozen —from the sky and the ground.

Who—or what—the hell were these things? If they had come from Winter Court, I was sure they would have identified themselves by now. They would have given me orders to comply so they could return me to their princess. Maeve wouldn't have told them to attack and kill me . . . would she?

Using magic and plain old hand-to-hand combat, I fought, but I had to admit, this many might have been more than I could handle. I had spent too much time on my ass at the Winter Palace, eating and lazing around instead of practicing and sparring. Maybe that had been Maeve's plan— to weaken me and make me an easier target. Maybe these were her men after all.

But that didn't feel right, in my gut. The energy off these fighters was different and much darker than anyone in the Winter Court. These were outsiders, reminding me that I was wanted dead or alive by pretty much everyone. Usually the dead part.

"Use your power." The gravelly voice came from somewhere around me, but I was still fighting in the complete darkness so I couldn't see to whom it belonged.

"I am!" I grunted. My beast sprang to her feet, energized by both the fight and the dark energy encircling me.

"No, you're holding back!"

A long talon swished by my head, then sliced across my shoulders, through the cloak and even my leathers, which should have been impossible. A deep growl formed in my chest as my beast prepared for release. I feared unleashing her, though. I had to keep control. *No, you don't. If there's ever a time to let her loose, it is now.* The problem was not knowing if I could ever regain it.

My wings burst free, but unlike my attackers, I couldn't fly blind, so I made the feathers hard as titanium and sharp as razors. I swept my wings outward, connecting with at least two more assailants, slicing through flesh and bone. I released a few feathers, sending them like darts through the wall of darkness, hoping they would hit a mark.

Then everything suddenly fell silent, and the air shifted and thinned. As though the black wall had disintegrated into nothing more than smoke, it drifted away. Actually, more like it was sucked away in a vacuum to a point in front of me. The moon's light on the snow was nearly blinding before my eyes adjusted. I blinked several times as the scene came into focus, and then my breath caught.

Over a dozen dead bodies surrounded me, dark blood staining the snow. Up ahead, the ridge only another twenty yards away, was the Circle of Knowing, and between me and the floating stones, the black smoke gathered and began to settle, taking the rough shape of a man. From my vantage below him, he looked nearly as tall as the stones, his shoulders about as broad. The smoke circled and undulated around him, cloaking his body, but clearing just enough for me to see blazing silver eyes glaring down on me.

"There you are, little shade," the familiar raspy voice filtered through, and my whole body froze. "Do you know how long I have been looking for you?"

Shit. Shit, shit, shit. This couldn't be happening!

I glanced behind the form, to the stones, where runes carved into their surfaces glowed in soft colors as if lit from within. The magic of the circle pulsed almost as strongly as the figure before me. My shoulders tensed, my wings flaring as I wondered if I could make it—to my answers, to home, to my family.

"I wouldn't," the smoky shape warned, and my eyes snapped back toward him.

Fuck me. I was *so* close!

"We have a deal," he reminded me. "You do not want to

break a deal with a fae, now do you, little shade? Surely you know better than that. Especially a fae king."

And I'd bet my life that was not just any old king—that was the Shadow king himself standing before me.

Fuck me again. I should have known. Damn it! Stupid sixteen-year-old me made a deal with not only a fae but a fae king. If I could, I'd go back and stab her all over again.

"I already held up my end," the king continued. "You went home and then even disappeared for a while, but now I am here to claim what is mine. You know what will happen if you do not uphold your end, yes?"

Sometimes while we were growing up, my mom would take time out to do our English and literature lessons herself. She'd been a famous author in the Before time, and our lessons would include writing stories together. She'd taught us about the trope of the heroine who was too stupid to live—a trope we wanted to avoid, she'd said, if we didn't want to tick off our audience. I was feeling like that stupid bitch right now. Too stupid to live. I'd been caught by two different factions of our enemies already—three if I counted Dorian as the Daemoni—imprisoned twice, freed, and now caught again by another foe.

On the other hand, I was still alive, so I supposed there was that. That made me not entirely stupid, right? And the only way to stay that way—and to ensure my sister did as well—was to not piss off the Shadow king. To not break a deal with him. He was right. He'd upheld his end.

I blew out a harsh breath. "Yes," I nearly growled. "We had a deal."

"I am a king!" He didn't *nearly* growl. He practically roared it. The dark energy thickened, the wall returning momentarily before he reined it back in. "Show your respect."

Internally rolling my eyes, I dropped to a knee and lowered my head, mimicking what I'd seen others do before Maeve, though she'd never asked it of me.

"We had a deal . . . your majesty?" It came out as a

question because I wasn't quite sure how he wanted to be addressed.

The dark form huffed. "You need proper training, but I suppose that will do."

Then the smoke suddenly swept toward me and surrounded me, a black energy that at once made me sick and made me want to sing. When it cleared as quickly as it had come, I was no longer on the slope of the ridge with the stone circle ahead and the forest behind me, but on the top of a tower overlooking a city enshrouded in mists. Through the layers of fog rose steep roofs and towers with spires pointing accusing fingers at the dark sky. Dim lights glowed and blurred in the hanging waves of mist.

Did we flash? Was it possible to flash in Faery? I'd tried it once from Winter Palace, quite unsuccessfully, of course. I didn't know, though, if it was because flashing magic didn't work in Faery or specifically *my* magic didn't.

"We sifted," the king said from my side, as though reading my mind. Having grown up with a telepath for a mother, I was skilled at blocking her out, and I immediately slammed that protective wall in place, just in case the king hadn't made a simple guess. "Much like what you call flashing but using fae magic." He swept his hand out before him. "Welcome to the City of Shadows, your new home."

Not for long, if I can help it. I had to figure out a way out of this. I needed to know what he wanted and what his endgame was. Then maybe I could make a new deal. Or kill him. If that was possible.

"Why?" I asked, turning toward him and nearly gasping out loud.

The smoke had cleared away completely, revealing the Shadow king's appearance for the first time. His skin was the color of dusk on a cloudy day, of dark storm clouds gathering on the horizon, glimmering in the dim light as if sprinkled with stardust. In stark contrast, white hair donned his head, pulled back into a fat man-bun that spoke of its great length and exposed his sharply pointed ears. His slanted eyebrows and closely cropped beard and mustache were just as white, nearly glowing against his dark skin. His face was a study of angles, from the sharp cheekbones to the straight nose and pointy chin, the only curves that of the fae markings faintly shining in silver. If he were human, I'd guess him to be in his forties, but his dark energy was truly timeless.

He wore armor made of a material I was unfamiliar with and must have been native to Faery. A cape attached to his shoulder pieces and waved in the breeze behind him like a black flag. His overall appearance seemed to answer the question that had been bugging me since arriving in this realm —everyone in Faery had an affinity for times long gone on Earth.

His eyes narrowed as his thin upper lip curled.

"Why, your majesty?" I quickly corrected.

"Why what?" he demanded.

"Why do you want me here?"

His silver gaze pierced into me, a tangible probe into my mind, my soul. "After what happened on that ridge, I ask myself the same question."

"Because I killed your people? *They* attacked *me*." I refused to let guilt worm its way in.

"No. The fact that you took so long to do it." He grabbed my arm, and we must have sifted again, because we were suddenly indoors, in a dark, gloomy parlor, for lack of a better word. The space was small but the ceiling high, and the king seemed to take up every inch of it. A round table with a single, black-upholstered chair were the only furnishings, thick, heavy drapes hanging on one wall, presumably over a window hidden behind them. A chandelier of actual candles provided the only light, flickering shadows over the walls and the king's face.

"So you don't care that I killed your men?" I asked, picking up the conversation from where we left off.

"I have plenty of men. What I do not have—until now—is a weapon like you." He stepped closer, towering over me, and when I looked up, the lines and whorls of the fae markings on his forehead and cheeks glowed as bright as his silver eyes. His dark energy intensified, tendrils of black smoke rising off his body and licking at mine. My beast, who still hadn't quite settled after the fight, rose again, mewling in response. The king bared sharp, pointed teeth, much like Maeve's had been that one time, but so much worse. When he spoke, his voice reverberated into my bones. "You have power like no other. Power I need. You will use it, little shade. You will make it mine. Or your family will die."

With that, he left, and I was alone in another strange castle, another strange room, another threat hanging over my head. But I knew this one was very real and much more frightening.

I wasn't alone for long. A throng of waifs who reminded me of Ena flittered into the room, chattering quietly with each other in a foreign language unlike anything I had ever heard before. Well, sort of like the Faelic language I'd heard in the Winter Court, but I'd learned a few words and had begun to understand the basics of their grammar, and this was different. The Shadow fae seemed to have their own dialect or maybe even complete language. I wondered if that were true for the Seelie fae, too, or if it even differed among courts and kingdoms.

Before I could stop the servants, my leathers were gone, and I was shoved into a tub the size of a pool, then scrubbed from head to toe with some kind of concoction that smelled divine. There must have been something in it that made me more docile, because all the fight left me, and I relaxed.

I did, but not my beast. She was up and moving about, sniffing the air and soaking in the dark energy that seemed to hang over the City of Shadows along with the fog. Like a cat, she stretched and slid against my restraints on her, gently pressing into them, as though testing their hold. Which, admittedly, was weakening. The king had called this my new home, which it never could be, but my beast certainly felt at home here.

The Shadow fae hurried me out of the bath and into a dress. With deft fingers, two combed my hair, drying it with faint magic as they did, then molding it to their liking. Another coiled elaborate metal bands around my forearms and placed a headpiece over my forehead. One touched my chin with a trace of weak power, but what she did, I didn't know. When I saw myself in the mirror, though, I couldn't help but be pleased. And here I thought leaving the shiny world meant forever looking drab.

I looked like me—not glamoured—but the best version of me. Though they applied no makeup, my brown eyes popped, bright yet alluring. My cheeks held a faint trace of color, and my lips were slightly redder than usual. My hair was arranged in an elaborate display of braids and curls tumbling down my back. The simple metallic headpiece scrolled across my forehead with a large oval amethyst at its center. And the dress . . . All black, straps crisscrossing my chest with the two widest barely covering my nipples and ending just below my breasts. A center strap connected to the waistband of the skirt, which flowed to mid-calf with a slit all the way up the front. I wore no undergarments, so the wrong move would have everything on display. It was sexy as hell, but this wasn't the place nor the time.

There was a knock on the door, and the fae ushered me into the main room, where a tall male fae entered. He was dressed in armor, a sword swinging at his hip. The servants who had been dressing me fell back, their faces averted. Were they like Ena—slaves? In their own land? A knot formed in my gut as I felt the truth in this theory. The guard wrapped his hand around my forearm, then we were no longer in the same room.

We appeared in a much more spacious area, on a stage at the front of it. The throne room, I assumed, since the Shadow king was sitting on a large throne that looked to be carved from onyx. We'd sifted to the far right of the dais, where the guard shoved me into a golden gilded cage. A fucking cage, like I was a bird. Or a beast. The king glanced over at us with a smirk.

"My children," he said, lifting his hand and wiggling his fingers in a beckoning gesture. Five fae stepped forward, all of them male. I had a feeling he spoke English for my benefit. "Let the auction begin."

CHAPTER 13

*W*ait. What?

Another cage floated forward from the far side of the dais, hanging in the air before the king and his sons. Crammed inside were a half dozen waifs much like Ena and the others, except they were smaller, more child-like, most of them trembling and some crying, waves of fear wafting from them, which seemed to please the king, based on the glint in his eyes as he appraised them. *Ew.* He was feeding off their torment, just as Maeve had said.

I eyed the five male fae who had stepped forward when the king beckoned his princes and wondered which one was the Tormentor. I expected him to give off the same energy as his father and be gloating right now, as well, but none were like that. In fact, their energy felt extraordinarily weak in comparison. How disappointing.

A woman—a fae—sauntered forward from the shadows, standing off to the side on the dais. When she spoke, I understood nothing, but apparently the auction had begun because as she chanted in their faerie language, brief shouts came from the crowd, bids I assumed. The bidding didn't last long, though, and the auctioneer tried to prod for more. A dark energy lashed out from her, slamming into the cage, and the fae inside screamed, one yelling something I couldn't understand, but her desperation was loud and clear. A few more bids piped up.

I wished I could bid myself. I'd buy them all and figure out how to free them from this cruelty. My own darkness ached for violence and blood and death, and I had no problem hurting or killing those who deserved it, at least in my mind. But I stopped there, the other side of me—the Amadis, the angelic—needing to protect the weak and innocent. It was my way of maintaining control, I supposed. Or, at least, a sense of control, though it may have been a false sense at times.

The bidding quieted, and the auctioneer wrapped that one up. Then another cage floated forward, this one containing two naked fae, a male and a female, totally getting it on as though oblivious to their situation. The energy in the crowd blossomed, and I wondered how many of these Shadows fed from lust. By the way the bids flew in rapid succession, I'd say a good portion of them. Three of the princes were the most adamant bidders, and eventually one of them won. I supposed there were worst things to feed off of, but wasn't there enough lust naturally in the world without the need of sex slaves? As anger waved from the crowd when the prince won—the king feeding from it, no doubt—I supposed there wasn't enough lust for them all, at least not here in the City of Shadows.

That cage floated away, and the auctioneer and the king exchanged a glance. The king lifted his chin in a sort of nod, and the auctioneer dipped hers in acknowledgment. Then her arm swept out, gesturing toward my side of the dais, and my cage lifted and floated as she switched from Shadow Faelic to English, again for my benefit.

"Now we present the most coveted possession anyone could desire, including our enemies—the demons, the Seelie and Unseelie, the Daemoni, even the angels." As she named each faction, the crowd booed and hissed, their disgust and hatred growing, again feeding the king. "She may not be full fae, but her beauty is still lovely, in an exotic sort of way. More importantly, within her is the power to defeat them all. While she will remain the property of King Caellach, the winning bidder will be the one to break her and train her, using her in whatever way you wish until the time comes that our kingdom needs her. And even then, you will be her handler, ensuring victory for our king. Nobody except his majesty himself will experience such glory."

I would expect the crowd to cheer with some kind of patriotism, but that wasn't exactly the type of energy exuding from them. Lust, yes, on all sorts of levels. Lust for me physically shone in many eyes, but also lust for admiration, for power and control. When she'd referred to breaking me, the dark energy had spiked even higher and thicker, especially from the king himself. Fuck them. If any of them thought they could break me, they had another think coming. Well, except maybe the king. He might have had a chance.

"Shall we begin?" the auctioneer purred seductively, feeding the crowd.

She rang a bell, her version of a gavel, and an energy blasted at me. My wings sprang out on their own volition, as though my magic couldn't contain them any longer, and spread as wide as they could within the confinements of the cage. The crowd gasped, and the bids came in a flurry. They bid in their native tongue, so I had no clue what my going price was, but as excitement and lust escalated, it must have been high.

Then the king himself spoke up. The auctioneer lifted her brows in surprise, then acknowledged his entrance into the bidding war. The crowd fell silent, not responding when the auctioneer pushed to raise the king's bid.

"Bid, you cowards," he ordered, his energy slamming down in a sharp command. "What is my appreciation worth to you?"

They started up again, but it didn't seem to be enough, as the king kept chiming in. He was obviously just trying to raise the total, milking every little bit he could steal from his people. Otherwise, what was the point of auctioning me in the first place when he already had me?

The bids began to slow, and when they stopped, the king slammed his hand on the armrest of his throne. "You *fir darrigs* do not seem to understand."

He looked over at the guard who'd brought me in, lifting a single finger. The guard nodded, and he and four of his peers surrounded my cage, their hands lifting and fingers undulating, their dark power building. Their eyes became fully black—no whites or irises, like those of demons—and as they continued, their fingers began to blacken, too. The more the discoloration spread, the stronger their power became, reaching black tentacles through the bars of my cage, into me, straight to my soul, to my beast.

She immediately reared, pushing against my cage of control harder than I could ever remember. I dropped to my hands and knees, curling my fingers into fists, my breaths coming in pants as I tried to maintain control. My eyes rolled up, and the Shadow faes' flesh had darkened completely, the points of their ears curling, looking more like horns. Then all I saw were demons before me as their black fae magic found the darkness within me and pounced.

The power rippled through me, awakening parts of my heart and soul I'd forgotten had existed. The deepest, darkest corners that should have remained dormant. My upper lip curled, baring my teeth as a growl rumbled in my chest. I pushed myself to my feet as the Darkness with a capital D grew, and all I saw before me was death—death I would bring to all of them. A black haze enshrouded my vision as I flexed my fingers at my side, pushed my shoulders back as my wings spread and hardened, and threw back my head, mouth wide open as I finally let go of the reins of control.

My beast burst free, and my Darkness exploded. I screamed with both despair and elation. Power—*my* power—swirled around me, crackling and thundering like the darkest of storms, and I'd never felt so strong. So free.

Yes, you have. You only need to remember.

I shoved the thought aside as the guards attacked me. They tried to feed on my power, but it was all mine. *Mine, you fuckers!* Nobody could have it. Not these acolytes and definitely not the king. He would not imprison me. He would not control me. Nobody would ever control me again! I was the fucking king here now, and I'd annihilate whoever got in my way. Their souls meant nothing to me. *Nothing!*

I gathered my power, feeding my beast with it as it surrounded me in a wall of Darkness. But this time it was all mine, and I would be the one unleashing it. With another scream, I blasted the force outward.

The ground shook. Shrieks pierced the air. Dust and debris filtered through the dim light as the air slowly began to clear.

A deep-throated laugh bellowed. The king's laugh.

"That is only an inkling of what this little shade can do," he said.

He let out a small wave of his own power—that one little push more powerful than my blast because I'd only fed him more—completely clearing the air, as well as the energy around me. As though he'd doused the fire within me with a bucket of cold water, my power sizzled out, leaving me completely drained. Falling back to my knees, I gasped at the sight before me.

Bodies littered the ground. Not just the guards that had been surrounding my cage, but most of the crowd, too.

I *had* killed them all. All but the king and his princes, the auctioneer, and a dozen or so fae at the back of the room.

What have I done?

A sob lodged in my throat as the Amadis part of me, the angel blood running through my veins, mourned the loss of souls that might have had hope for redemption. But I pushed it down and forced the burn in my eyes away, knowing I could show no regrets. Doing so would reveal my weakness. The dark side of me knew just how fatal of a mistake that would be.

So I lifted my chin and glared at the king, who only responded with a wicked curl of his lips.

"Shall we continue?" he said to what remained of the crowd, completely ignoring the bodies as though they didn't even exist. The bodies of *his* people. His own courtiers!

The remaining fae pushed their way forward, also ignoring the corpses, stepping over them as they tried to move closer to me. Their bids started firing off again. Fine. I would kill them, too. I wasn't done here. I'd lost control—this time. And it probably wouldn't be the last time either, but I would learn. And all the heavens and hells help them when I did.

The auction continued, growing more heated and louder by the heartbeat. If I only knew what they offered now. My beast, lured back into her cage that was so different than my physical one, prickled at the thought of being owned by any of these assholes. I soothed her, promising her revenge, but only after we used them. They obviously thought they could break me and then train me. They'd never do the former, but I'd embrace the latter. If they really had the means to do so, it would only make me stronger. Would only make it easier to end them all. Fucking fae.

The room suddenly fell silent. I'd already grown so accustomed to the dark power, I hadn't noticed the new strain of it. Not until its intensity slammed into me at the same time the crowd parted, dropping to a knee. Even the princes cowered from the new presence. As did my beast. She'd felt this kind of force before, directly from the king. But this was even stronger. Even darker. Possibly darker than our own.

Sitting back on my heels, I tilted my head, trying to steal a glance of the newcomer. Like the king had been when I first met him near the Circle of Knowing—no, when I first met him at the Vault—the man's form was barely distinguishable through the black smoke enshrouding him. As he approached the dais, coming closer than anyone else had dared to come, even the princes, the smoke cleared, drifting away. Remnants of the dark energy caressed my skin, and my beast no longer cowered but purred. Interesting.

When he turned my way, I understood.

At first, his hair was as white as the king's, pulled back in a ponytail behind his pointed ears, the tip of it falling below his shoulders. His skin was that same dusky color, but more shimmery, not as though stardust had been sprinkled on it, but as though an entire galaxy graced his body. And that body —tall, broad, all muscles and strength and sex under metal armor over a silk tunic. His silver eyes glowed brightly as he took me in, licking out tendrils of his power over my skin. I felt the cold burn of it and wanted more. Wanted him to lick every inch of me and not only with his power, but with his tongue, too.

Then his power pulled away, my beast mewling at its retreat, and his features transformed. His hair became a deep black, the color seeping down from roots to ends. His skin lightened, taking on more of a brown than gray, though still dark in tone. Color seeped into his eyes, a bright aqua blue taking over the silver, but just as piercing and unnerving. His power pulled completely back from me, and I practically threw myself at the bars of the cage, already missing it. Missing any touch he would give me.

Fuck. I didn't even like men! I'd never been so affected by the fae before, not like the humans who would strip naked and writhe with lust as soon as they saw one, especially one this strong. Not even Maeve had managed that. Only now did I understand. That had to be the explanation. Because it was taking every bit of my focus to keep from peeling my dress off and opening myself to him.

To a male! Ugh! I hated him already.

He turned back to face the king, not an ounce of deference to the older fae.

"This one is mine," he declared, his voice deep, loud, and commanding. *Oh, hell no!*

The king cocked his head as his eyes narrowed. "She is not the one you want."

"I said she is mine." His voice was calm, but forceful. Nobody dared to contradict him.

Not even the king. "You will do what needs to be done?"

"Don't I always?" the sexy fae replied. *Ew.* I needed to not think of him like that! "I am sure you have already begun plans for the ceremony. Have you not drawn this out because you were waiting for me?"

The king's gaze darted to me, then around the room, skipping over the much smaller crowd and the princes, all of whom still stared at the ground, and finally sweeping across all the dead bodies. Appreciation glinted in the silver pools when he looked at me again before returning his attention to the fae before him.

"So be it." He gave a curt nod. "She is yours, my son."

The cage around me disappeared as though it'd only been an illusion, and before I could utter any kind of protest, that delicious power lashed out and encircled me, swallowing me in its depths. A lust like no other consumed me, heating me from the core outward. My breasts swelled and strained against the confines of my dress. An ache throbbed between my legs, growing to become an exquisite need to be touched. To be taken. To be completely ruined. The power was both brutal and beautiful, and I lost myself in a combination of pain and pleasure as the room around me faded away.

Only when I found myself in a completely different place, the power released, and the black-haired, aqua-eyed fae standing before me did my senses return. *My son*, the king had said. Another prince.

Oh, shit. I should have known.

I'd been claimed by the Tormentor himself.

CHAPTER 14

"*W*hat happened to your dress?" the faerie prince asked, his first words spoken directly to me.

I looked down, horror overcoming me at the sight of my completely naked body, my breasts pert and my nipples hard with need. The only items remaining were the bands on my arms and the jeweled piece on my head.

"You tell me," I snapped as my wings sprang back out and wrapped forward, around me.

"You blame me?" Arrogance dripped on every word. He knew damn well this was his doing.

"I'm not normally in the habit of stripping for a man," I growled. Or even wanting one.

"You mean for a man you just met? Though I am not exactly a man." His voice was so damn seductive.

"First of all, we haven't exactly met yet, have we? And secondly, I mean for *any* male, asshole."

He chuckled, and something stroked over my feathers on the outside of my wings—his finger or his power, I couldn't be sure. Nonetheless, I moaned in pure ecstasy as the pleasurable sensation jolted through every nerve of my being. My body convulsed as I came undone right then and there. I came down from the impromptu orgasm as fast as it had come, and fury exploded in my chest.

"I hate you," I snarled.

"Forgive me. I thought you were stronger than this."

"Fuck you."

"Possibly in due time, if you so desire."

"Never!"

He continued as though I hadn't spoken. "For now, you can open your wings. I have clothes for you."

"I don't want your clothes. I'll glamour my own." So I did, conjuring my fighting leathers, while wondering where my real ones were. I opened my wings and hid them, resting my hands on my hips.

The prince's gaze traveled from my head to my toes, then his full, beautiful mouth lifted in a smirk. "You must do better than that. I am a powerful prince, and I can see right through your glamour."

Ugh! Another growl built in my chest, but I decided I wouldn't give him the satisfaction. I squelched it as I continued standing there, still naked to his eyes. He must have reined in his own power, because I no longer had the overwhelming urge to climb all over his body, so now *he* could deal with *my* wiles. I pulled back my shoulders, lifting my breasts, and slightly bent a knee, rolling my hips forward.

The fucker snorted, looking away as he threw something at me. It took me a moment to realize it was my leathers—the real thing. With a flick of his hand, I was suddenly dressed in the leather corset and pants, knee-high boots on my feet. He strode over to a table I hadn't noticed before, laid out with food and drink. He poured two glasses of thick amber liquid, lifting one of them out toward me. I shook my head in rejection of his offer. With a shrug, he lifted it to his lips and threw back the full contents in one gulp.

While he seemed to be distracted with that, I let my gaze sweep across the room, different than the one I'd been in before, taking in the details. No windows. Only one door. Probably locked. The only furniture besides the table was a settee covered in dark gray velvet, squatting in front of a cold hearth. Dozens of candles provided light that flickered shadows over the walls. We were completely alone, it seemed. No slaves or guards nearby, from what I could sense.

"Where are we?" I blurted, the words tumbling out before I could stop them.

"Still at the Court of Shadows, for now. My former wing at the palace. We will be leaving soon, though. Your training must not be delayed."

I peered at him. He was more forthcoming than I expected. I wondered what information I could extract from him. "Training for what? For the ceremony your father is planning?"

He smirked. "I imagine neither of us need training for that, although you might, considering your distaste for men. Even for me."

My eyes narrowed. "What is that supposed to mean? What kind of ceremony is it?"

His eyes glinted to match the smirk. "A bonding ceremony, of course. You and I are to be married."

My mouth opened and closed and opened again, like a fish out of water.

"Wait . . . *What?*" I managed to sputter out.

"You made a deal with my father, did you not?" One corner of his mouth lifted even further, deepening the smirk. "I know you did. I was there."

I remembered now. He'd been the other shadowy presence in that room at the Vault, after Brielle and I had died. Or whatever we had done.

"I didn't . . . I didn't know . . ." I still couldn't form words properly as the memory—and our exact words—swirled in my mind, my breath trapped in my lungs. The smirk became an all-out grin as the Tormentor watched my face. "I can't . . . I can't *marry* you!"

"Believe me, it is not my preference, either."

My mouth clamped shut as I tried to figure out if that was a good thing or if I should be insulted. Wait. "But *you* claimed *me*."

"I did. I have my reasons."

"Which are?" I demanded when he didn't continue.

"You will see soon enough. There is no way out of this, Elliana Knight." He held out the other glass. "Would you like that drink now?"

I snatched the glass from his outstretched hand and threw back the contents just as he had done. The thick liquid was warm, a pleasant burn down my throat. Almost immediately, my mind and body relaxed.

There is a way out of this, I thought. *There has to be.* I just had to figure it out.

"I will prepare the horses and return in a few minutes. Do not go anywhere." He chuckled with these last words before striding out the one door. I flew at it, but in the split-second it took me to reach it, it disappeared. Only a smooth, solid wall stood there now. Heh. I got his joke now.

I couldn't say how long I remained in the room alone, but I walked the perimeter a few times while fuming about my predicament. I should have accepted Maeve's proposal and married her. Better yet, I should have never left college and stayed with Sadie. Oh, how I missed her! I hadn't realized how much I'd fallen for her in the few months we'd been together until now. *She's better off without you.* Yes. Yes, she was. I had to keep reminding myself of that to keep the heartache at bay.

"We have a long trip ahead of us."

I jumped at the voice, spinning and crouching into a fighting stance. The Tormentor lifted a brow.

"You have no need to fight me," he said. "But if you try, you will never win."

My eyes narrowed as I studied him for a moment before slowly rising from my crouch. "We will see about that. One day I *will* kill you." I paused then tacked on, practically spitting the words, "*Your majesty.*"

His lips twitched, whether suppressing a grin or a scowl I couldn't be sure, except for the glint in his piercing eyes. "The plan is that one day you will kill *for* me."

"What makes you think I'd do that?"

"I know you will. First, you must be trained, and we will not do that here in my father's castle." He strode for the door, holding it open for me. "And please, call me Tor."

I snorted. "Tor? Short for Tormentor?" His nostrils flared at this. "Yes, I've heard about you, possibly as much as you've heard about me. I know how you get your kicks."

His brows gathered in a scowl as anger lit up his eyes, the silver glowing behind the aqua blue.

"You know nothing," he growled, grabbing my bicep and shoving me out the door.

He didn't let go, tugging me along through the corridors and down the stairs until we came out into a courtyard where two horses waited. Another horse. Yay. What was with fae and their horses? Hopefully this one was as easy to ride as Moonbutt had been. She was just as pretty, gray with a silvery mane and tail and purple eyes that matched the purple fae markings across her hide. I hesitated before mounting her.

"The horse is not good enough for you, princess?" Tor asked from behind me. "I thought it would be easiest for you, since they are all that you have in your realm. Perhaps you can work your way up to a gryphon or a dragon."

"I can fly myself—wait. What?" I turned to see his face, to determine if he was serious. I didn't see any humor, but I scoffed. "Dragon shifters let you ride them?"

"Not shifters. Those are beings of your world. We have the real thing here."

"Real dragons?" I tried to conceal the excited curiosity to

see one—let alone ride one—but it tinged my words anyway. "And gryphons? For real?"

His lips curled into a real smile—small, but not a smirk. "This might be more fun than I expected." His large hands wrapped around my waist, and he practically threw me on to the horse's back. "This is Needan. She follows my thoughts, so do not entertain any lofty ideas. She will not obey you even if you do, but she will share them with me."

Fabulous. The Tormentor was a damn horse whisperer.

He'd just sprang into the air and landed gracefully on his own horse when a shadowy figure appeared before us, an image of the king magically projected into the courtyard. He spoke in their version of Faelic.

Tor blew out a harsh breath, the energy around him changing, darkening. He replied, then looked over at me, the brown of his skin leaking away as the dark gray took over. His hair whitened, and the teal color of his eyes gave way to silver. "You think you know so much, princess? You should come and see this."

His dark power rose off him like black smoke and surrounded both of us. My own darkness stirred, exciting my beast as we sifted again. At least this time my clothes didn't come off. He must have kept that part of his power in check.

When the smoke cleared—at least from me, it still surrounded Tor—we had returned to the throne room. The bodies had been cleared away, and a new group filled the audience, all of them cowering from Tor's presence. The king still sat in his onyx throne on the dais, slouched into it casually as though he were bored. Before him knelt four Shadow fae females, on their knees, their hands behind their backs, and their heads bowed. Their white hair fell in curtains around their faces, and their ashen skin was dull, the markings barely visible.

The king said something to Tor, again in their language. Tor's power, darker than ever, lashed out in four tendrils, each one striking a kneeling fae over and over like a whip. The women screamed and writhed with each hit, and at once, my beast rose with excitement while a lump lodged in my throat. The tendrils stopped their lashes, and I thought it was over, but then the smoke wrapped around them. The agonized shrieks made my heart stop and my beast cry out.

The king leaned forward on his throne, his interest obviously piqued now. His mouth stretched in a sharp-toothed grin, and his eyes shone with greed and lust. He was drinking it all in—the torment giving him power. The smoke around Tor grew too, in both size and intensity, as the fae women's cries pitched higher and higher. Through the mist around them, I could see four bodies convulsing on the ground.

"For fuck's sake, stop! You're killing them!" The words shot out of my mouth as I stepped forward without thought.

The king's silver glare nearly leveled me. "Mind yourself, unless you want to join them."

"It is done anyway," Tor said, the smoke clearing from him as well as the fae women.

Their bodies stilled, and their voices fell silent, but they no longer looked like women. They'd diminished into small, thin waifs, like Ena and those who had been in the cage earlier. They weren't dead, but I had a feeling death would have been better.

"Break her good and hard," the king said to Tor, whose hand swept out and gripped my bicep again, sifting us away without a response to his father.

"Why?" was the only thing I managed when we reappeared in the courtyard.

"They disobeyed, and the Court of Fates needs new slaves." He shrugged, as though not caring, but there was something different about him. He seemed almost . . . smaller than before. No, not smaller, just not as much power radiating off of him. I thought he would have received a boost from all the torment he'd created to feed on, but perhaps he'd expelled more than he consumed. Tired, even exhausted—that's the kind of energy I sensed from him now. Interesting.

His physical strength remained, however, evident when he threw me on to Needan's back again, but rather than springing up on his own like before, he used the stirrup to climb on. Without a word, we took off in a trot, exiting the courtyard through a stone archway. Our horses' hooves clip-clopped on cobbled stones of a terrace and then the bridge that crossed to the City of Shadows.

The fog hung low, concealing the roofs with their sharp points and spires that I'd seen from the castle tower earlier. Had that only been hours ago? Had I only been in Winter Court just last night? It already felt like weeks. I wondered how much time had passed in my home realm, then decided I probably didn't want to know. There was nothing I could do about it anyway.

We passed through the narrow cobblestone streets of the city, where low lights still glowed in many windows and from candles in lanterns that hung on wall hooks and posts. The energy was heavy and thick, as though despair clung to the mists themselves, a blanket of sodden misery. The large bricks of the buildings created patterns of dingy grays and browns, seeming to reflect decades or even centuries of desolation. Narrow windows and wooden doors broke up the solid lines of buildings, some doors plain and others wide with beautiful, ornate metalwork scrolled around them. I wondered what kind of metal, since fae were allergic to iron.

By the time we passed through a gate and crossed another bridge, exiting the city, Tor was back to his old self, sitting taller in his saddle and his coloring returned. Then he told me to "hang on." We took off at a full gallop down a dirt road, the surface almost as hard as stone, packed down from heavy use. We passed a few homes and farms on the outskirts, with buildings of stone and thatched roofs, then the trees started coming closer together, and I could see a forest ahead. I looked over my shoulder at the city and its looming castle on the edge of the horizon. Once we entered the forest, we were devoured by it.

At first, it was so dark, I could barely see Tor in front of me. The trees looked blackened, as though by fire, their trunks and branches thick, almost threatening, but their leaves small and sparse. It reminded me somewhat of the forests at home, especially as they'd been when I was young, when we'd first been able to emerge from the Loft—dead, yet not, and frightening.

But the farther we traveled from the City of Shadows, the more alive the forest became.

I had never seen such beautiful colors and shadows in real life. The lighting was so strange in the Shadow Lands. It seemed like the sun should have risen by now, and through the glimpses I caught between the branches and leaves overhead, it appeared as though the sky had lightened slightly. Rather than midnight blue sprinkled with stars, it was more of a dark royal blue like that on a full moon evening just after dusk, though in no direction came the light of a rising sun or even a moon. As we continued, the lighting *within* the forest grew brighter and more ethereal. The edges of the trees themselves, as well as faerie runes carved into some of their trunks, glowed in various jewel tones as though lit from within, creating their own play of shadows and light on their branches and leaves. The pathway shone, too, as well as the rocks, including clusters of faerie stones that looked like crystals of our world, growing out of the ground. This was more like I'd imagined Faery to look like in my little girl dreams.

"How is it so pretty here?" I mused aloud at one point. "I thought the Shadow Lands were supposed to be a place of nightmares."

"Some places are, such as the City of Shadows," Tor replied, surprising me. I'd only been talking to myself, not expecting him to listen or care.

"I can't imagine why," I muttered, to which he did not reply.

We eventually came to a clearing of tall grass and wildflowers, waving in an unfelt breeze. They, too, glowed softly, and tiny light orbs danced about, probably some kind of faerie creature. On the far edge of the clearing sat a thatch-roofed cottage, more faerie runes glowing in some of the stones of its walls, and beyond it a stream, then more forest. As we crossed the clearing, I looked up at the sky, checking again for the sun or moon now that I could see more of it, and my breath caught. It was even more beautiful than the diamond-studded sky had been in the Colorado mountains of our college, so close then, it felt like we should have been able to feel the heat of the stars. But here . . . The sky was not just blue, but also pinks and purples and teals, an aurora borealis dancing in the heavens, either stars or more faeries twinkling among it.

"We stop here," Tor declared when we reached the cottage, dismounting from his horse.

"This is where you live?" I asked with surprise. I couldn't imagine such a powerful and dark prince living in such a small yet inviting home. His presence was so large, it didn't seem the cottage could even fit him within its walls.

"This is where we train," he replied. "I will bring you to my home when I know I can trust you."

Well, I never said he was stupid.

The cottage was as quaint and charming on the inside as the outside. We entered into a cozy living room, a fire already blazing in the hearth, and two bedrooms were in the back, a bathroom between them. He led me to mine. Though smaller than the one I slept in back at Winter Court, the bed looked just as soft and welcoming. I hadn't realized how bone tired I was until now.

"Sleep," I murmured aloud with longing.

"Not yet," Tor said. "We must begin."

"Right now?" He couldn't be serious.

"Do not worry. This first step is easy: you simply need to remember."

"Remember what?"

"What you can do. My father and I watched many of your fights in the Pits at Shadow Vault Citadel. We saw your potential then. We also saw your lack of control. We thought you would have learned it by now, but apparently, we were wrong."

I shifted from foot to foot. There was a number of reasons for that.

"I understand your memories and your powers were bound with a spell. It seems some still are. You need to remember before you can properly learn what you have and how to control it." His hand darted out, his fingers touching my forehead much like Dorian had done before leaving me at Winter Court. This time, though, I felt magic seep into my mind, a muted zinging through my gray matter, and it was like I could *feel* hidden pockets revealing themselves. "That is all. Good night."

He turned and left me in the tiny room, shutting the door with a flick of his hand. When I fell asleep, I dreamt again— remembered more. And he lied. It was not easy. Not at all.

I would have done anything to never remember again, but now that I did . . . I would never forget. I *couldn't* ever forget again what I had done.

CHAPTER 15

ongues of Tor's dark power stretched away from him, licking at my own, calling it forth. Trying to anyway. My hold on it was tighter than ever, my beast growling in protest. She wanted free. She wanted to play and frolic with Tor. No way could I let that happen. Never again.

Tor let out a string of what I assumed to be profanity in his native tongue—the tone was definitely right. I'd slept three times since being here at the cottage, though I had no idea how many actual days and nights that equaled. The sky and lighting hardly ever changed. The colorful, dancing lights in the sky drifted away and returned, drifted and returned, but I didn't know if that was any indication of another day passing. So in other words, I didn't know how long we'd been at this, but enough that he was losing his patience.

"Why do you *still* hold back?" he demanded, frustration thick in his deep voice. "I know you remember what you can do. What you did at the Vault against your opponents."

Of course, he knew that I remembered. I saw how those memories haunted me in my own reflection. I heard how raw my voice had become from waking up screaming over and over again. I noticed his gaze on my trembling hands for the hour or so it took to calm myself enough to eat, let alone train. Except he was partly wrong—it wasn't just the Vault where I'd unleashed my true power.

"I know precisely what I can do," I snarled. "And I will *never* do that for you or your father. I can never do such horrors again—unless it is against you. Against *him*."

He cocked his head at this, the points of his ears twitching as those aqua eyes studied me. "Except you cannot, can you? Because you lack control. The only reason you were able to kill your opponents and nobody in the stands is because you were deep in the Pits and the crowd was far above, out of reach. You are like your earthly bombs. You do not have the control to kill me or my father without wiping out innocent lives."

I hated that he was right, but it was all the more reason to not use my power at all.

"I have other ways," I said. "I'm well trained in the diverse arts of combat. I can wield three types of magic and am proficient with a variety of weapons."

"And how have those helped you come to this place at this very moment?"

I scowled, frustrated that he was right once again. None of my powers and training thus far had helped me escape the demons, the Unseelie, or the Shadows. Of course, since arriving in Faery, I hadn't fought as hard as I would have at home, considering I had no idea how to return to my own realm or whom to trust to help me with that once I regained my freedom. I still didn't know the lands or what kinds of dangers lurked here. But I did know enough to appreciate that magic and even weapons often elicited surprising results when used on unknown types of creatures—not often in a good way.

He would never teach me what I really needed to know—where the other stone circles were or any other portals to my realm; what strange creatures and other threats I could face in my travels around Faery; how to kill a fae, particularly the Shadow fae, since they were my biggest threat at the moment.

My beast pawed at me. She knew how to kill them. We'd already done so, hadn't we? And threatened to do it again? But while in my right mind, without her looming and ready to take over, I knew there had to be another way. If anything, leaving a wake of dead bodies in my path would likely start a war—a war I didn't know if my parents and people were prepared to fight. Of course, killing the prince and the king would probably do the same, but at least I knew without a doubt that they deserved it.

But that brought me to my biggest dilemma of all: how to break a deal with a fae—and not just any fae, but a fae king. Tor's father. And basically, Tor himself, considering the deal was to marry him. Would killing them both break that deal or free me from it?

Pacing between me and the cottage, Tor shoved his hand through his black hair, loosening the ponytail he kept it in while we trained. So far, since I refused to draw on my darkest power, my training consisted of him attacking me and me staving him off the best I could. I'd never tell him this, but he was the strongest opponent I'd ever faced, including any of the worst demons in the Pits or any of the multitudes of creatures at school. My magic—angelic, sorceress, and fae alike—continuously fell short, and my weapons failed to find their mark because *his* magic was always on point.

He blew out a harsh breath and eyed me. "You have a unique power—unique to you and your siblings—that you refuse to use. It is your best weapon against any opponent, including that which you hate most."

"You have no idea what I hate most," I interjected.

"You hate the demons most. That was very obvious in how you fought in the Pits."

"Maybe that's changed. Maybe I hate the Shadow fae more now." I crossed my arms over my chest.

"You are such a petulant child," he said on a rough sigh. "Listen to me, Elliana. Shadow fae, Unseelie, Seelie, the demons—you have the power to end us all."

"Eh. I'm not really into genocide. That's my one saving grace compared to all of you."

His patience was waning, I could tell, and while part of me really wanted to learn to use and control my true power, I wouldn't. There was no convincing me—because I knew that once I did, I'd lose myself.

"You are not listening!" He suddenly stood right in front of me, all up in my personal space, looming over me so I had to crane my neck to look up at him. "*End* the demons, Elliana. Not just send them back to Hell but end them for good."

I blinked. *Shit*. Maybe I could be convinced. But no . . . I couldn't let that be a good enough reason.

"That's not possible," I said in denial. "Only my mother can do that."

"You know that's not true. You have done it before."

One of those nasty memories—one I'd refused to examine, even in my unconscious mind—tried to push forward, but I shook my head. I needed to change the subject, re-route this conversation before I gave in.

I shoved him back a pace. He had let me, of course, since he was much stronger than me. Fucking fae prince and all.

"*You're* not listening to *me*," I said. "I do not *need* this power you want so badly. *You* do. Your *father* does. All these other factions who think they can use me—only to force me to turn it on my own people, on humanity. Or to end *me* before it can be used against *them*. My sister and I have become pawns in everyone else's war because they all assume we *want* this power. That we want to use it. Nobody's ever considered that if they just left us alone, they'd probably have nothing to worry about."

"You are so very wrong." He came at me again, dark energy lashing out at me, reaching for my own.

I cast a shielding spell to block it. Unfortunately, my shields weren't strong like Charleigh's, and his power easily broke through it, but not before I was able to flick a star at his throat while conjuring an icicle as long as a spear and sharp as a dagger that I aimed at his chest. My shields might have been weak, but I had enough offensive moves to make up for it. Unfortunately, again, Tor was good at both. He easily plucked the throwing star out of the air and shattered my icicle before it even came close. At the same time, a cage of dark energy slammed down around me, throwing me to the ground, and wrapped up in it was that special fae power that had me writhing with lust.

"Stop it," I hissed while my hands began to undo the bindings of my corset. My breasts swelled against the tight confines, needing to be freed and groped, by whom I didn't care.

"Use your power," Tor replied evenly.

"Never," I said between gasps for air.

His powers bared down harder, and one of my hands gave up on the bindings, sliding inside over my breast, squeezing and pinching, while my other hand glided down between my legs, pressing against the building heat. My beast roared inside, kicking and clawing her way out.

"Fight me," Tor ordered.

"Fuck you."

"You seem to be doing a fine job of that yourself."

I groaned, in ecstasy at first and then in anger, jerking my hands away from inside my own clothes. Crossing my arms over my chest, I fisted my hands in my armpits to keep them from drifting again. My breath came out in shallow bursts, my body still wanting to give in to the lust he created and my beast to his power. I pulled my knees to my chest, curling into a ball on the ground to try to contain it all. He finally pulled it all back, releasing me.

"You're an asshole," I said as I climbed to my feet. "That was practically rape!"

His eyes narrowed. "Trust me—you would know it if I fucked you. But it's not rape if you're begging for it, now is it?"

Fury filled me, and I charged, shooting a ball of flames at him while using my magic to summon the sword at his waist. I sprang into the air to catch the hilt, then swung down, putting my whole body into it. It all happened in a split-second, fast enough to take out anyone else, even a vampire. But not a fae prince. Tor sifted six yards away, and I nearly impaled myself when the sword and I both landed on nothing but hard ground.

"I will never beg for anything from a man," I growled through a clenched jaw as I once again pushed myself to my feet. "Especially not for sex. And especially not you!"

I hated him with every fiber of my being. Mostly because he was right. I'd never felt so violated, so vulnerable . . . yet, so damned turned on. Not once had I ever found a man sexually attractive, but even without his power on me, I couldn't deny Tor's sexuality. If I were to be honest, his power only heightened real desire that already existed deep within. For the first time in my life, I wondered what it would be like to see a man naked, to feel him between my legs . . . inside me. And I hated him all the more for that.

"You see?" he said. "Your power could have stopped me. You *do* need it, precisely because everyone does want to use you for it or destroy you for it. The only way to protect yourself and your sister and even your parents is to ensure that you can use it for *you*."

"And for you and your father."

"I do not have the same plans for you as my father."

"But you still want to use me."

"Is it using you when we have the same enemies? Or is that just two allies helping each other with a common goal?"

I lifted a brow. "Your father is my enemy."

This was met with silence.

"If I were to use this power on anybody, it would be to destroy him," I said, just to be clear. Still, Tor's only reply was to glare at me with hard aqua eyes before turning and stalking away.

"It would not be genocide if you learned control and proper use," he threw over his shoulder. He paused, turning slightly toward me. "You only need to become an arrow rather than a bomb. Eliminate the right targets and you can end any battle, any war."

He left me to stew in this, and stew I did. And I realized he was not entirely like his father. The Shadow king didn't give a shit when I killed his soldiers who attacked me on the hillside by the Circle of Knowing or his guards and the others in the throne room during the auction. The king only wanted me broken and trained to obey. He didn't care how many lives I took in the process, even those of his own people. He probably wouldn't care on the battlefield, either.

Tor, however, seemed to have a different objective. What, exactly, was it?

I sat by the stream behind the cottage, taking in my surroundings. This was the longest Tor had left me alone. If he wasn't trying to instigate a fight and elicit my power, he was shoving food in my face or locking me in the tiny room. Which I honestly couldn't complain about, because by then, I was exhausted from trying to fight him *and* control my beast.

I didn't know where the food came from, but he prepared the meals himself. Surprisingly, he wasn't a bad cook. I wondered when he'd learned and why. After all, he'd surely been raised by slaves, every whim served his entire life, however long that was. I wondered where all the prince's slaves were now.

The forest surrounding the cottage was dark and beautiful. Faerie lights and otherworldly types of bioluminescence caused the trees and foliage to glow in various colors. I'd seen a few animals, including a buck that looked much like an earthly deer, if not for his glowing blue antlers that were broad and flat, shaped more like that of a moose, and a small rodent-type creature that somewhat resembled a rabbit with wings. If it were ten times bigger, it would have been terrifying. That had me wondering what other beasts lived in the forest and if I could take them. If I ran now, would I be able to escape or only run into more danger?

Was there anything more dangerous than the Tormentor himself?

It felt like hours passed, and Tor still hadn't returned. The longer I sat there alone, the more my mind started to drift toward my parents, to Charleigh, to Brielle, and the more my heart, my gut, my very soul ached until I thought I would be sick. For as long as I could remember, I'd dreamt of going on adventures by myself. I'd always believed myself to be an outcast, the black sheep never able to live up to my family's standards. I thought it would be a relief for all of us once I was out on my own, never considering just how much *I* would miss *them*. Especially my twin.

Brielle was my rock, who kept me grounded and centered. The earth to my fire, she was always able to tamper my heat and keep me from burning out of control. I may have had the passion and the confidence and the power, but she had the brain and the compassion and the heart. She truly cared for other people, putting their needs first, and most especially me. Not that she was weak—our powers were matched and she had no problem standing up to me and putting me in my place—but I'd always felt the need to protect her. Only now could I truly appreciate just how much she did for me.

I missed her logic and how she counted things under her breath—everything, from the steps as she walked to the clouds passing overhead in the sky. I missed her love for learning and reading, frequently sharing random little tidbits just to make me laugh. I missed our late-night conversations, how we used to chat with each other in our own little language when we were little. I missed the way she could comfort me and make me feel loved when it seemed like I was up against the world. I missed my sister. We'd never been separated like this since the moment we were conceived and our cells split.

I'd never felt so alone.

I needed to do whatever it took to get home.

Swiping at my wet cheeks, I finally stood. Although my stomach ached from longing, I returned to the cottage, knowing I should keep my energy up and wondering what was stocked in the cabinets. Tor had been in control of that until now—and when I walked into the kitchen, I realized he still was. A bowl of warm stew and a big chunk of hearty bread waited for me on the table, tendrils of steam rising from both. But no sign of Tor himself, except for a note.

Saoirse will be taking over your training. And you thought I was difficult.

I did a quick check of the cottage for this Saoirse person, but found nobody else here. After forcing myself to eat the stew and bread, I went into my room, feeling like it was time to sleep. But, of course, I couldn't. Facing the memories that I knew would come in my dreams was bad enough when Tor was here. The prospect of doing it alone, however, was somehow worse.

I must have dozed off, however, because the next thing I knew, I bolted upright, screaming as visions of fires and bodies scattered around me faded away.

"Ach. No wonder you're afraid," said an unfamiliar female voice to my right.

I snapped my head toward the chair, the only other piece of furniture in the tiny room. A female fae rose from it, taking her full height of nearly six feet tall. A brown armored corset and black low-cut pants showed off tremendous amounts of flawless, golden brown flesh over perfectly sculpted muscles. Her deep black hair—as black as mine—was cut asymmetrically, cropped close to the head in the back and on the sides, with long, spiky bangs swept to the side, revealing eyes like amethysts.

"Who are you? And what the hell does that mean?" I demanded.

Her angled brow lifted as her gaze traveled over me. "Come now. It's time to conquer that fear."

She strode out of the room, her ass a work of perfection in those tight pants. Thick, round, and muscular. But besides the admiring thought, I felt nothing for her—or from her. Not like I did with Tor. All that ass made me think of—all it made me want—was Sadie.

"Yasta!" she barked from the living room.

I slid out of bed and into my fighting leathers, finding her holding a mug of coffee and a cinnamon bun out to me.

"Yasta?" I asked, though I didn't expect her to reply since she hadn't bothered to answer my other questions.

"Make haste," she said. "And I am Seer-sha. Tor said he warned you I was coming."

I glanced at the note still on the counter. "He said Say-or-see . . . Ser-see?"

She rolled her eyes. "Ach. Saoirse. It's pronounced *seer-sha*. Come now. We apparently have much work to do."

"What did you mean about me being afraid?" I asked as I hurried out the door after her. "You can't possibly know what I'm afraid of!"

She spun on her heel, her face suddenly transformed into one of those still bodies from my dream . . . from my memory.

I sloshed coffee all over my front. "How the hell?"

Her face morphed back into the beautiful fae. "I was bored watching you sleep, so I did a little dream walking." She shrugged, as if invading my unconscious mind meant nothing.

She must have seen the rage forming on my face, because she held her hands up in a *stop* gesture. "Tor sent for me for a reason. If we're going to break you of whatever is holding you back, I need to understand you. Now I do."

"You know nothing about me," I seethed.

"I know enough."

Without warning, she went on the attack, trying to provoke me as Tor had done all the days before. Her power was not like his, though. Not quite as dark—not dark enough to interest my beast. So I had no problem only using my magic and weapons, no temptation to tap into my own dark power as she poked and prodded, attacked and withdrew. So much for breaking me, I thought as this went on for hours. Why had Tor even bothered sending for her? And where had he gone anyway?

"You need to eat. It's inside. I'll be back." And with that, she disappeared.

She didn't return by the time I finished the meal of meat and parsnips, the plate indeed waiting for me when I entered the cottage. Although no sun or moon ever shone here, I did notice a darkening of the sky as more time passed. I went outside and back to the stream, peering into the forest for any sign of Tor or Saoirse.

I wasn't exhausted like I had been while working with Tor. Bed didn't beckon me, and my stomach didn't ache with hunger. The only thing preoccupying my mind was a single thought:

Now's my chance.

CHAPTER 16

*M*y wings exploded from my back, and after doing a quick check that all weapons were in place, I sprang straight into the sky from the clearing in front of the cottage. I needed a bird's eye view to gain my bearings and see the lay of the land. Perhaps discern the best direction to head. As I circled around, however, all I could see to the horizon in all directions was more of the dark forest, the bioluminescence hardly noticeable from up here. Far in the distance one way appeared to be mountains—dark, jagged points against a slightly lighter sky—but with no sun or moon and no real idea what time of day it was anyway, I didn't know if that was north, south, east, or west. Not that it mattered. The Shadow Lands hadn't been on the maps I'd seen while in Winter Court. I had no idea where I was in relation to anything else. Especially not to home.

I needed to find a Circle of Knowing. That was my only hope.

We had entered the clearing that first time on the far side of it from the cottage. I knew I did not want to go back that way, toward the City of Shadows, so I flew in the opposite direction, past the cottage, over the stream and the forest beyond it. Once over the trees, I could see nothing of the ground through the canopy of leaves, and as I flew, the landscape remained the same. I banked a bit to my right, my gaze sweeping over the lands but not finding even another clearing. I turned sharper to the left until I soared parallel to the mountains, and still the terrain was unchanged. Just more and more dark forest.

Flying was supposed to give me a vantage point, but how much below the treetops was I missing? For all I knew, I'd flown over several stone circles already. Angling my body downward, I prepared to dip below the canopy, hoping there was enough space between trees and branches to fly. If not, I could run, but flying was easier and faster—and so much more fun.

I hadn't even broken through the tops of the trees, though, when a paw the size of a car tire swiped out and batted at me, sending me tumbling through the air and crashing through branches until I hit the ground with an unimpressive thud.

"Son of a bitch," I grumbled, jumping to my feet, my sword already in hand as I surveyed my surroundings. My head craned back to see what had hit me, and I swallowed a gasp as a huge feline-type creature crawled down the tree. She looked like a lioness, though her fur was a powder blue color with highlights that glowed an electric blue, and two horns curled out from the top of her head, between her ears. Her tail, big and fluffy like a fox's, swished back and forth, painting a galaxy of stars in its wake. The size of a large horse, she was terrifyingly beautiful, and I had no idea how to respond. Freeze? Play dead? Try to look as big as I could make myself? We'd read in a brochure about such techniques when facing a wild animal in the mountains around our campus. I couldn't recall reading anything about feline faerie beasts, however, so I did nothing but harden my feathers, just in case she attacked.

A snap in the woods behind me made both of us freeze.

On the ground now, the cat-beast crouched, blue eyes

peering into the space beyond me. I remained perfectly still, sending out all of my senses.

The darkness was thorough.

The faerie feline sensed it, too. With a hiss, she sprang away, darting through the trees until she disappeared a second later.

Slowly I turned, bracing myself. A swirl of black fog pulsed and throbbed between two trees, slashes opening and then closing, revealing Tor's eye here, his mouth and chin there, the side of his cheek, and the other eye next. We watched each other for a long moment, and then he disappeared.

I spun, finding him again—no. Not him. I didn't sense Tor anywhere. The ebbing and flowing of black night behind another tree was not Tor. Hatred immediately bubbled up in me, awakening my beast.

"What a pleasant surprise to see you again, little shade," the black mist purred. "Though I see my son has failed to break you. That is a shame."

The mist sucked into the form of the Shadow king, a nasty grin stretched across his inhumanly beautiful, ageless face.

"It'll take more than a few days to break me," I said as I continued scanning my surroundings, wondering if I could make a run for it. Not at all wondering what happened to Tor.

"For anyone else, perhaps, even for my son. But not for me." A tendril of black mist swished out and sliced through the air, slashing at me like a whip, dark energy curling around me, needling into my flesh, into my veins.

My beast sprang fully alert, a roar building in her chest. In *my* chest.

I surveyed the area again. Sent out all of my senses once more. Was the king really alone? If so, I could let her loose. Explode that bomb with no risk of casualties.

The king laughed. "You can't kill me, little shade. How I'd love to see you try, but you won't, will you? What do I have to do to break you? Kill your sister? Would that do it?"

"You promised," I hissed through a clenched jaw. "We made a deal."

"Ah, yes. So we did. Then how about that sorceress friend of yours?" Did he mean Charleigh? She was a powerful witch, but not a sorceress. If he wanted to believe that, though, I wouldn't correct him. "I wonder how loud she'll scream as I drain her magic. How her torment will taste." A pale tongue swiped over his lips. "I wonder who might pay highly for her as a slave. Perhaps she can join Ena at Winter Court."

His taunts were enough. He did know how to break me.

No, not break me. I would make this choice—this choice to end him now. This was an opportunity, not coercion. I had made a vow to myself to kill him, and I would follow through. Now was as good a time as any.

I allowed my power to build, the Darkness flowing freely through my veins, into my flesh, swirling through my torso until I could hold it in no more. I threw open the cage and freed the beast. And exploded like the bomb I was.

"Son of a fucking bitch!" The familiar female voice came from where the king had been a moment ago.

"I warned you." Tor's voice approached fast, and when the dust cleared, I found him bending over, his hand stretched out toward Saoirse.

They were in a shallow crater—a crater I'd created, trees laid out, roots upended.

Saoirse took Tor's hand and let him help her up. She looked quite a bit worse for the wear, her hair disheveled, and multiple slashes across her face and her arms. She moved slowly, groaning a bit as she straightened up. Still, as she brushed leaves and dirt off that perfect ass, she gazed up at me with what might have been a little awe mixed with a lot of triumph.

"You definitely pack some punch," she said. "Just not enough. Yet anyway. We need to hone that power of yours, and it will be deadly, even to a king."

I dropped my hands to my hips. "But you're not the king. You tricked me."

She shrugged. "I got you to break, didn't I?" She gave Tor a pointed look. "I told you it would work. You should listen to me more often."

My mouth gaped opened, then shut, and open again as I struggled to find the words I wanted to spew at her. Renewed hatred grew, and my beast clawed at the cage I'd already clanged around her. The longer I glared at Saoirse, though, the taller she stood, the clearer her skin became as the cuts healed, and the bigger her grin grew. At the same time, the heat of the hatred I felt for the king, first, and then for her, cooled.

"Fuck you," I managed to bite out with the last bit of loathing I could muster. She shuddered with the sentiment, her purple eyes glowing contentedly, as though I'd literally just fucked her.

"Saoirse, we'll meet you at home," Tor said, the command clear in his tone.

The fae female pushed her bottom lip out in a fake pout before the corner of her mouth curled into a small smile.

"I can't wait," she said, her voice the sound of a delicious promise, then she winked at me before sifting away.

I turned fully at Tor, my hands still on my hips and my mouth open to unleash on him the anger that was already rebuilding. But the look in his aqua blue eyes, in the stoniness of his expression shut me up right quick.

"You were leaving," he said, not quite a question but not quite an accusation either, his voice low and frighteningly calm. Before I could answer, he went on. "Did you have a route for the thousands of miles to the border? A plan for how to feed and shelter yourself for the weeks it would take to reach the closest one? Do you know how to protect yourself from much more deadly beasts than the *cait sith* you just met? Or were you just . . . how do the humans say . . . winging it? In a land where everything and everyone wants to kill you?"

I shrugged. "That's pretty much the norm wherever I go. And as you keep reminding me, I have a most deadly power."

"Which you don't know how to use."

"I just did, didn't I?"

"What, do you expect the beasts to insult you and your family first? Will it take the threat of rape or worse from my father's men before you fight them back? That seems to be the only way for you to even acknowledge your power. You react emotionally. That is not control or use."

I pressed my lips together, unable to argue because he was right. From what I'd heard about my mother, I came by that talent naturally. Of course, Mom had been trying to use herself as a cautionary tale when teaching us about the difference between reacting and responding.

"Even if you had made it all the way to the borders and managed to escape the Shadow Lands, you made a deal with a very powerful fae. I don't recommend breaking it, if you care for anyone in any realm. He won't kill you. He will torment you and all you love."

Of course, he would. "So do you have any other recommendations?" I tried, cheekily. "Besides marrying you?"

"Would that be so bad?" His aqua gaze traveled over my body, leaving a trail of heat I both despised and basked in. *Would* it be so bad? Was I really asking myself that? Then he turned, shrugging. "You'll just have to learn to trust me, Elliana Knight." He swished a finger in the air, and Needan and Tor's horse came trotting through the forest. "We're leaving."

"To where?"

"To my home."

Giving him a wary look, I paused before striding over to Needan. "So you trust me now?"

He shrugged as he handed me the reins. "You could have tried to kill me, if you really wanted to. There have been no innocent lives around us to become collateral damage. There will be many at the Court of Souls, however, so I presume that I will be safe."

Shit. I should have let him teach me control while I had the chance. To make my power an arrow rather than a bomb so I could shoot it into his heart, if he even had one. What had I been thinking?

"You will learn eventually," he said. "I believe Saoirse may be a better teacher than I. Besides, I have business to attend to." He paused, his mouth stretching into a wide grin that bared his teeth. "A wedding to plan."

I rolled my eyes and flipped him off before hiding my wings and swinging myself onto Needan's back. I really needed to figure out how to disentangle myself from this damn deal, preferably the right way that wouldn't endanger myself or my family.

We rode through the forest in silence for what must have been hours when the path started winding up a hill. The forest gave way to patchy clearings, the air growing colder as we climbed. Eventually, it gave way completely to nothing but stone. We hadn't been climbing a mere hill but a mountain. When it became too steep for the horses to carry us, we dismounted and led them upward. My breath caught when we reached the pinnacle. Before us spread a mountain range in blues and purples, blanketed in layers of dark fog, and beyond it appeared to be a valley lost in the shadows.

"That is true *Annwn*, and the Court of Souls is there," Tor said, pointing vaguely toward the valley.

"And that is your home?"

"It is my creation."

That was an interesting way to put it. The name he'd given it was also intriguing.

"Wouldn't it be easier if I flew and you sifted?" I asked as we remounted the horses for the climb downward. "Or you could just sift us both?"

"I want you to see the beauty of my lands," he replied,

pride filling his words. "What will become the lands of my lady . . . and eventually my queen."

If I'd been drinking anything, I would have spewed it out, showering Needan's mane. Queen? I didn't much like the sound of being anyone's lady, but queen had a whole different ring to it. And if I kept the deal I'd made, that's what I would become.

Perhaps I could wait to kill Tor.

Ahead of me, Tor snorted. I'd forgotten Needan would share my thoughts with her true master. Now I began to think of all the ways I could kill him and his father.

"You have to be more creative than that," he said after a few minutes of this. I envisioned slicing off his ears and using them like my throwing stars, jamming their points into his father's eyeballs. Tor laughed. "Better, but that wouldn't kill him."

Scowling, I changed my train of thoughts. Otherwise, he'd undoubtedly start haranguing me about the only way to kill any of them—by using my power. So I internally admired the beauty of his lands instead.

The snow-covered mountaintops reminded me of school in the shiny world, and then my mind drifted to Sadie. As I recalled our time together, Tor stiffened in his saddle. No, that was not a good train of thought either. I needed to simply meditate, not think at all, but as I watched his back, that didn't work either.

"You want to kill your father," I blurted and immediately wished I could take the words back. What had come over me to say them in the first place? He could kill me in an instant for suggesting such a thing. Even if I was right—*especially* because I was right.

"And why would I want to do that?" the prince asked, his voice even as though I hadn't just accused him of treason.

I hesitated before answering. Was this really his response or was he setting me up?

"Because you want the throne, of course." As if that wasn't the most obvious reason.

"Do I?" he asked. "I have the Court of Souls. You haven't seen it yet, but when you do, you will understand why it could be enough for me."

My brows pinched together. *Could be* seemed to be the operative words there.

"So why do you want to kill him?" I dared to ask since he hadn't attacked me on the initial accusation. I knew it was true. He hadn't once argued with me or given me any reason to not kill King Caellach. In fact, he often seemed amused when I mentioned—or thought about—murdering his father.

"Why do you want to kill us?" he asked in return. "Why do you hate my father so?"

A sort of laugh-snort burst out of me. "You're kidding, right? The king made me *kill* people, simply for his amusement and gain."

"Such as in the Pits?"

"I killed for my life and my sister's then," I corrected. "No, he surrounded me and terrified me, making me fight for my life when he didn't need to. We had a deal. He had the power. I didn't have to kill those people first. And then in the throne room . . ." My throat tightened at the memory . . . a memory not unlike others.

"But I have done no such thing."

"Perhaps why I haven't killed you yet," I muttered, but then my voice grew louder again. "But you do want to enslave me, too. Which I kind of get, since you think I have some great power you can use, but why the others? Why are you so keen to enslave your own people?"

"There were no slaves at the cottage. You will find none in the Court of Souls."

This made me pause. Was it true? I supposed I'd find out soon enough. "*I* am your slave, am I not? Besides, I saw what you did to those women. Drained them of all their power to feed your own. You said yourself they would become slaves. That makes you no better than him."

"Or," Tor said, his voice dropping to be nearly inaudible, "maybe he uses me in the same way he wants to use you."

The truth rang through his words, pain lacing his tone. He'd tried to hide it, but I not only heard it but felt it in my soul. I'd learned the hard way to trust my intuition, but I'd nonetheless learned.

"Princess Maeve claims you do it to boost your own power. The tormenting people thing. She says all Shadow fae feed off the worst things in life, such as torment and despair, and create more of it to gorge themselves."

"*Princess* Maeve?" he scoffed, though I didn't know why he stressed the title, spitting it with disgust. "Be careful what you believe from that one. Like all fae, she twists truths, especially when it comes to the Shadows. We do feed off precisely what the other fae had tried to discard of themselves—the aspects of life and existence most care to hide, such as grief and death, fear and despair. But there is plenty of all of that in simple day-to-day living. After all, not even the most powerful royal fae can truly banish all of life's darkness. We do not need to create more, and if they were smart, they would know that we could actually bring them relief."

I pondered this for a few minutes. "Saoirse—she feeds off hate, doesn't she?"

He glanced over his shoulder at me. "Excellent observation."

"She grew stronger, her injuries healing, as my hatred drained away." I started putting more of it together. "When I first saw her in the woods—when she looked like you—her power was weak."

Tor cut me off with a hearty laugh. "Don't ever let her hear you say that."

"I'm pretty sure I can take her. I practically did back there."

"But you did not, even when you thought she was the king and hit with all of your power. She may not be him, but she is of royal blood."

I shrugged. "Compared to you, she *was* weak. And definitely compared to your father. But when she appeared as the king, her power strengthened as my hatred grew. Strong enough to lash out at me."

Tor tilted his head in appreciation. "And that is how I know I can trust you with my life, Elliana."

My brows furrowed. "I don't follow."

"You didn't feel hatred when you saw me. Only when you saw my father."

Well, damn if he wasn't right.

"So you do want to kill your father," I said after a while. When he didn't reply, I pressed further. "What is the plan?"

Apparently obeying a silent command, Needan took a few steps quicker, sidling up next to Tor's horse. The prince cut a sideways glance at me.

"Maybe I will tell you when I know I can trust you," he said.

"You just said you already did. And you're taking me to your home."

"I said I trusted you with my life. With my secrets is yet to be determined."

I didn't reply. I already knew he did. After all, hadn't he disclosed a major secret—his motive?

CHAPTER 17

"Ye'll need to sift from here," Tor said when we finally crested the last ridge of the mountain range. Below us the fog hung thickly, obliterating any view of the valley below, besides the spindly tops of evergreen trees that poked through like bony fingers reaching out of a misty grave. Needan strode up next to Tor's horse, and he reached over to wrap his long fingers around my arm.

His power momentarily swirled around us then disappeared. We no longer perched at the top of the mountain looking into a valley of shadows, but had come some ways down, on the banks of a turquoise pond at the edge of a cliff. He'd sifted all of us—horses and all. If sifting was truly like flashing, then that required immense power. Another display of the strength of this prince.

A waterfall to our left fed the pond, which in turn spilled over the edge to somewhere I couldn't see from this vantage point, but I could hear the splash of water on rocks far below. There was more color here than there had been in all of our travels, or, at least, it seemed more natural than the bioluminescent hues of the forest, and I realized the lighting had brightened. It wasn't full on daylight, but more like that morning twilight time just before sunrise.

Tor grabbed my arm, his magic swirled, and once again we transported to the side of another pool. I looked up the mountain to a series of waterfalls that flowed over and down what could have been stairs made for giants, the pools gathering on the ledges before cascading to the next level below. Mists hovered around the falls and pond, where the sun sparkled on the ripples. The sun . . . I tilted my head back to look up at the sky, feeling the sun on my face for the first time in what felt like forever—since coming to Faery. I closed my eyes and let it wash over me, sending paradoxical goosebumps over my skin.

"It's so good to feel the sun again," I murmured aloud. I opened my eyes and looked over at Tor. "But how?"

"Shadows need light to exist, do they not?" he replied, glancing to the far side of the pond.

I noticed for the first time several fae lounging on the bank over there, dressed scantily in gauzy camisoles and skirts, basking in the brilliant warmth of the sun. They waved at the prince, their faces lit up with joy.

"So why is the rest of the Shadow Lands so dark?" I asked.

Tor frowned. "That is my father's doing."

I snorted. "Did his black soul snuff out the sun?"

He laughed—a genuine, beautiful sound. "He certainly wishes he had that much power. He does create the fogs, however." We began moving again as he talked, the horses circling the pond and heading toward an archway that led away from the mountain. The joy left his voice as quickly as it had filled it. "The constant darkness feeds the despair of his people, which in turn feeds his own power while theirs withers away."

"Wouldn't he want his people strong, though? I mean, the Shadow fae have plenty of enemies, from what I've been told. What if they're attacked?" I didn't know why I cared so much.

No, wait. Ena. That's why. And all of those fae at the Court of Shadows, the ones in the cages and the ones in the crowd . . . the ones I killed. I couldn't fathom why a king would be so cruel to his own people.

"My father only wants power and control. The Seelie and Unseelie hate us, yes, but they never attack. They never come to the Shadow Lands. They created the Shadow fae and banished us to our own lands—"

"Wait. The Seelie and Unseelie created your people? How could they hate you so much then?"

We passed through the arch and onto a path that led down a gradual slope toward what appeared to be a town in the distance. Behind the town rose a stone wall, the face of another mountain, jagged peaks scraping the sky. Picturesque cottages out of the pages of fairy tales with their stone walls, thatched roofs, and flower gardens were scattered among the trees that lined each side of the wide path.

"Yes, we came about during one of their big wars eons ago, before the Seelie and Unseelie delineations, when they were all simply Light and Dark. They go to war frequently, often out of nothing more than boredom, but the War for *Emain Ablach* was one of their deadliest and most realm-changing. The Light and the Dark clashed like never before and never since, so violently and vehemently that parts of themselves separated from their very souls. They kept what they deemed worthy and discarded the rest—the parts they desired to keep hidden in deep, dark places. The parts of themselves they hated. The souls of the Shadow fae were created as a result, but they banished us to our own lands where they would not have to see us, allowing them to forget what had once been a part of their very beings. Of course, they want nothing to do with us."

"Except as slaves."

"Except as slaves," he echoed, then added, "Only my people here at the Court of Souls are free."

"And your father allows it?"

"He never comes here. He abhors the light, which is exactly why I chose this as my lands. He does not understand it, and he is too arrogant to suspect I would be doing anything against him."

"I meant, he allows the oppression of his own people?" I was trying to wrap my head around it all but couldn't fathom how Caellach was their king.

"Ah, well, that my father encourages. Like I said, he covets power and control. He gives the Seelie and the Unseelie what they want, which puts them in debt to him. That gives him power."

"And they're okay with that as long as they get their free labor," I said bitterly.

"They need their fields worked, their palaces cleaned, and their food served, but never by their own. They would never do to their own people what they are so willing and happy to have done to the Shadows. Draining us of our Shadow powers means they don't have to be reminded of what once was part of them. As they see it, fae with no powers are not fae at all, but merely soulless creatures to own like property." His voice had grown heavy, anger threading the words together.

"Another reason you want the throne," I said.

"Someone must do something. At one time, I thought the people would rebel, but those who dare step out of line in even the slightest manner . . . Well, you saw what I had to do to those three fae."

"*Had* to?" I challenged.

"Had to," he confirmed. "If I do not, I become one of them. Then I could never free anyone. And yes, that is exactly what I plan to do—I *will* free my people, Elliana. Saoirse was one of my first, many years ago."

"Really? How?" I found this all fascinating but also wanted to keep him talking as I collected more key pieces of information, recognizing their value and tucking them away for when I needed them for my own goals.

"Saoirse is my sister. More precisely, my half-sister, a product of one of the king's many affairs."

That explained how she'd survived my power when other fae hadn't. I didn't find it in the least bit surprising the king was a womanizer, but— "I was under the assumption he had no daughters."

"None that he acknowledges. His actual claim is that he only sires princes. He's sent all the daughters away, pretending as though they don't exist. I don't know how many or where they all are, but Saoirse's mother came to court when she was young, begging for food and shelter." His voice dropped, regret lacing it as he said, "Fearing she'd disclose his secrets, my father made me drain her and ordered me to find and drain the daughter, too. I told him the child got away before I could find her. It was the first time I defied his orders and risked everything—my name, my title, my life. I would do it every day again to save her. In fact, I *do* it every day for her and the others."

My heart weighed heavily in my chest as we rode in silence again, my mind processing this. Was this prince known as the Tormentor a softie at heart? A noble man with a noble cause? Well, maybe not quite noble, but he claimed to at least have the right intentions. If he could be believed, which I wasn't sure of yet. And what plans did he have after he freed his people, I wondered. What would the Seelie and Unseelie do when they no longer had slaves delivered to them on demand? Did Tor plan to go to war with them? He surely had to know that would happen, whether he wanted it to or not. The earthly realm served as a prime example of how far slave owners and elitists would go to ensure they could oppress others for their own gain. Would such a war be good or bad for my people? For my own world? I didn't know those answers. He probably didn't care.

I wasn't one to fault a being for having to do whatever necessary to protect their own. I'd done the same in the Pits.

And other times, that persistent voice tried to remind me. Yes, other times I didn't want to think about. Though not thinking about those memories didn't make them any less real. And if I would admit it, I'd realize I was no better than the Shadow fae prince. In fact, maybe even worse. My motivations had been selfish—to protect my own heart from losing those I loved, and I hadn't even done that. His motivations would change the entire Faery realm for the better.

The horses slowed as we approached a tall, white wall that appeared to be made of marble and surrounded the town, another archway stretching over the path, its gates opened wide.

"Welcome to the Court of Souls," Tor said as we passed through.

It appeared to be everything the Court of Shadows was not —its complete opposite. Where the Court of Shadows was all dark with sharp angled roofs and pointed spires stabbing the sky, the Court of Souls encompassed architecture of round buildings, domed roofs, curved archways, and white marble walls. A dark, low-vibrating energy weighed heavily in the Court of Shadows, the stench of agony and despair permeating the very walls, trapping the residents into mere existences and survival. Here, fae bustled about, on foot and riding various types of creatures, as they went about their business, the air fresh and their energy buzzing with life.

We trotted down a wide avenue through what seemed to be the center of the town toward the largest structure that appeared to butt up against the mountain cliff behind it. The fae stopped and grinned as we passed by, their heads dipping in respectful acknowledgment, but not a single one actually bowing or taking a knee to their prince. He didn't demand it either, but only nodded and waved in return.

We entered what I supposed would be called a plaza—a wide, semi-circular area bordered by shops and bistros with a large fountain in the center. The archway to what I presumed to be Tor's palace was on the far side of the fountain, though the beautiful structure beyond it was no palace. Mansion? Yes. Awe-inspiring? Definitely. But in size alone, it was not at all comparable to King Caellach's gothic castle or Maeve's icy one at Winter Court.

We'd barely rounded the fountain when two male fae came rushing through the archway, hailing Tor down. Our horses stopped, and Tor dismounted. They spoke in their native tongue, and whatever they had to say was obviously important and urgent. Tor glanced at me, and with a tilt of his head, Needan started moving while their discussion continued, carrying me through the archway and stopping at the short flight of marble steps that led to a covered veranda. At the top of the steps stood a domineering and fiercely beautiful female fae. Eyes the color of amethysts gazed down at me, and she lifted a slanted brow—in appreciation or annoyance, I couldn't tell, so I only glared back, raising my own brow.

With the tiniest curve of her cupid-bow lips, Saoirse lifted her chin. "Well? Do you plan to sit there all day or are you coming in?"

Dismounting Needan, I ascended the curved steps to the round portico, the roof supported by white marble columns, taking it all in. The domed ceiling was made of an opaque glass tinted blue, filtering the sunlight so that it gave the marble a bluish glow, making it feel as though we were under water. Scrolling metal and colored glass decorated the edges of the dome and its frame, crawling partway down the columns.

"Yasta!" Saoirse barked, turning on her heel and striding for the tall arched doors that led inside. "The longer you take, the longer we have to wait for mealtime."

My stomach growled just at the thought, so I hurried after her, only to stop in my tracks as soon as I entered the wide, round space. The ceiling curved several stories overhead, another glass dome at its top, elaborate scrolls and runes decorating the curved walls all the way to the marble floor. At the center stood what looked like the wide marble base of a fountain, but rather than water cascading downward, purple, pink, and teal faerie light streamed upward where it combined into a large spherical shape that hung in the air. The light flowed like water, and the sphere rotated slowly like a small sun, the movement artistic, otherworldly, and quite mesmerizing.

"Elliana," Saoirse bit out, urging me on. We circled around the light sculpture fountain thing as she flipped her hands in different directions, gesturing toward some of the archways off this chamber that she called the mezzanine. "Throne room. Ballroom. Tor works down that way. Library over there."

We passed under the archway that seemed to lead to the back of the manor, entering a hallway where ivy crawled along the walls and around the large windows on the outer curved wall and paintings of fae lined the inner one. I slowed again, admiring the artwork, the images at once realistic and magical.

Saoirse groaned. "Yes, I know, Tor is quite talented."

I pulled back in surprise. "Tor painted these?"

"You'll have plenty of time to look at them later. Yasta, yasta!"

I was about to pick up my pace again when a certain image caught my eye—a younger, softer version of Saoirse sitting on the back of a dragon. On the back of a gods-damned dragon. The beast was beautifully rendered, making me wonder if it was from Tor's imagination or reality. He'd said dragons lived in Faery, but I'd still yet to see one. And Saoirse . . . he'd captured her perfectly. At least, if a younger, softer version of her had ever truly existed.

"My dad was an artist," I murmured.

"Was?" she asked, her tone quiet and less urgent as she suddenly stood back by my side.

I flinched at the realization of using the past tense.

"I don't know the last time he painted. I don't know anything about what's going on with my parents," I admitted, and the pain of missing them bloomed into an ache in my stomach. I no longer felt very hungry. "I don't even know where they are."

"Tor may be able to help you with that," she said as she began moving again.

"He'd find my parents?"

"Are they in Faery?"

"I have no idea. Only rumors that they could be."

She stopped and turned, giving me a long look, then shrugged. "You should have said something to him. The Shadow Lands are far removed from the rest of Faery and the Court of Souls even farther, so we don't follow all the goings-on of the continent—only what interests us—but this is something he needs to know. He would want to find them."

My brows arched. "Would he now? And at what cost?"

"Of course, he would and at no cost. You are his future family. Your family is his family." She hurried on again with me following on her heels.

She said it so easily, but I couldn't quite believe that Tor would do anything for my family. I supposed it wouldn't hurt to ask, especially if we were truly going to be united.

"Oh, ew!" I nearly choked. "I promise you this—*his* family will never be mine!"

She glanced over her shoulder as we turned a corner. "No offense taken."

I said no more, following along as she rattled off other rooms, gesturing toward a doorway to the kitchen and rushing us through a sitting area full of plush settees and pillows as large as beds, with several large glass doors that opened to a terrace. Of all of the Shadow fae, I hated Saoirse the least. Well, no, that wasn't true. Not anymore. Tor had been right— I didn't hate him at all. I didn't want to admit how or what I did feel for him, but it wasn't hatred. I wasn't sure about his sister yet. She aggravated the hell out of me, but I knew the only harm she'd done was an attempt to help me.

I'd meant the king and Tor's brothers—they would *never* be my family. I may have to kill them before the wedding to make that true.

We passed through an archway off the sitting room, entering another hallway with curved walls, the outer one again lined with windows, these framed by blue drapes, and more whorls, scrolls, and fae runes glowing in various jewel-tones along the inner wall. Saoirse stopped at a set of double doors painted a green that was the color of the ocean.

"Your room. You have enough time to clean up and change. If you take too long, however, and Tor makes me wait on you to eat, it may be your heart that I'll be consuming." With that, she strode off, back the way we came.

Standing against the door, I took in my new quarters, and for some inexplicable reason, the room's décor pricked the backs of my eyelids. The far wall rounded outward with floor-to-ceiling double doors that flooded the room with natural light. The bed sat in the center of the space, with a pointed canopy and white sheers draping down and gathered to each of the corner posts, making me think of a palanquin— perhaps to transport a noble lady rather than royalty because it was elegant, but not ornate. Several large, thick pillows sat on a fat comforter decorated with mandalas in soft hues of mauve, blue, and teal. What I could only describe as a large pouf sat next to the bed to serve as a nightstand, sitting on top of a shaggy white throw rug. Faerie lights lit up the canopy, and two pendant lights flanked a dresser against the side wall. The other side wall contained a door to what I presumed to a bathroom. Live plants and flowers were scattered around the room. It was all so pretty in an understated and comfortable way, especially compared to my opulent room at Winter Palace. Although the Loft was nothing at all close to this, the simple beauty almost felt like . . . home. Which made me ache for my real home, for my family.

Dad. Mom. Brielle. Charleigh. Sasha. Even Sadie came mind. What were they all doing now? Where were they?

Heaving a harsh exhale, I fell back on the soft bed and threw an arm over my eyes, fighting a strange desire to cry.

I wasn't a crier. But my whole life had turned upside down, and I was in a strange—and dangerous—land with otherworldly beings and no idea where anyone I loved was. I wondered if they were okay . . . and knew they probably were not. Would I ever hug any of them again? Would I even *see* any of them again? My throat thickened, and I drew in a stuttered breath.

Stop being so dramatic. Suck it up and do what needs to be done.

Giving myself another minute to gather my feelings and stuff them back in the box where they belonged, I finally forced myself to sit up. I was right about the other door—it led to a private bathroom, where I filled a large tub that appeared to be made of sea glass or some kind of crystal, the warm water faintly scented with lavender and chamomile. It should have been relaxing, and I did feel loads better when I emerged, though that ache of loneliness still lingered. A large closet with only a few outfits hanging from one of the many rods was off the bathroom, and I grabbed the only dress, not knowing what to expect for mealtimes here, especially dinner.

Leaving my room, I went back the way Saoirse and I had come, through the sitting room and toward the kitchen, but I hadn't been paying attention to where the dining room was located. Following my nose, I passed through another doorway and gasped. An arched ceiling of stained glass topped the broad corridor, the dark, shiny marble floor reflecting the various colors like a mirror. I marveled as the same colors danced along my skin as I walked through. About halfway down, I was pulled to the right, and I turned into a much darker hallway.

No natural light flooded this corridor as there were no

windows, colored or otherwise. A few faerie light orbs were scattered along the ceiling, their light dim, just enough to see by. More paintings lined the walls, both sides, and these were not at all like the portraits Tor had painted and hung in the other hallway. These were dark . . . full of rage and anguish and pain . . . of torment. One to my right was only broad, harsh strokes in black and red, thick blobs of paint left on the canvas. One to my left showed the naked body of a fae, skin flayed, a pool of deep crimson surrounding it. Another appeared to be a stormy sky over an angry sea, but so blurred and abstract, it could have been a vision of the mind rather than that of the eye.

But at the end of the hall, I paused, my breath catching. Becoming trapped in my lungs as I remained frozen—all but my hand, which lifted and reached for the scene before me.

A blurred background of mostly brown stone walls, smudged faces gathered across the top, as though looking down. Down upon a pit where two female figures with copper-colored hair were surrounded by dead bodies on the ground around them—

Brielle and me, facing each other . . . our arms reaching for each other . . . a spear rammed through the hearts of both of us.

This was the image of our deaths in the Pits.

CHAPTER 18

My heart seemed to stop as renewed pain shot through my chest, as though I were feeling the killing blow all over again. The expressions on our faces—shock, agony, love—so beautifully and realistically captured. The same bedlam of emotions churned through me, all dark and full of anguish and rage, swallowing my breath and bringing me to my knees. What had happened to us? *Why?*

Tears once again filled my eyes, and I allowed them to spill this time as I pressed my hands against my chest, my gaze still locked on the image even as my head craned back to see it now. I sobbed for the innocent girls who'd somehow ended up in that prison and for the lives that were stolen from them.

But were they? Were they innocent? Were their lives stolen? Or are they traveling the paths they're meant to—the ones they deserve for what they've done?

The dark voice of the beast inside me spoke truths I'd been trying to deny. I still wanted to deny. I knew what I had done, but Brielle . . . she didn't deserve what had happened to her. No, I could not believe our time in the Vault was a dish served up by karma, a punishment for something we had unintentionally done at six years old, too young to understand or even know what, exactly, we had done. The Vault was done *to* us. Why, I did not know. By whom, I did not know either. But as my eyes drifted to the painting right next to ours, I began to wonder . . .

The cruel eyes of King Caellach stared at me, silver in color against the dark ash tone his skin became when he turned on his full power. The portrait was only of his face and white hair against a black background of broad, swirling brushstrokes. I glared back at him for a long moment, until a red haze blurred my vision and a storm of hatred filled me. I rose back to my feet, my beast doing the same within. As my gaze bounced between the cruel king and the death of my sister and me, new truths formed in the back of my mind, and the cage within began to rise, my beast's tongue sliding along my veins, leaving a trail of Darkness.

"So you've found the Hall of Sorrows," a soft, deep voice said from directly behind me, his breath hot on my ear, he stood so close.

And immediately, the anguish drained away, Tor absorbing it, taking it from me. Without hesitation, I leaned against him, feeling his power grow as my beast settled down, the cage back in place. My breaths still came unevenly as I tilted my head and looked up, his beautiful face over me as he glared at the same images. The hatred built in him, too, his skin darkening and his hair bleaching out. I stepped away as the power grew, lashing off of him in black tendrils of smoke. Rather than settling me now, his dark energy reached for my own, and my beast stirred again.

"I have to get out of here," I gasped, rushing back down the corridor for the hall of light and color.

"Don't know if I need food anymore, between the two of you." Saoirse stood in the doorway, her own skin blackening and her short, spiky hair whitening. Though she'd shed her normal armor, wearing a loose silk top and harem-like pants that should have softened her appearance, the purple glow in her eyes made her look fiercer than ever. She inhaled deeply, consuming Tor's hatred in large gulps until his own power settled.

I rushed past her and leaned against a wall, gasping for fresh air as I tried to calm myself. When I finally looked at the two of them with wide eyes, their hair, skin, and eyes had returned to normal, though now dappled in bright colors from the stained glass overhead.

"You painted those, too?" I asked Tor. He dropped his head in acknowledgment. "But why keep them? Why put them on display?"

He didn't respond but strode off.

"When you have memories like his, there's no need to torture others to feed off their torment," Saoirse said quietly before following him.

I stared after them as I began to understand. The Hall of Sorrows, as he'd called it, created enough torment of his own to feed his power. And that last picture was the being responsible for it all: his father. The hatred that face alone must have created within both of them kept Saoirse's power well fed, too. This was how they remained strong without harming others.

We ate, just the three of us, a quiet meal of a white fish with a light sauce and greens, perfectly prepared by the prince himself. The siblings disappeared right after, giving me freedom to explore the manor as I liked, but I returned straight to my room. Sitting on the balcony beyond the double doors, which overlooked the plaza, I watched as the final light of the sunset disappeared and night took over. Colorful light orbs danced and hovered around the small city, casting purple, pink, blue, and turquoise hues on the white marble of the buildings. Many of the domed roofs glowed softly, as well. It was all straight out of a fairy tale, including the prince himself.

Too bad I already knew this could never end with a happily ever after.

Unlike the previous evening, the manor bustled with activity the next morning when I emerged from my room for breakfast. The sitting room and kitchen were still quiet, but a platter of pastries was laid out. I chose a croissant, poured a cup of faerie tea, and followed the sounds to the front of the home. Fae seemed to be everywhere, chattering and a few even humming as they cleaned, polished, and hung swaths of fabric across the domed ceilings of the mezzanine, and more could be heard in the directions of the throne room and ballroom.

"Ready?" Saoirse asked, appearing next to me, dressed in tight pants, a cropped tank top, and armed to the teeth.

"Ready for what?" I choked out, wondering what everyone was preparing for. "And I thought Tor didn't have slaves."

"He doesn't," she snapped. "Hired work is not the same as slavery."

"So they're paid?"

"Very well paid, in fact."

"Do they do this every day?"

Saoirse snorted. "The prince does not get engaged every day, now does he?"

My heart stuttered, and I turned to stare at her. "Whoa. What does that mean? What's going on here?"

Her pretty little mouth curled into that smirky grin. "You are to have an engagement celebration, of course. The fae love their parties, don't you know? Even the Shadows." She chuckled at the horror that was clear on my face. "Come with me. I know what you do like."

She walked off, and at first, I only watched her, wondering what exactly she had in mind as her round ass sashayed across the room.

"Yasta, Elliana! Yasta!"

I hurried after her, following her through the halls again to the back of the home and out to the rear lawn. A large terrace of more marble, with a few distinct seating areas scattered about, gave way to luscious green grass. The mountain's gray face that was as vertical as a wall rose just beyond the marble wall bordering the lawn. Stopping in the middle of the grass, Saoirse turned to me and gestured to put my teacup down on the nearby table.

"What are we doing?" I asked, though I was pretty sure I already knew.

"You are scared of your own power. You need to overcome that, or you will never gain control, and eventually, you will explode. I imagine you wouldn't like the repercussions of that."

I shrugged. "Depends on where I am at the time and who's around me. I don't regret what happened in the throne room at the Court of Shadows."

She smiled. "No, I don't figure you do. But that's a dangerous way to defend yourself and no way to live. We're going to do whatever it takes to solve the puzzle that is Elliana Knight, so you don't have to live in fear of yourself."

How could I argue with that? I'd spent years fearing what the beast inside me could do. Now that my memories had returned, I knew exactly the carnage she could create, so much worse than the greedy, soul-sucking fae in the throne room at the auction. If I could harness that power, though . . . destroy the Shadow king . . . that might be worth the effort it would take to learn to trust myself.

Except it took a lot more effort than either of us expected —or, it seemed, that I could muster.

I trained with Saoirse for days, only seeing Tor in the evenings. I assumed he was planning our wedding, which annoyed me because if I had to actually marry him, well, I'd like to be a part of the plans. But when I asked, he insisted he was attending to court business. Our evenings together were, well, nice, if I had to admit. We sat on one of the balconies each night after meals, drinking faerie wine and discussing life in the Court of Souls. The pride for his people and love for them came through in the stories he told and details he shared, and I could almost imagine myself happy here. You know, if my family weren't scattered across the realms and who knew what was happening to them.

"I'll send some scouts to the Light lands to find out if your parents are there," he promised me, and for the first time since that day in the mirrors at college, I felt the tiniest bit of hope.

During the days, I worked with Saoirse, yet barely made any progress. I knew how to find the power and even tap into it, but I couldn't bring myself to embrace it. To allow it to run through my veins freely, without fear of what it might do if I lost control. Without fear of decimating all of the fae busily preparing for my engagement ball. Saoirse's glamour tricks to become the king no longer worked, since I now knew it was her. A trip back through the Hall of Sorrows brought my full power rising once again, but voices in the rooms beyond reminded me of the risk, and I sucked it all back in.

"You'll get a break the next couple of days, but then we're back at it again," Saoirse said one afternoon when we ended early. "I no longer care if you use your power to help us, though I hope you will. Now you've just become a challenge I *must* overcome. The fae in me just can't go on knowing that there's such immense power in that body of yours. The Shadow fae in me who's seen so many drained of their powers, including my own mother, can't fathom the idea of all that power being suppressed . . . all that potential wasted."

I scowled at this perspective, not liking it either. But it seemed nothing we did could change it.

"What's going on the next couple of days?"

She smiled. "Tor has plans for you tonight, and tomorrow is the big ball." My mouth gaped, and she laughed at my reaction. "Have fun."

She flitted her fingers in a little wave, then sifted away.

I found two female fae waiting and a beautiful dress laid out for me when I returned to my room. After a luxurious bath in that perfumed water, the duo went to work on my hair and face, making me into a piece of art. The gossamer dress, an almost sheer dark blue fabric with sparkles that made it look like the night sky, fell perfectly over my curves, the back completely open almost all the way down to my butt.

"Are you sure this isn't for tomorrow?" I asked them.

The more outspoken one scrunched her brows together. "No, my lady. This is just a simple gown."

I could only imagine what the dress I'd be wearing tomorrow would be like then—or the one for the actual ceremony. I couldn't wait to see either. Just trying to find the silver lining in the fact that I was not only marrying someone I didn't love, but a male at that. At least this male was . . . bearable. I didn't know if he was better or worse than Maeve. I just knew neither were the one I truly wanted to be with.

Neither was Sadie.

Tor waited for me on the back veranda, which was lit up with colored faerie lights, a table laid out like a fancy restaurant at the center. He sipped from a glass of wine as he leaned against the balustrade, wearing a black jacket and dress pants, a turquoise tunic underneath that brought out his eyes. As if they needed any help. At least he was handsome. When the time came to, uh, consummate our marriage—after all, I wasn't a fool and knew the king expected a grand-prince or two out of this—I could easily remind myself there were much worse males to have to lay with. His power could help things along, though I feared he might not have to use it. Still . . . this was not *my* fairy tale ending.

"Before the true chaos begins, I thought you and I should have some time alone tonight," he said, his piercing gaze traveling over me from head to toe. "You look . . . divine. The dress is perfect."

I dipped my head in thanks, then realized what he meant. The backless dress was on purpose. I snapped my wings out, and he grinned in approval.

"You and your sister are simply amazing."

My brows pinched for a moment as I wondered why he said it that way. Why he even mentioned her. Before I could ask, the *very well-paid* attendants came out and began to serve us.

Dinner was out of this world. Faerie food was so much . . . *more* than even that of the shiny world.

Afterward, he looped his arm through mine and led me out of the front of the manor for the first time since I'd arrived. We walked the perimeter of the plaza as he introduced me to the owners and employees of the shops and cafes, reminding me of the stories he'd already told me about them and their families—how he and Saoirse had prevented them from becoming property of other courts. As we spoke with them, I noticed how much they revered their prince, and I myself was in a bit of awe, but as we headed back for his home, another feeling began to override that, tightening my gut in knots.

He walked me all the way to my room, stopping just outside the double doors. His head cocked to the side as he studied me.

"Something is wrong," he said, not as a question.

My gaze averted for a moment before I looked him in the eye. "You speak so highly of yourself and what you have done for your people. It is truly impressive. Yet . . . this . . ." I gestured between him and me. "You're still allowing this. You're still making me your property."

The light in his eyes dimmed as they filled with sadness. He lifted his hand, as though to brush his fingers over my cheek, but then stopped himself and dropped it instead. "If it were up to me, none of this would be happening. Not like this."

"Then why don't you stop it?"

"You made a deal with a fae—with a king, no less. It is not my place to break it."

"So you took advantage and claimed me."

"I'm trying to do what I think is right," he ground out, his jaw clenching at my accusation. "You are better off with me than with my father or any of my brothers."

Crossing my arms over my chest, I lifted a brow. "So you think you are *saving* me? I don't need to be saved."

"You don't know what you need!" he snapped, his voice a near growl. I pulled back, and he blew out a sigh. He pushed a hand through his dark hair, loosening the ponytail. When he spoke again, his words were calm, soothing. "I had hoped tonight would make you feel better about all of this. That perhaps you could find a way to be happy here." When I didn't reply, he released a long breath, and his voice lowered even more. "This is not exactly what I want either, Elliana, but I have a plan. I have my reasons. I just need you to trust that I will do all that I can to make it right for both of us."

Then he turned and strode away, leaving me more confused than ever. I wasn't sure if I should be insulted or relieved.

As I slipped into my room, I knew it really didn't matter how I felt. How he did. He was right—I had made a deal. I had committed to this long ago to save my sister, and I would go through with it. And for whatever his reasons were, Tor had committed to it, as well. I would just have to trust that he would, indeed, make it good for both of us.

CHAPTER 19

*S*leep evaded me, and the closer morning light came, the more nauseated I grew. The knots in my stomach created their own knots until I was just a big, tangled mess of tension and queasiness. Not that sleep brought much rest anymore, always filled with real-life terrors of the past posing as dreams. When the sun rose and I could hear a swarm of activity elsewhere in the manor, though, the last thing I wanted was to be awake, because that meant facing my current reality—which was better than the past, but not by much. I lay in bed as long as I was allowed, wishing for a last-minute miracle to save me from the disaster my life had become.

To be honest, I couldn't explain why this day, this party made me so sick. In my head, I knew it really meant nothing. This was not the ceremony. The Court of Souls already knew why I was here. Probably all of the Shadow Lands knew about the Tormentor's inevitable wedding by now. It was not like some big secret was being revealed, an unexpected announcement being made. As I had been told and witnessed myself at Winter Court, the fae loved their balls, and this was simply an excuse for one.

That said, I was not full fae, and as far as I knew, not

Shadow at all. I didn't know how the people felt about this union, especially those of the Court of Souls, knowing this mandate came from the man they despised. They might have felt some sympathy for my predicament, but they also might have felt suspicion and disdain, seeing me as an outsider. Still, I had never really fit in anywhere, not even in my own family, so that wasn't what had me all tied up either.

I really couldn't pinpoint the why. I just knew that dread was eating me alive.

A pounding on my door brought me out of a doze sometime later in the day, and when I didn't respond, Saoirse stormed into the room, spewing a string of what sounded like Faelic profanity by the tone and sharpness of it all.

"What the hell are you still doing in bed?" she demanded as she threw open the drapes. "You should be getting ready! And you haven't eaten all day? No faerie wine for you until you have something in your stomach."

"What's wrong with you?" I croaked, pulling the thick comforter over my head.

"Me? You're the one who looks like *cait sith* shit warmed in the sun."

"You're acting like a mother hen instead of a drill sergeant," I muttered.

I was suddenly laying cover-less in the bed, Saoirse having ripped the blankets off of me. She stood over me, hands on her hips.

"I was going for future sister-in-law," she said with a cheeky grin.

Grabbing my hands and jerking me out of bed, she dragged me into the bathroom. By the time I finished cleaning up, the two fae from last night were there, along with a third and Saoirse overlooking them all, because today I had to look extra-special, I supposed.

When they were done, I stood in front of the mirror, and rather than notice the beautiful dress or how they'd fixed my hair, all I saw was terror filling my brown eyes—eyes that reminded me so much of my sister. My heart clenched at the thought of doing this without her. I'd never considered ever marrying anybody, but if I were going to, surely my twin should have been by my side. How I wished she was here with me.

No, wait. I did not wish that. Not at all. I hoped she was safe and with our parents. I didn't want her anywhere near the Shadow Lands and King Caellach. This was something I had to do on my own . . . which made it all the more frightening.

Saoirse stood behind me, her head tilting as she watched me, then she said something to the other three, and they hurried out of the room.

"Prince Toridhan will not force you to do anything you do not want to do," she said once they were gone. "He would never force anything on anybody. He knows too well that kind of torment himself."

Toridhan. I hadn't even known that was his full name until now. Tor wasn't short for Tormentor after all. For some reason, that knowledge made me feel slightly better, and the iron grip on my heart eased.

"Then why are we doing this at all?" I asked.

She shrugged. "It's just a party. We do love our parties. And it's a way to appease the king, because word will surely travel back to him that Tor has formally announced his engagement. It's buying Tor some time, Elli. That is all."

I studied her reflection in the mirror, her gaze locking with mine. I could see the truth in those amethyst eyes, and relief flooded through me.

A sigh escaped as my shoulders dropped from my ears and my chest loosened. "I wish he would have said so. I wouldn't have wasted the day in bed."

"He's a male." She rolled her eyes, and as if that explained everything, she turned for the door. "I need to get dressed myself. There's wine on the balcony, if you want an early start. But please make sure you eat something too."

From said balcony, I watched the attendees enter in an endless parade below, all of them dressed scantily to show off the swirls and runes decorating their flesh, as I sipped on a glass of sweet wine and nibbled on a piece of cheese. I had only just finished it when Saoirse returned, dressed in a gauzy dress that left nothing to the imagination. Not only were her well-defined muscles and fae markings on display, but so were her breasts, dark nipples hard and pierced with little pearls dangling from them. If I hadn't still felt a little queasy, despite her earlier reassurances, I might have been turned on. On the other hand, she was already feeling more like a sister, and I really had no interest. I could admire her powerful beauty and sexuality, but I felt nothing more. *Shit*. What was happening to me?

"Ready?" she asked.

I followed her through the back halls, avoiding the crowds at the front of the manor. Merry chatter and music grew louder as we approached, but then we ducked into a room where Tor waited in what appeared to be his office. He gave me a once over, followed by an approving smile. I tried to return it and failed.

"It's just a party," he murmured. "It only means what you want it to mean."

I didn't know what to make of that. Saoirse was about to leave to announce us when several male fae rushed into the room. One, who seemed to be the leader, began speaking in Faelic, but Tor cut him off, saying something curt as he tilted his head toward me.

"I am sorry, my lord, my lady," the fae said in English with a brief bow to each of us. I stifled a snort. "The situation in the Elven Lands has escalated. Word has been sent that an emissary with a small company is headed for the Shadow Lands, seeking the king's help."

Tor's brows came together in a scowl as he looked at me. Of course, my interest immediately piqued at the mention of the Elven Lands, but also because he'd said none of the other fae ever came to the Shadow Lands. Perhaps he only meant the Light and the Dark fae. Maybe that didn't apply to other races of the realm, such as the elves.

"We need to intercept them before they reach the Court of Shadows," Saoirse said. "Caellach will never align against the Winter Court."

My face must have shown my confusion, because Tor explained further. "He sent his men to Winter Court to scuffle with them as a distraction so he could get to you. That is not the same as forming an alliance against them."

"Maeve has gone too far, though," the one who'd spoken before said. The others had all lined up near the door, remaining silent as though awaiting orders. "The elves need our help."

Now Tor looked to his sister.

"We need all the allies we can muster," Saoirse said.

Tor nodded slowly, stroking his chin. "Yes, we do. But we must be careful. Send a party to intercept and bring them to the Mistwood outpost. I'll meet you there later."

The leader inclined his head in a small bow, and the fae filed out.

"I want to go," Saoirse said.

"Of course," Tor replied.

"I'm going too," I blurted, and they both looked at me with raised brows. I shrugged, trying not to look overly eager, though something told me I needed to go, to help.

Tor shook his head. "It's too dangerous."

"I thought I was the most dangerous creature in this realm."

"Exactly. It's too dangerous for everyone else." He held his arm out to me, crooking his elbow. "We'll keep the torture of this ball to a minimum here, then when we leave, you can choose to stay and enjoy the party or you have a perfect excuse to skip out and call it an early night, if you prefer."

I scowled, not liking his answer and change of subject. "I know how to fight without killing everyone around me. I've kept my power suppressed for years. I actually have a lot more control than either of you give me credit for. I can help you. Isn't that what you want?"

"Why are you so interested?"

Pressing my lips together, I searched for the right answer—for me as well as for him. "I don't know," I finally admitted. "Maybe because Maeve is involved? That feels . . . I don't know, personal for some reason. Besides, I've been in this manor, in this town for weeks. You say I'm not a prisoner. Prove it. If anything, let me stretch my wings. I can scope the situation out from the sky."

Saoirse laughed. "Oh, love, you are not the only one here who can fly."

She strode out, and I turned to Tor.

"I do not think this is the best time for you to be seen, especially by potential enemies. You are wanted by many, and not necessarily alive," he reminded me. "But I promise I will personally take you out beyond the walls and allow you to fly as soon as I return. Now speaking of your wings . . . I do love to see them."

He tilted his head, his turquoise gaze traveling along my neck and over my shoulder, and I could almost feel the caress tangibly, a warm spray of tingles spreading over my skin. My stomach dipped with a different kind of anticipation—one of need and desire to be physically touched. My wings sprang out on their own, and his long fingers trailed over the top edge, causing a shudder to rack through me and my thighs to clench. And I didn't mind my body's betrayal one bit.

"Weapons, Elliana? Do you really think they're necessary?" he asked, obviously seeing through my weak cloaking powers that hid my sword on my back. There was also a throwing star under the waistband of my dress.

"Always," I said. "A girl can never be too vigilant. Someone might try to steal my wine . . . or my virtue."

He laughed. I didn't tell him that it was him I feared would steal my virtue—if I even had any.

He held his bent arm out again, and I slipped mine around his, for some reason surprised at how much larger, thicker, stronger it felt than I was used to. Most men weren't built like him, let alone any women. Saoirse probably came the closest, but still a far cry from the muscular prince. I understood now why some women gawked over men's arms— the strength was steadying, reassuring . . . and turning me on. *Shit.* I really was a hot mess anymore.

The introductory announcement of our entrance was as awful as I'd expected, horns blaring, a booming voice declaring, "Prince Toridhan and his future lady, Elliana Ames Knight," and all the following gasps and whispers, as if this really was news to them. Taking my hand, Tor led me in a dance around the center of the room, guiding me expertly through the twirls and turns of a choreography I didn't know. We finally made it to the head table, the guests returning to their conversations and their own revelry. I barely had time to lift a glass of faerie wine to my lips or a chance to admire the sparkling silver and gold décor when a female soldier hurried up to Tor by my side.

"My lord," the fae whispered. "We found the group and have intercepted them."

"Did you take them to the outpost?"

"I'm sorry, my lord, but she refuses to go anywhere until she speaks with you personally."

"She? Who is *she?*"

"The leader. She claims . . ." She dropped her voice to a low whisper, but I still picked up her words. "She claims to be relation."

Saoirse must have heard, too, because her head whipped toward us, her eyes narrowing with suspicion.

"She was near the borders, but closer to here than to the Court of Shadows. She was specifically looking for you, my lord."

"I will go soon. I must—"

"I am sorry, sir, but it is urgent that you come. She was being followed. A band of Winter Court soldiers is closing in on her. If they come near our borders . . ."

Tor gave a curt nod. "Understood. Call the *Skaelach*."

He motioned to Saoirse, who unceremoniously disappeared.

"I am sorry to have to leave so abruptly," Tor said to me. "But again, feel free to stay for the party or return to your room—the choice is yours. I promise nobody will notice either of our absences." I doubted that but nodded. He gave my hand a quick squeeze, turned to leave, but then turned back once more. He leaned in close, his mouth by my ear, his breath cool on the sensitive flesh. "And you are wrong, Elliana. You could be very easy to love."

Scowling, I watched him and several others leave the party. That was one of my most protected secrets I shared with nobody, not even Brielle. How did he know?

I was glad he'd left. Because with a little too much faerie wine, I might have felt the urge to admit to him the same: he could be very easy for me to love.

One glance around the large room, I realized he was right —nobody paid much attention to his exit, everyone already drunk and oblivious. I returned to my room and out to the balcony to stew and pout under the full moon, but my attention was immediately diverted. Below, in the courtyard, Tor, Saoirse, and a whole company of fae were gathered, almost everyone mounted on various types of creatures, some with wings, some not, including a couple of gryphons. A few of the creatures looked quite similar to Sasha, which surprised me, since she was an angelic being and not of Faery. Many of the fae sprouted their own wings, some thin and colorful, like those of butterflies, and others gauzy with rainbow flashes, similar to those of dragonflies.

Tor and about half of the company—those who could fly —launched into the air and flew off toward the south, Tor leading them in a V-formation parallel to the mountain behind his home. My brows pulled together as I watched the prince, wondering if he was like my brother, able to fly without wings. Then I saw them, nothing more than dark smoke floating on the air, the stars shining through them: wings of shadow.

For some reason, as I watched, I felt as though my heart flew off with them.

A few minutes later, Saoirse led those on foot as they filed out of the courtyard through a side gate, slipping into the dark cover of night. As the tail end disappeared from my extensive sight range, an indescribable yet very real sensation tugged on my gut, so hard that the breath flew out of me.

"I need to go," I said aloud, my voice full of conviction. I couldn't explain it, but my intuition was practically shouting at me, shoving me off the balcony. I snapped my own wings out and not bothering to even change out of my dress, I took to the air, hurrying before I lost their trail.

I caught up to those on the ground quickly, slowing my speed so as not to alert Tor, whose group was much farther ahead. They were such small specks in the sky, they could have been birds or even bugs, only discernable because of the moon's bright light. When those on the ground rode into a forest and I lost sight of them under the trees, I had no choice but to catch up a little closer to the airborne company, so I didn't lose track of them, too. We banked to the left and lifted up, over the mountain, and the farther we flew, I began to wonder why they hadn't sifted—though I couldn't be sure all fae had that ability. Something I'd failed to ask.

Below us, Saoirse exited a tunnel in the mountain, leading the ground troops across a narrow valley before they entered into another tunnel, the rear end of the group yet to emerge from the first. Tor's flyers tilted up to clear the next mountain, but when they passed over the peak, they disappeared completely.

"What the hell?" I muttered. I'd lost sight of them altogether. Same with those on the ground. All I could do was keep flying and hope I caught up with Saoirse's company when they came out the other side.

As I crested the mountaintop, though, magic zinged over my body, and everything changed. A portal—we'd crossed through some kind of fae portal.

And on the other side was a snow-covered field, a small battle raging in the bright light of a huge, full moon.

Tor's group dropped to the ground, merging with Saoirse's as they appeared seemingly out of nowhere, and they all joined in the battle.

Knowing I could be easily seen now, I conjured an invisibility cloak as best as I could to hide myself. I was no Charleigh, though, and lacked her more powerful cloaking magic. I knew Tor could spot me, and perhaps Saoirse, too. Hopefully none of the others were as powerful as them to see through it. Not that it really mattered. What could they do about me now?

I circled the battle, searching for Maeve, though I didn't expect her to actually be here. It depended on her motive, though. I didn't know why Winter Court had attacked the elves. I knew Maeve hated them, and her brother probably did, too, but I didn't think they were still actively at war. Tor's man had blamed Maeve for this—not her brother, the king—which had made it feel personal to me, but I honestly couldn't fathom why. After all, if it was about me, why didn't she just attack the Shadow Lands?

I didn't see or sense Maeve anywhere, but I did notice two

figures engaged off to the side from the rest of the battle. One wore a cloak, a pale green that looked almost silver in the moonlight, a quiver of arrows and an unused bow slung over his back, and a deep hood hiding the warrior's face. The other was a female fae dressed in blue and silver armor with Winter Court's runes marked all over it. They were both skillful sword fighters holding their own, and I began to circle away when there was a shout and what sounded almost like a sonic boom. When I turned back, the Winter fae lay on the ground, a large crack in the ground between them.

Then a dozen Winter soldiers swarmed on the cloaked figure.

I looked over at the others, Tor, Saoirse, and all of the Shadow fae fighting with more Winter troops. I was closest. But did I want to get involved? When a scream came from below me, that same sensation that jerked me off the balcony tugged me downward. My intuition once again taking control.

Releasing my sword into one hand and a throwing star in the other, I dropped in front of the cloaked warrior, who lay prone on the ground, Winter surrounding him. Whipping weapons and magic, I fought as they turned their attention to me. One down. Two now. Another ran away. Numbers four and five tried to take me at the same time, but I easily parried their blows and blasted them with fire, melting the snow around them. They ran, too, but then three more attacked at once. They were stronger than any of the others and used their own magic to block mine.

A sword swung out, carving a shallow gash below my ribs, and I shouted in anger before stabbing him in the neck. My flesh began to heal immediately, but the other two pounced before I could free my weapon from the first one's throat. Calling on my air magic, I created a tornado of snow and ice around one, blinding him. The other, though, circled my throat with large hands and squeezed. I kicked out, landing a hard blow to the groin, but the armor protected him while sharp pain shot through my foot. He lifted me into the air, and taking advantage of it, I beat my wings, trying to free myself from his grasp.

Then suddenly he was shouting, releasing me to clutch at his own head, falling to his knees. The others around us did the same, blood pouring from their eyes and ears, dripping crimson in the white snow. The screaming was horrific, blood-curdling, nightmarish . . . and then over. Silence falling as the battle ended.

The only sound that could be heard were Tor's warriors dropping their weapons to their sides. I looked up at them, standing several yards away among a half dozen dead bodies, him glaring at me with hard silver eyes. I shook my head. That hadn't been me.

Then came the only other sound from behind me. A familiar female voice. One I thought I might never hear again.

"Elli?"

CHAPTER 20

I whirled around, my breath hitching. The cloaked warrior was not a male but a woman. She stood in the snow, her hood thrown back, revealing long blond hair and electric blue eyes. Oh, those electric blues that I missed so much, that had haunted my good dreams that snuck in between the nightmares.

"Sadie?" I choked out, and I immediately burst into a run. She ran for me, too, and we crashed into each other's arms, falling into the snow. "Is it really you?"

She grinned at me. "Is it really *you*?" Her gaze seemed to be drinking in my face as her fingers reached for my wing. "It is. It's really you," she whispered, and I nearly came undone at her touch. My wings began to curl in around us until—

I remembered we weren't alone.

Springing to my feet, I turned back toward the others, and when I saw Tor watching us with a bewildered expression, my whole body froze. *Shit. Fuck. Damn.* Well, this certainly complicated things.

"Do you know each other?" Tor asked, suspicion clear in his tone.

"She's—yeah, from school," I said, knowing how lame it

sounded and not at all the full picture. I hurriedly added, speaking too fast, "We knew each other in school. In the earthly realm. Well, a different earthly realm than mine, where I was when we had to escape and hide. Well, you know, I told you all that." I clamped my mouth shut as his brow raised a notch higher with each word.

During one of those evenings on the balcony after dinner, I'd divulged to him where Brielle and I had been when we'd "disappeared" and his father couldn't find me. It would be impossible for him to figure out exactly which earthly realm we'd been in unless he found Dorian's gate, and there was a fat chance of that because Dorian kept that very well hidden. Not even the Daemoni knew where it was. I had to give Dorian credit for that, at least. Still, I needn't say more than necessary. Especially not now, with Sadie in the picture. I had no idea what this meant, but I wasn't stupid enough to think it changed a damn thing. In fact, it would be best if nobody knew about her and me, our relationship. It would only endanger her, too.

"And you are . . . ?" Tor prompted, turning his attention to Sadie, who'd risen to her feet next to me.

"Princess Sareirdre Angrec," she said, and I turned slightly toward her, still unable to believe she was here, that I was really seeing her next to me. She sounded so different, stating her full title and name with an accent I'd never heard from her before.

"Angrec?" Familiarity filled the prince's tone. "As in King Angrec."

"Yes, he is my father." Sadie's gaze flickered over the other soldiers—mostly Tor's but a couple of elves, too—before coming back to Tor's face. She tilted her head and gave him a significant look, sending him an unspoken message. "I've been sent to seek an alliance. The queen, my mother, specified I speak with you and only you."

Saoirse stood just behind Tor, watching Sadie closely. As

they stood so closely together, I saw the resemblance for the first time, even as their coloring returned to normal. They had the same black hair, and although their eyes were different colors, they had the exact same slant; all fae's eyes tilted up to some degree, but the angle of theirs was identical. More than that were their noses and chins. The cut of their cheek bones didn't match, and their lips were different, too—Tor's full and Saoirse's uneven, the bottom full but the top thin—so I'd never really noticed before. And then I looked at Sadie, her lips like Tor's, her nose like both of theirs . . . The fae earlier had told Tor that Sadie claimed relation. She'd once told me that she suspected her father was not actually her father.

Holy shit. I tried to keep the realization to myself, because it was not my secret to divulge, but—fuck. What did this mean?

Tor lifted his chin as he strode toward us, studying Sadie's face carefully. I wondered if he saw the similarities like I did.

He looked over his shoulder at Saoirse. "I'll take care of these two. You lead the others back."

She gave him a curt nod, then turned toward the troops, lifting her hand and twirling a finger in some kind of signal. What it meant I didn't know, because Tor wrapped his arms around both Sadie and me and sifted us away.

We appeared in his office at the Court of Souls, and he immediately rounded on Sadie.

"Explain," he demanded. His voice was calm, but I could feel his dark energy swirling just under the surface.

Sadie looked at me with those electric blues, and I swore she was trying to tell me something, but then she turned back to Tor. "My father requests an alliance with the Shadow fae. A . . . permanent one."

Tor's slanted brow rose. "I see. But you came to me and not the king?"

She nodded. "As I said, my mother insisted that I see you first. She believes that you would understand . . . that you would . . . that she knows . . ." She stammered under Tor's commanding gaze, wringing her hands together. "Um, oh—" She swore something in Faelic or perhaps Elf, which made Tor chuckle. She looked up at him in surprise, as did I. His features had softened somewhat, which must have been enough for Sadie to relax to spit out her truth. "I cannot align with anyone in your family permanently, because I am part of your family. The Shadow king . . . my mother . . . he . . . he forced—"

Tor lifted his hand, stopping her. "You needn't say more. I remember meeting your mother at the Court of Shadows many years ago. The Elven king showing off his newest bride, so bright and fresh. Of course, my father couldn't allow her to leave unsullied." He shook his head, his sorrow clear in his eyes, the downward turn of his mouth. "Your mother was right to send you to me. I've been looking for my half-sisters and had suspected I had one in the Elven Lands."

Sadie heaved a sigh of relief, her shoulders dropping and her whole demeanor changing. She gave him a tentative smile. "I'm Sadie. It's nice to meet you, brother." Then she added under her breath, "I hope."

Tor rubbed a hand over his face. "It is late. You have been traveling for days, from what I understand."

"The Shadow Lands are not easy to find," Sadie replied.

"For a reason," he said. "I will provide you a room for tonight. You will need to meet with me and my council in the morning and explain everything you know. They can be trusted. Whether the same can be said about you is yet to be determined."

Sadie dipped her head. "I understand."

"Saoirse will show you to your room."

As though she'd been standing right outside the door— which of course she had been—the female fae threw it open and hurried Sadie out. I turned, a million things to say to her and not knowing when or if I would see her again, but Tor stopped me by magically shutting the door in my face.

"Do you know her well?" he asked me.

I gnawed on my lip while staring at the door for a long moment, deciding what to tell him—and what he didn't need to know—before turning back to him. "I do. We were . . . close. I thought I'd never see her again."

"Do you trust her?"

"With my life," I replied with no hesitation, then, remembering what he'd once said, I added, "And with my secrets. She knows things about me that not even my twin does."

One side of his mouth tilted upward as he nodded slowly, processing this. "Thank you. That means a lot."

"Yes, it does," I agreed. "It means everything to me." I left it at that.

Brielle was the other half of my very soul. I wished I could say we shared everything, but there were some things I couldn't admit to her out of fear of what she'd think about me. I had shared some of these secrets with Sadie, though. I didn't know if that meant I didn't care what she thought about me—which didn't feel right—or if I just knew in my heart and soul she wouldn't judge me. I did know that she hadn't told a single person. At least, not at school. If she had, it would definitely had gotten back to Brielle or Charleigh, who would have been all over me about it.

"You will not seek her out tonight," Tor said, making me rankle. He must have sensed the change in my energy because he lifted a finger. "I know you trust her, which already leads me halfway there. But I ask that you honor my request. I must know more myself and so does my council. If she passes our inquiry in the morning, which I believe she will based on *your* word, then you can see her after. I imagine you have much catching up to do. You can give her the good news." He gave me a wicked smile.

I rolled my eyes. "Fine. But please don't make her leave without at least letting me say goodbye. It would mean a lot to me."

He nodded. "Very well. Good night, Elliana." His tone wasn't dismissive, but I got the message anyway. As I reached for the door, though, he added from behind me, "We'll discuss your blatant disobedience of my command later."

My spine stiffened, and I turned on him, seething. "My *disobedience*?"

"Or now," he muttered with a sigh. "I am the commander of the *Skaelach*, the Court of Souls army. I also command the Court of Shadows troops when my father so directs. As a warrior yourself, it is absolutely imperative you recognize that for all of our sakes."

My anger immediately dissipated. *Shit.* I hadn't even considered that—how I'd undermined him, what kind of message that sent to his men. I averted my eyes and apologized.

"What was that?" he asked.

"I'm sorry," I murmured.

"Still didn't catch it."

I looked up at him to find him grinning at me. The same grin that made my knees weak and my stomach dip when no other male had come close.

"Did Elliana Knight apologize to me? I shall write about this in my diary."

"Asshole," I snapped. His grin widened. "Wait. You keep a diary?"

"Well, someone will need material for my historical biography one of these . . . centuries, will they not?" The light tone remained, so I couldn't tell if he was being serious, arrogant, or teasing me.

"Good night, Tormentor," I said before walking out the door. I tried not to feel too guilty for throwing that nickname in his face, understanding now how much he hated it.

I couldn't possibly sleep, knowing Sadie Angrec was under the same roof as me once again. Every single cell ached to find her, to hold her in my arms, to feel her lips against mine, but I wouldn't jeopardize anything. I especially didn't want to put her at risk because I couldn't control my hormones. But holy hell. My Sadie was here.

Here, at the Court of Souls. Here in the Shadow Lands. Where I'd already made a deal to marry a prince—and one I thought I could, in time, actually love.

But could I now? Knowing Sadie was just in reach? I couldn't be with her. I knew that. Not if I wanted to keep my deal and protect my sister and the rest of my family. Could I overcome my feelings for someone who was very real when I thought she'd only be a nice memory and fall in love with Tor?

I did believe he could make it so easy.

If it weren't for Sadie.

"Argh," I groaned aloud as I rolled over for the hundredth time, my mind and emotions chasing each other in circles. Never would I have thought I'd be in such a predicament. Of course, the smart thing to do—the best thing for them both— was to send Sadie away and keep Tor at arm's length. Otherwise, it was only a matter of time before I broke them both.

At some point I dozed off, just long enough for the sun to rise.

"Of course, the day I can't work with you is the day you decide to get up at a decent hour," Saoirse said when I entered the kitchen.

"Like you're ever up at this hour," I snipped back as I poured a cup of tea. I missed coffee almost as much as my family, but that wasn't a thing here in the Shadow Lands.

"Only if I haven't gone to bed yet," she replied on a chuckle. "Except today. Off to find out who this mystery woman is and if she's truly my sister."

Tor must have talked to her after dismissing me. I wished I

could be a fly on the wall at the council meeting, but I meandered outside to not so patiently wait.

And wait.

And . . . fucking . . . wait.

"What the hell is taking so long?" I finally snapped out loud, thinking nobody was around.

"She went to change," Tor said from the doorway.

I jumped to my feet. "And . . . ?"

He seemed to drink me in, cocking his head as he did. "Something's different about you."

"What?" I shook my head. "Just tell me, will you?"

"Such demands of your prince." He gave me that crooked, one-sided smile. "Sadie will be staying with us. Indefinitely." I sucked my lips in, trying to suppress the huge grin that wanted to fill my face. He could tell, so he was sure to drop his teasing tone, his voice quiet and dangerous when he added, "Unless she gives me any reason to believe she is a threat to me, my people . . . or what is mine."

I swallowed, my throat going dry at how he said *mine,* then dipped my chin. "I understand." I peered back up at him. "What about her father's—the one who raised her—his desire for a, uh, permanent alliance with the Shadow Lands?"

He scowled. "That situation needs my attention. You'll be glad to know that our ceremony will be delayed for a bit now. I need to find out why Winter Court is suddenly so interested in starting war with the elves again and then figure out exactly how to appease both King Angrec and King Caellach while creating a new ally for my own cause."

"Sounds like . . . fun."

He chuckled, and a cruel gleam lit up his eyes. "The games of kings are always *wickedly* fun. Enjoy your time with your friend, Elliana, but Saoirse's been ordered to stay back just for you. Hopefully when I return, you'll finally be able to impress me. You have two weeks."

He turned and strode into the house as I flipped him off.

Two weeks. Two weeks with no Prince Toridhan to distract me and make me question everything about myself, including my own sexuality. Two weeks of Sadie Angrec, who was an even bigger distraction. Two weeks I never thought I would have with her—and two weeks to find a way to let her go. Again.

I had been watching through the open doorway as Tor's form retreated farther into the manor when movement from the other side of the room caught my attention. I turned as Sadie slowly walked toward me, pausing in the doorway as she gave me a tentative smile that didn't reach those big blue eyes.

"Elliana Knight," she said quietly.

"*Lady* Sareirdre Angrec," I replied just as quietly as I studied her face. I'd only seen it by the light of the moon and for a few, brief minutes in the dim light of Tor's study last night. I hadn't noticed how her cheek bones looked sharper now, her skin tone, usually a soft creamy hue, seemed awfully sallow, and purple smudges circled her eyes . . . and those eyes. An electric blue that always made my heart stop for just a moment had lost some of their spark. My brows drew together as I took in the rest of her—how thin she'd become. "You . . . are you okay?"

She looked away, toward the mountain face behind me, and lifted one shoulder in a half-shrug. Her voice remained low, barely more than a whisper. She sounded exhausted. "It hasn't been exactly easy since I returned to my world. I told you before about the expectations of me. When Winter Court attacked, it all became very real very fast." Her gaze came back to me. "It's been hell, Elli. And it's nowhere near over."

I stood there like an idiot, not knowing what to do. I wanted nothing more than to take her into my arms and tell her everything would be okay now, that we were together and nothing else mattered, but that would have been a lie. A huge, fat lie. We couldn't be together, and everything most definitely would not be okay.

She seemed to sense it, too, because she didn't come rushing toward me, either.

We stared at each other in awkward silence for a long time before I turned and walked over to the balustrade, staring at the mountain face but not really seeing it. She joined me, though remained several feet away.

"Where are Brielle and Charleigh?" she asked. "Are they okay?"

"I have no idea," I admitted, and I started to tell her the story but then stumbled when it came to the part about Winter Court.

"They held you prisoner?" she asked, her eyes wide. We'd moved inside by then, a cup of tea in front of each of us as we sat at the breakfast table by the kitchen's picture window. "I can't imagine how awful that was!"

I stared at my teacup, guilt squeezing its fist around my heart. It really hadn't been awful at all. Not where I had wanted to be, but nothing like, say, the Vault. But Maeve was her sworn enemy, had killed her brother.

"I'd rather not talk about it," I said, which was the truth. Maybe someday I would tell her about Maeve and me—if we were ever given the opportunity—but today was not that day.

She nodded. "I imagine you wouldn't. So how did you end up here?"

Shit. I didn't want to tell her about my deal either. I didn't want to hurt her. I didn't want what little time we had together to be so deep and heavy. I didn't want to put more strain between us, especially when everything already felt so strange. New and awkward, nothing like how we'd left things.

But that was a different world, literally. A whole different life, for both of us.

"Wait," she said before I even opened my mouth, "before you start, are there any flowers here?"

I blinked, caught off guard. "Flowers?"

She shrugged while her cheeks pinked—the most color I'd

seen in them yet. "Winter Court froze our lands when they attacked. I haven't seen a flower in weeks, and I'm craving some."

I laughed. That was so much more like my Sadie. "I know where we can find some."

Shrubs of various colors bordered the back veranda, but none of them were currently flowering, so I led Sadie around the side of the house, no fewer than five of Saoirse's men following us. An archway in the fence led to a park that was still within the city's walls—still within safety, in other words. I didn't know if we could go farther, such as to the falls over the giant steps Tor had originally brought me down when we came to the Court of Souls. Sadie and I were both wanted, and the Court's best men had left with their prince. And considering the mission they were on, I didn't want to jeopardize anything by pulling more protectors away from the city and the people just because we wanted to frolic in the woods. So to speak. Anyway, the park offered plenty of flowers for Sadie to choose from.

"Oh, gods, these are divine!" she mumbled around a mouthful of petals as she plucked another pink bloom from its stem. "Who would have thought the Shadow Lands could be so lovely? It's not at all like what everyone says, but I could seriously live here. Like right here, in this park. I'd sleep in that tree over there." She pointed to one of the largest specimens with low, wide branches, broad, velvety leaves, and flowers the color of her pale, full lips. "I could make clothes out of the leaves, and I wouldn't even have to leave it to eat. I would, though, at least to visit the other trees. See how the limbs are perfectly arranged? I could skip to each beautiful soul and never need to touch the ground for the rest of my days . . ." She drifted off, the last of her words growing quieter as shadows skimmed across her features, dimming the flicker of hope that had sparked in her eyes.

"You are such an elf right now," I teased, trying to hang

onto the moment a little longer as the corners of my mouth curled upward—perhaps my first real smile of joy since I had last seen her. That's what she did for me.

It didn't last long, though. The smile or the feeling. But it was enough to know that joy was still possible, making my heart feel a little lighter, life a little more bearable.

If only for the most fleeting of moments.

CHAPTER 21

*S*omehow, Sadie scarfing down flower after flower as though she hadn't eaten in a year—which she surely had as flowers were treats to the elves, but not sustenance—helped to bridge the chasm between us. It wasn't like it had been before, but I rediscovered that sense of comfort I'd always had with her. The reason I could tell her anything with no fears of how she'd react, what she would think of me. I wasn't ready to tell it all, but as we meandered through the park, I did spill everything about Shadow Vault Citadel and my deal with the king.

"Wow," she breathed. "We talked about the Vault at school, remember?"

I nodded. "I had no memory of it then."

"But you do now. Someone did something to you, Elli."

"I know."

"And now they've undone it?"

I shrugged. "I guess. I think . . . I think it was my brother. I just don't know if he put us there in the first place or if King Caellach did or someone else. But I've been thinking about it all and the timing and everything, and I think it was Dorian who made me start to remember. He broke the spell or something."

"Why? Why take your memories in the first place, and why give them back now?"

"So all of this could play out? To torture me with them?" I shrugged again, trying to conceal my flinch at the thought of those memories—especially the ones I hadn't shared with her yet. The ones I hadn't truly acknowledged for myself. "I honestly don't know."

"Well, at least you know why everyone wants you and that you have this badass power."

"You're one to talk," I said. My elbow jerked out to bump hers, but she was too far away, and for some reason, neither of us could quite close the remaining gap between us. Like we knew that it represented what we hadn't yet spoken aloud—what truly kept us apart as though an impenetrable wall stood between us rather than empty space. "What did you do to those Winter Court soldiers?"

She frowned. "Do you remember what I did when you were trapped in the mirrors?" I nodded, recalling the pile of rubble she'd created in the library, trying to get me out. "I can do that with minds, too."

"Whoa. You can make minds explode? Wait—can you do it to the Shadow king?"

"Something like that. Break them, anyway. Most elves can. Some of us are just stronger—but no, I'm positive I'm not strong enough for the minds of any fae royalty, but especially not King Caellach." She paused, gnawing on her lip. "Last night . . . that was the first time . . . I had never taken it so far before. I had never killed anyone until last night." Her last words came out as a near whisper, as though her remorse made them too heavy to lift with her voice.

Perhaps that was the change I had sensed—the change over her, over us. Neither of us were the same as when we'd been together before, just two college kids having the time of their lives. Maybe that was a good thing since we couldn't be together anymore.

"You did what needed to be done," I reassured.

"Oh, I know." She lifted her chin and looked out across the pond we had come to. Strings of faerie stones hung from some of the tree branches overhanging the banks, the sunlight catching in the crystals and throwing prisms across the water's still surface. "I'm sure it won't be the last time, and one day I'll probably get used to it."

My stomach dropped at that possibility. "Oh, Sadie, I hope you *never* get used to it."

Our gazes locked, and those electric blues were nearly overflowing with tears. She blinked them back, though, and looked away again. "I wish the same for both of us, Elli, but I would rather get used to killing if it means protecting those I love than get used to watching them die."

Her words felt like a dagger cutting into my very soul. I could one-hundred percent agree—but for me, not her. Not my Sadie, whose light was supposed to counteract my dark.

She must have seen something in my expression, because her eyes averted and her mouth turned down as she let out a sigh. "It's growing dark. We should probably get back."

The awkward tension between us continued throughout the evening and over the next couple of days, but we fell into a routine. Though I hated wasting any time Sadie and I might have had together, I was actually grateful when Saoirse insisted on training several hours every day. It helped with the nervous energy growing in my veins. However, when Sadie was anywhere close by, I only clamped down harder on my power. I knew she wasn't fragile—she could kill a man, no, a *fae*, with her mind—but I feared losing control and hurting her. And even if she could heal herself almost instantaneously, I would still never be able to forgive myself.

Without the prince home to be our personal gourmet chef, the three of us spent most evenings dining on the plaza. We enjoyed the live music, conversed with the locals, and shared drinks and delicacies with many whom Saoirse introduced as friends, which honestly surprised me—for some reason, I'd never expected her to have friends. No slaves, no judgment of others, no ongoing torment to suffer while simply trying to exist under a cruel king or in a post-apocalyptic world.

It felt a lot like what I imagined Heaven would be.

❦

"Do you know the story of Milano?" Saoirse asked as she danced around me one morning on the back lawn.

Turning with her, my sword held out in preparation for her attack, I shook my head. "Let me guess. It's a faerie tale?"

I smirked at my own joke, but the Shadow fae wasn't impressed, swinging her blade toward me. I blocked it with my own, spinning away from her.

"Milano was a fair fae, as they say. A princess of the Seelie Court, perfect in every way. Long blond locks that flowed down to her ass. Full pink lips and eyes the color of luscious grass."

"Very poetic," I quipped.

"She'd always lived a life of charm, sheltered away from any harm," Saoirse continued, circling me, blade held at the ready. "She was innocent as can be, you see. So when she met the male named Lect, she knew not quite what to expect. So fine he was, with a disarming grin, a powerful build, and a strong, chiseled chin. She failed to see the smoldering of his eyes, the glint of fire that brought others to their demise. Blind to the signals and warnings of witches, all she could see was the prodigious bulge in his britches." Saoirse winked at me. I pulled a face of disgust, but she went on.

"Milano's own thoughts seemed outlandish to one so pure, until Lect told her all he wished to do to her. His amatory whispers turned to kisses fluttering over her skin, and she gave

234

into the ravenous hunger growing within. His hands were adept at undoing her laces, and wandering down into warm, wet places. Her breath came fast as he lifted her skirt, but she cared not at all when he warned this might hurt. He spun her around, and she had no inkling what next would come. Then his fingers drove deep, as he clamped his teeth down on her bum!"

Saoirse fell silent, and I went still, no longer following her movements.

"What's the rest?" I asked when she didn't continue.

She shrugged. "Nothing. That was it."

My brows scrunched together for a moment. "Wait. Was that some kind of weird fae porn? Did you just tell me an erotic faerie tale?"

Saoirse rolled her eyes. "What I'm trying to tell you, you obstinate, argumentative child, is that if you remain blind to what's right in front of you, you're bound to get bit in the ass!"

And with that, she was suddenly directly behind me, pressing the point of her dagger against my butt cheek.

"Point taken," I said on a snicker, and I thought I might have actually made the warrior fae smile. "So tell me, wise one, what's right in front of me?"

She leaned in, her breath hot on my ear as she whispered, "If you look close enough, perhaps the answer to everything you want."

I stiffened, cutting a sideways glance at her face that was still so close to mine. Was Saoirse seriously hitting on me? Her gaze, though, was on the side yard, where Sadie held her bow up by her face, three arrows notched at once and aimed at a target mannequin. *Shit.* Had Saoirse figured us out? Did she know we had a past together? We'd been so careful to hide it, to pretend it had never happened, as much as that hurt. At least, it hurt me. I didn't know how Sadie felt anymore. That was how good she played the role—if she was even playing it. So what did Saoirse see?

The fae pulled back, her voice growing louder with each word as she added, "And by closer, I mean within. Your gods-damned power, Elli. You're looking everywhere outside of you for answers when they've always been right here." She pressed the tip of her dagger against my sternum.

Scowling, I pushed her hand away. "Point rejected. It's grown dull from overuse."

She heaved out an angry sigh. "Fine. Then don't expect your situation to change if you won't."

She stalked off with that, crossing the terrace with angry strides, and I released my own sigh. I was growing frustrated with myself, so I couldn't blame her, but I just didn't know how I could allow myself to release the lethal power within me without destroying everyone here.

Feeling a penetrating gaze on me, I looked up to see Sadie watching me. Well, not me, per se—more like my ass. She was totally checking me out! A delicious sensation curled down my spine and into my belly, and I dared to wink at her. Her cheeks blossomed in a pretty shade of pink, and she quickly looked away, focusing back on her archery. Except when she released the string . . . for the first time that day, every arrow completely missed the target, one so far off, it flew through the open terrace door. A second later came a crash from inside and Saoirse cussing up a storm. Sadie and I looked at each other with wide eyes, then we both burst out laughing.

I lay in bed that night alone and giggling out loud like a lunatic at the memory. My Sadie still wanted me as much as I wanted her. Did it make me a masochist to find pleasure in that when I knew nothing could ever come of it?

"I know what your problem is," she said the next afternoon after watching Saoirse and me once again in a literal power struggle on the back lawn. As usual, the Shadow fae kept attacking me in a myriad of ways, with her many different abilities, and as usual, I used my own various brands of magic to fight back, but never with the one power she tried so doggedly to provoke. But now we both stopped and turned toward the blond elf who sat on the steps of the veranda. Her long hair was arranged in an array of braids, her eyes brighter than they had been before but still not quite like they used to be, the rest of her coloring improving, as well.

"Well?" Saoirse prodded.

Tilting her head, Sadie trained her focus entirely on me, making me internally squirm as though she could she see right through me. "I always admired you because you embraced that dark side of yourself." I opened my mouth to argue, but she held up a hand. "You maintained control, yes, but you also used to accept it as part of yourself. You knew it was there, and you didn't deny it, any more than you do that birthmark—" She cut herself off, glancing at Saoirse, while my own stomach fluttered as I recalled her discovering it for the first time. The birthmark was on my hip, not anywhere sexual but also not easily seen by the casual friend. "But not now. You're in complete denial because you fear it so much."

"I keep telling her that," Saoirse chimed in.

Sadie stood and strode over to me, coming closer than we had yet. "You think it's evil."

"Well," I began. If she knew what I'd done, she'd know I was right.

She cut me off before I could go further. "But how can it be, if it's a part of *you*, Elliana?"

"Perhaps because *I'm* evil," I sniped, growing more uncomfortable by the second with the direction of this conversation.

Saoirse snorted. "You've met evil at the Court of Shadows. If you really believed you were, you'd have no problem wielding your full power like the king does, consequences be damned."

I frowned, unable to argue with that.

"You're not evil, so stop with that bullshit," Sadie added. "Just because you possess some really dark and powerful energy doesn't mean you're on the brink of becoming a murderous villainess."

If she knew the truth, though, she would know I already was.

"It doesn't matter if the energy is dark or light," she continued, her tone growing more impassioned, her hands moving in the air to accentuate her words. "It only matters how you use it. And I know that sounds trite, but it's true. It's just power, no different than your angel magic or sorcery magic or fae magic. You don't judge those, do you? But for some reason, you've led yourself to believe that dark energy means evil and can't be anything else. You try to separate it out rather than accept that it's simply part of you. A part of you that I—" She stopped herself again with another flicker of those eyes toward Saoirse before returning them back to me. "A part of you that's just as incredible as the rest of you. And because of that—it can't possibly be evil."

While Sadie and I held each other's eyes, I could feel Saoirse's gaze bouncing between the two of us. Her own energy shifted a degree, and I was pretty sure she'd just figured out that Sadie and I had been more than friends. Or, at least, confirmed it in her mind. She didn't acknowledge it, though, not out loud. I wondered if she'd tell Tor.

"That's all well and good and not much different than what I've been saying," Saoirse said, dropping her hands to her hips, "though you do seem to have a better understanding of our girl Elliana here." She let that hang for a moment, confirming that she did know about us, before continuing. "But what ideas do you have to overcome it?"

Sadie's eyes glinted as they still held mine. "You learn to use it like you do your other magic—small bits here and there integrated with your other powers." She broke our hold and turned to Saoirse. "You may or may not have noticed that Elli naturally and expertly combines her various types of magic into her own unique brand. Take her wings—they're feathery like angel wings, but when she needs them to be a weapon, those feathers harden into double-edged blades—that's demon or sorcery magic at work." She glanced at me when I frowned at the word *demon*, and I could practically hear a finger shaking at me. "Don't even get that way with me. That's exactly what I mean when I say it's a part of you—*you* make it what it is." She looked back at Saoirse. "Now take her fire ability. You can tell by its properties and the way it behaves that it's fae elemental magic versus sorcery, right? But she uses her sorcery magic to control and wield it."

"No, I don't," I argued. "I just do what feels right with it."

"Exactly," Sadie said pointedly.

"She's right," Saoirse said. "You don't wield fire magic like fae do. Go on. How do we overcome her fear and hatred for her own power?"

"You take a little bit of this and a little bit of that, and you don't even realize you're doing it, right? It's just part of you," Sadie said to me. "So you do the same with that oh-so-dark-and-scary power of yours. Instead of putting all of your focus on it, separating it out even more from the rest of you, bring it into the mix. Add it in to your other magic, just a little at a time until you figure out how to use it as you need to, when you need to."

Saoirse tapped a finger against her chin. "It makes sense. You're obviously too scared to open the floodgates completely, unless you're really pissed off, but that's not control. So maybe you just slide it open enough for a trickle at first."

"Yes." Sadie nodded. "Just enough to boost your other magic. Learn how it works together, what you can do with it."

I gnawed on my lip. It could work—in theory. But my beast inside was already pacing, and I couldn't tell if she liked the idea or hated it. *There's only one way to find out.* Sadie was right. I needed to stop treating my beast as a separate part of me and learn to become one with her. After all, wasn't that what shifters did? Weren't the human and the animal two sides of the same soul? My beast sat on her haunches within her cage, and I could *feel* her cock her head and twitch her ears forward at this thought. Sadie had no idea just how right she'd been about mixing all the different parts of me, including the shifter blood.

The mixed DNA of the Amadis bloodline went back to Ancient Greece, to Cassandra, the first matriarch, and her twin brother, Jordan, who became leader of the Daemoni. He'd been the one to first sully our angel blood with that of various creatures, and the results continued down the line, but my parents, each in different ways, were the products of a new mix. Each more powerful than anybody before them, greater than the sum of their parts. And then together they created us —Dorian, Brielle, and me. Perhaps it was this more intense concoction or maybe because of the circumstances of our conceptions and births and lives, but we did, indeed, have our own brands of magic. Together, as siblings, but even as individuals.

At least, Brielle and I did. I didn't know much about Dorian.

Brielle leaned more heavily on witch and fae magic, tapping into the energies of nature and earth, blending her angel magic with it to create spells and potions or to manipulate energy around her. She was trained to defend herself, but she preferred being on the sidelines, strategizing and manifesting behind the scenes, using her brain to help on the fringe and stay out of the fray. I, on the other hand, relied heavily on whatever powers I could use offensively and defensively. I wanted to be *in* the fight, protecting those who needed it, taking down those who deserved it.

If this dark power within me—what I'd always referred to as Darkness with a capital D or as my beast—could be useful in that way, without killing everyone within a half-mile radius around me, then why wouldn't I want to learn to use it? Why wouldn't I want to meld with it instead of pushing it away?

My dad's voice popped into my mind, repeating what he'd taught us countless times over the years during our Aikido lessons: "*Move with the energy, my little warriors. Be like a palm tree in a hurricane, bending in the wind but never breaking. A warrior who stands tall and resists the oncoming force will snap. One who moves with it, adapting and blending the energy into her own, gains control and eventually victory.*"

As though relieved that I'd finally made that connection, my beast purred, lay down, and rolled over, exposing her belly.

I supposed that was my answer.

"I guess we can try," I said, hesitantly. But first—

"One thing, though," Saoirse said. "Do you think you can learn to forgive yourself?"

"You will have to face your truths," Sadie added. "Head on. No turning away from them anymore."

But first . . . I had to accept every part of me, fully and completely, including the past.

I nodded in agreement.

And then I ran.

CHAPTER 22

I rounded the corner of the manor, originally headed for the park, seeking peace and solitude, but then the sounds of the plaza called to me. Late afternoon meant the cafes were preparing for the dinner crowd, and fae were finishing their shopping and other business for the day, others joining them for a shared meal before going home.

After crossing the side lawn, I slowed, passing through the courtyard to the archway that led into the business part of town. The sun was setting behind the mountain, washing that end-of-day golden light over the white marble buildings and cobblestone pavers. Some of the domes of the surrounding buildings were already glowing in blues, pinks, purples, greens, and yellows. The fountain in the center grabbed my attention, and I stared at it for a moment, the cascading water twinkling as it caught the colored lights before pooling in the basin. A couple of faelings chased each other around it in a game that had their heads thrown back and their little pointed ears wiggling in laughter. Other fae were gathered in small groups, chatting about their days, I presumed, as they waited while the musicians set up for the evening's entertainment.

The whole scene was breathtaking and magical.

If I'd come upon it before being whisked away to the shiny world, I would have thought it impossibly magical and surreal. But except for the architecture and all the pointy ears, it wasn't all that different from any other town. Even in our own dark, war-torn world, the days ended similarly with a gathering of family and community for a shared meal and conversation as everyone wound down for the night. Funny how across the dimensions, we were all much more alike than we were different.

A few of the nearby fae saw me enter the plaza and gave a small wave, while others smiled shyly before turning away . . . and a handful still watched me with guarded expressions, even after all the time we'd spent with them in the evenings.

The engagement ball hadn't gone as planned, meaning not everyone was won over by the idea of the prince marrying an outsider on the king's demand. Most, however, seemed to have adopted the view that if the prince himself was happy—and they fully believed he wouldn't have brought me here if this wasn't what he wanted—then they were happy. They owed him so much. He deserved a good wife, they said.

A good wife.

As if.

My pace was slow as I started to circle the plaza. I didn't know what I thought I would find here. Escape, I supposed. Escape from what needed to be done. But as the shop owners greeted me and the cafe servers invited me in for dinner, it became clear that this was not an escape. This was reinforcement. Because these people—these fae—they would be my people. In some ways, they already were.

While my life would not play out the way I would prefer —namely with Sadie on my arm, not the sexy prince—I could easily make this place my home. These could easily be my people. It was even easier to fall in love with them than with Tor.

Which meant I needed to protect them. I needed to ensure

they didn't unintentionally become like those of another town in a far away land.

"I told you she would come to her senses." Sadie's voice floated over to me as I approached the last bistro, the one closest to the manor, on the far side of the circle from where I'd started. She and Saoirse sat at an outdoor table, a wine glass in front of each of them and a third at the empty chair, waiting for me. I swallowed it in one gulp while still standing.

"Are you ready to face your fears?" Saoirse asked, her purple eyes studying me as I finally sat.

I shrugged. "It's time."

"We can help," Sadie said. "We can be there with you. You don't have to do it alone."

My head cocked. "What do you mean?"

"You're part fae," Saoirse said, always having to remind me. "We have the ability to project our thoughts and memories to others."

That's right. I remembered my grandmother telling us about this ability. Our mother had also told us the story about the trials and tribulations she and Dad had faced to be together, including an actual trial with testimony from our fae grandmother who did just that—shared her memories with the entire courtroom.

Homesickness washed over me with the memory, a waterfall crashing through me. I felt like I was drowning as heartache burst in my chest and gut. My hand pressed against my heart, as though ensuring it was still there because it suddenly felt ripped out of me as my sister's and my parents' faces danced on the outside of my vision. Oh, how I missed them! Oh, how I ached for them! How long had it even been? I didn't know. Time meant nothing anymore. I just knew I didn't want to do this without them. Especially not without Brielle, who'd been there, who would understand more than anyone.

Or would she?

Sure, she'd been present, but had her experiences been the same? Had her emotions and intent matched mine? Or had she watched in horror as her twin allowed the Darkness to win? She was the good daughter. She was driven to make the world better by serving with her heart and mind and soul. I couldn't fathom the idea of her giving in to the Darkness. Yes, it still resided within her as it did me, and yes, I'd seen her lose control. And I'd also witnessed how harshly she had judged herself for it. How harshly she had judged me when she thought I was to blame.

Maybe she wouldn't understand. Maybe, when the memories all came back to her, too, she would. Right now, I couldn't possibly know because she wasn't here. And a large part of me didn't want to—didn't want my quiet, softhearted sister to know the horrors we'd survived, let alone about my contribution to it all. So it was probably a good thing she wasn't here.

And that Sadie was.

"You'll probably want a couple more of these first," Saoirse said, pushing a refilled glass of wine toward me.

After a meal I hardly touched and a few more glasses of faerie wine, the three of us returned to the manor and changed out of our fighting leathers and into comfortable sleepwear of silk pants and tops of the softest cotton-like material I'd ever felt. We sat on colorful, oversized pillows in the middle of the sitting room, a fire crackling in the hearth. The only other light came from dozens of candles scattered around the room and several arranged in the space between us. Crystals and faerie stones were also laid out carefully, and Saoirse painted our skin with fae runes representing strength, insight, and other virtues we may need to call on. Using my mage magic, I'd already called on the four directions and the four elements to create a circle of protection. We were bathed in magical energy, making Saoirse's natural fae markings glow and Sadie's . . .

"I've never noticed that before," I murmured, brushing my fingers over her cheekbone, where her skin was raised in intricate swirls and whorls not unlike fae markings.

"You're avoiding," Saoirse accused impatiently. She'd thought all of this was unnecessary, but she'd only had a small glimpse while dream-walking in my head. She didn't know everything, and a part of me feared how we'd all react—how much hatred may bloom that Saoirse would consume. That could be helpful for Sadie and me, unless the Shadow fae lost control of her own power and came to the same conclusion as Maeve's brother and others—that I shouldn't exist and needed to be eliminated. "Yasta. Let's be done with this already."

She reached for my and Sadie's hands, and when Sadie's and my palms pressed together, an electric energy zapped between us. Our gazes locked, and a knowing light filled her eyes, but she shook her head. *Later*, she seemed to say, the word almost as clear in my head as my mother's would be when she used her telepathy.

Saoirse, whose fae blood flowed most strongly of the three of us, instructed us to close our eyes, and she led the way into my mind, guiding me to open it and find the truths we sought. The room around us vanished, and we appeared in a forest, three teenaged girls sprinting around the trees ahead of us.

"Brielle, hurry your ass up," I called over my shoulder as we chased the demon through the woods. "We're losing it!"

She lagged behind Charleigh and me not because she couldn't physically keep up, but because we'd already passed through the protective wards of the Loft, leaving the safety of the shield a few hundred yards back. Which meant we'd broken our word to our dad when he'd allowed us to help Charleigh forage today while he and Mom were at Amadis Island on the other side of the world. Technically, we'd already broken his word when we didn't wait for Sasha, who had left long before we did for her early morning hunt, and had left without our loyal guardian. Brie cared a lot more about those technicalities than I did.

I just wanted to kill this demon that had come too close to the Loft, as far as I was concerned, making it a serious threat to our people. I may have also wanted to prove to my mom that I deserved to be on her demon assassination squad.

The demon seemed to be taunting us, darting in and out of the forest, flying up above the tree canopy and then dropping down in plain sight to run on cloven hooves, always staying just out of reach of our weapons. The colors of its oily, mottled skin flickered with various hues, sometimes blending in with the trees in greens, browns, and grays, and other times shining a bright yellow or orange.

"Screw this," I muttered under my breath as I pulled out a silver throwing star. It probably wasn't enough to end the beast's existence here on Earth, but the silver might at least slow it down. As soon as I flicked the star, though, the demon soared beyond the trees and didn't come back. I slowed to a jog, knowing we'd lost it. "This sucks balls! If we'd only come into our powers by now or at least had our wings, we could have taken it down and killed it already!"

"But since you don't, if we do catch it, what then?" Charleigh asked from my side, the August sun filtering through the leaves setting her orange hair on fire.

I gave her a wicked smile. "You kill it, of course. After Brie and I take it down."

Charleigh's magic was powerful enough to send the beast back to Hell, where it belonged. But not today. We came to the edge of a ravine, the demon flying out of sight. I stopped abruptly, feeling the need to punch something.

"Fucking demons," I growled, hating the taste of failure in my mouth. "One of these days, I swear to the angels, I'll annihilate them all!"

I turned in a circle, peering as far as I could see in every direction, trying to catch a glimpse of where the demon might have gone. I hoped maybe it was still taunting us, but it seemed we'd lost it for good.

"Can we go back to the Loft now?" Brielle asked. "I promised I'd help clean the medical ward."

Sheesh. My sister, the goodie two-shoes. We'd been out here today to help Charleigh with her chores. Now Brielle couldn't wait to do someone else's. I was sure she also itched to get back inside the wards as quickly as possible. Our sixteenth birthday was in two days, and she took Dad seriously that we wouldn't see it if we broke our promise to stay within the shield.

"You know, you volunteer way too much. You deserve a break. You already do more than your fair share of work," I said.

"Well, someone has to do yours, don't they?" she retorted.

"The sun will be setting soon," Charleigh chimed in to prevent an argument before it started. She bumped her shoulder against mine. "And when you get back, you can finally talk to your parents."

I frowned. "They have more important things to worry about."

Brielle opened her mouth, surely to argue, but then a twig snapped not too far in the distance, and we all went still and silent. Thinking the demon was back, I grinned before spinning on my heel to the right and taking off again.

And nearly ran into a pack of zombies.

Mom and Aunt Vanessa's sperm donor had created what was probably the most unnatural part of everything in our world, which was saying a lot. He'd mashed up a highly contagious virus with necromancy black magic and spread it at the beginning of the war. Whether he had any idea it would continue to infect humans seventeen years later, nobody knew, but pretty much every *human who died reanimated with a craving for flesh worse than a newborn vampire's thirst for blood.*

The demon's odor of brimstone and sulfur must have masked the stench of this herd, the only explanation for why we hadn't smelled the decaying bodies before. All three of us unsheathed our weapons, fell into formation, and went to work at cutting them down, making them dead-dead. We were almost through the pack when I fought with a half-corpse dragging itself on the ground by its hands, its teeth snapping at me. It nearly bit me because I was all caught up in the hot-pink roots of a young colata *tree that were lifting out of the ground, encircling my legs and growing upward for my waist. I gritted my teeth as needle-like spikes pushed out of the tentacles, pressing into my leathers, poking my skin. At least this was just a sapling. In a year or so, those spikes would be venomous flesh-eating teeth. It took both my sister's sword and Charleigh's magic to kill the thing and free me.*

"So now can we go back?" Brielle asked, offering me a hand to help me to my feet.

Taking it, I sighed. "Yeah, I guess."

Passing the pile of zombie corpses, we began making the trek back toward the Loft, walking rather than running now.

"So would you rather be bitten by a zombie or a colata*?" Brielle asked, starting one of our favorite games to pass the time.*

"Colata," Charleigh and I both answered easily.

"Faster death," I added.

"I don't know," Brielle said thoughtfully. "If you were bitten by a zombie, I'd put you out quickly. Wouldn't want you developing a taste for me."

I snorted. "So you've said a hundred times, but whether you could do it or not is another story. I'd be eating your brains before you finished listing out the pros and cons."

They giggled, but we all knew her hesitation would be more than that. I hated the thought of ever having to give her a merciful death, and I knew she'd struggle with it even more.

"*Would you rather* eat *a* colata *or zombie flesh?*" *I asked to lighten the mood.*

"*Gross, Elli,*" *Charleigh said, gagging.* "*I just threw up a little in my mouth.*"

Brielle only laughed. "*Colata. At least it's alive.*"

I nodded. "*Good point.*"

"*So . . .*" *Charleigh poked her elbow into my ribs.* "*Would you rather tell your parents or be kissed by Corbin Morty?*"

"*Ew!*" *Brielle and I groaned. The thought of kissing the greasy-haired new kid—*

"*Now I just threw up in my mouth,*" *I said.*

Charleigh laughed. "*I'm sorry. That was a bad one.*"

"*Would you rather tell Mom and Dad or I tell them?*" *Brielle asked, the teasing gone from her tone.*

"*Brielle,*" *I gasped, feeling like I'd been punched in the gut. She and Charleigh were the only souls I'd ever told about my sexuality and Charleigh only in the last few months. Brie had known for years. How could she threaten this?*

"*I'm sorry, Elli,*" *she said,* "*but it's nearly impossible to keep this secret from Mom and Dad any longer, especially Mom. I'm pretty sure she already knows, and if I'm too relaxed and she decides to confirm with a peek into my head . . .*"

"*It's my secret to tell,*" *I said quietly.*

Her hand squeezed my forearm. "*I know,*" *she said as quietly.* "*Consider it an offer, if you think it would help. Until you decide, I promise I'll still keep it to the best of my ability. I have this long, right?*" *She paused, waiting until I acknowledged her with a nod.* "*But seriously, El, you need to tell them. I'm one hundred percent sure they'd want to know and one thousand percent sure they won't be mad or sad or anything but happy. I mean, Mom might be hurt because you hadn't told her sooner, which is why you just need to do it.*"

I knew she was right—about their reaction and also that Mom already knew. She'd given all the indications not too long ago in an attempted heart-to-heart. But I hadn't been able to open up. I honestly didn't know why. Probably because I hated disappointing them, especially Dad, even though it seemed like that was all I knew how to do.

"Fine," I finally said. "I will. Soon."

"Promise?" Charleigh asked, and we all stopped when she held up her hands with the first two fingers of each raised, as though giving us the peace sign.

I blew out a heavy breath, then held my hands up the same way, pressing two fingers against Charleigh's and holding the other hand out to Brielle. She joined us, pressing her fingers to each of ours.

"Promise," I said, and I knew I'd have to keep it. This had been our way of making unbreakable vows to each other since we were little. Aunt Blossom said they used to do pinky swears when she was young, and Aunt Vanessa had told us all about blood promises, but being a vampire, she loved to talk about anything bloody. We did this. We used to pretend magic bound us to the promise. Now, Charleigh could make that a reality, but we chose to trust each other instead. Our bond as family—by blood and by choice—was stronger than any magic anyway.

We walked in silence for a few minutes when an odd sensation tugged at me as though a fishhook had lodged in my gut and was reeling me in.

"This way," I murmured aloud, abruptly turning to the right. "We have to go this way."

Unable to stop myself, I broke into another sprint. Surprisingly, Brielle ran after me. She must have known I wasn't chasing a demon this time. She must have felt what I had. A compulsive need to go this way. There was something here. Something we needed to find. I ran harder, Brie right on my heels.

When we charged into a clearing, the energy shifted, and I came to a sudden halt, Brielle crashing into me. As we collided, a force rocked through me, radiating from deep within and outward. Then the air itself seemed to explode, knocking us to the ground. We climbed to our feet, looking around. Though shaken, I felt as though this was exactly where I needed to be, but it was nothing more than an unremarkable small clearing.

"You feel that, right?" I asked quietly, to be sure I wasn't imagining things.

"What is it?" she whispered back.

I had no answer. Our backs to each other and our hands clasped tightly together, we turned in a circle. The trees around us appeared to be thicker, closer together than I'd realized while we'd been running. The clearing itself was only about six feet in diameter, black tree trunks creating a perfect circle—except for one place where it protruded to make it more egg-shaped than round. And right in the middle of that place, as though hanging in the air, was what appeared to be a portal, the space beyond it dark. Very . . . fucking . . . Dark.

Without thought, I grabbed Brielle's wrist and took a step toward it, as though my feet moved on their own. She balked and debated, and even Charleigh protested, but in the end, neither Brielle nor I could fight the pull as it once again strengthened. Our pace quickened.

"Do you feel it?" I asked, hearing a touch of fear in my own voice. Then realization hit me. "Oh! I know where we are!"

Brielle's eyes widened. "Me—"

She screamed, the sound one of agony. At the same time, I felt as though a knife carved over my shoulders and down my back. We both fell to the ground, writhing in agony.

"What's happening?" Charleigh yelled, panic filling her voice.

"Get . . . help," Brielle gasped. Charleigh disappeared, the only one of us able to flash since Brie and I hadn't come into our powers yet.

I could only hope we lasted long enough for her to return with help, both of our backs arching up and down as though our spines tried to escape the pain.

"What. The. HELL?" I screamed as another wave shot through me, feeling like every bone in my upper torso was *breaking and reforming. Like my skin was stretching beyond its limits and then shredding apart. Like something was carving me from the inside out.*

Then with a terrifying ripping sound, two huge, dark appendages sprang from Brielle's back. I felt the explosion through my own flesh. And just as suddenly as the pain had come, it was gone.

"Holy . . . shit," I gasped. "Our wings."

One moment we stood there, marveling at them, and the next, we were both suddenly at the portal, reaching into it.

And then everything went black.

I didn't know how long I'd been out, but I came to in a small cell made of three stone walls, the fourth consisting of metal bars.

CHAPTER 23

I had forgotten all about the would-you-rather game the three of us used to play all the time. We'd never played it again after waking from the supposed coma. Now I knew why.

I still didn't know how we ended up at Shadow Vault Citadel. The world beyond our gate was definitely not the Vault, but somehow it had led us to the pocket realm of the supernatural prison. Which meant it had been my fault we landed there from the beginning.

If I had never insisted on chasing that demon, Brielle and I would have never suffered the atrocities of Shadow Vault Citadel and the Pits within.

As though we watched a movie play out, Sadie, Saoirse, and I observed my experiences at the Vault. I didn't shy away from these memories. In fact, I was admittedly proud of them, handling a horrendous situation the best way I could, learning and growing my own powers while ensuring my sister remained safe. As safe as she could be in such a place, anyway. At least, until that final time in the Pits.

I was slightly drawn out of the memory when I felt a hard squeeze on my hand when the spear drove through Brielle and me . . . even tighter when we both went down in a pool of blood. I could feel Sadie's grief coming through at the sight of my death.

I had good news for her there: Brielle and I couldn't be so easily killed. The self-healing magic in our DNA possibly made us indestructible. Not that I wanted to test that theory.

While I hadn't protected Brielle from the brutality entirely, I was still proud that I'd been able to get us out of there. Though I was paying for it now, I would make the deal with the Shadow king all over again.

"We have a deal," the shadowy form said, the other one in the corner growling something in the black fog, but whatever he said didn't change anything.

The room filled with their power so thoroughly black that I momentarily wondered if I'd ever be able to see again, then suddenly Brielle and I were standing in the center of Ravenbury. We were in the town square, surrounded by homes and buildings, but all I noticed at first was Brielle's hair—no longer coppery brown but now bluish black. Was mine the same? People emerged from their homes and stared warily at us, having suddenly appeared out of nowhere.

"Hold on a minute," someone said. "Are those the Knight twins?"

"Send someone for Alexis and Tristan!" barked Scout, the mayor, as she ran for us.

My memory blanked out, the vision returning with me waking in a small room with two twin beds, Brielle sitting up in the other. I sensed Scout nearby and heard my parents outside.

Something was going on out there. Something not good, the charge of magic in the air.

This—this was what I'd been avoiding. Consciously anyway. My subconscious knew, had given me enough glimpses of it here and there to know how awful the next several minutes were. I braced myself, fighting the urge to pull out of the memory and stop it all from coming to light.

But I had to do it.

For myself. For the Shadow fae of the Court of Souls. For my family and the people I loved.

And so we watched.

Brielle and I looked at each other, and in an instant, we were outside, blinking against what at first seemed like the bright light of the outdoors. No, wait, it was night. Night in the outside world, with stars and a moon, so much more light than we'd had for all that time while we were in the Vault. But something blocked the moon. Not eclipsing it, though. Something much closer. A dark mist, swirling overhead and closing in on my sister and me before I could see what all the commotion had been with my parents. It sped toward us, then spun around Brielle and me, creating a black tornado, blocking out everything else. Wind raged in my ears, whipping my hair and lashing it against my face.

"No!" I gasped.

My younger self didn't know then that the deal she'd made was with the Shadow king. She didn't know his name or where he was from. But she was certain now he hadn't let them go after all. That this was his darkness surrounding them.

I knew better now.

Through breaks in the black fog came the rotting faces of

zombies. Younger me blasted magic at them, killing them for good. Next came a pack of demons in their Hellish forms of wings, horns, and mottled skin. I fought them off, too, and I realized now I'd also killed them for good. At least—if they'd even existed. Because what came next . . .

⚔

The fog suddenly cleared as fast as it had come, and Brielle and I were in the middle of a deep crater.

"We're back in the Pits," I screamed with complete and utter desolation. "We didn't get out! We didn't fucking get out!"

Creatures came from all directions, attacking Brielle and me. Again, my twin fought only enough to keep them at bay, refusing to kill them if she didn't have to.

"We have to kill them! It's the only way we live!" I shouted. "I have to!"

I pulled on that dark power within me, releasing the beast who had kept me alive throughout our time at the Vault. She charged outward, exploding from me in a dark fog just as impenetrable as that of the form I'd made a deal with. Magic burst from me in uncontrollable waves, obliterating everything in its path but my sister and me.

Then there were screams in the distance. The crowd cheering? No, it didn't quite sound like shouts of encouragement and victory. More like agony and grief.

"Elliana!" a voice called through the darkness still surrounding us but thinning. A familiar voice I'd been longing to hear since that day in the woods. My mother's voice. "Brielle! Stop!"

The black fog cleared.

We were not in the Pits. We were not at the Vault at all. There were no zombies or demons.

Brielle and I stood side by side, still in the middle of the street in Ravenbury. What remained of it anyway.

The building closest to us was demolished. Another vomited black smoke into the air, flames licking out its windows. People . . . people were everywhere. Many of them prone . . . still . . . lifeless?

"Elli," Dad called out, a strange edge to his voice. My dad wasn't afraid of anything, but I swore I heard a tinge of fear as he said my name.

I spun in their direction. But demons surrounded them— hovering over their heads, coming up from behind them. So many demons.

I lifted my hand toward them, about to blast them with my demon-ending power.

"NO!" my mother screamed, and I paused, turning to see where she looked next to me. Where my brother suddenly stood, holding Brielle by the head. I watched as he twisted his wrists, then dropped her to the ground, her neck at an unnatural angle. My mouth opened in a scream as he flew at me . . . slammed his hands against the sides of my head . . .

The memory deteriorated in a haze of silver, then shifted, and we were at the Loft, in the room Brie and I shared. I bolted upright, gasping for air, my eyes wild as my gaze bounced around, taking it all in. My sister still slept, but she'd awake soon, too. This memory I knew well. It was one I hadn't forgotten. One that hadn't been taken from me.

"It's okay," my mom had said, sitting on the floor between our beds. Her warm brown eyes filled with tears before she lunged in and wrapped her arms around me in a hug only a mother could give. "You're okay now. You're okay."

I thought she said it just as much for herself as she did me.

"What do you mean? What happened?" I asked, pulling back with concern. "Aren't you supposed to be at Amadis Island?"

"You were hit by a powerful curse," Mom said quietly, studying my face as she pushed a lock of hair out of my eyes. "All three of you. Charleigh wasn't hurt as bad as you and Brielle."

"What? While we were sleeping?" My eyes squinted with confusion. *Who at the Loft would do such a thing?* my younger self had wondered. At that time, all I could remember was Brielle convincing Dad to let us go foraging with Charleigh the next day while he and Mom went to Amadis Island for a meeting with their greater council. Then we'd gone to bed to wake up to this.

Mom shook her head. "You two have been in a magically induced coma for a couple of months."

"*What?*"

"It seems you and your sister have come into some of your powers, but, unfortunately, most have been repressed. Blossom, Owen, and the other mages did everything they could to . . . to ensure you have some magic to work with. When you're ready, you can start learning to use it." She smiled, and at the time, I thought it had been one of pride and love. Now I knew the love was there and perhaps some pride, but I also saw the strain of fear—fear of her own daughter.

As we pulled out of the memory, I couldn't blame her. She'd seen what I'd done. The town I'd nearly destroyed. The human lives I had taken.

Her own daughter was a monster.

"You're not a monster," Sadie said a few minutes later, when I voiced it aloud once our minds had returned to the sitting room.

"You were a young girl who was traumatized," Saoirse added. "And I wouldn't doubt the king was messing with your mind when you returned. You only did what anyone else would do in the same circumstance—tried to protect yourself and your loved ones."

"I killed them," I whispered as I stared at the flickering candles. "I killed innocent souls."

Sadie's hand landed on my knee, squeezing gently. "It's not like you were trying to."

"Wasn't I?"

"I saw a young, fear-filled girl with a deadly power stronger than she knew," Saoirse said. "A girl who'd experienced things nobody ever should. Of course, you lost control."

"So badly that my parents felt the need to suppress our magic because I was such a danger to everyone around me." I understood that now. There had been a spell, all right, that had knocked Brielle and me into a coma and suppressed our powers. But our own parents had been the ones to cast it. Well, not them—they'd had Dorian's warlock do it—but they'd given the order. I was sure of it now. "Except it didn't hold."

Before I could change my mind, I grabbed their hands and dove us into another memory.

We appeared in Misery's Edge, two years after the events in Ravenbury, our backs against the wall of tight living quarters. The single room felt even smaller because of all the bodies filling it. Dani and I shared an oversized, threadbare chair, and Brielle sat with Mom and Dad on the couch, while Dad and Papa Miguel shared stories in Portuguese. The fragrance of Papa Miguel's delicious stew filled the air, making my mouth water even now, and music from outside filtered through the flimsy walls. This night—at least, this hour—might have been one of my favorite memories ever.

Until it became my worst.

I'd never found out how the meeting with the mayor had gone. I supposed it didn't matter now. Maybe if I'd known more then, I could have insisted we leave immediately. Instead, I'd insisted we stay.

Now I could see what I hadn't then—the strain in Mom's eyes when she and Dad exchanged a look, probably holding a telepathic conversation at the same time. I could now hear the activity outside, feel a dark energy growing in the center of the market, sense Uncle Owen and Aunt Vanessa and other Amadis guards rushing toward us.

We watched as Mom and Dad flew out the door, ordering Brielle and me to stay put. Of course, I never listened. Papa Miguel's residence was right across the street from the edge of Market Square, so I only had to step outside to see all the commotion, Brielle right behind me despite her protest. We watched in horror as the mayor grew and transformed into her true major demon self.

"You should not have rejected our offer, Alexis," her deep voice boomed, purplish black smoke spewing with each word.

"Did you really think I didn't know, Shamara?" Mom asked before she launched into the air. "You cannot have my daughters."

Chaos erupted as Mom shot her power at the enormous demon and Shamara fought back. People screamed and ran for cover from falling debris. Others—Mom's people—ran the opposite way, straight toward the center of the action.

"We didn't come alone," Mom said.

"And I have my own army," Shamara replied. "Half of this town is possessed by my followers."

Then came the dark purple fog that filled the spaces between buildings, surrounding the demon and our parents until we couldn't see them anymore. People ran through the streets and alleys, shouting for help and shrieking with pain as their possessed loved ones, friends, and neighbors attacked them, trying to devour their souls.

I recalled now the clashing power of light and dark colliding within me. How my beast tried to escape her cage, the demon's energy calling to her. How my angelic powers began to build, supporting my mother to strengthen her own.

Then I remembered the undulating shape on the roof of the building next to us. The words that filled my mind . . . *"Remember me, little shade? We had a deal."*

Dark energy engulfed me, overpowering the light. Then, I thought it had been the demon's power. Shamara letting it loose. Now I knew differently.

The Shadow king had been there that night.

"You cannot have them!" Mom shouted.

Shamara swung her bus-sized hoof through the flimsy buildings around the market and swiped a claw at my mother who soared to the side, and I could feel her gathering her power. Drawing on the Amadis who'd come with us, strengthening her own and preparing to unleash it.

And all I could think, as I saw hundreds of black-eyed humans flooding the area and then Papa Miguel about to attack his own daughter, the girl I thought I could love with all my heart and soul—was that it wasn't enough. Mom needed to send these evil creatures back to where they belonged, and I didn't know if she had the power to do it. Not this many.

A new energy grew within me, traveling through my veins and into every cell—I'd thought at the time that had been Mom pulling on my Amadis power, but I knew differently now. It was foreign yet familiar. Dark and powerful and lovely at the same time. Exactly what she needed, I'd thought then. Gathering it within me, I formed a ball of the intense energy and grew it until I couldn't hold it any longer.

"Do it now or your sister, your family, everyone you love is mine," that voice—all too familiar now—ordered.

I thought then that I had pushed my power to my mother, feeding her everything that I could. Just wanting, like her, to rid this town of their demon infestation. To keep my sister and me and all of the humans there safe.

But that wasn't the case. I'd blacked out then, but now I knew better. Now I knew that crossing dimensions hadn't been what broke the spell repressing my and Brielle's powers.

Now I knew it had been the Shadow king all along.

And when that bright light burst from my mother, turning her form into an angelic silhouette, my own beast exploded from me.

The blast thundered through the air and the town, shaking the buildings and even the ground.

The demon souls didn't just disappear to Hell only to revitalize themselves. They were truly ended—for good.

Except the purple demon-bitch, who burst into thousands of ravens and took to the sky, disappearing somewhere among the stars. Saving herself.

And all around us, bodies dropped. Dozens of them. Hundreds. I would never forget the sight.

Screams came from every which way, echoing each other into a dreadful song of angst and sorrow.

Directly behind me, though, came the loudest. I would never forget the sound:

Dani's sobs as Papa Miguel fell in her arms, dead.

CHAPTER 24

"*I* killed Papa Miguel," I whispered.

As we came out of the memory and returned to the sitting room in the Court of Souls, I swiped at my face and was surprised to find it wet with tears. I'd had it all wrong. I'd been solely blaming my mother for the death of Dani's father all this time.

"How do you figure?" Saoirse asked.

"That was *my* power, not my mother's. I didn't know it then. I didn't even know I had that kind of power."

"Still, the demon killed her father when it possessed him. There was nothing of him left. You know that, Elliana," Saoirse said.

My brows scrunched together, and my lips turned down. I did know that, in my brain. But the image of Papa Miguel's body in Dani's arms. The scream that had echoed in my ears all this time . . .

"Are you sure it was even your power?" Sadie asked. "I thought it was suppressed."

I nodded. "It makes sense. My mom is powerful, but nobody ever thought she could *destroy* demons. She can only return them to Hell. So it had been a shock when that happened. According to Tor, I can destroy them completely. I did it in the Pits. But yeah, Brie and I thought crossing dimensions had broken the spell that suppressed our powers, but apparently not."

Saoirse rose to her feet and crossed over to the wet bar by the hearth to pour three glasses of faerie wine. "Seeing it for myself now, it is obvious King Caellach broke that spell. Having your powers suppressed doesn't serve his purposes all that well, now does it?"

"I thought he never went to the earthly realm," I said, watching her from the floor, no energy to move myself.

She came back over and handed each of us a glass. "For you, Elliana, it appears he will do whatever it takes. It seems your people stripped you right out of his grimy hands when they took you away. And if it makes you feel any better, Tor said it took the king quite a while to recover from that blast of yours. You'd almost taken him out, too."

"Too bad I failed," I said bitterly before sipping on the wine. I hadn't realized how chilled I'd been until its warmth slid down my throat and spread over my skin. "He did say he'd been looking for me."

Saoirse sat back down, and I realized she'd completely disregarded my circle of protection, breaking it not once but twice. I sighed, silently opening it anyway, because I could hear Aunt Blossom and Charleigh both yelling at me about sacred circles and energy disruptions if I didn't.

"So you can stop now with the guilt," Sadie said, almost as a command.

"If you want someone to blame, blame our father," Saoirse agreed.

And I did. He'd been behind it all—our deaths at the Vault and the carnage afterward, releasing my powers and more carnage as a result. Papa Miguel . . . the vengeance Dani swore on my mother, when it wasn't her fault. So much blood and death and ruined lives, and so much more that would still come.

Rage and hatred stormed through me now. I was going to kill that motherfucker the first chance I had.

"Mmm . . . that's more like it," Saoirse said, licking her lips as she basked in my hate. A few moments later, my emotions deescalated to a more manageable level.

But my guilt still lingered, the memory a stain that would forever remain as another black blemish on my soul. Regardless of the Shadow king being the one to push me into the pile of tinder, I'd still chosen to light the flames.

"So now you have your powers back and the maturity to learn that control," Saoirse replied, standing once more. "We begin again in the morning."

She sifted away, I assumed to her room for the night.

Sadie stood, then leaned over and grasped my hands, pulling me up in front of her.

"Let's go to bed," she said, keeping one of my hands in hers and leading me through the archway toward my room.

Trying to ignore the electric energy zapping between us, I slowed as we approached the double doors, forcing her to come to a stop, too. We needed to say goodnight here, because if I let her in my room . . .

"Sadie," I began.

She stepped up to me, placing a finger to my lips. "Not now."

She opened the door and stood back, gesturing for me to enter first, and I thought I'd misunderstood her intentions. I turned to apologize when she shut the door, her body between me and it. The look in her eyes—lit up like I'd never seen them before—made my insides quiver, my breath catching in my very suddenly dry throat. Then her hands darted over my shoulders and wrapped firmly around the back of my neck, tugging me up against her, as she pressed her mouth onto mine.

The softness of her full lips was everything I remembered it to be. Her sweet floral scent flooded my senses, and I could taste her even before the tip of her tongue brushed over the crease of my mouth, teasing me until I opened for her. My hands gripped her face as the kiss deepened, our tongues plunging and dancing together, and everything we'd been holding back began to rush to the surface. My whole body heated when she pressed herself closer into me, eliminating anything but the thin fabric of our nightclothes between us. Then she spun me around, crushing me against the door with her body as our tongues continued their duel, making her moan into my mouth. My breasts swelled and tightened at the mewl, my core enflaming with need.

Releasing my hold on her, I ducked under her arms, stepping away. "Fuck," I gasped. "This isn't . . . I can't . . . we shouldn't—"

"Oh yes, we absolutely should." She pushed me just hard enough that I stumbled backward several steps until my legs hit the side of the bed and I fell onto it.

Grabbing the hem of her shirt, she lifted it over her head, prowling toward me with a look in her eyes that made me think of a lioness stalking her prey. Unable to help it, my gaze drifted down her glorious body, and the throb between my legs became a desperate ache, making my thighs clench, even when I knew this was all wrong. We were only setting ourselves up for something we could never have. For heartache and agony and grief.

But . . . would one time really be so bad?

Her pants were gone, too, by the time she reached the bed, leaving me gaping at miles of creamy flesh, pink nipples tightened into points, and beautiful ornate elf markings scrolling across her chest and into a V between her breasts and another V stretching between her hips just below her belly button, pointing downward. She'd kept those hidden from me before, and my tongue slid over my lips, wanting to run over those raised markings . . . and the rest of her.

"Don't tease," she said, her voice husky as her hands gripped my knees and pushed my legs apart so she could step between them.

"Not teasing," I whispered. "It's a promise."

Her full lips curled sexily, those electric blues becoming like lightning, striking straight into my heart, my soul. And then she pounced.

I landed flat on my back, Sadie on her knees, straddling me, her mouth crashing down on mine. My hands went to her hips as hers traveled under my top, lifting it as she went, her fingers skimming over my sides, my ribs, under the swell of my breasts, which craved her touch. A moan escaped my lips when she pinched my nipples, causing my hips to buck against hers. She laughed against my neck, where her tongue swirled and her teeth bit.

It wasn't long before I was naked, too, and we explored each other, sometimes with slow reverence and other times with urgent hunger. We'd never been able to do this before, too rushed with everything going on at school, never quite having the privacy to properly make love—and suppressing our physical needs because we'd known then what we still did now: this could never last. But I'd made the mistake then of holding back when it should have been all the more reason to experience at least one time together. So it was more than just the last few days of sexual tension, of forcing ourselves to ignore our bodies' longing for the other. It was months and months of desire and need and ache that had been building into such a force that we couldn't possibly restrain it any longer.

This was not just the elf princess Sadie Angrec and the dangerous hybrid angel Elliana Ames Knight. This was us becoming . . . *more*. One, I might dare to say, as foolish as that was. But as we soared over the edge together, that's exactly how it felt—like our very souls had fused together into one incredible, infallible, indestructible being . . . and then shattered into a million pieces only to come together once more and do it all over again.

I didn't know how long we'd made love into the night. I'd lost count of how many times each of us had climaxed. But finally, it all caught up with me—the emotional and physical exhaustion pressing me into the soft bed, Sadie in my arms.

"Ten stars," she whispered against my neck as her fingers traced random shapes between my breasts and over my stomach.

"At least," I agreed.

"But I won't highly recommend," she said. "I don't want anyone else to have this with you. You are mine." She licked my ear lobe, followed by the scrape of her teeth before her breath came hot on my ear. "I love you, my beautiful dark angel."

My heart grew for a beat, then shrunk into a tiny stone, a lump lodging in my throat.

"How?" I choked out.

She tilted her head, using her finger against my chin to turn my face toward her. "How could I not?"

Our eyes locked, and I saw it, felt it in those blues that enraptured me so much. The truth of her words, of her heart. "After what you know . . . even now?"

She lifted up onto her elbow and pressed a soft, lingering kiss to my lips before snuggling back down. "Especially now."

I opened my mouth but didn't know what to say. How badly I wanted to say it back. I certainly felt it. But at some point—as in very soon—I'd have to say other things that would be devastating to us both. Because I couldn't be just hers, just as she couldn't be only mine. I should have spit it out now, but then I heard her soft breaths become deeper and even out, and I peered down to see she'd fallen asleep. I wasn't too far behind her.

✦✦

Now that the memories had fully returned to my consciousness, they didn't torment me in my dreams, but their effects remained. I woke up gasping, my heart pounding, though I couldn't remember what I'd been dreaming about now. Loss. That's all I could recall—complete and total loss.

"I had hoped you'd sleep better now," Sadie murmured, wrapping her arms around me and pulling me against her.

"How did you know I hadn't before?"

She sniggered. "Besides your haunted eyes, the circles beneath them, the screams I may not have heard but could feel?"

I pulled back to see her face. "You could feel my screams? You make no sense."

She smiled, her fingers raising to brush over my lips. "I feel everything about you."

Our gazes held, and I felt like she was trying to tell me something—or search for something from me. But what I had to tell her . . . I needed to just do it. I'd chickened out last night, but I couldn't prolong it. It would only hurt more if I waited. If we did *this* again.

As I searched for the words, my mind snagged instead on how different she looked now. Her coloring had fully returned, her eyes brighter than ever, her energy stronger and more intense. Perhaps that was why her elf markings had become so prominent now.

Her cheeks flushed as I studied her, then she wiggled out of my arms and out of bed. I rolled over to watch as she strode toward the bathroom, her light blond hair flowing down a slender but strong back, her hips swaying naturally yet still seductively, and I recalled with pleasure the feel of her perfect ass filling my hands.

"Sorry, but I got hungry in the middle of the night," she said as she passed the dresser where a vase of flowers stood.

Well, not flowers anymore. Just stems. I laughed, the full, deep-bellied sound almost foreign to my own ears.

"Sadie with no flowers is a very sad Sadie," I said as she returned, sauntering toward me. "I think you need them more than you realize. They make you . . . glow."

She laughed, too, pushing me over as she climbed back in bed. "I'm not better because of the flowers, silly. This is because of you."

Shit. I wasn't expecting that. I rolled onto my back and stared at the ceiling, again searching for the right words. "Sadie, I have to tell you something."

Pushing up on an elbow, she leaned over me, and I didn't miss her bare breast sliding against my arm. How could I? I was hyper-aware of every inch of her. "I have something to tell you, too. Something I've known for a while, even back at school. But with our circumstances . . . both of us having to return to our own worlds, not knowing if we'd ever see each other again . . . I didn't think it fair to lay it on you then."

My brows came together, unease setting in as I wondered what kind of truth she kept. A different unease than what I was already feeling in regards to my own truth.

We both opened our mouths at the same time, words tumbling out and over each other before we stopped ourselves and laughed awkwardly.

"I need to say this first," we both said, again at the same time.

Then there was a knock at the door, and I sighed. "I guess Saoirse gets to say her thing first."

I grabbed a wrap off the chair on my way to the door, bracing myself for Saoirse's reaction. She already knew Sadie and I had a past. I could tell she'd sensed the tension zapping between the elf and me every time we came near each other or our arms brushed at dinner. She also knew about my future, and I didn't know if she'd be more pissed off about the betrayal to her brother or to Sadie. With a deep breath, I pulled open the door, about to spew something about how this wasn't what it looked like and I'd explain later, but my breath caught in my lungs.

Tor's large, powerful body stood at my bedroom door, not Saoirse.

His aqua gaze traveled over me as I finished tying the wrap under my breasts, his nostrils flaring. Heat flushed up my chest and neck when I realized what he scented—lots and lots of sex. His eyes flicked behind me, to Sadie sitting up in my bed, covers held to her chest, making it even more obvious she was naked underneath. There was no denying what had gone on in here. Tor's laser sharp focus came back to me, his expression like stone, a flicker in his eyes the only sign of any kind of emotion.

My stomach sank, and my heart squeezed into a tight ball.

"Saoirse said you had a breakthrough," he ground out between gritted teeth. "She's waiting for you outside."

He turned on his heel and stalked away.

I closed the door and leaned against it, a string of curses rumbling under my breath. I would explain to him that I knew this could be nothing, that I still planned to keep our deal, that I understood if he felt the need to send Sadie away. My heart cracked at just the thought, but I'd known all along this would happen.

I just . . . I hadn't thought about how much this would hurt him. Truthfully, I hadn't really thought about his feelings at all, which made me feel even worse. Of course, I hadn't expected him to be home already. It hadn't been two weeks yet. Had it?

I looked up. Staring at me from the bed was another heart I was about to break. I probably should have gone after Tor, but some kind of realization slid over Sadie's face, that crack splintering all the way into my soul, and I thought my whole being was about to shatter.

What a wonderful morning this had turned out to be.

"What was that about?" she asked, her voice small. She hadn't missed a thing.

With heavy steps, I crossed back to the bed and sat on its edge. Unable to meet her eyes, I stared at the quilted pattern of the duvet, tracing a finger over it.

"I think I should go first?" I said, trying to be a smartass and partially hoping she would stop me. But she remained silent. I blew out a long sigh and finally looked up at her. "The deal I made with the king . . . It wasn't just to serve him, to let him use my power. I'd—I—" *Damn.* This was even harder than I expected it to be.

Her hand landed on my mine. "Elliana, I know about your deal. I know that you're supposed to marry Tor."

I looked up at her in surprise. "You do?"

"Of course. You think anybody here could keep that secret for this long?" She lifted a shoulder in a small shrug. "I'd been waiting for you to tell me, and I thought I understood why it was so hard. Until just now. You care for him, don't you?"

My gaze dropped again, my hands squeezing together in my lap until my knuckles turned white. "More than I ever thought I could."

"Do you love him?"

I pondered this for a moment before lifting my gaze to hers. "No. I thought maybe I could, but now . . . He's not you, Sadie. But—"

"That's all I need to know. You know about my own predicament. I'm supposed to marry Shadow royalty, too."

"Still?"

"Of course. My people need the alliance."

"But . . . you're related."

"Not to the entire royal line. There's some cousin on Tor's mother's side who will qualify. I think that's one of the many pieces of business he's been gone to attend to."

I studied her face as questions tumbled over one another

in my mind. "Even knowing that we can't be together . . . you still—"

"Elliana Knight, I have full confidence that we will find a way to be together. I will not break your heart."

I pulled away. "You can't make such promises."

"I can. I know because—"

There was another pounding on the door, this one much harder. We both glared at it as though we could see through it.

"Yasta, Elliana!" Saoirse barked through the wood. "Get your ass out here now!"

CHAPTER 25

I stopped in the kitchen for a cup of tea and something to eat, then met Saoirse out on the back lawn. Tor was nowhere to be seen, and I didn't know how I felt about that. I'd never meant to hurt him, and not only because of all he had done for me, considering the circumstances. I truly cared for him, and my own heart ached for what he must be feeling right now. For what I had done to him. I wished I could be the wife he really did deserve, but everything else aside, if I could choose between him and Sadie, it would always be Sadie.

The thing was—I didn't have that choice.

Sadie had high hopes for something that could not be changed, not without risking my sister's life, and I wouldn't do that. No, I had to keep my deal. Sadie needed to understand that and let any other lofty ideas go. We had our moment together, and it was without doubt the best night of my life, beyond anything I had ever expected, but it could be nothing more than that. It could never happen again. I needed to find a way to apologize to Tor and, if necessary, spend the rest of my life proving to him that he could trust me. That nothing like this would ever happen again.

And the only way to ensure that was to avoid Sadie. Even when it felt like doing so just might kill me.

So I did everything I could to stay away from her, which I thought would be a feat in itself, but apparently she was right. Tor had been arranging a possible "alliance" with a cousin, whom he'd brought to the Mistwood outpost outside the Court of Souls. And when I heard she'd left with some of Tor's men to meet this cousin, the truth struck me like a punch to the gut. Nobody else came to the Court of Souls. Tor wouldn't allow it. Sadie really would be removed from my life. Gone . . . never to be a part of it. My heart felt ripped in pieces just thinking about it. And where would she go? To the Court of Shadows? No, I couldn't allow that either. Absolutely not. But what could I do? The longer she was away, the worse I felt about the whole situation. Faerie wine, lots and lots of faerie wine, was the only way I could numb the pain enough to sleep.

In the meantime, Tor seemed to be doing everything he could to avoid me, because I hadn't seen him since he'd come to my room two mornings ago. That made apologizing to him and trying to mend things between us impossible, and also meant Saoirse and I spent a lot of time together over the next couple of days, as I put every waking moment into trying to use my power. Instead, I just grew more and more miserable. And bitchy.

"Did we miss something?" Saoirse asked the middle of the third day of trying Sadie's idea of using just a hint of my dark power combined with my other magic.

"I don't know," I snapped. "You're the trainer. I'm just the lowly pupil."

"I can't train someone who doesn't want to be!" she bit back. "And you apparently still don't want to be. You shy away from your power every time you get close. Did we miss some fear or past grievance of yours that you need to own up to?"

I snorted. "Well, if we need to hit them all, we could be here for months."

"Seriously, Elliana. I'm at my wit's end. I honestly don't think you're even trying."

I couldn't argue with that. I really wasn't trying, to be honest, my mind bouncing around between Tor and Sadie and my sister and my parents and everywhere except where it should have been.

"I'm sorry," I said half-heartedly. "I've got too much going on in my head."

"There's certainly something going on in there." Her voice softened when she asked, "Do you want to talk about it?"

I walked over to the marble steps and dropped down on one, resting my elbows on my knees and my head in my hands. Saoirse sat next to me.

Rubbing circles into my temples, I closed my eyes and posed the question, "Have you ever cared very deeply for two people, but the one you loved more than anything was the one you could never be with?"

Saoirse chuckled. "Can't say that I have. It sounds miserable."

"It is," I muttered into my palms.

"But if you care for them both, then at least you're not entirely losing, right?"

I blew out a sigh. "I guess. But why does it feel that I am? That I'm losing everything?"

Stupid tears sprang to my eyes, and I pressed the heels of my palms against my eyelids, willing them away.

"I know you're in an awful situation, Elliana. Nobody should have to commit to someone they don't truly love and want to be with."

"But a deal's a deal," I finished when she didn't continue.

"A deal's a deal until you can negotiate a better one," she said.

I turned my head, peering at her between my fingers. "Go on." She only shrugged. "Saoirse, if you have any ideas on how I can get out of this deal—preferably without hurting Tor any more than I already have—you must speak up!"

"Not me. I'm not the politician of the family. But you need to talk to Tor when he returns. I think you'd be surprised at everything he would do for you."

"Wait. He left again? He hasn't been avoiding me all this time?"

Saoirse peered over my shoulder, at the veranda above us, then stood. "I don't know about that, but you'll be able to ask him soon. For now, we should get back to work."

"Can I try?" a familiar voice asked from behind me, sending an electric current through my veins. That's who Saoirse had seen before she stood, trying to help me with my avoidance maneuvers. I mouthed *no* to her.

"Do you have another great idea up your sleeve?" Saoirse asked. "Because the last one isn't working too well, and if not, best to let her focus."

"Please," Sadie nearly begged. "Elli, we need to talk. And I promise it will make a difference."

Saoirse's gaze slid from Sadie to me, and her brows rose in question. I groaned internally then nodded.

"She's all yours," Saoirse said. "Maybe you can use that mind-bending trick to knock some sense into her."

The Shadow fae disappeared, and I reluctantly stood, slowly turning to face Sadie. I was shocked to see she looked as bad as I felt. My brows immediately pressed together.

"What's wrong?" I hurried up the steps to her, my hands fluttering around her face, but holding back from actually touching her. She'd looked so much better the other day, and now— "Are you sick?"

A small smile curled one side of her mouth. "Some call it a sickness. Let's walk, okay?"

She took my hand, warm energy flowing between us, feeling like a balm to my aching soul. We went around to the side lawn and through the gate to the park. We didn't stop until we reached the pond, and when we sat on the side of the basin, I noticed she already looked better.

"Flowers," I said. "You needed flowers."

She stifled a laugh while swallowing a mouthful of petals. "They are delicious, but it's not the flowers that make me better, Els. Like I said the other day—it's you." She inhaled a deep breath and hurried on before I could stop her. "It's because we're mates, Elliana. Fated mates. Bonded mates. Soul mates. Whatever you want to call it."

I held up my hand, my lungs locking up as I processed this. "Mates," was all I managed to croak out.

She nodded, taking my hand between hers. "I felt the connection almost immediately, but I'd had to deny it then. Too many expectations with my family, as you know. Then when we pushed past that, I became more and more certain. I'd wanted to tell you at school, after the stupid project and you almost got trapped in that hall of mirrors, but then what you told me about needing to go home . . . And I found out I wouldn't be returning to school either . . . Well, it seemed selfish to drop that bomb on you when we could do nothing about it. But now, Elli . . . the bond completed between us the other night. I know you felt it."

She finally stopped talking, allowing me to think, but I couldn't. I could only *feel*. Feel the bond between us, strengthening both of us even as we sat here. Feel the sadness that she'd been holding this within all of this time. Feel the elation that Sadie Angrec, the one person I knew could love me as much as I loved her, was my mate. Feel the despair that in the end, it meant nothing.

"Wait. Did you know the bond would complete the other night?" I asked, and she answered with a small smile. "So you knew about my deal, about your need to *align* with someone else, and yet you allowed our bond to complete?"

Her smile turned into a frown at my tone. "It wasn't exactly that I allowed it. I simply stopped fighting it. Doing so was hurting both of us, and it would only get worse if we didn't go through with it."

"And now what? We were apart barely more than two days, and we were both a mess. How the hell are we supposed to live the lives we're committed to—very separate lives—without destroying ourselves?"

Her frown deepened. "First of all, we were only a mess because the bond is so fresh. We'll get over that. But don't you see? A fae mating bond is more sacred than anything—even more than a fae's word. More than a deal."

I blinked at her as hope dared to rise. "No shit?"

She laughed. "No shit."

"I get to be with you—be your mate—and at the same time get out of my deal with the Shadow king?"

She nodded, grinning widely, but even as the last words fell off my tongue, my hope sank with them. The Shadow king. Since when would he honor the sanctity of a mating bond over our deal? He would laugh in my face if I suggested such a thing, and then punish me by making me kill more of his men.

My shoulders sagged with defeat. "He'll never do it," I murmured. "King Caellach will never give up on possessing me and my power."

Sadie's finger slid under my chin, lifting it so she could look into my eyes. "We'll figure out a way. But you're going to need to talk to Tor first."

I wished I could have her same confidence, but I didn't think she'd ever met the king. I knew for a fact she'd never seen the gleam in his eyes or the way he salivated all over me. He fed his men to me just to see me in action. No, there was no possible way this was our answer.

But she was right about one thing: I needed to talk to Tor.

"He hasn't returned from Mistwood, though," she continued when I started to stand, pulling me back down. She turned on the ledge of the basin, crossing her legs in front of her. Tiny rainbows from the suncatchers hanging in the trees danced over her face. "In the meantime, we're going to work together on getting to know your beast. Turn and face me." I did, mimicking her position by crossing my legs in front of me. She took my hands in each of hers. "Now close your eyes and sit for a few moments."

I followed her orders, but within a few heartbeats, I began to squirm as my mind reeled over everything we'd just discussed.

"Elli, settle," she said, quietly but firmly, like my mother used to do. With a deep inhale followed by a slow exhale, I settled. "Ground yourself." She paused as I imagined my body growing roots into the earth, grounding my energy. "Now let me in."

I didn't understand at first, but then I felt her energy pushing at my mental walls. It felt similar to when my mom used her telepathy to "knock" on my mental door. When I opened up to Sadie, though, she did the same for me, and that feeling of the other night—the feeling of becoming more, of becoming one—washed through me. We were connected not physically, but in every other way possible.

"Feel my darkness?" she asked, and I was surprised when I did. Our eyes remained closed as she went on, our hands held in the air between us. "You're not the only one with dark power. You've seen what I can do by simply touching a man's mind. Tor and Saoirse, I imagine your parents, too . . . everyone has darkness in them."

"Not like mine, though. Not everyone has the insane DNA mix my brother and sister and I do. Not everyone was conceived among the dust of black magic. Not everyone visited Hell while in their mother's womb. And nobody ever has opened an inter-dimensional gate to a world of evil."

She chuckled. "Okay, okay, I get it. But not everyone is as strong as you. And you're not alone, Elli. You always think you have to do this all on your own, but it's not true." I wanted to argue with her, but she gave my hands a reassuring squeeze. "Now show me this beast you've told me about. I'm excited to meet her."

Said beast circled her cage I still held her in, pushing the side of her head against the walls, that purring sound rumbling through her, through me. Sadie chuckled quietly again.

"I think I found her," she said. "And she's not so scary." I —my beast—purred louder. "Let her out, Elli. Let her free. Let her in to become one with you just as you and I have." I hesitated, and she squeezed my hands again. "You're not alone," she reminded me. "Let me help you."

Slowly, I lifted the cage, some of that power leaking out, ice-cold and pitch-black, and Sadie gasped when she first felt it.

"No, keep going," she insisted when I stopped. "We can do this."

Squeezing my eyes—and her hands—tighter, I lifted the cage more. I'd never truly looked at my beast myself. Not dead-on like this. My heart pounded with both fear and excitement.

The beast dropped her head under the cage, peering out. Bluish-black fur. Big brown eyes. She was cold and feral and absolutely terrifying but at the same time, fucking beautiful. A beastly version of myself. Together we pushed the cage higher until she was free. Instead of charging forward like she had before in my times of distress, she meandered her way out, sniffing against both Sadie and me, then rubbing her head against our combined energy, the purring louder than ever.

"You're actually purring out loud," Sadie said with a giggle. "Embrace her, Elli. She's part of you."

Hanging on to Sadie's energy, which felt so much lighter than mine in both weight and color, I let loose a tendril of my own force and slid it around the beast. She felt like . . . me. Like I was hugging myself, a long, lost part of myself. For the first time, I truly understood what Sadie had meant. I hadn't noticed that a piece of me had been empty all this time, a hole in my very psyche gaping open until I allowed my beast to fill it. She fit in like the last piece of a puzzle, completing the whole picture—the picture of me. Once she did, Sadie's energy swirled around us, filling in the tiny gaps between pieces, solidifying us into a whole.

"You did it," Sadie whispered. "Open your eyes."

I did, and shock racked through me.

The pond was dry, all of the water gone. Sadie's gaze swept around us and to our other side. Ice crystals hung in the air like frozen raindrops, but most shocking of all was the figure next to us.

I hadn't realized Saoirse had come to the park, but she stood there frozen, surrounded by icicles the length of my arm like spears, angled toward her and poking into her flesh. Everywhere the sharp points touched, black lines crawled under and up her skin.

"It doesn't exactly tickle," she ground out between clenched teeth.

I immediately shattered the icicles, lighting them with fire until they melted, returning the water to the basin.

"I wouldn't call that control," I growled.

"It's progress," Saoirse said as she inspected herself for any lasting damage. "A lot more control than you used to have."

"Only thanks to Sadie's power holding me back."

"You're wrong," Sadie said. "You have what you need within you." She squeezed my hand before letting it fall, sending a message through our bond. And I understood—I felt what she meant. I could feel her energy still within me. No, *our* energy, united, bonded. There for me to call on, to mix with my other magic, intensifying it without losing control. "Now let's go practice some more."

"I have something to do, but I'll meet you two back at the manor shortly," Saoirse said before disappearing.

"Are you going to tell me about the cousin?" I asked Sadie as the two of us walked through the park, heading back to the manor and the openness of the back lawn for more practice.

"Farran?" Sadie shrugged. "He's okay, I guess. I suppose he's good-looking, for a male, although I'm not sure about the goatee he wears."

"Ew," I said as I tried not to imagine that between my legs and failed.

"Yeah," she agreed. "He seems nice enough, though."

"But not your soul mate?" I teased.

She laughed, bumping her shoulder into mine. "He can't compare to you, Elliana Knight."

"That's good to know. Not sure if I can say the same about my own betrothed . . ."

She looked at me with mocked shock, pressing her hand to her chest. "I have competition?"

"If I was forced to be with a male, I could do worse. You can't argue with that."

Sadie wrinkled her nose. "He's my brother. I can't even think about him like that."

"I wish I could say the same," I murmured. We fell silent, but I could feel a slight change in Sadie's energy as we walked, so I grabbed her hand and gave it a reassuring squeeze, not dropping it until we came to the gate to the prince's estate.

We returned to the back lawn of the manor, and the two of them helped me fumble my way through blending the newly embraced power with my other abilities. Maybe someday I'd become good enough where it was simply second nature, like the rest of my powers and magic, but today was not that day. At least I was finally making progress, though.

As dusk fell and we decided to call it quits for the evening,

I looked up to see Tor standing on the balcony. I wondered how long he'd been watching. Apparently long enough, because he gave me a nod of approval before turning to go inside.

Now if only I could believe things would go as well with him as they had with Sadie and with my beast.

CHAPTER 26

*T*he next afternoon, after finishing some tortuous training with Saoirse while Sadie was forced to make plans for her own upcoming . . . engagement . . . I paced in front of Tor's study, mentally running through ideas of how to start this conversation and coming up with nothing I particularly liked.

"Are you going to hang out here all evening, carving a ravine into my floors?" Tor stood in the open doorway, his powerful body leaning against the frame. I didn't know how long he'd been watching me.

"Were you just going to stand there all evening and watch me as I did?" I sniped back. *Shit.* That wasn't anywhere close to *any* of the ideas I'd had for launching into this conversation.

"We need to talk," he said, turning and striding into his study, around the large desk.

I followed him in, and the door shut behind me. I sat in the chair in front of the desk as he sat behind it, and we stared at each other for a long, drawn out moment.

"I'm sorry," I finally blurted. I was beginning to realize I pretty much sucked when I was under pressure. Well, at least when it came to pressure from someone I cared about. "I had a moment of weakness, but it changes nothing. I will still marry you and keep my deal. I'm learning better control of my power, and I will help you free your people and whatever else you need me to do. It was a mistake—I make a lot of those, if you haven't noticed. But this particular one won't happen again."

He watched me carefully as I spewed my ridiculous speech that was not at all like I'd practiced. I was oh-for-two so far, in that regard. The weight of his aqua gaze became almost tangible, but when he lifted one black, slanted brow at the final promise, I clamped my mouth shut. He leaned forward in his chair, resting his arms on the desk and folding his long fingers together. His head cocked as he continued to study me.

"What, exactly, are you sorry for, Elliana?" he asked quietly.

I inclined my head, dropping my gaze from his to stare at my hands. "For betraying you," I said even more quietly. "For hurting you."

He let out a sort of snort-chuckle. "Look at that—Elliana Knight does have a heart."

My head snapped up, and I narrowed my eyes, my mouth opening for a retort. But when I absorbed his expression, I realized he wasn't taunting me. There was an unfathomable glint in his eyes.

"It is nice to know you care," he said, his voice even. "I care about you, as well. But seeing you with Sadie didn't hurt me in the way you think it does. Do you recall me saying that this union between us is not exactly what I want, either?"

I felt a prick in my heart, the pang of rejection, and frowned. "Yes."

"I've never intended for this marriage to actually happen. I've tried to tell you that before. I am buying us as much time as I possibly can."

"I understand, but being with Sadie doesn't help any of us.

Like I said, what happened the other night—it changes nothing."

He chuckled, leaning back in his chair and wiping his hand over his face. "Oh, it changes everything. We cannot go on pretending to be engaged when you are mated with another."

"She told you," I breathed, feeling a hint of betrayal. After all, she would have done so before she told me.

"No, she didn't need to. For fae, the bond of mates is clear. Not necessarily seen by the eye, especially after the bond settles, but still unmistakable. Word will undoubtedly get back to my father."

My whole body sagged deeper into the chair. This was not what I'd hoped to hear. "I know he won't honor the bond. He won't allow it to override our deal."

"No, he will not," Tor confirmed. "I have my own idea for you and your deal with him, but I still need more time. Until then, however, my biggest concern is not about you and me. It's about your mate. My sister, for whom we both know my father has no lost love."

My heart stopped in my chest as his meaning set in, my stomach knotting up so I thought I might vomit. I looked up at him in horror. "We just gave him another reason to kill her."

I couldn't breathe. Horror swiftly became rage and more hatred when I thought I couldn't possibly despise the king any more than I already did. My vision blurred as my heart thundered in my ears.

"I need to kill him first," I gasped.

Tor grunted and shifted, his fingers turning black and his eyes glowing silver. My emotions ebbed enough to sense Saoirse outside the door, helping him to bring me back down to a more controlled level.

"Thank you," I uttered.

"My chair, Elliana?" he replied, and I looked down at the

purple flames licking from my palms over the armrests I grasped so hard, my knuckles glowed white in the smoke.

"Son of a bitch!" I jumped to my feet, releasing my grip and the fire, too. Thankfully, the chair remained intact, though a little smoke-stained now. "Still need to master control."

"I'd say that has more to do with the mating bond than your power," Tor drawled.

"So what are we going to do about Sadie?"

"I'm working on it."

"Working on it?" I echoed, then slamming my hands on his desk and leaning in his face, I yelled, "Working on it! There better be a gods-damned patrol all over her ass!"

He glared at me. "My desk."

Shit. A blue crystalline frost spread over the polished wood surface. I jerked my hands to myself, fisting them and tucking them under my armpits.

"What are you doing about Sadie?" I grit out between clenched teeth.

"First of all, I brought her back here to the Court of Souls, where she is protected by our wards. Secondly, her future husband—" I couldn't help it—I growled at the words. "—has gone back to the Court of Shadows as a distraction. As long as she doesn't go anywhere, she will be safe. In the meantime, I did get a lead on your parents."

"It's not good enough—wait. What?" My heart stopped. "Where are they?"

"W—" he began, but then his door flew open with a bang.

"The wards have been breached," Saoirse announced. "Sadie's—" Her eyes cut to me, and it was all I needed. "I can't find her," she finished while I was already running out the door. "Nobody's seen her since this morning."

No. No, no, no. This couldn't be happening.

"Elliana," Tor called after me.

"You just said she was safe here!" I snarled over my shoulder.

I ran to her room and charged right in, hoping to the angels she was simply in the bathroom, but already knowing she wasn't. My gaze swung around, trying to catch any pertinent detail without wasting a single second. All I noticed was her cloak, quiver, and bow were missing. As I was about to run back out the door, I noticed a vase of stems, the tops of the flowers all picked off—except for one. Glancing around the room, I walked over to it, and as soon as my finger brushed over the tops of the petals, they became paper. A piece of parchment had been rolled and folded to look like a flower. And I already knew this was meant as a private message for me.

Elliana,

We're in danger here. Everything has been a lie. Tor is setting us both up with his father and the Winter Court. We must get out of here immediately. When the ward alarms go off, that's your signal. They'll be busy searching for the problem, so fly. Fly high, up and over the falling steps. Find the outpost. Farran will help us. I'll meet you there. Be safe! All my heart ~ Sadie

My heart thundered so loudly, I almost didn't hear the footsteps behind me. I quickly scrunched the letter in my hand, allowing just enough water from my palm to dissolve it before turning around.

"The breach is somebody leaving, not coming in, to the south. Would Sadie have any reason to leave?"

I shook my head, swallowing, forcing my shoulders to sag as though with relief. "Of course not. We're safe here, right?"

He glanced around the room, though whether he really saw any of it, I didn't know. His mind seemed somewhere else. Which was good for us. "It doesn't make sense that she'd leave without you."

I forced a smile. "She absolutely wouldn't. I'm sure she's fine. She probably went out to practice her archery in the park. I'll find her."

"I'm going with my men to double-check the wards. Find

Sadie and come straight back here. Don't leave until we know for sure it was a false alarm."

I nodded, and he sifted. I could finally inhale a much needed deep breath. Then I hurried to my room to grab the weapons I wasn't already wearing, tucking them away in my pants and boots, then headed out the back of the manor and toward the park, watching for Tor's men. Everything seemed calm—they'd had enough time to go their way. Calling on a cloaking spell, I snapped my wings out and took high to the sky, flying in the opposite direction of their destination, toward the giant steps up the side of the mountain, and over into the dark mists of the Shadow Lands.

CHAPTER 27

*C*onfusion, rage, and fear rushed through me as I flew over the mountain. Could it possibly be true? Had Tor—and even Saoirse—been lying to me this whole time? Had this all been a set-up so I'd be more docile and cooperative for him? Trying to charm me into thinking we were working for some greater good, only to hand me over to the Shadow king?

And what was this about Winter Court? That's where the fear came in—the fear of Tor being so cruel as to just hand Sadie over to the Winter Court. My imagination tried to run wild with what they would do to her—what Maeve would do to her in retaliation of her parents—but a red haze of hatred and anger filled my vision, making it difficult to see below me.

A gust of wind nearly sent me reeling, forcing me to snap out of it and focus on my mission. I needed to calm down and search for the place of our rendezvous. Tor and I had never passed an outpost when he'd brought me to the Court of Souls. Or perhaps I'd been too blind, too taken up with the thought that the Tormentor was actually a good guy, to notice. What a fool I'd been.

Spotting a smattering of tents and buildings on the top of

a ridge, I soared for what I assumed to be the Mistwood outpost, banking left at the last moment to alight at the top of a tree. From here, I scoped out the situation. There were two permanent buildings, one quite a bit larger than the other, and the smaller one seemingly stables for various faerie beasts. I couldn't identify them if I tried. A few open structures made of wooden poles and roofs stood here and there with a couple of Shadow fae under each one, some working on weapons, another on body armor, and another preparing food. A dozen or so canvas tents created the perimeter, a half-circle dipping down the side of the mountain. In a somewhat flat clearing to the far right, several fae practiced hand-to-hand combat techniques.

Sending my senses out for her, I couldn't find Sadie anywhere, not her physical self nor her energy, not even that bond that had formed between us. Had I beat her here? Or was I not fast enough and she'd already been forced to flee without me? She wouldn't have left me unless desperate or coerced. Right?

Watching for a while longer, I used my keen hearing to try to listen in on any conversations, but I heard nothing useful. Such as, whether I could even trust these soldiers. Did they work for Tor or for King Caellach? Was there ever really a difference? Not according to Sadie's note. I tried to identify Farran, but nobody I saw from here fit the description Sadie had given me. She'd only said to come to the outpost, though. No warning about who or what I'd be running into here.

Finally, with a sigh, I dropped to the ground, releasing my sword and calling on my beast to be ready. As soon as my feet hit the snow, several Shadow fae surrounded me. I immediately crouched into fighting stance, sword held out with both hands as I turned, measuring each one. They just kind of stood there, eyeing me with bemusement.

"You're Tor's bride-to-be, are ye not?" one asked, his English not as smooth as other fae I'd spoken with.

Shit. I hadn't expected them to recognize me.

"I was sent here for Farran," I hedged.

A deep, commanding voice barked something in Faelic from behind me, making me jump. The others disappeared into thin air as I spun to find a tall, broad fae with a goatee, just as Sadie had described.

"You're Farran? Sadie—"

"I am," he said before clamping his hand over my forearm and sifting us away.

We transported to a snow-covered field, the sky near dark, whether with dusk or that constant darkness of the Shadow Lands beyond the Court of Souls, I couldn't tell.

We also appeared right on the edge of a raging battle— dozens of fae fighting each other with both weapons and magic.

Farran tried to keep his grip on me as he surveyed our surroundings, as though he searched for somebody specific and not at all surprised at the fighting around us. Zapping him with a touch of my power, I jerked myself free, but barely made it one step before he tackled me into the snow. Damn, he was fast. I shot a fireball at him, but he had some kind of shield around him deflecting it, so I shoved my foot into his groin while trying to scramble the rest of my way out from underneath him.

"What the hell?" I muttered. "I thought—"

Pain ripped at my scalp, and at the same time, I was jerked back to my feet.

"You thought what?" he snarled quietly in my ear as his hand gripped tightly on my hair. *This* was the man Tor was going to give my Sadie to? I would slaughter him right next to his father. "You thought I would go along with this dangerous game you and that elf are playing? You thought I would betra —" He fell silent mid-word, every muscle in his body tensing against my back.

"I knew you would betray somebody," Tor said, "though I

wondered who it would be. Too bad you chose poorly. Now, please remove your hands from my bride."

I'd been trying to lean away from Farran, so when he released me, I stumbled forward before catching myself and whirling around. Tor stood behind Farran, a blade pressed into his cousin's throat, crimson beading along the silver edge. The prince's skin was no longer dark tan but that shimmery dusky color with fae runes on full display. His hair had bleached white, and the beautiful aqua of his eyes was pure silver now as his gaze traveled over me, as though ensuring I wasn't hurt. When his eyes returned to my face, relief flickered in them, and I wondered if it was real or still part of his game.

Then his focus returned to Farran.

"What is your plan?" Tor demanded. "Why bring us to Winter Court for this?"

"Because I asked him to." The familiar female voice rang across the field.

The fighting suddenly stopped, half of the fae dropping to a knee as she glided past them toward us, the other half—Shadow soldiers, the *Skaelach*—appearing to be in a stupor. I knew how they felt. She looked like a warrior goddess, dressed in armor rather than revealing dresses, her ebony skin glowing in the moonlight against the snow.

"Maeve?" I breathed.

Her bluish-silver eyes fell on me, and her mouth curved in a slight smile. She also seemed to be assessing me for any injuries.

"You're not harmed," she said, confirming it out loud before turning her attention on Farran. "Thank you, shade. Your deed is done."

She flicked her hand dismissively, and Farran suddenly collapsed against Tor, who dropped him to the ground, his full focus on Maeve.

"What have you done?" he demanded.

"It is nice to see you, too, Toridhan. It's been too long."

She gave him a coy smile full of cruelty and hatred. She barely glanced at Farran, who was on the ground, clawing at his throat. His eyes rolled back in his head as his mouth moved like a fish's while his heels dug into the ground. He appeared to be choking to death on nothing but the princess's power. Maeve's upper lip curled in disgust. "I asked him to fetch the girls for me, and he did. I'm done with him."

We both stared at her in utter shock for the length of a heartbeat.

"Where's Princess Sadierdre?" Tor demanded, recuperating faster than me.

Maeve cocked her head. "She's important to you? An *elf?*"

She practically spat that last word, and I stiffened, seething. Something flickered in her expression, but so quickly, I wasn't sure if it was in reaction to me or something else.

"Where is she?" Tor bit out each word individually.

Maeve studied him for a long moment, and it almost seemed like she was purposely ignoring me while not ignoring me at the same time. Like I could feel her monitoring every muscle twitch, every blink, every breath without actually looking at me. Finally, she shrugged. "She's back at the castle. Along with Elliana's family."

My breath caught. My jaw dropped open. My heart pounded in my ears, growing so loud, I thought I must have misheard her.

"My . . . my family?" I managed to fumble out.

She turned toward me, and the smile she bestowed on me was completely different than the one she'd given Tor—beatific and warm, seductive in more ways than one. "Of course, doll. I thought you would want to see them. To know that they're safe."

I blinked, then looked sideways at Tor. He was studying the Winter princess, calculating, trying to figure out her game.

Maeve rolled her eyes. "Go see for yourself, Toridhan. Take your men. Mine will escort you. I'll even let you take your stupid, disgusting elf back—but then you can get the fuck off my lands." She snarled those last words, the threat clear, though her gaze remained locked on me. Did she see my body tense when she spoke of Sadie that way? Did she hear my heart stammering? If so, she didn't let on. "Go on while I'm feeling generous."

Tor glanced at me, then at Saoirse, who stood off to the side with the *Skaelach*, all of them full-on Shadowy with dark skin and white hair. Saoirse lifted her chin slightly in acknowledgment or agreement of some kind.

"Elliana?" Tor asked.

"Oh, she stays here with me," Maeve replied, her voice turned seductive and full of all kinds of promises—promises I wasn't sure I wanted her to keep. "The elf for Elliana. I think you're getting the shit end of the deal, but that's really all you Shadows deserve anyway."

Tor's eyes narrowed, but then he quickly glanced at me. I inclined my head, trying to tell him to go, to save Sadie. I didn't know what the hell was going on here. If Farran had betrayed Tor—and apparently King Caellach, too—then Sadie's note must have been a lie. Regardless of what he'd planned to do with me, it was obvious now that Tor had no intentions of turning Sadie over to Winter Court. I had to trust he would take care of her until I could figure out what to do with Maeve myself.

Tor must have understood my expression, because he and Saoirse exchanged some words in Shadow Faelic, then he took off, half of his men leaving with him. Saoirse and the others remained with me.

Maeve turned her nose up at the Shadow fae before striding toward me.

"Close enough," Saoirse warned, and I understood. If Maeve could touch me, she could sift with me.

"Would you like to end up like that one?" Maeve retorted, glancing at Farran.

Saoirse smirked. "I'd like to see you try."

Maeve's chest heaved, and I thought she was going to meet Saoirse's challenge, but then she must have decided the Shadows weren't worth her time, because she angled her back to all of them, facing me fully.

"I have been so worried about you, doll," she said, true concern ringing in her voice. "I couldn't come to the Shadow Lands to rescue you. I'm so sorry. I've been working ceaselessly to get you out of there, though."

My brows gathered. "What do you want, Maeve?"

She took another step forward. Behind her, Saoirse's hand landed on the hilt of the sword hanging from her hip. Maeve stopped. "I want you, Elliana. What else? Who else? Only you."

I shook my head. "I . . . I can't."

"Of course, you can, darling. We can work this out. We can be together like we are meant to be. When I walked in your dreams while you were here and saw your memories of the elf, I have to admit I was disgusted at first. But I realized you didn't understand at the time how awful the elves are. You were in a different realm, under different circumstances. I tried to ensure she wouldn't be a problem here, in this realm, even before you were taken from me. I'd already sent our men to the Elven Lands."

"You attacked the elves because of me?" I asked in disbelief.

"Yes, doll, of course. I needed to eliminate her and ensure she was removed from your life for good."

My beast growled, the sound nearly escaping my throat as she clawed at me to let her take control. *Not yet. Not now.* But hell if I didn't want to rip this fae's throat out for even saying such a thing, let alone actually doing it. Never mind the invasion of privacy of walking through my dreams. Walking through my fucking dreams. Scraping details to use against me. The nerve!

Maeve didn't seem to notice the anger churning in my chest and boiling through my veins, though, because she continued.

"The filthy bitch ran away like a coward, and we would have had her on the borders of the Shadow Lands, but I saw my opportunity. A hostage trade. They can have her. I just want you back, Elliana. When she went to Tor instead of the king, well, that threw a little kink in things, but I figured it out. Because that's what I do. I found the weak link and made my move." She glanced at Farran's prone body, lifeless now.

What the actual fuck? Want me back? As though I would have any interest after all this!

"I can't come back to you, though," I said, the words grinding out from a clenched jaw as I tried to hold on to every bit of self-control I could muster.

"You cannot be with *her*," she snarled, making me flinch.

I couldn't let her know just how much Sadie meant to me, though. She couldn't know the truth. "I know I can't—if I actually wanted to be." Her lips trembled as though she suppressed a smile, though her eyes remained cunning, sharp as daggers. "I have a deal with the king."

She scoffed, waving her hand in the air. "Oh, that. I'm practically queen myself. I can get you out of that."

My heart stuttered for a moment. Could she really? She said it so easily, so confidently. Tor had promised his own solution, but I wasn't sure if I could trust him anymore. And he kept asking for time, more and more time. For what? It wasn't like he'd shared his plan with me. Did Maeve really have more power than him to be able to finagle me out of the deal? Did she have a better one to offer the king in exchange? Or was it a scheme that would only land me in bigger trouble? Trust Maeve or trust Tor?

Trust your intuition.

My intuition was screaming at me loud and clear. Tor may have been known in outer circles as the Tormentor, and he'd violated me in ways I'd never forget, but never like Maeve had done, now that I knew. He'd used his seductive fae power over me to prove a point that in the end helped me—and with the ultimate goal to save his people. Maeve had used her powers to plunder my mind and then manipulate me for her own personal pleasure and gain.

"I made a deal," I said again. "Until I am actually released from it, I won't renege on it."

Maeve's pretty lips turned down in a frown. When she spoke, authentic remorse seemed to fill her tone. "I guess I'll have to take a different angle with you to make you understand."

With a wave of Maeve's hand, Sadie suddenly appeared, standing like a statue in the snow to my right, her face badly beaten and bruised, her clothes torn, and her expression seemingly frozen in a perpetual though silent scream.

CHAPTER 28

From my left, Saoirse charged for Sadie, but she'd barely taken two steps before a loud crack reverberated in the silence, and the Shadow fae plunged head first into the snow as though something tackled or tripped her. The *Skaelach*, who'd been standing behind their leader, drew their weapons at the sight of the phantom attack and ran for the remaining Winter Court soldiers with Maeve. But then they went completely still and silent. My mind barely registered the commotion, though, as I stared at Sadie with horror.

"What have you done to her?" I gasped.

"Nothing worse than the Shadow king will do when he gets a hold of her. Which he will, as soon as I'm done. Unless . . . you could make her agony stop, Elliana. I would put her out of her misery for you. Your choice."

My trancelike focus broke, and my head snapped toward Maeve where she still stood several yards in front of me. That small, alluring smile returned as she lifted one shoulder in a shrug. At the same time, my attention broadened, taking it all in. Saoirse flat on the ground, a hand on her leg that was bent at a sickening angle, obviously not healing like it should have been. The *Skaelach*, who stood frozen, literally, ice coating each of the soldiers in mid-step. A half-dozen of Maeve's men encircling Sadie, her cloak, quiver, and bow on the ground between us, the snow stirred up as though there'd been a skirmish. Had Sadie been here the whole time, cloaked from us?

"In exchange for what?" I growled, though I had a feeling I already knew the answer.

"For marrying me, of course. I'll renegotiate your deal with Caellach, and you'll be freed from that. It should be easy enough. Toridhan has already released you. I do believe he'll find a way to convince his father."

I cocked my head. "Tor hasn't released me."

"He indeed has. Just before he left, he told Saoirse to grant you your freedom. Isn't that right, shade?" Maeve watched Saoirse, who still lay on the ground. When she didn't immediately answer, a second crack shot through the air, and Saoirse screamed, grabbing her other leg.

"Yes!" she groaned. "Tor has freed you, Elli."

"See?" Maeve said, pride filling her face as though she'd been the one to make that happen. "Now, I think I can find a way to forgive you for even wanting to be with the revolting elf. You'll have some making up to do, certainly, which will hurt me as much as it will hurt you, but we can eventually move beyond this, Elliana, and be happy. You and me—we're meant to be together. We are mates."

"You're fucking insane," I barked out on a laugh that held no humor.

Maeve's chest rumbled with a savage growl, her eyes enflaming with hatred. Her upper lip lifted in a snarl, exposing a mouth full of pointy teeth. Good. At least she'd be empowering Saoirse, who might finally be able to heal herself. I was surely feeding her much of my own hatred. But then torment was added as Sadie's scream was silent no longer, piercing my ears while her agony broke my heart and soul.

I watched in horror as she lifted her hands to tremble in front of her, her fingernails flying off of her fingertips, as though being jerked free by a phantom force, blood dripping down her hands, staining the snow crimson at her feet.

"Stop it!" I yelled at Maeve, conjuring an icicle that I threw at her like a spear, but a flick of her finger shattered it in mid-air.

The princess stilled, though, her eyes growing wider with each passing heartbeat as she looked at me, then Sadie, then me, then Sadie. She shook her head, her mouth opening and closing.

Perhaps it was the agony in my own voice. Perhaps something else that made her realize the truth.

"No!" she roared around those sharpened teeth. "Not possible!" She jabbed a finger toward me, her nail elongated to a lethal point. "You and *I* are mates! Not—no! I will not allow it!"

"I don't think you have a choice in the matter," I said, now giving her my own smirk.

"Of course, I do!" she bellowed. "I am the Winter Court queen!" Her chest heaved as her gaze swung around, daring anyone to challenge her on that claim. What that meant about her brother, I wasn't sure. Perhaps she was only posturing, trying to make herself sound more important and powerful than she was. Or maybe she had killed him. I wouldn't be surprised at anything she did anymore.

Except I was.

Her voice dropped as she reined her anger back in. "I will give you one more chance to do the right thing. One more, Elliana, or everyone you have ever loved will die. I promise you that."

She swirled a finger in the air. Nothing happened for a moment, and I began to think she really had lost her mind.

But then the stone in my chest heated at the same time a male fae appeared next to Maeve, squeezing my twin's bicep.

"Brielle!" I gasped.

Her brown gaze swung around wildly before landing on me. "Elliana! Oh, my angels!"

I ran for her, but an invisible force threw me back, so powerful, I went flying several yards before landing on my ass.

"You know what to do," the male fae snarled, shoving Brielle forward, toward Sadie.

"Sadie Angrec?" Brie asked, seeing her for the first time, confusion filling her tone. She turned back for the male and Maeve, shaking her head. "No. I won't."

"You will," Maeve declared coldly, a cruel glint in her eyes.

Brielle stumbled forward, seeming to fight herself as she slowly lifted her hands, a falchion gripped in her right, the broad blade dull and dark, and a blue flame dancing in the palm of her left. Her body jerked forward, as though against her will. The blade swiped at Sadie, who screamed as her skin sizzled from the shallow gash. Iron. The falchion was made of iron.

"Why, Elliana?" Sadie cried out. "Why are you doing this to me?"

Her focus was on Brielle, even while she blamed me.

"Oh, did I mention that Sadie sees *you* attacking her, not your sister?" Maeve said nonchalantly. "She can't seem to differentiate between the two of you. She must not know you as well as you think she does. Or maybe it's that little mind trick I planted."

"What?" I gasped at the horror of it—of Sadie thinking I would ever try to hurt her. "No, don't do this, Maeve. Please. Make it stop."

"Hmm . . . no, I don't think I will," Maeve said, whispering something in Faelic under her breath.

The blue flame flew from Brielle's palm and slammed into Sadie's stomach, singeing the bottom of her leather armor to leave blackened bare skin. Sadie glared at my twin, hurt and anger marring her beautiful features, as her own hand lifted, her palm up and bloody fingers curling inward.

"Don't make me do this, Elli," she half-pleaded and half-warned.

Brielle swung the falchion again, the move awkward as she still fought against the power controlling her, but nonetheless finding its mark across Sadie's thigh.

Then my twin was suddenly falling to her knees, the sword dropping with her as she grasped at her head.

"I suppose the elf should at least be able to fight back, should she not?" Maeve asked nobody in particular. "I wonder if she's strong enough to break a Knight's mind?" She glanced at me, before lifting her chin.

Brielle screamed louder, falling over and convulsing in the snow.

"Enough!" I shouted, my beast roaring through my chest. She exploded free, her power rocking through my limbs, my torso, filling my veins and every cell of my being. Threading that dark force into my other magic, I blasted a wall of frozen air at the male fae next to Maeve, sending him flying to his back, then pierced a yard-long icicle into each shoulder, pinning him to the ground.

Mimicking Maeve's own power, I froze the rest of her soldiers in a sheet of ice, then turned my attention fully on her. Sadie and Brielle continued their awkward fighting as Maeve and I went at each other.

She was Winter—I'd have to be the opposite. Surrounding myself in flame, I snapped my wings out and launched into the air. She threw her magic at me, but it sizzled and evaporated when it hit my fire. I shot fireballs at her, but she easily lobbed them away with mere swipes of her hands. Pulling my wings in and calling on my sword, I engulfed it in white-hot fire and flew at her. She met me with her own sword. The clang of the blades meeting so powerfully made my teeth clatter, and an electric jolt shot up my arm. I flew back, then soared at her again. My sword connected with her shoulder, but her blade slid across my wing, only a scratch but still making me grunt as piercing cold pain shot through the sensitive nerve endings.

I dropped to the ground, and we fought in hand-to-hand combat, weapons parrying each other sometimes and drawing blood at others, but we seemed to be evenly matched. Neither of our magic did much damage to the other, and my wings gave me an advantage, allowing me to fly out of her reach, but when I released and shot my hardened feathers like titanium darts, she easily batted them away.

The ice coating the soldiers on both sides broke off at some point, and they engaged in their own battle. Metal clanging against metal mixed with the sizzles and pops of magic, creating a cacophony I may never forget. Brielle had managed to fight against Sadie's mind-bending power, climbing back to her feet, but the two of them continued their brawl. I flew back, higher into the air, taking it all in.

The snow around us was no longer a pristine white, but a slush of mud and blood. Shouts and cries of pain rang out, mixing with the weapons' songs of battle. Bodies littered the ground, some leaking blood and others dead still. Saoirse kept trying to push herself to her feet, only to fall back into the snow, her broken legs unable to hold her weight, her expression contorted with a mix of pain and desperation to fight alongside her men.

And my sister and Sadie . . . trying to kill each other.

The ground rumbled and buckled under Sadie's feet, making her fall to her knees, as Brielle pulled on her earth magic, but roots grew up and out of the snow at Sadie's call to them, wrapping around Brie's legs and yanking her to the ground again. While she sliced at them, trying to extricate herself, Sadie took advantage and squeezed her mind. My twin screamed, her back arching in agony.

I threw a shielding spell between them, which stopped

Sadie's attack on my twin, but only for a moment before I could literally feel the magic shatter.

"There's only one way to end this," Maeve said, dropping her hand back to her side, "and that's not it. Kill the elf, Elliana. *You* can end this."

I could end this. Yes, I could. And not in the way Maeve wanted.

As the battle scene before me continued to rage, I also saw another scene. Ravenbury first, buildings burning, bodies scattered, people shouting for help. And then Misery's Edge— more dead bodies, everywhere. Shouts of help intermingled with wails of pain and grief.

Dani's loudest of them all.

I blinked, the other scenes disappearing, yet their ghosts still there, a reminder of what I could do. What could happen with a simple blast of my beast's power. Yes, I could certainly finish this and even kill Maeve herself. But who else would die with her? The soldiers, who were only doing their commanders' bidding? Saoirse . . . Sadie . . . Brielle?

Who would be left to sob and scream and mourn their losses? Me. Only me.

The two most important people of my life—two souls that were embedded in mine—groaned and grunted as they fought each other. Both of them battered, bruised, and bloody, but neither giving up. Because they couldn't. They had no choice, their wills taken from them.

Brielle's sword had somehow ended up several yards away. Magic crackled over Brie's hands as Sadie crooked her fingers again, trying to twist my twin's mind once more. But Brielle stood her ground, whipping her power at Sadie, the elf's flesh splitting and shredding, and I gasped with each strike, practically feeling the pain myself. I quickly realized how easily my twin could kill my mate. I blasted another shield between them, this time fortifying it against Maeve's attempt at shattering it again, and absorbed my sister's attack, siphoning it from Sadie.

Brielle's power slammed into me. Surrounded me in a Dark cloud—so fucking Dark. So fucking familiar. It took my breath away. Made my own beast pause. It was possibly even Darker than mine when it had never been before. What had happened to my sister to cause this? What had she endured while we were separated?

I felt my own skin breaking against its force. Blood leaked from my nose, and a gash opened across my forehead as her energy came in surges. I began to gather my own to fight back, to stop her, when I saw them.

The huge horses consisting of nothing more than black smoke towering over my twin. The riders with horned heads and glowing crimson eyes looking like devils in black armor. And pouring off of them in waves on the smoky air was the worst kind of evil. Darker than me. Darker than my twin. Darker than my beast.

My heart stuttered. My mouth dropped open.

"*ENOUGH!*" Maeve shouted.

I blinked, and the horses and their devil riders vanished. As though they'd never been there. Had Maeve seen them? Had Brielle? Had she *brought* them?

The single word still echoed off the mountains, and those warriors who remained standing instantly dropped their weapons as though the word itself forced them to. Brielle's power evaporated, too, as she and Sadie flew off the ground and into Maeve's hands that looked more like claws, each one curling around a throat.

"I'm bored, Elliana," the Winter princess declared. That answered that question: no way did she see the horses and still proclaim boredom. I hoped that meant Brielle hadn't either. That nobody had but me, just another vision with really bad timing. "Since you don't have the courage to do what needs to be done, to kill the putrid elf, I'll just end them both and make it simple for you."

Her fingers squeezed, and both Brie and Sadie squirmed and thrashed as their faces began to swell, their skin turning purple.

I didn't want to fall for her taunt, but no way in hell would I let her kill them.

I could still end this.

I had to.

My power roiled through me again. How dark and delicious it was as it flowed freely through my veins and my flesh, gathering and building, becoming something completely Other within me. My beast nothing but an energy force— dark, dangerous, deadly. Beautiful. And all mine—to control.

My mother once told me that during her darkest times, Uncle Owen would incessantly tell her, "In the end, good always wins." But, she'd said, over the years she'd come to her own conclusion and tweaked the saying: "In the end, *love* always wins." Sometimes she would add it to our family motto: "In the end, love always wins, and I will love you until the end of always and forever." I'd thought at the time it was something a mother would say to make her children feel better—*we'll always win because I'll never stop loving you.* It felt trite, if I was being honest. I even felt it was condescending. After all, she couldn't say good always wins if her own children weren't good.

I understood better now. Good was subjective. When your papa lay dying in your arms, who did you believe was good? Not the people you felt responsible for it, even if they were angelic beings claiming to serve the higher good. Who was considered the good guys in the battle between the elves and Winter Court when both sides lost loved ones at the other's hands? Good and evil were only a matter of perspective, and depending on yours, good didn't always win.

Love, however, was love, plain and simple. Love trumped

fear. Love trumped hate. Love trumped bigotry and greed and the need for power and control. Real, unconditional love transcended ego and jealousy, the need to be right, to avenge, to get what you want at any cost.

"In the end," I murmured, "Love. Always. Wins."

"Why do you think I've done all of this?" Maeve replied, her head tilted back to watch as I still hovered in the air. "For love. For you."

"Except you have no idea what real love is, do you?" As I dropped to the ground, wonder and awe glowed in her eyes but fear flickered in them, as well. I wondered what she saw in me. Brielle and Sadie continued clawing at her hands around their throats, but they were obviously growing weaker by the moment. My power raged. But I remained in control. "If you wanted me to love you, you probably should not have gone after those I do love most."

I bent over and picked up Sadie's bow, plucking an arrow out of the quiver.

"If I eliminate all others, there is only me left. I know you, Elliana. You pretend to believe you're a loner, that you can do it all on your own. But you really cannot stand the thought of being alone, can you? You *need* someone in your life. Truly, though, who else can love you but me? Not these two. You know they can't. You know they deserve better. But I will always be here for you. I am the only one who can handle you. They cannot." She shoved them to the ground, where they both lay unnaturally still. "Let me be the love you crave. Forget everyone else and focus on me."

I knocked the arrow in the string and lifted the bow. "Oh, I am definitely focused on you."

She tilted her head, her slanted brows pinching together in a sharp V.

"What are you playing at, doll?" she asked. "You know an arrow will not hurt me."

"Maybe not an ordinary arrow," I said, as I brought all of

that dark power swirling within me, weaving it into my witch magic and threading within it all the power of love—love for my sister and love for my elf princess. Yes, I could end this, and I knew how. For them, I would be a fucking bomb if I had to be and raze everything in sight. But I did not have to be. As Tor had said, *Eliminate the right targets and you can end any battle, any war.* And I saw that target directly in front of me. "But you don't know what I'm truly capable of."

I lifted the bow higher and pulled back the string, aligning it with my cheek. Her eyes narrowing as her brow dropped lower, Maeve must have understood. I felt her power—full of fear and hatred and everything that was not love—push against my hands, and I let it. I let her redirect my aim so the arrow pointed at my twin . . . then pushed harder to target my mate. The arrow even began to vibrate against the string as she tried to force its release.

Licking the dried blood off my bottom lip, I let one side of my mouth curl upward as I easily sliced through her power, returning the aim to her. Her eyes grew wide, her head shaking slowly in denial. Murmuring my spell, I released the arrow, blowing my unique brand of magic over it as it flew. A black mist plumed from my mouth and snaked around the wooden staff as it soared for its mark. Maeve tried to deflect it, but she could not. Not even Winter Court royalty could match my power.

The arrow drove straight through her armor and into her chest, eliciting a scream of hatred and defeat and wrath like no other. And then she fell silent.

CHAPTER 29

I didn't check to make sure she was dead. If I did—and if she was—I'd have to stop and think about the ramifications, and I didn't have time for that. Not now. Later, I knew, the moment would haunt me. Right now, though, I had to get Sadie and Brielle out of here.

Rushing over to them, I squatted between their prone bodies, shaking them both. Brielle pushed herself to her hands and knees.

"I'm okay," she said, though she didn't look okay at all. We stared at each other for a breath, then launched ourselves into each other's arms. My twin. The other half of my soul. I'd missed her so much but hadn't realized just how badly until this moment.

But we didn't have time for this either.

"We have to go," I said, releasing my hold on her.

Sadie didn't stir so easily, but when those gorgeous electric blues did finally flutter open and looked up at me, she started thrashing and screaming. *Shit.*

"Sadie, it's okay," I soothed. "You're okay. That was all Maeve. Not me. Not Brielle. Not you. Shh . . ."

She barely calmed down, her body trembling as I scooped

her into my arms and stood, Brielle rising next to me. Just as I was about to launch into the air, Saoirse caught my eye. Damn it.

I didn't know what to think about her. Or Tor. Or any of it. And again, I didn't have time to sort through my feelings.

"Just go," she called out. "Her power is released from me. I can heal now. Go!"

I nodded, swallowed, then launched into the air, holding Sadie's limp body close to my chest.

"*Any idea where we are?*" Brielle asked in my mind, our twin bond returned, as she followed me into the air.

While fighting Maeve, I hadn't really paid attention to the landscape, so I circled the area. A snowy field surrounded by forest on all but one side, where a mountain range rose. A little ways in the distance I could see the deep chasm between the nearest mountain and the next, and I knew exactly where we were. I'd stared out the window at that ravine with the beautiful waterfalls for weeks, possibly months.

"*This way to the Winter Court castle. Let's get our parents!*" With strong flaps of my wings, I soared toward the palace.

"*Elli, our parents aren't there.*"

"*Maeve said—Fuck. Maeve lied.*" Though I supposed she hadn't technically lied. She'd said my family was there, and, indeed, Brielle had been. "*So where are they?*"

"*They're in our own world, not at all in Faery. And Elli, they're in danger. Charleigh . . . Charleigh is, too, and Skylar . . . Everyone is in trouble.*"

I glanced down at Sadie, glad she'd passed out. I hated bringing her to our dangerous realm, but I couldn't leave her here, either. Not when I wasn't sure if anybody could be trusted. Fucking fae. I'd have to bring her with us. At least we could be together. She would keep me balanced, and I would . . . Well, I didn't know what I had to offer her, but we were mates, so some greater mind must have seen something there.

"*This way still. I know how to get home.*" Sort of. I did know that just a ways beyond the castle—not far now that we could fly—was the Circle of Knowing.

Home. I was finally going home. I had my girl. I was reunited with my twin. Soon we'd be with our parents. Not long ago, I thought I might not see any of them ever again. I knew we had a lot of danger to still face—not the least of which was the Shadow king because even though Tor might have released me, I was pretty sure Caellach wouldn't. But for now, maybe I could disappear from his reaches again, long enough for Tor to do whatever it was he had planned to get us both out of the deal. In the meantime, I knew that as long as Sadie and I were together, we could face any challenge that came our way.

Because love always wins.

"*Wait,*" Brielle said, slowing as she gazed down at the ground.

A crowd of fae was gathered below, mounted on various creatures, not far from the castle, which we'd already passed, off to our left. My heart stuttered when I thought at first that it was the Winter Court army below—after all, I had no idea where Maeve's brother, the Winter king, had been throughout all of this. But then I realized it was Tor and the rest of the *Skaelach*. He was directing some of his troops to head back toward the battlefield, and a handful in the opposite direction, toward the stones, the Circle of Knowing. *Shit.* Had he changed his mind about releasing me? He must have realized he'd been tricked by Maeve.

At that moment, Tor glanced up at the sky, spotting us.

"*Go!*" I mentally shouted at Brielle as I continued forward, picking up speed.

I glanced over my shoulder, watching as Brielle followed, though not flying as fast as I wished she would. Tor's beast took off in a gallop, much faster than Moonbutt had been, managing to keep up with us although he stayed on the ground rather than flying, which I found odd, but whatever.

Maybe he was letting us go without it appearing so? I didn't know. I didn't care. I just wanted to reach those damn stones and go home.

"*Come on, Brielle,*" I urged. "*Hurry!*"

We flew over the forest, the trees slowing Tor down, though only slightly. Good. It was enough that now we could beat him to the Circle of Knowing and figure out how to use the stones to go home before he tried to stop us.

Not grasping my sense of urgency, Brielle slowed even more.

"*Brie, what are you doing? We're almost there!*" In fact, I thought I could see the ridge from here, tiny objects floating above it.

"*I . . . I can't, Elli.*" She felt farther away, and I whirled in the air, staring at her as she beat her dark wings slowly, hovering in place. Her brows pinched together as she looked at me with bewilderment.

"What do you mean you can't?" I demanded out loud, but I noticed what I hadn't before—how bruised and bloody she still was. She should have fully healed by now, but she looked tired and weak. "Are you okay?"

"I . . . I don't know." She looked down at the ground, her gaze coming to rest directly below us. Tor had caught up again, staring up at us from a clearing in the woods. Brielle tilted her head, and when she lifted her eyes back to me, some kind of realization dawned in their brown depths. "I have to stay here."

"What are you talking about? We have to get home, Brie! You just said our parents need us. Charleigh and everyone else!"

"I know, but—" She started dropping downward.

"But what? Let's get the hell out of here!" I spun away, toward the mountain, toward the floating stones with their colorful glows. I knew for sure those were them. So close. We were so damn close.

"He'll help us," Brie said.

"I doubt that," I muttered, turning back toward her. "We don't need him, though. Stop being a pain, and let's go."

She landed in the snow only feet from Tor, studying him for a long moment before looking up at me, a new expression filling her face that I couldn't place. "I really can't, Elli. I have to stay with Toridhan."

Wait. What? How did she even know him or his name? I shook my head. The last thing I wanted was for her to become wrapped up with the Shadows. Yes, I still had my own problems with them I'd have to figure out at some point. And I supposed Sadie did, too. I had made the deal with King Caellach to save Brielle in the first place, though. I'd be damned if she fell into his sights again.

"No, you don't," I insisted. "Our parents need us. Our family does. And I won't leave you again. Until the end, Brielle."

"Until the end." Brielle nodded. "But I do have to stay here," she said firmly, glancing again at Tor, then back up at me. "I made a deal."

EPILOGUE

I sat by the window in Sadie's room back at the Court of Souls, staring out it but seeing nothing. I wouldn't let Brielle come here on her own. I hadn't decided yet if I could trust Tor or not—especially when he'd never bothered to tell me about his deal with my twin. That he even *knew* her. Two days later and I still fumed about that.

He said it was between him and her, but she could tell me if she wanted to. She still hadn't explained, although she'd only been awake for a few hours since we'd returned, exhaustion overcoming her when we arrived. We didn't normally need so much time for our cells to regenerate, so I figured I could give her a little bit longer and let her eat breakfast and bathe before pouncing on her. I just hoped she was all right.

What kind of deal she had made—and when—had been niggling at me so hard, I could barely sleep myself. That and the fact that Sadie still hadn't truly awoken. Tor's healers had been coming in every few hours to work on her. When she did arouse some, she'd thrash in the bed, see me and grow hysterical, then pass out again. Maeve had really done a number on her.

I hoped I'd done the same to Maeve. We still didn't know

if I'd killed her or not. Tor said it was smart to come back here with him, where we'd all be safer from whatever ramifications came about. Whether Maeve died or not, I could be tried for attempted assassination at best. She was high court royalty, after all. I didn't know if self-defense was a mitigating factor here in Faery.

Of course, one ramification was inevitable, already brewing for years and now coming to a head: war.

I was sure now that was what I had seen in the mirrors—a war of all the factions tearing our worlds apart. Destroying them both once and for all.

"Elli?" Sadie's voice was barely a whisper, but I sprang from the chair and crossed the room to the bed. She looked up at me with those electric blues, clearer than I'd seen them in days. Sunken, but clear. Her usually creamy skin was so pale, it was practically translucent.

When she didn't freak out upon seeing me, I gingerly sat on the edge of the bed next to her and took her hand between mine. "How are you feeling?"

"Um . . . weak. Thirsty." I reached over to the bedside table for the glass of water and held it to her lips. She smiled after swallowing. "Thank you."

"I'd do anything for you, Sadie." I brushed away a lock of blond hair matted to her forehead. "I was so worried about you."

She smiled thinly. "Fighting a Knight twin—I give it one star. Do not recommend."

My own mouth curved upward. "I'm pretty sure Brielle felt the same about fighting an elf princess. She's slept for days and awoke with a killer headache."

"She's okay?" I nodded, and she breathed a sigh of relief. "You're okay?"

"I am if you are."

Now she nodded. "I think I will be." Her head tilted, her eyes glossing over as she stared at me. "I love you, my dark angel."

I leaned over and pressed a kiss to her forehead. "I love you, too, my warrior princess."

Her smile broadened as her eyes drifted closed, and her hand in mine went limp. I thought she'd gone back to sleep, but then her eyes popped open, wide and full of fear as she stared at me. Then she began screaming. "Don't make me do this, Elli! Please! No!"

I jumped away from the bed, hands in the air, but then she fell silent, unconscious again. Tears stung my eyes as I watched her, my heart breaking for her pain.

"Elliana?" Tor stood in the doorway. "We need to talk."

Inhaling deeply, I rolled my shoulders back, blinking away the tears, then turned and strode out after him. "Are you finally going to share details with me?"

"Did Brielle?"

I scowled. "No."

"Then I will wait for her on that matter." He led me to his study, closing the door behind us.

"And other matters?"

"Maeve is not dead."

"Oh." That wasn't what I'd expected to hear at this moment. I didn't know what to make of it.

"But she appears to be psychologically . . . broken."

"Broken?"

"Her mind is, yes."

My brows pinched. "Do you think Sadie . . . ? But she was already a mess herself."

Sitting behind his desk, he leaned forward, pressing his long fingers into a temple over the wood surface. "I think it's possible you could have a touch of your mate's magic. Or it's possible Sadie had already tried before we even arrived on the scene. From what Saoirse has reported, Maeve was especially . . . neurotic the other night."

"That's an understatement," I muttered. "By the way, how

did *you* arrive on the scene? How did you even know where to go?"

He slid his hand under the lapel of his jacket and pulled out a folded piece of parchment. "I found this in Sadie's room."

When he held it out, I stared at it for a moment before taking it.

Sadie, we're leaving. Tor is setting us up. Meet me at the Mistwood outpost. ~ E

"I didn't write this," I said, looking him in the eye as I did. "I swear."

He nodded. "I know. I figured you had been fished out of the Court of Souls in some other way, possibly with a promise of where to find your parents. The information I had just been about to share with you was to tell you they were at Winter Court."

"So you just went straight there."

He nodded.

"But they weren't there."

He shook his head. "No. They had thoroughly set up all of us. I still do not know why Maeve would practically invite me and my men there. She should have known I would not have given you up for Sadie . . . or visa versa. I think she'd gone mad long before that night."

"The mad queen," I murmured, then tilted my head. "But why were you so interested in saving my parents? Or was this an excuse to attack Winter Court, since you were there anyway?"

"I *attacked* Winter Court because Maeve took my sister," he growled, his eyes flashing. "I initially went to see if I could negotiate the release of your family."

"But why?"

"Because that's what we do for those we love. Their family becomes our family."

I pondered this and wondered if he'd say the same thing if

the elves turned on the Shadows. Would he consider Sadie's other family his? It seemed too many politics was involved in that, which made me not fully trust the answer. But I let it go. And completely ignored the statement about those he loved. I could not at all go there right now.

"How is Brielle?" he asked, though I sensed in his voice that he already knew. He hadn't wandered too far from her room until she'd awoken earlier today.

"I don't know. We have a lot of catching up to do."

"I imagine you do. Just know that I will keep her safe. I will keep all of you safe to the best of my ability."

My eyes narrowed as I heard the "but" in his tone. "Except . . . ?"

He sighed, averting his eyes to stare at his folded hands. "Except that Maeve managed to send word to the Court of Shadows about both Saoirse and Sadie."

I gasped as my stomach clenched, feeling like I'd been punched.

"Your father knows about them," I breathed as the horror washed fully over me. "Who they are."

"Indeed, he does," Tor said quietly.

I could barely see as I stumbled out of the room, my mind whirling over this news. What were we going to do? How could I save Sadie from the Shadow king?

I had brought this on her. If it weren't for me, Maeve would have never paid her any attention. Instead, my love for Sadie was the spark of a new war between Winter Court and the elves. Who else would be drawn in? Likely the Shadows, but on which side would remain to be seen. Though who would lead the Shadows in the near future might remain to be seen as well, if Tor was ramping up his plans against his father now.

So much destruction . . . and I couldn't help but feel responsible for it.

As I started for Sadie's room, I passed the open doors to

one of the balconies and saw Brielle standing out there, a mug in her hand as she leaned against the balustrade.

"It's so much prettier here than I expected it to be," she said, sensing my presence.

I walked out to join her. "What did you expect?"

She shrugged as she turned toward me, my mirror reflection. "Darkness. Lots of shadows." She chuckled. "I know. Sounds cliché."

"Well, you'd be right, in the rest of the Shadow Lands, anyway. The Court of Souls is definitely different."

"You've been . . . you've been to the Court of Shadows?"

I nodded. "And I will do everything possible to keep you out of there."

Not that I was doing a good job so far. She was closer than ever to the Shadow king. If he learned about Brielle being here like he had Sadie and Saoirse . . . I swallowed the lump in my throat, blinking as I realized Brielle had said something.

"Come on. Tell me all of it. Because I'm still really pissed at you for going back to Misery's Edge that night," she said.

More guilt pierced my heart. Where would we both be if I hadn't snuck away from her to try to save Dani? Definitely not here. Of course, then I wouldn't have found Sadie again. On the flip side to that, Sadie might not be a broken mess at the moment . . .

"Elli! Tell me your story!" Brielle took my hand, leading me over to the seating area.

We settled in, and I told her the truncated version of everything that had happened since I left her in that camp back in our own world. She listened intently, and I could see her mentally taking notes for topics we'd discuss later. There was *so* much to discuss. But I wasn't sure what she remembered yet, and I didn't want to push that topic at the moment. It took so long that by the time I finished, we were starving and went on the hunt for food. I wanted to take her to our favorite bistro on the plaza, but I also didn't want to wander that far from Sadie. So we found some snacks in the kitchen and returned to the balcony overlooking the plaza and all of the evening hustle and bustle.

"I guess I'm not surprised about the Court of Souls being so beautiful," Brielle said as we stood at the railing again. "Not if it was created by Toridhan."

"So how exactly do you know him? When and how did you make a deal with him? And where are our parents?"

She sighed. "That's a long story, too. All of it."

"So? It's your turn now."

"I guess it is." We went back to the chairs, poured ourselves some faerie wine, and settled in again. "I suppose it begins at Shadow Vault Citadel and when you and I died in the Pits."

My stomach sank, forming its own pit. I hated that she'd remembered our time there. Our deaths. I hated that she'd been there in the first place. Another thing I felt responsible for.

There was no denying it—I was a danger to the people I loved. Maybe it was time to start rethinking my role in their lives. Perhaps they really would be better off without me. For a moment, I had a glimpse of understanding of Dorian and why he stayed away from us. Perhaps he truly did care but knew he would only hurt us in the end. My brother and I might have more in common than I ever thought. Something to keep in mind as I made my future plans to keep Sadie, Brielle, and the rest of the people I loved safe.

"No, actually, before then," Brielle continued, bringing my attention back to the present. She inhaled a deep breath, blowing it out slowly as she stared at the stone floor of the terrace. "To when I first saw the smoky horses and their riders."

My mouth dropped open. "What?"

She nodded, her eyes lifting back to me and full of such depth and pain, I felt like she'd lived a thousand years without me. "I know exactly what you saw in the mirrors. I've seen them myself. I'll tell you everything I can, starting from the beginning. And then, when I'm done, we have to figure out how to kill our brother. He has our parents."

What happens next? Subscribe to my newsletter for news on Book 2 in the Knights of Souls and Shadows series. If you haven't yet, be sure to read the Sun & Moon Academy series about the twins' time in the shiny world and the Soul Savers series for their parents' story that started it all.

Word of mouth is very important for any author. If you enjoyed the book, please consider leaving a review, even if it's only a sentence or two. This is one of the most important and appreciated things you can do for an author.

GLOSSARY & CAST

A reminder of who and what you've discovered so far in the Knights of Souls and Shadows and Soul Savers world.

Aidan - Gargoyle shifter from Scotland.

Alexis Ames Knight – Amadis matriarch. Married to Tristan Knight and mother of Dorian. Youngest daughter to ever go through the Ang'dora and to become matriarch. Her bio father is the leader of the Daemoni. Known abilities include telepathy, electricity, telekinesis, super strength, speed and senses, Amadis power.

Amadis (uh-MAH-dees) – Secret matriarchal society that serves as the Angels' army on Earth, currently led by Alexis Ames Knight. Their purpose is to defend human souls from the Daemoni and to convert Daemoni souls to Amadis. Consist of a variety of supernatural beings.

Amadis daughters – Women of the bloodline of the original creator of the Amadis. Each daughter eventually serves as the matriarch.

Amadis power – A special power of love and light gifted to the Amadis by the Angels. The Amadis daughters receive it during the Ang'dora. Other society members are granted a lower level of power upon conversion and official acceptance into the Amadis.

Ancients – Major demons who created and still oversee the Daemoni.

Ang'dora – Literally means "gift of the Angels" (Ang = angels, dora = Greek word for gifts). An enigmatic change all Amadis daughters go through to receive their powers and supernatural abilities. Usually happens in middle age, after the daughter has experienced major milestones of life as a human, but Alexis went through it quite early. Except for Sophia, no Amadis daughter has given birth after the Ang'dora.

Angels – Spirits of Heaven who (primarily) remain in the Otherworld. Most fight in the age-old war with Demons, battling for human souls.

Blossom – Alexis's best friend and council member. Amadis witch from the Daytona coven.

Bree – Tristan's birth mother. Fae.

Brielle Sophia Ames Knight – Daughter of Alexis and Tristan, twin to Elliana, sister to Dorian. Angel hybrid with unknown powers.

Caellach – Shadow king.

Camila – Mayor of Misery's Edge who's not quite human.

Charleigh – Best friend to Elliana and Brielle, considered their cousin, a witch who's their sworn protector. Daughter of Blossom and Jax.

Cloak – A magic spell performed by mages that hides or makes invisible its subject. Often used in conjunction with a shield.

Court of Shadows – The main court of the Shadow Lands, ruled by King Caellach.

Court of Souls – Minor court of the Shadow Lands, ruled by Prince Toridhan.

Daemoni (day-MAH-nee) – Satan's servants as the Demons' army on Earth, currently led by Lucas. They turn humans to harvest their souls and build their army. The Amadis try to stop them.

Daniela / Dani – Former love interest of Elliana, part demon

Demons – Spirits from Hell, some being angels that fell from Heaven with Satan as his followers and others being his creations. They take various physical forms, including horned and winged beasts and possessors of human meat suits.

Dorian Knight – Son of Alexis and Tristan, unknown creature but currently human. Known abilities include self-healing and flying. Converting to Daemoni?

Dragons - One of the many creatures that had disappeared from this realm when they were captured by Satan and held prisoners in Hell

Earth's Angels – Newly created by the Angels, on the lowest rung of the Angel hierarchy, includes Alexis, Tristan, the Summoned sons who have converted back to Amadis, as well as their offspring. Alexis leads them.

Elliana Katerina Ames Knight – Daughter of Alexis and Tristan, twin to Brielle, sister to Dorian. Angel hybrid with unknown powers.

Ena – Shadow fae slave at Winter Court.

Faeries/Fae – Little is known about the fae as they tend to stay away from human affairs, as well as those of the Amadis and Daemoni. A handful do enjoy wreaking havoc in the Earthly realm, and sometimes they may even help out. They're considered Otherworldly creatures, because their world is not exactly part of Earth. They closely guard their secrets about the Faerie realm.

Fintan – Winter Court king.

Flashing – The supernatural ability to transport to another location up to a hundred miles away (give or take) in the blink of an eye.

Gargoyles - Little is known about them, as Aidan is the

first to be seen in many centuries. They're somehow connected to the dragons.

Jax / Jaxon – Croc shifter from the Australian Outback who's become part of Alexis's team. Blossom's beau. Charleigh's dad.

Loft, The – A massive underground nuclear bunker given to the Amadis as their new HQ.

Lykora – An Angelic being that is extremely loyal and highly protective of its master. When in hidden form, looks like a small white dog, but when in defensive mode, can grow as large as necessary to protect, has a wolf head and body, tiger stripes on a white coat, and feathered wings.

Maeve – Princess of Winter Court, sister to the Winter/Unseelie king.

Mages – The wide classification of supernatural beings that can wield magic, including witches/wizards, warlocks, and Sorcerers/sorceresses. These general sub-classifications are based on strength of power. Some may call themselves by other names, depending on the type of magic they use, preference, or other reasons (e.g., Shamans, Druids, etc.).

Misery's Edge – Large trading town that sprung up after the war south of St. Louis, on the Mississippi. Home of the great massacre.

Noah – Sophia's twin brother, Rina's son, a Summoned son with the Daemoni and controlled by Kali.

Norms/Normans – Normal humans.

Owen Allbright – Warlock and Alexis's so-called protector. Also like a brother to her and Tristan's best friend. Vanessa's love interest.

Portals – Magical doorways that can only be created and controlled by sorcerers/sorceresses and extremely powerful warlocks like Owen. They allow teleportation to anywhere in the world just by stepping through.

Ravenbury – Small town about 50 miles from the Loft, their closest neighbors besides the dragon clan.

Sadie – Elven princess, love interest of Elliana.

Saoirse – Shadow fae warrior, disowned princess of the Shadow fae, Tor's half-sister.

Sasha – Dorian's lykora, now loyal to the twins.

Scout - Mayor of Ravenbury.

Seelie – Also known as the Light fae, considered to be the more benevolent of the fae, but don't be fooled. Ruled by Summer Court with Spring Court as its secondary.

Shadow Fae – Hated by both the Seelie and Unseelie, often become their slaves. Ruled by King Caellach.

Shadow Vault Citadel – a/k/a The Vault, a supernatural prison in a pocket realm controlled by the fae but for all sorts of supernaturals who have committed the most heinous of crimes but cannot be killed.

Shamara – Major demon who took over Misery's Edge

Sheree – An Amadis were-tiger who'd been bitten and turned against her will by the Daemoni. She was Alexis's first ever conversion from Daemoni to Amadis. Now she helps with conversions of others and is a close friend to Alexis.

Shield – A magic spell performed by mages that puts a protective barrier around its subject. If the subject is not also cloaked, the subject can still be seen, so it's often used in conjunction with a cloaking spell.

Skylar – Young woman from the marketplace who Brielle camps with.

Sorcerers/Sorceresses – The most powerful of the mages that can boost their energy by siphoning more from the earth and everything around them. Their greed for power, narcissism, and general disdain for pretty much everyone make them loners and also not part of the Amadis.

Toridhan / Tor / Tormentor – Shadow prince, ruler of Court of Souls.

Tristan Knight – Former Daemoni converted to Amadis by Sophia. Matriarch's second, best friend, and husband. Dorian's dad. Sexy AF warrior. Known abilities include shooting fire from his palm, quickly determining the best solution if he knows enough of the facts, telekinesis, paralysis, instant killing power, super-duper strength and speed, brooding with guilt, giving a girl multiple Os.

Unseelie – Also known as the Dark fae, considered to be the more malevolent of the fae compared to the Light/Seelie. Ruled by Winter Court with Autumn Court as its secondary.

Vampires – Supernatural beings that are sustained by blood. They can also feed on fear and other emotional energy. There are vampires on both the Amadis and the Daemoni sides.

Vanessa – Formerly one of the Daemoni's star vampires recently converted to Amadis. Alexis's half-sister, Owen's partner-in-crime, Victor's twin, and Lucas's daughter.

Victor – Vanessa's twin brother, Alexis's half-brother, Lucas's son and Daemoni vampire who's not too bright.

Warlocks – Part of the mage classification, supernatural beings who are born with the ability to wield magic and physically endowed with strength and speed, making them excellent warriors. They are not gender specific and are on both the Amadis and Daemoni sides.

Witches/Wizards – Part of the mage classification, supernatural beings who are born with the ability to wield magic, usually using a wand as well as spells, incantations, potions, elemental energy, etc. While they can be quite powerful, their powers and physical strengths aren't as strong as Warlocks or Sorcerers. Using the term Witch or Wizard was traditionally by gender, but really is up to each individual's preference. There are Witches and Wizards on both the Amadis and Daemoni sides.

Were-creatures/animals (a/k/a Shifters) – Supernatural beings with two combined spirits—human and animal—and they can physically shift between their two forms. There is a were-creature/shifter for nearly every predatory species on Earth, and they're on both the Amadis and the Daemoni sides.

Zombies – Reanimated corpses with deadly bites. Created by mixing necromancy magic with fatal and highly contagious viruses, such as Ebola. Lucas made them as an experiment and to provide meatsuits for the Demons he planned to let loose on Earth.